CAROLINE GEORGE

Evernight Teen ®

www.evernightteen.com

Praise for THE VESTIGE

"With her amazing grasp of the English language and her sophisticated understanding of the human heart, Caroline George weaves together a simple romance in the midst of a complex world."

—Sharon Wilharm, award-winning producer and writer of PROVIDENCE, THE GOOD BOOK, and other films.

"Few stories have had the ability to haunt me long after closing the book. This was one of them. From the first page, I was drawn into Julie's world, and I soon became swept away into a pulse-pounding adventure. George delivers a sci-fi story that shadows our present day, and she accomplishes this in a way that adds a unique flair to the sci-fi apocalyptic genre. THE VESTIGE is more than another YA novel—it's a thought-provoking (if not prophetic) masterpiece."

—Tessa Emily Hall, award-winning YA author of PURPLE MOON and UNWRITTEN MELODY

"Mistrusting world. Untold destruction. When the action begins, there is no coming up for air."

—Christine Rees, author of THE HIDDEN LEGACY

CAROLINE GEORGE

Copyright© 2017

Caroline George

ISBN: 978-1-77339-338-4

Cover Artist: Jay Aheer

Editor: Audrey Bobak

DEDICATION

To those who have shown me the truth and challenged me to see the unseen, and for every person who's been crazy enough to say what no one wants to hear.

CAROLINE GEORGE

THE VESTIGE

Caroline George

Copyright © 2017

FIRST LAYER
Chapter One

"The loneliest moment in someone's life is when they are watching their whole world fall apart, and all they can do is stare blankly."
F. Scott Fitzgerald, *The Great Gatsby*

"What's your blood type?" Jack yells over the intense rattles and rippling slosh of a red sea. Blood type. Mom didn't tell me. She kept that sort of information stored in Dad's filing cabinet.

"I … don't know." Air leaves my lungs and doesn't return. A metallic liquid pollutes my throat—I choke. I roll over and vomit blood. The floor's star-shaped grooves dig into my forearm, branding me with this hell. Flesh peels off my fingers as I claw at the metal ground. How is it possible to be in so much pain? Am I breathing? Am I screaming? Maybe. Not sure. The tires crunch and squeal. Police sirens wail in the distance. They're alive—I won't be for much longer.

"So if you don't bleed out or die from sepsis, my blood will kill you. Great." Jack kneels with an armful of first-aid kits, flashlights, and alcohol. He braces himself against a stainless steel toolbox and inserts a needle into his forearm, attaches a tube, and then connects the opposite end to my central vein.

Thirty minutes ago, I was meeting Jon. I was wearing a floral print sundress. Now it's all ruined: my life, my illusion, my dress. This doesn't happen to people like me. I get good grades, I brush my teeth—I'm a good girl. What did I do?

Jack feels beneath my ribcage. His fingers are vultures picking at my necrotic corpse. "The bullet must be lodged beneath your false ribs, within your external oblique muscle." He uncaps a bottle of vodka. "This is going to hurt." Before I have a chance to respond, he pours the clear liquid onto the wound. A searing pain spreads through me. Yes—I *am* screaming.

Tremors of resilient determination replace the hot agony, and an icy sensation numbs my limbs. Death—this is what dying feels like, isn't it? *Help. Mom. Dad. Jon. Sybil. Save me. Please. Someone. Anyone. Don't let me die. I'm not ready to die.*

My dress gets wetter and the world spins, mixing blood with vomit, faces into the cosmic roar. Angry voices and sharp pain. Dust and crimson plasma. I never got to try the new brand of hazelnut flavoring that just arrived. Where did I put those shells we collected? Jon promised he would keep me safe. Liar. I'll never believe him again.

"You better move fast. She's going into shock." Tally glances back from the driver's seat. "Wow, that's a lot of blood. How is she not dead yet?"

"Be quiet." Jack lifts the vial of alcohol to my mouth and forces me to drink. There must be something wrong with his voice. It's muffled. Wait. Why is his face blurry? Why can't I taste the vodka or feel pain? I really am dying. This is happening. Right now. *No, I can't die yet. God, don't let me die. I'm too young. There's so much I've yet to do.*

Jack unwraps a package of scalpels. "Stay with me, Julie."

I'm in the ocean, rocking back and forth with a surging current. These waves are safe, warm. They embrace me in a sort of unnatural quiet. I'll stay and swim for a while. Maybe Jon will show up to dive for sand dollars. He likes how they fit in his hands.

Jack removes his t-shirt and tucks the fabric between my teeth. "I don't have any anesthetics so once I begin surgery, you'll feel everything. The pain's intensity should make you pass out. Stay still. If I make a mistake, you could die." He sticks the blade of his scalpel into my flesh and cuts.

The wad of sweaty, blood-drenched clothing straddles my teeth like floss—putrid, boy-tasting floss. Death sears through my nervous system as Jack digs into me. It's more severe and harrowing than anything I've ever felt. This is torture, torment. Dying might be better. No more suffering. No more heartbreak. *I want to die now. Please let me die.*

Jack curses when a gust of blood explodes from the incision. His bare chest and arms are splattered with red. He clasps a hand over his mouth, clutches his head. He seems to be scared. Because he's covered in me. Because I am about to leave the world. "There's a tear in the abdominal wall. Julie, I need you to be still while I make sutures."

"Make her shut up," Tally's voice echoes with ferocious authority.

"She hasn't passed out yet."

"Duh, that's why she is still squealing like a freaking baby. Do something."

Angry voices. Pain and numbness, sharp and dull—they twist inside me. Something stifles my screams and then eyes. Those eyes, blue. No cobalt. Indigo? Azure? Sapphire? No just cold blue. Hateful eyes. Cold, hard blue eyes. Eyes that were so pretty an hour ago. Eyes that sparkled and laughed.

His face is pinched, serious, and I hate it. How could you? Jon loves you. Jon believed you and you've betrayed him. Stabbing pain ... an angry face. A face that only a few seconds ago I thought was my friend. A face I had finally started to trust.

He removes his hands from my torso and lifts me into his lap. "You're not going to die. I'm a good surgeon. I will keep you alive." His bloody fingers rest directly above my collarbone. "Don't give up. Keep fighting. This isn't over." His grip tightens. The universe spirals. I'm saturated in safe, warm waves—slowly, and then all at once.

****

If I had known what would happen to me, maybe things could've been different, but that's what we all believe, isn't it? That awareness of future events offers us a chance to make changes to our fate, that knowledge gives us power to play God? If Jon hadn't come home, if I hadn't met Jack, if we had been at a different place at the right time—maybe things would have been different. None of those scenarios matter now, though. What happened, happened. I can't change the past, so I must look to the future while drowning in memories.

Rewind. Repeat. Relive.

There are certainties, small infinities this world offers like ocean breezes, skies streaked with white lines like mega Etch-A-Sketches, people's voices as they rush like currents through civilization. Life will forever exist, no matter what happens to us or around us. The sky will remain blue, wind will still blow, and somewhere a voice will mutter. Jon says my obsession with simple things is cute, but when things aren't simple and certain, I get hurt. Cling to what is infinite. Avoid change.

I roll over and stare through the dark lenses of my sunglasses at the manicured green space nestled between Porter's Lodge and Randolph Hall. Students lounge on the lawn, basking in the midafternoon heat. Their white-noise chatter, the clip-clop of horse hooves, and the occasional car horn blaring from the streets outside the College of Charleston create a rhythm, and I tap my foot to the beat.

When my cell phone alarm detonates, playing a repetitive acoustic strum, I climb up from the ground and fold my quilt into a neat, grassy wad. Students glance at me with upturned noses. Whatever. They're jerks, whispering about how my handmade sundress looks like it belongs to a grandma, gossiping about my dead sister and semi-crazy parents. I don't care. Well, maybe I do. Just a little.

Everyone wants to deny what hurts them the most, to be strong and untouchable, but it's easier to fall than stand upright, easier to break instead of stumbling through life wrapped in my own duct tape, easier to accept what I see in the mirror rather than let the pain of someone else's tongue tear me down. Easy isn't always best, but what's complex is hardly ever worth the struggle.

I move toward the antebellum arches of Porter's Lodge where my vintage, 1950 Schwinn Spitfire is propped. With a swing and a shove, I peddle down George Street and arrive at The Grindery moments later. It's a coffeehouse located on Broad Street—a pastel-blue building with yellow trim and massive, arching windows. A full-grown palmetto sprouts from the curb.

Missy sighs when I enter the café. "There you are. This place has been a madhouse all day."

I grab a red apron from the employee coat rack and fasten it over my dress.

"Whew, it's too warm outside for people to be drinking this much brew," Dax says as I restock the mini-fridge with milk. Her t-shirt and jeans are caked with grounds.

"Julie, you didn't leave your bike out front again, did you?" Philip strides from the back room with a crate of fruit. "Trees are not bicycle racks."

"I parked in the alley."

"Good girl." He pats my shoulder and unloads the produce onto a concrete counter. *Good girl*—the stereotype has ruined my social life. *Good* isn't fun. *Good* isn't interesting. *Good* gets you home and in bed before ten, decent grades, respect from adults, and zero friends your own age.

Missy leans against me and lowers her soprano voice to a muffled whisper. "Want to hang out in the park tonight? I have things I need to tell you."

"Anything wrong?"

She shrugs. "Your mom was in here a few hours ago. She bought an Italian soda and showed me a picture of her latest masterpiece…"

Missy isn't a secretive person, quite the opposite. We've been close friends since my first day as a barista, when I accidentally spilled coffee grounds onto Philip's favorite couch. Missy spent hours helping me clean the upholstery. It was the first kind deed anyone had done for me in years and since that moment, she's been like my sister. In appearance, we are a great contrast. She's tall and full-figured with long, braided hair and a smooth, chocolate complexion. I'm barely five-feet-six-inches, flat-chested with dyed blonde hair and skin in desperate need of a summer tan.

I reach under the counter and remove a stack of new magazines to replace the tattered copies on the rack. Their glossy covers are adorned with thin bodies and white teeth, perfect except for a single flaw. The same model plasters three issues of *Vogue*. Was it an editorial mistake? Did they only have enough money to hire one gorgeous, freak alien model?

For the next few hours, Missy and I mix lattes and seep herbal teas. I clean the grinder and make an espresso for a man playing his guitar. She wipes tables and dusts sugar over a batch of lemon squares.

Some drink coffee to complete their stereotype: that woman in the corner attempting to write a novel and the teenager pretending to be a philosophical poet. I drink coffee because I like its warmth, its consistency. The bitter taste that ignites my blood with caffeine.

As I swirl whipped cream onto an iced coffee, Missy grabs my bicep in a crazed death-grip. Her eyelids stretch apart and her jaw drops. She motions to the café's threshold.

"Holy ... wow, I didn't know they could look like that," she says.

I follow the path of her focus to a man standing near the coffeehouse's entrance. He looks to be around my brother's age—twenty-three or twenty-four—with a perfectly chiseled body and short brown hair. His eyes are blue, a shade so unnaturally cobalt they must be contacts. Framed beneath thick, arching eyebrows and matted by stalwart features, his irises contrast like stars in the night sky, like Missy and me. He's beautiful. I know men aren't supposed to be, but he is.

The stranger moves toward us with his gaze transfixed on the menu above our heads. For a man so incredibly handsome, he's dressed plainly—denim jeans, a gray t-shirt, sneakers, and a leather jacket similar to Philip's. He sways back and forth, hands stashed in his pockets.

"I'm surprised his shirt hasn't burned off," Missy whispers.

That'd be a sight—guy in a coffeehouse, t-shirt rolling off his sculpted abdomen in a cloud of ash. I laugh, and then my stomach twists with a hurricane of hormonal butterflies and I can't breathe. I'm not this shallow. Good looks do not affect me. Even so, the closer he approaches, the faster my heart beats. Stop looking at him. Be professional. He's not an explicit image from a trashy tabloid. He is a human. Treat him like a normal, coffee-loving human who isn't at all attractive. *Think of Jon. Okay. Better.*

"What can we get for you today?" Missy props herself against the counter and leans far enough forward to showcase her not-flat chest.

"An espresso, double-shot." He places a ten-dollar-bill near the cash register.

"Sure ... are those real?" My friend leans further to inspect our customer's blue irises.

"Excuse me?"

"Your eyes. Are they real?"

He takes a step back and flashes his bleached smile. "Yes, they're real." A chain hangs over the collar of his t-shirt—ID tags. He's in the military, like my brother, Jon.

"You can sit down, if you want. We'll bring your drink to you," I say.

His pupils explode, melt, and evaporate me all at the same inconvenient time. They decipher my expressions like mathematical equations. Then, the intensity of his hypersonic analysis subsides. His lips twitch into a small, understanding smile. "Keep the change." He moves to a table set against one of the many antique windows, pulls a book from the pocket of his jacket, and flips through its stained pages.

Missy needs to turn on the air conditioning. It's too hot in here. Sweat beads on my neck, slides into my dress. I hold a chilled gallon of milk to my chest where lungs sink against the back of my ribcage, expand and ache. Blue eyes touched my skin, reached into my head. Now they linger by the window, probing a more interesting open book. If I could, I'd ball up on the cool, tile floor and hide from them because I know better than anyone that to be truly seen is to be changed or hurt.

"Go talk to him," Missy says and offers me a cup of espresso.

"No. You should take him the coffee. My shift ends soon and I promised Dax I'd clean the toilets." I slide past her and scoot toward the bathroom. Wiping up pee and soap spills are preferable to speaking to a dagger-eyed, hot-bodied customer. Besides, no one wants to watch pathetic me try to converse with a man way out of my league, like in another universe *out of my league*. A simple hello would be so embarrassing, it'd evoke the apocalypse.

"That won't be a problem. I'll go clean the bathrooms and *you* can give that pretty boy his espresso." She shoves the mug into my hands and leaves me to confront the stranger, his soul-rupturing eyes, and my hurricane of hormonal butterflies alone.

I hold a breath captive behind smiling teeth and stand up straight. Boys sense fear—they're like dogs or bears. There's no reason to be afraid. He is a normal, coffee-loving human. But what about me? I'm the problem. I have a tendency to trust easily and I get hurt. At first, the betrayals and rejections only knocked me down for a short time, like tripping and scraping a knee.

Then it became harder for me to get up after falling. One day, I didn't get up. I stayed with my face pressed to the pavement. It seems like I've been lying on the ground for years, incapable of trusting anyone.

Why am I shaking? Gross, I have sweat stains underneath my armpits. Ugh, I'm going to throw up. What's wrong with me?

"Here's the espresso you ordered." I lower the steaming cup to his table. "Let me know if you need anything else." Maybe he'll be a jerk and not respond. Please let him be a jerk.

He looks at me. It's as if I'm transparent. "Your name is Julie?" He motions to my nametag.

I nod because the violence of his stare makes speaking impossible. After several seconds of word vomiting, I say, "I've never seen you here before. What's your name?" Stupid. I should've said yes and left. It's the southern girl in me—I love people even when I hate them. I mask distain with cordiality, disgust with compliments, and stabs in the back with sweet hugs. Geez, I'm so passive aggressive.

"Jack," he says and shuts his book—some obscure zombie novel. "Was the espresso made with Ethiopian Harrar? It smells like it was." He sips the coffee like fine wine. Crema gets stuck in the stubble above his lip and glistens. Would it taste good? Ugh, gross thought. Back pedal. Refocus.

"Yeah. We purchase and import the beans from a special seller."

"Awesome. I'm sort of a coffee snob. People don't realize the importance of a quality bean, you know? Generic-brand grinds from the local Walmart do not make a decent cup of coffee." He lifts his tattered novel. "Do you believe in the possibility of a zombie apocalypse, Julie?"

"Uh, not really." My heartbeat roars within me. It says to stare at him, lower my guard, and flirt. Really flirt. Like a smitten teenage girl. But I can't. He is so beautiful, looking at him seems like an insult to God. And I don't want to insult God.

"Yeah, me neither. There are a million other more likely things that'll kill us first: nuclear bombs, disease, global warming, aliens, the closing of all fast food chains." His pupils look me up and down like the airport's full-body scan. "You'd be one heck of a zombie slayer, I can tell. You'd blast my brains with your old-fashioned shotgun before I could eat you. That's a compliment, just so you know. I rarely let somebody kill me in my doomsday scenarios. Besides, if there did happen to be a zombie apocalypse, I wouldn't be a zombie. I'd be the leader of a hardcore survival clan."

"Oh … okay." What a weirdo. Why do the hot ones have to be crazy?

"I'm really not a weirdo. I see the concept of zombies as a metaphor."

I choke on a wad of saliva. Is he a mind reader?

"There are two types of people in this world: dead and alive, corpses versus the living. Just because someone's heart is beating doesn't mean they're alive—at least, not really. To truly live, one must feel and experience new things, find joy, connection. *Zombies* are depressed, lonely people caught in routine, void of emotional ties. It's easy to be infected by the *dead*, but we must put up a fight. We must always choose life." His eyes narrow to squinty lines. "You're staring at me like I'm crazy."

"No, I just … I've never heard that perspective before."

He laughs, drinks from his cup, and gazes into me a few seconds longer than what is socially acceptable.

"You're pretty, Julie, and I know stating my observation aloud is considered fresh, an indiscreet come-on, but frankly I think more people should hear the truth about themselves. Screw what society thinks, right?"

A huff of laughter escapes my throat. Pretty? Me? He must be weird and crazy. How can something that was once deemed ugly become beautiful?

Jack's smile stretches into a full-fledged grin. "Wow, that's more than a pretty face. What I'm looking at now is painstakingly gorgeous." When my eyes widen, he waves his hands as if they're white flags in surrender. "Sorry, sorry. I didn't mean to freak you out. I have a tendency to be awkward around attractive people. It's a problem I'm trying to fix."

"You didn't freak me out," I say and rub the heat from my cheeks.

"Then why won't you look at me?" He leans forward to connect our line of sight. His pupils meet mine with searing intensity. "That's better."

The butterflies in my stomach morph into a stampede of horses, tsunami waves ramming against the cliff face of my emotions. Boys sense fear and they also sense attraction, the little devil that springs from poor girls' hearts when they meet an awkward, endearing guy who buys their coffee and talks about zombies. Sadly, I have both fear and attraction—Jack's hit the mother lode.

I cough. "So, do you live in Charleston?"

"No, I'm here on business." His smile has yet to fade, bright and reticent as if he knows a profound secret. He could easily be the poster boy for a toothpaste company or a Calvin Klein model in town to shoot a spread for next season's fashion line.

"You're in the army, aren't you? I caught a glimpse of your ID tags."

"I was but ... I'm not anymore. Things happened

and it became clear to me that I needed to choose another career. I'm a freelance researcher nowadays," he says. "Would have been a biochemist, but college takes too long. Even thought about becoming an artist, that is, if I didn't completely suck at art."

A moment of silence passes between us, offering a polite escape. I snatch an empty cup from a nearby table to make myself appear busy. "It was nice meeting you, Jack. I better get back to work."

"Would you like to have coffee with me sometime?"

My legs freeze, and I spin around to see if he's kidding. His eyes shimmer with sincerity—he really does want to have coffee. With me. Why? This must be a joke. Hot guys don't flirt with average girls unless they have a hidden agenda, a dark secret, or believe average equals easy. I'm not easy. I won't be hurt. Not by him. Or anyone.

"Sure, you work at this coffeehouse but even a barista must enjoy a cup of coffee every once in a while. I'm not a total freak. Let me prove it to you."

"What would we talk about? How you think I'm pretty?"

Jack laughs. It's a deep, infectious rumble. "No, we'll find something we have in common." He motions to his half-read novel. "Do you like to read?"

"Yeah, I guess."

"I bet there's a stack of books on your nightstand right now."

"Are you a stalker?"

He smiles and leans back in his chair. "I'm good at pegging people."

"Oh, really? How would you peg me?"

Jack leans against the window and scratches his chin. "Barista Julie, you aren't as complex as you think.

Let me guess. You've lived in Charleston your entire life…"

"Yes. Not hard to guess, though. I have a distinct accent."

"Don't give up on me yet. I still have to impress you," he says with a snicker. "Okay. You didn't go to a normal high school. I can tell this because of the way you talk, articulate and with confidence. But you aren't confident. You don't see yourself as beautiful, which is a bummer because you are stunning. And although you dress like a 1950s pin-up girl, wear more makeup than you need, and try to make it seem like you've accepted yourself, you haven't."

Seen and changed. Seen and hurt. He undressed me, sliced off my skin to peer into my heart and soul. He's a Know-It-All with a Pretty Boy attitude. Why should I allow his few observations to affect me? I'll be the bigger person and walk away like I usually do. But why am I still standing here?

Jack's smile vanishes. He shakes his head and mutters a self-aimed curse. "Gosh, I'm sorry, Julie. I just … have a habit of putting my foot in my mouth, especially around people I don't know. You seem to be a nice girl and I promise, I'm not a horrible guy."

"Would you like a biscotti with your espresso?" the passive aggressive southerner in me asks. Love when I hate. Compliment when I insult. Hug those who stab me and hug when I stab back.

"I can tell you're strong," he says before I have a chance to leave. "You are a survivor and even though you look fragile, you are unbelievably strong."

"You're sounding more and more like a flirt." Sugar and venom fill the words. Maybe they'll shut him up. Maybe he'll get the hint and leave my insecurities unexplored.

"Nah, I'm not trying to flirt with you. There's at least a five-year age difference between us, along with other conflicting details." He pauses for a second and then emits a reluctant sigh. "I have the habit of saying what I see because it's easier to point out other people's flaws and perfections rather than let them notice my own. Besides, why withhold a compliment from someone who might be in need of it?" His grin flickers into place. "By the way, I can be normal. I'm not sure why I've been creepy today."

Raw, unfiltered honesty—that's a new concept. Around here, people douse the truth with butter, sugar, and elaboration because no one wants to break a commandment by hurting their neighbor's feelings or reveal their own dirty sins. Instead, they are honest in private where the truth can't hurt anybody. I'm one of them. Holding my tongue has kept me safe from a lot of pain, but it's also caused a rift between who I am and how others view me. To be fully revealed is to be fully vulnerable.

Maybe that's okay.

Maybe I am ready to be seen.

Chapter Two

"There is no ideal world for you to wait around for. The world is always just what it is now, and it's up to you how you respond to it."

Isaac Marion, *Warm Bodies*

Tires grind asphalt when I swerve to a stop in front of my home on East Bay Street, otherwise known as Rainbow Row. It's a yellow building—tall and narrow with blue shutters. Grandpa bought us the house, at least, that's how Dad interprets his inheritance. He says colonels don't make a lot of money, and we should be grateful. Grateful for the creaky pipes. Grateful for the lack of decent air-conditioning. Grateful for the neighbor's demonic cat. Sure, there are a gazillion good things about my house, but without Jon and Sybil, it seems empty, almost eerie. I still use a nightlight.

"Mom, I'm home." I cross into the foyer and toss my purse onto the grand piano, next to a stack of colorful paintings. Gardenias fog the air with a perfume that smells of The Citadel in springtime, strolls along the Battery, and antebellum rooms.

"How was your day, sweetie?" Mom shouts from her studio.

Weird. Invasive. Humiliating. Filled with Know-It-All strangers, gossiping college kids, and a pushy best friend. "Same as usual. Any word from Jon? He was supposed to call us today."

A voice drifts down the spiral staircase—Mom forgot to turn off her audiobook again.

"Not yet."

A painful knot twists my stomach, makes me

cringe. Why hasn't he called? Has something happened to him? No. He's fine. Maybe the government assigned his platoon a lot of work today or something. He will call. He will come home. Like always.

I saunter into the living room. Unlike the rest of my house, photographs clutter these walls. It's the one place Mom and Dad have left personalized, untouched since Sybil's death. Paintings hold no memories. It's easier for them to replace the vestige of their past happiness with insignificant, aesthetic artwork. I understand but sometimes I want to remember the pain. It's the only way I can remember *her*.

A picture of my family hangs over the couch. It was taken eleven years ago on John's Island before Sybil's leukemia was discovered. Jon was thirteen at the time, I was seven, and Sybil, only five-years-old. Life was okay. Nothing was broken … yet.

Weeping. Sobbing. Sybil is intubated, eyes closed. My parents slump over her sallow figure, crying and praying. But their begging doesn't change God's mind. An eternal beep—the heart monitor flatlines. My body slams against the doorframe, then my butt hits the floor. Where are our mountains, the red notches that belonged to Sybil and me? She said her heart was creating a new world for us and through the monitor, we could catch a glimpse of it, a sketch of what our heaven will be. Did she go to our world without me? Why can't I go with her?

A loud shrill bursts from my mouth and echoes through the sterile halls like an ambulance's siren. Nurses try to hush me with soothing words, but I continue to wail. Tears stream my face. Anger explodes out of my mouth. I kick and claw as Jon throws me over his shoulder and drags me away from the threshold.

"She's not dead," I squeal. "We have to fix her. Let me go." The pain of infinite heartbreaks cuts through

my chest like a dagger. Beep—mountains. Beep—castles and princesses and no more cancer. Flatline—Sybil is gone.

Jon carries me into the empty waiting room and collapses on the floor. His warm t-shirt absorbs my tears, and my I Heart Nick Jonas *tank-top soaks up his jagged sobs. God could've taken me—why didn't he take me instead of her? The doctors said Sybil wouldn't get better, that she only had a short amount of time to live. I didn't believe them because accepting that my sister was dying would be like giving permission for her to go.*

"It's not fair," I say. "Why did she have to die?"

"We all have to die, Jules. Nobody can live forever," Jon says in a broken whisper. "Sybil just ... wasn't given much time. But she's better now, no more doctors and chemo."

"Is she in heaven?"

"Yeah ... she's in heaven." He pulls my knees into his lap and rocks me back and forth. "I don't fully understand why people live and die. It's a stupid, screwed-up system, and if I could, I'd change it all, but I can't. We are going to die too someday, which means we'll see Sybil again. She's not dead to us forever."

"You can't die too, Jon." I press my head against his chest and squeeze him tight. If I let him go, I may never get him back. "Do you think Mommy and Daddy will be okay?"

"They'll get better over time, but for the next few months, we're going to be on our own. They are really sad. We have to take care of them, be strong when they're not. You get that, don't you?" When I nod, he hugs me again. "You're brave. We can face this together. I promise."

Sybil's death stunned my family. For years, we lived in what felt like silence. Dad retired from the military, spent his time in local bars and rarely came home at night. Mom locked herself in her studio and stared out the window, speechless and distant. Jon took care of me. He drove me to school, made my meals, and kept me hopeful. Then one day, my parents came back to life. We resumed our daily routine and slowly healed back into a family. Things weren't perfect, but we survived.

Mom uses the tip of her foot to push open the studio's door. She smiles—blue paint specks her teeth. "There's peach tea in the fridge, if you're thirsty." She sits in front of her easel, working diligently on a portrait of Charleston Harbor. A blue sailboat is anchored off the watercolor shore. After Sybil died, sailboats took precedence over her other muses.

"I brought home tonight's rations." Colonel Stryker appears in the foyer, wearing his professorial Citadel uniform, with an armful of takeout. He winks at me. "Guess what's in these bags."

"Sushi from downtown." His wink and the chopstick stabbing through a bag gave away the answer. Eel rolls, soy sauce, miso soup—saliva fills my mouth. "You're the best, Dad."

"Let's eat on the patio tonight." Mom jumps up from her workspace and rushes to the kitchen. Within a matter of minutes, the three of us are seated outside beneath strings of lights, talking about college, Dad's students, and Mom's commissioned painting of the USS Yorktown. Exams with grades. Faceless names. Inanimate objects. My sushi is more personable than them.

Hey, I shouldn't complain. At least they're talking like normal human beings instead of wobbling around the house, grunting and staring into space. I'm thankful, really. The silence was killing me. What hurts now, though, is worse. It's what comes after a war, that devastating aftermath where soldiers dwell in numbness, terrified of the day when they might have to refight their battles. We're all living in a universal tragedy where people die, love fails, and wounds run so deep, they can't be healed. The trick to surviving such a pessimistic reality is to build walls around our hearts so we won't be in pain, or we could live life to the fullest. I'm not sure which option is more beneficial.

Jack's bleached smile and blue eyes appear on my plate. Did I forget to eat lunch? Yes, I only had an apple. If I eat more sushi, maybe he'll disappear. Maybe I'll stop thinking about him, what he said, the crema glistening on his upper lip. There's something strange about him, as if he knows a dark revelation that will change everything, but as much as I want to forget about our meeting, I can't rid myself of the unsettling feeling that our lives are somehow intertwined.

"May I be excused?" I ask midway through my parents' conversation on the building project downtown. "There's homework I need to do." This excuse always works with Dad, whose greatest peeve is late homework.

"Yeah, go ahead. I'll put your leftovers in the fridge." Mom pours herself another glass of wine. "Remember, you're going to the Market with me tomorrow morning. We leave at seven o'clock, okay?"

"I'll be ready." I stuff two pieces of sushi into my mouth and go upstairs.

Polaroids dangle from wire over my wrought-iron bed. Shelves, brimming with books, cover the crimson walls, along with my collection of vintage typewriters. What Jack guessed about me is true—there's a stack of novels on my nightstand.

Words have the potential to build exquisite cathedrals of syntaxes, illustrious syllables and picturesque verbiage, but also have the power to start wars and drive men to suicide. I'm addicted to their dynamism like a junkie to cocaine. I write. I read. I listen. I speak.

If words were wine, I'd be an alcoholic.

Makeup-removing wipes are antagonists. When I press them to my face, they steal what I have of self-esteem and transform me into a clean canvas—bare, vulnerable, and honest. For months I've told myself that if I dress like I'm beautiful, I'll feel confident. So I cover up my figure with retro dresses and cosmetics, all in a desperate attempt to fix my ego.

It doesn't work.

There's a fat girl in the mirror who looks an awful lot like me. She's thirteen-years-old with braces, pimples, and mousy hair—someone the boys called ugly, the girls told to sit alone. I touch the curves of my waist, the flatness of my abdomen. I've changed. I've grown up. Why can't I see myself in the glass? Where are the flat stomach and slender thighs?

Jon told me there isn't a single person in this world persuasive enough to convince me of my worth, not even him. He said the day I fully accept what I see in the mirror is the day I free myself from the past. He's probably right, but how can I accept a lying reflection? I don't like the girl I see.

Hugh Grant and Julia Roberts appear in my television screen, lounging on a London park bench. She's pregnant. He is reading. And they are in love. Oh, romance movies, you strike again.

I change into pajamas and collapse onto my bed with a handful of dark chocolate and nail polish. The film fades to black and the credits roll, interrupted by a commercial I've seen a million times, one of those obnoxious advertisements for Charleston residents.

"Meet the Jones Family," the narrator says when a suburban, ranch-style home materializes on the screen. A father with gelled hair and a mustard sweater vest pushes a lawnmower across his pristine yard. The mother has her locks twisted into a bouffant and hovers over a flowerbed, sprinkling plants with her watering can. "They understand the value of stability and hard work."

A little girl and boy play hopscotch in the driveway. They giggle, wave at the camera. "Home is swell," says the kids. "We do not wish to leave such a neat place."

"Dinner is ready." Mrs. Jones pulls a meatloaf from an oven and sets it on the kitchen's Formica table. Her smile dazzles white against a mint-green backdrop. Then, the camera zooms out to showcase the family. They all grin as if they're high on Prozac.

"Golly, darlin'. The food looks terrific." Mr. Jones tucks a napkin into his shirt collar and pecks his wife on the cheek. "Why travel when we live in the happiest town on Earth? Home is our vacation."

"Enjoy the luxury of your inhabited paradise," the narrator states in a robotic tone. "Do not stray from your home-sweet-home. Be safe in the same, like the Jones Family, and remember, credence exuberates concord. Charleston, South Carolina—the happiest place in the USA."

My phone vibrates with a text from Missy.

****

Waterfront Park is quiet, locked in the serene shadows of dusk. For eighteen years I've come here to laugh, sob, and think. Not once has it changed. Fountains still bubble with illuminated opulence. Couples still weave between rows of palmettos, whispering and holding hands. Change leads to death, so by staying in my evergreen garden where time is irrelevant and replaceable, I am, in essence, saving myself. But if I'm frozen, when the past slides its fingers up my spine, how will I be able to escape?

Jon will save me, of course. He'll grab my face in his hands and tell the past to get lost. Goodness, I think too much. Life is normal, a paradise of beautiful sameness—the same rivers that welcomed the Swamp Fox into the harbor greet me each morning, the same churches that watched the first shots of the Civil War launch from Ft. Sumter observe my bike ride to work. Charleston is a bastion, a dig-in-your-heels-and-hang-on kind of city. It has stood, fallen, and been rebuilt after hurricanes. It has modified itself but remained largely unchanged. It is delicate and rugged and strong. It is a guardian of tradition. Same—I like same. Same is good. Same is safe.

Missy waits at our spot: a park-bench overlooking the Cooper River. "Took you long enough." She hands me a latte—hazelnut, my favorite—and pats the space next to her.

"What's wrong?" I sit down. Coffee washes across my tongue, warm and bitter, sweet as sin. It's a scandalous, caffeinated affair in my mouth. An espresso-based boyfriend. A guiltless romance free of purity-taking, love children, and heartbreak. Perfect.

"Nothing." Tears roll down her cheeks. She stares ahead at the dark, churning water.

"Something is obviously wrong. You're never this quiet."

She rolls her eyes. "Am I not allowed to be quiet?"

I drink from the paper cup and cross my legs. "Of course. Sorry."

She sighs. I sigh. She sighs again.

"I'm leaving Charleston."

"You're what?" Coffee spills onto my lap, waterfalls down my calves. Hold on. Back up. Why would she want to leave Charleston? This is our home, our paradise. "Leaving, like, moving away?"

"Yeah, that's what I'm doing." She wipes her tears and fidgets with her cell phone.

"Why? What about college? You're a semester away from graduation."

"I'm transferring to USC for classes in the fall." She presses my hand between hers and looks at me with what seems like desperation—lips parted, brow furrowed, brown skin flushed. "It's not like I want to leave. It's just … my mom was diagnosed with Alzheimer's last month. I need to be with her. Columbia is only a few hours away. You can visit."

Sybil's hospital room was in the oncology wing's pediatric ward, fourth door on the left. Mom made me use hand sanitizer each time I'd wander down the corridor or enter my sister's room, as if being around sick kids would inflict me as well, as if disinfectant was potent enough to prevent a testy thing like cancer. Then, Sybil died and hand sanitizer couldn't offer hope in the power of medicine. It was useless. Leukemia, Alzheimer's—they aren't much different. They both steal and destroy.

"Why didn't you tell me about your mom?" Pain trickles into my chest, fills the cavity caused by losing Sybil. I dig my fingernails into the bench and wheeze on the memories.

She shrugs. "You're my best friend. I didn't want you to worry."

Makes sense. I will worry because watching my sister die screwed me up real bad. Missy won't be the same after her mom passes. It's impossible to lose a loved one and not let a piece of yourself die with them. "When are you leaving?"

"In two weeks. Not much of a heads up, I know."

Fourteen days before my best friend abandons Charleston. That's not enough time. I can't read the Harry Potter series in fourteen days, remodel a house, or have a new dress made for me by the elderly seamstress in Isle of Palms. No, no. I need, at least, a month with her.

"Your mom ... it isn't bad yet, right? She still remembers everything?"

"Mostly. She's a tad forgetful, you know, misplacing things, not remembering names and places. She remembers what's important, though. It will be a while before her memory suffers a major loss. Forgetting is a slow process."

"Yeah, very slow."

How can I say goodbye to her? I'm terrible at saying goodbye. It feels like being stuck in a corner with no way of escape. Goodbye is imminent—unchangeable, uncontrollable, certain. So I fear it as I fear being cornered. I always need to believe there's an escape.

I rub the tension from my face and lean against Missy's shoulder. "Don't you ever wish you could rewind time, do things differently?"

"The past isn't something to regret. It defines who we are. Of course, there are things I wish I could've done differently, but nothing I'd change. Through tempest, we find strength."

"I must still be fighting my way through tempest then, because I've yet to find strength."

Missy turns her eyes from the star-streaked sky to me. "What makes you say that?"

"Strength is choosing to stand up after being knocked down. I am still on the ground."

"Then get up," she whispers.

A single blaze shoots across the horizon, then

another. One-by-one, streaks of stardust paint the eternal canvas, spiral into a cosmos display and ignite the atmosphere with a brilliant white light.

"Falling stars." Missy gasps. She entwines her arm around my shoulders and pulls me close. "It's a sign, Julie. Something incredible is going to happen, I'm sure." Her optimism and faith in happy endings are cute, but she won't have them for much longer.

"Maybe." The estuarine breeze ripples my hair, squeezes through my forced smile. Could the phenomenon be an omen of some sort? Is this God's way of telling me to follow Missy's advice?

Meteors enter the stratosphere, burning in descent. They fall. They stop. They bounce across an invisible surface and remain flickering, trapped above Earth like planets caught in orbit.

"How'd they stop falling? What's suspending them?" If I didn't have a heart condition before tonight, I'm sure I do now. "There are space rocks in the sky. I would say it's impossible but ... it happened so obviously, it's not impossible."

People search for explanations they can understand. Whether or not the final explanation is true doesn't matter. If it's plausible, if it can be written in a scientific journal, if no man will contradict it, the explanation must be valid. I'd rather accept the unknown than lie to myself.

"It's a sign," Missy says. "It's definitely a sign."

Chapter Three

"People generally see what they look for, and hear what they listen for."
Harper Lee, *To Kill a Mockingbird*

The City Market, a remodeled shed stretching four blocks, was once where farmers would barter their beef and produce. Now it's mainly a tourist attraction selling imported merchandise, local artwork, and Gullah sweet-grass baskets. Mom displays her paintings at a booth overlooking the cobblestone streets and talks with different customers. She sells a pastel picture of Rainbow Row to a couple from Georgia and an acrylic sailboat to an old man who appears to be more interested in her than the art.

Crowds flow past, sweaty and loud. The rank aroma of body odor and sulfur burns my lungs like acid. I weave between vendors to inspect a display of pearl jewelry and flip through a stack of photography— *Credence exudes concord* is written in calligraphy at the top of a vintage print. Who'd want to decorate their house with an ad slogan?

"I've been trying to get in touch with her for years," the lady next to me says to her friend. "I've spoken with other people who have family members living far away. They haven't been able to contact anyone either. Something is happening and it's bad. The airport has been closed for months. Construction's blocked off the roads heading north. I think … we're stuck here."

Stuck? We're not stuck in Charleston. Tourists come here and buy Mom's artwork. Missy talks to her family in Columbia every day. We could leave, but why would we want to stray from home-sweet-home? What place is better than paradise?

Magazine mistakes. Space rocks hovering in the sky. *Something is happening ... and it's bad ... we're stuck here.* No, everything is fine and normal and same. There isn't a grand conspiracy hidden under our noses. *Stuck here ... something bad ... it's happening.*

Mom waves me over to her table. "I'm almost ready to leave, Julie. When do you have to be at the college?" She packs her paintings in a plastic bin.

"Eleven o'clock."

Mom checks the time on her cell phone. "That gives us about an hour to visit Sybil." She must be kidding. We haven't gone to my sister's gravesite in years. "Go buy a few sweet-grass flowers from the boys outside." She hands me a five-dollar bill and camouflages the sadness in her eyes with a laugh. "Stop looking at me like that. Go. I'll close up shop and be out in a few minutes."

****

We drive in silence. Wind whips through the open windows of Mom's Land Rover, blowing our hair in a frenzy. Charleston's downtown district fades into the distance. Historic buildings have been replaced with depleted factories and rundown apartment complexes. Should I speak? What's there to say? Mom rarely mentions Sybil, never her death. It's something we don't talk about.

Everyone wants to deny what hurts them the most.

Gravel crunches beneath the tires as we drive into the cemetery. Headstones protrude from the manicured grass, final evidence of the once living. Hundreds of people buried in the earth, rotting like banana peels on the roadside, important people who are important no more. And that's what makes me sad because I want life to matter even when it's gone, I want the survivors who lowered their husbands, wives, mothers, fathers, and siblings into the dirt to know I understand their loss.

Mom parks the car and together, we walk to Sybil's grave. My heart beats a rhythm that sounds like a death-march. Nine years ago, my sister died from leukemia. Nine years ago, we buried her in this cemetery. Nine years ago, everything fell into ruin.

"Sybil Stryker was a joy to everyone she met." The grim-faced preacher clutches his Bible and gestures to the awaiting casket. "She smiled through adversity, laughed when everyone else wanted to cry, and left a legacy of perseverance and love. Do not despair, Friends. As children of God, we will see Sybil again one day."

Jon grips my shoulders tight as pallbearers lift our sister's casket from the ground. Although his expression is hard, tears pour from his eyes like waterfalls. I cling to him as if he's a lifeline. Where are Mommy and Daddy? Did they stay at the funeral home? They're not with the people in black. They're not with Jon and me.

A group of men I've never met before lower Sybil into the earth. The flowers fall from my hands. I slide out of Jon's grasp and run toward the hole, screaming through a curtain of tears.

"Get her out. She's scared of the dark." I beat my fists against them, hitting and clawing until my body aches with exhaustion. "She is not dead. She can't be dead. Get her out."

"Jules, stop." Jon yanks me away from the plot of dirt. He spins me around and looks at my weepy face. "Let her go. We have to."

"Jon..." What am I going to do with Sybil's

Barbie dolls? I can't play with them by myself. Will Mommy still take me to the teahouse? Sybil liked the cucumber sandwiches. I can make some and bring them here so we can have tea parties. But she's dead.

He lifts me into his arms and escapes from the funeral mob. We collapse at the base of an old oak tree. I curl up in his embrace and allow him to stroke my hair.

"We're okay, Jules. You don't have to be scared," he says. *"When you're afraid, think of me. I'll always be around to protect you. It's what big brothers do."*

I place the bouquet of sweet-grass flowers onto Sybil's grave. Mom stands beside me, motionless. If I could, I'd pick her up and escape all this like Jon did for me. I'd stroke her hair and tell her not to be afraid, but I can't fix the past. I can't bring my sister back from the dead. I can't do anything.

"Like most moms, I never thought I'd … lose a kid," she says after several long minutes of silence. "Sybil was the least of my worries. As a baby, she was healthy and full of energy. Your dad and I were positive Jon would be the first to get hurt or sick. He was a little daredevil and liked to put gross things in his mouth. And you were the curious child who was too smart to do anything stupid. But Sybil … when you and Jon got sick with colds, she didn't. She was *never* sick." Mom pauses and takes a deep breath. "When the doctors told us she had leukemia, I laughed. I actually laughed. And a year later, she was dead. My healthy, energetic baby was dead."

This is the first time Mom has talked about Sybil since the heart monitor flatlined. Her world, once she reentered it, consisted of paint, small conversation, and Kelly Ripa. Nothing personal. I started to believe she couldn't remember the past. Block the memories. Block the hurt.

"You and Jon never gave up on me. Every day you brought me food and water. Once, I think you even tried to force me into the shower." She snickers with bitterness. "I'm surprised you don't hate your father and me for abandoning you the way we did. I regret it … every day of my life."

"None of that matters anymore. We're okay."

"It *does* matter," she says. "You're my kid. I love you and Jon more than anything. It hurts to remember what I put you through, what I went through. After all these years, I've tried to be a better…"

"You have," I say. "You've been a *great* mom. I wouldn't trade you for the world."

She embraces me. A single tear slips down her cheek and drips off her chin. We stay huddled next to Sybil's grave, finally able to breathe without pain.

Together, we remove our faces from the pavement. And after a while, we stand up.
****

The remainder of my morning is routine. I attend classes at the college, spend an hour lying in the green space between Randolph Hall and Porter's Lodge, and commute to The Grindery for an afternoon shift. Missy helps me tie on my apron with a perturbed look on her face.

"What's wrong?"

"We're out of milk."

Easy problem to fix. "Okay … I'll go to the store and buy more."

"Don't bother," she huffs. "I was just there. Every grocer in the county is out of stock."

"What? Why? We can't make most of our drinks without…"

"Yeah, I know." She pours black coffee into a ceramic mug and hands it to a customer. "Dax and Philip are out looking for milk now."

Weird. How can the city be out of milk? Who screwed-up the shipments and distribution? From where does our milk usually come?

I plate a slice of quiche. "Should we close the café until they get back?"

"No, let's serve what we can." She pours ice into the blender. "You're not mad at me for what I said last night, are you?"

"Of course not." I rinse the coffee grounds out of the portafilter and flush the machine's group head.

"Good." Missy drapes an arm over my shoulders and grins. "Oh, and that guy from yesterday is here. He bought you a cup of coffee and is waiting by the window."

Please let her be thinking about another guy customer. Nope, it's Jack. What possessed him to come back? He can't bribe me with coffee. Well, yeah, he probably can, but I don't want him to want to bribe me. Why? I'm not sure. Maybe because all this is too incredible to be real. Maybe because I've watched too many girls be hurt by gorgeous, endearing men. But I need to know why he's here. I need to know if there's even the smallest chance this could be real.

"You could've led with that, Missy." I turn my head, meeting Jack's observant gaze. He waves at me from across the room and motions to an awaiting mug of coffee. Nausea dissolves my stomach. Never mind. I don't want to talk with him. Talking leads to liking. And liking leads to heartbreak. Hot guy flirting with an average girl—the equation doesn't add up.

What if I'm just bad at math?

The march across the coffeehouse is turbulent and physically impossible, like swimming against a riptide during a thunderstorm. Heart pounds. Knees buckle.

Jon's voice in the back of my head tells me to be gutsy, have gumption, swallow my fear and swim against the current with Olympic speed. Jack smiles before closing his zombie-novel. His cobalt eyes pierce through me like daggers. Swim, Julie, swim.

"What's your problem?" If I appear angry and confrontational, it's possible he won't be able to break me. "Do you flirt with every girl you meet or only the ones who bring you coffee?"

"I don't understand." He tilts his head, furrows his thick brow. "I'm not flirting with you."

No man should be that handsome. It's unfair and offensive to all the other guys on Earth. If we were made in God's image, then he was made to look like someone else. His face is perfectly chiseled—I want to touch it. I want to run my fingers through his soft, styled hair without anyone batting an eye. Goodness, he can break me.

"Then, what do you want? Is this all a big joke, a game?"

"I don't want anything from you. I don't have a motive. I'm not an evil supervillain." He scoots his chair closer to me and looks up into my illusionary bastion. "Listen, Julie. I'm not around people often, due to my job. So when I do find someone I like, I try to build a relationship. And as surprising as it is, I actually like you." He said my name. Why did it sound different from his mouth, like poetry, like it belonged to someone more charming and elegant than me?

"We're strangers."

"You're different, and I know that's probably the most cliché response ever given, but it's the truth. When I look at you, it's as if I'm reading a novel. No matter how much time I spend studying your pages, there will always be more for me to learn, deeper layers of complexity to baffle me, and plot twists that'll leave me speechless." His lips lift into a cheeky, puerile grin. He's teasing me.

"So I'm a specimen for observation, like a lab rat? We don't know each other. This is the second time you've been here. What if I don't want you *reading* me?"

"You're definitely more spectacular than a lab rat." His smile returns, an incandescent contrast against his summer-tanned skin. "I'm not going to be in Charleston for long. Once I finish my tasks, I'm leaving. No harm done. So please, sit down. I'm not drinking another cup of coffee and I certainly do not want five-dollars to be poured down the drain. You can even chug the stuff if you're that set on *not* talking to me." He pushes out the picnic chair across from him. "Come on, Julie."

The chair is restricted area. If I sit and cross the line between customer and barista, bad things will happen. Is coffee worth compromising my safety? Is Jack worth the risk?

I slide into the chair. Foam warms my tongue, sweet and familiar. "A hazelnut latte?"

"Missy told me it's your favorite. She used the last bit of milk to make it for you." Jack's like one of Mom's paintings. Up close, I see his imperfections: several acne scars and slightly crooked teeth. Ugh, his flaws only make him prettier.

"She's so thoughtful." Sarcasm, of course. Missy is a devious matchmaker. She once tried to pair me with her cousin. Now that I think about it, she tries to pair all her single friends with her cousins.

"What sort of books do you read, Julie? Don't lie and say you hate reading." He gulps what remains of his espresso—curse that crema on his upper lip—and leans forward.

"I'm a literature junkie. I read everything. Chalk

one up. Your guess was correct." Figment fire burns my cheeks when his mouth twists into a goofy, gorgeous smile, as if I'm funny and captivating and totally out of his league. Hazelnut latte and a hot boy. Awkward eye contact and bizarre conversations. He's my type, isn't he? "Now, what about you, Jack? What kind of books do you like?"

"I'm a literature junkie. I read everything," he copycats. His piercing eyes and grin soften. "I am a huge fan of end-of-the-world scenarios. At the moment, *zombies* are my forte."

"You don't look like the breed of guy who enjoys reading."

"Because I'm not gangly and nerdy, I must be an idiot, right?" He snickers. "Nobody can place me in a category. I'm the peculiar sort of person who doesn't fit any of society's stereotypes, which annoys the mess out of humanity. People want to have the power to stamp a name on the foreheads of others, even themselves. They have to classify everything to understand the world. Without a name, they don't have an identity. It's like attending a huge convention where everyone wears nametags. One person joins the midst without a sticker on their chest and the entire system is botched, chaos unravels, and what was meant to be a quiet day filled with lectures and exhibitions becomes pandemonium."

Long answer—I was expecting a brief chuckle, not a societal analysis. "Why are you interested in end-of-the-world scenarios? Does it matter how we end, or that we ended at all?"

"After *the end of the world*, there is a world. Life doesn't stop. It changes. Mankind may fade away, but unless the planet explodes, something will reside here." He rubs his neck, blushing. "I've read every book and article dealing with the subject and have formulated a theory of my own."

"Let me hear it." This must be a dream because in front of me sits a boy who could have anyone, do and be anything, yet he's red-faced for a girl who's spent her whole life at the cruel mercy of others, who is still thirteen and can't fit into her homecoming dress. It's true—life has changed without notice.

"Okay." Jack leans until he's inches from my face and then cups a hand around his mouth like a kid ready to tell a secret. He's close enough to kiss. "People have always expected *the end of the world* to be a dramatic, thematic event: war, disease, a sudden explosion. But what if *the end of the world* has already occurred? What if our final demise happened slowly, secretly … and we've been oblivious to it all?"

"That's an interesting thought. So you think we're living in the apocalypse, right now?"

"Yeah, right now."

He must be one of those conspiracy nut jobs. "Wow, you're serious."

"It's just a theory. Don't worry. We live in a messed-up world and I'm weirdly observant. Those two factors don't mix well." Jack pushes his coffee-stained novel across the table. "For you."

"But you haven't finished reading it yet."

"I've read it six times, actually." He laughs. "Yeah, the plot is mainly fixated on zombies, but the book is about so much more than that. The author is utterly brilliant, like, he changed my perspective of humanity. Read it and tell me what you think. Maybe we can discuss the underlining meaning next time you have coffee with me."

Next time. He wants a next time.

The tattered pages flip between my fingers. "Zombies, huh?"

"Yeah, zombies."

"I'm surprised you didn't write your phone number on the first page."

"You know, I thought about it," he says, "but I didn't want to seem too average. Instead, I'm going to come here every day, leave notes, and remain completely mysterious."

"Oh, wow. You've decided to be a stalker."

Jack laughs. "Well, I was aiming more for endearing, but I guess stalker is also an appropriate classification." His thin lips stretch into a smile so genuine, I can't help but smile back.

And this is how it starts, the beginning of a friendship that might just ruin me. I want it to be real as much as I want it to disappear. Walking away isn't an option because I made a promise to Jon last summer, during one of Mom's bad days. He took me onto the pier. I told him I loved him and he said, "You're loyal, Jules. Loyalty and love are very different."

I asked, "How so? What is love?"

He gave me a look I won't forget, a beaming gaze that transmitted across the gap between us. "You don't know what love is until you find it," he whispered, "but when you do, promise me you won't let it go. Promise you'll seek it out even when you're scared it'll hurt."

Jon is the one daring me now to swim faster, let Jack the Coffeehouse Stalker be my crazy, flirty friend. Okay. For Jon, I'd do anything.

"Fine, I'll read your book." I tuck the novel into my apron pocket. "Where are you from, Jack?"

"Are you interrogating me now?" He raises his eyebrows and sits back in his chair. "Tell me about you and I'll tell you about me. Fair?"

"You said I'm a complex novel. Read me and find out."

"I'm liking you more and more, Julie."

Be safe in the same, like the Jones Family—what the heck am I doing? This isn't safe. This isn't same. Who do I think I am, Taylor Swift, Jennifer Aniston? Superstar? Sexiest woman? No, I'm Julie Stryker, change-hating, coffee-drinking, dress-wearing bibliophile. Boys … what are boys? Why should I care if one wants to buy me lattes and talk about zombies?

To end the madness before it goes to my head, I turn my empty mug upside down. "I'm out of coffee." For some reason, the small movement hurts, sends an agonizing ache through my body. "Thanks, but I need to get back to work. See you later, Jack." Ouch, he's already caused me pain.

If I were daring and fearless…
If I were more than what I am…
If I knew I wouldn't get hurt…

The afternoon crowd comes and goes. Dax and Philip return with three cartons of milk, the only available dairy in a sixty-mile radius. Missy works at the cash register and I stay behind the counter, mixing drinks and baking pastries. Comfort relaxes my muscles and extinguishes the fire from my cheeks, but with it also comes loneliness and a twinge of failure. Upside-down cup. Ended conversation. Goodbye Pretty Boy and blue eyes and thoughts of happily ever after. Nice meeting you.

"What happened between you and Sexpot?" Missy asks.

"You gave him a nickname?" I groan and swirl a milk tulip into an espresso shot. "Nothing happened between us. And why did you encourage him to buy me coffee?"

"I didn't *encourage* anything. He asked which drink was your favorite and I told him. That's all." She snickers. "He must like you a lot."

"Why do you say that?"

"Because he's still here."

Sure enough, Jack is at his spot by the window, reading another book. Doesn't he have a job? How can he afford to spend an entire afternoon loitering at a coffeehouse? Has he stayed for me?

"This is weird." I untie my apron and grab my purse from the coatrack. If I run fast enough, maybe he won't catch me. "My shift is almost over. I'm going home. I'll see you tomorrow, Missy."

"Julie, wait!" Jack emerges from The Grindery as I roll my bicycle out of the alley. He chases after me and grabs the handlebars. "May I walk you home?"

No way. He cannot come to my house. What if he murders me or worse? Missy is inside the coffee shop. If he tries to make a move, she'll come to my rescue. Or I will electrocute him with my Taser. But he has a voice that makes my skin feel like more than skin and a crooked smile meant for me. How could a person with a face like that be dangerous?

Boys are unpredictable and stupid and brash. They do creepy, stalkerish things because they believe in extreme measures. They love to the fullest and ignore completely. They heal hearts and grind them to dust. To have nothing from a boy is devastating, but when he gives his all, the world becomes an electric place, and that is why women love them so—their all is worth the risk.

"How do I know you're not, like, an axe murderer?"

"Oh, I totally am an axe murderer. Chopped someone up last night. Sorry. That wasn't funny." He sighs and lowers to eye level. "I'm not going to hurt you, ever. For a long time, it was my job to protect people. I protect, not hurt. You can trust me, I swear."

"I live near Waterfront Park." The words are pried from my tongue by an invisible force, maybe the lure of his eyes. Did he put truth serum in my coffee? Why don't I give him my social security number and credit card, too? Trust? He's a stranger, a man, and he likes me. Three strikes.

"Great. I'm staying at an apartment on Prioleau Street. We're practically neighbors." Jack stashes his hands in his pockets. He drags at my side like a ball and chain, and as the setting sun blankets downtown Charleston with shadows, he glances at me fast. His mouth becomes small and his pupils dilate—he resembles a hawk, a super-hot hawk with broad shoulders and a jawline that could cut butter.

"You're staring," I say after we've walked two blocks.

"Oh, sorry. I'll stop." He uses his hands as blinders. "I just like the way you look."

His compliment is devoured by my heart before I can block it with a shield of self-talk. Beautiful is what girls expect to be called. Pretty is the second best compliment. Jack didn't tell me I was either. He simply said he likes the way I look as if I have an appearance as unique and desired as a good wine or French Roast. I've never been given a better praise.

I wipe sweat from my forehead and grip the bike's handlebars. They imprint my palms with rectangular grooves. "People usually like you, don't they?"

"Usually." He smiles. "I'm determined to make you like me, Julie."

"Why? Why do you want to be my friend? We just met and you're already walking me home. I know nothing about you except that you like apocalypse books and good espresso."

"It's a feeling I have," he says after a moment of thought, "like we need to be friends."

Music resonates from bars. People crowd the sidewalks, wait in line at restaurants. They all smell of sunshine and sea breeze, alcoholic joy, southern pride. Their laughter drifts through the streets. Welcome to the happiest place in the USA.

"I moved around a lot as a kid," Jack says as we stroll toward the harbor. "My parents divorced when I was seven years old. I moved to Athens to live with my mom but ... she died five years later in a car crash. So I packed up and moved to Albany to live with my bigwig, military dad. Simply put, we didn't get along. He worked constantly, practically hated me, and I never liked him."

"Gosh, I'm sorry."

"Now you know something about me." He stretches out his arms and walks backward so we're face-to-face. "What about you? Any family problems? I don't want to guess your life story."

"Dead sister." Is anything sacred? What's wrong with my tongue?

"Damn, I was hoping you'd have a perfect life. You *deserve* a perfect life."

"Nobody *deserves* anything. We live each day trusting in a tomorrow we may not have, trusting that our hearts will keep beating, trusting we'll be able to provide for ourselves and our families. Life is a game of survival and in the game, we're all equal and undeserving." A monologue—isn't that attractive? Boys adore chatty girls, said nobody ever. "I don't understand why bad things happen. I don't understand why my sister died, but she did. There's no use dwelling on what I cannot change so I cling to the hope of a brighter tomorrow. Believing that life could get better helps me survive the day."

"I'm glad you're an optimist." He jumps and high-fives a crosswalk sign. "I don't entrust my hope in a brighter tomorrow because tomorrow is just another day. The world doesn't change because the sun sets and rises. We can either adapt to survive our circumstance or we can change it. And I know we can't control fate, but I'm sure not going to spend whatever time I have left sitting around and waiting for my life to get better."

There's something to be said about an assertive lifestyle, but I'm not sure what. Is it productive, safe? Brave? Will battling my circumstance save me from it or worsen my discomfort? Jack's perspective is rational, daresay brilliant. And yes, change doesn't happen overnight. But do I really want a better life, or is clinging to the hope of it my excuse for staying the same?

We saunter past Vendue Wharf, along a path lined with park benches and oak trees. Jack grabs an old newspaper from a trashcan and folds it into an airplane. With a flick of his wrist, he sends the craft into darkness, a universe far from Charleston where beautiful boys fall in love with pretty average girls. If I could shrink myself down to size, I'd climb aboard and stray from home-sweet-home.

"Tell me more," he says, "about your game of survival."

One trip on his charm and I pour voice into what's been bottled-up in my head for the past nine years. I tell him about Sybil, Mom and Dad, even my thoughts about life and the future. After half-an-hour of my blabbing, he knows me on an above-personal level. I didn't want this to happen. I didn't want to give him exclusive insight into my life, but he'll be out of Charleston in a few weeks. No harm done, at least, no harm will come to my routine and singleness.

"You shouldn't let those college jerks screw you

over."

"They don't."

"Sounds like they do. Make them stop. You got to pull out your guns…"

"I don't have any guns!"

"Oh, you have guns. I can tell," he says with a smile. "And you really like sushi? That's gross. Ugh, raw fish and seaweed…"

"It tastes good." I laugh. "There's this incredible restaurant downtown that makes the *best* spicy tuna roll. And the calamari salad is to die for."

Jack's eyes sparkle like stars in the dim light. "We should go together sometime."

"Sure, okay." Dang it. I've broken my own rules. Not only have I trusted him, I've allowed him to become my friend. This was supposed to be one night of openness. Now there are strings attached, a commitment for more. To change the subject, I ask, "What does a freelance researcher do?"

"Researches things." He winks at me and helps lift my bike onto a cobblestone walkway. "It's not an interesting or particularly sexy job. Nobody wants to date a perpetual studier, but I bet there's an army of guys crawling over each other to get to you."

More like crawling away. "You're ridiculous. Who'd ever want to date me?"

"Someone like you? There'd be a line at your door as soon as work got out."

"Oh, would you be in the line?" Sarcasm. Not a real question. I don't care if he responds—heat burns my toes, ears, and everything in between—well, maybe I care a little.

Jack pauses and gazes into me. "Yeah … I'm in the line … and I'm better than all the other guys so you should really pick me. I'm funny. I'm strong, like, I could sweep you off your feet and run without breaking a sweat. I can also blow milk through my nose, but only if I'm drunk and the milk is warm."

"Gosh, that's weird." And random. Did he say he was in the line? For me?

"I know." He laughs. "I'm a freak."

"No, you're a flirt."

His grin swallows most of his face. "Shameless."

Electricity makes my hair stand on end. I grip the bike's handlebars. How could Jack do this, trip me on his charm? He is the person I'd want to catch fireflies with on hot summer nights when the cicadas hiss and the bullfrogs croak, the person who'd tell me to stick my head out the car window so I could feel the estuary's breeze on my face. He would be a plot twist in my story, a spark of different in my daily sameness. But he's leaving soon. If I get attached, if I like him more than platonically, saying goodbye will be another tragedy I'll have to survive.

Maybe I don't have to be daring and fearless...
Maybe I don't have to be more than what I am...
Maybe I won't get hurt...

Streetlamps illuminate the open space of greenery and reflect off the flowing river. An acoustic band, situated by the water's edge, plays for a crowd of onlookers.

Jack jogs toward the massive Pineapple Fountain constructed in the center of the green space. It glows with an array of colors: blue, yellow, white. He yanks off his shoes and removes his shirt.

"What are you doing?" I hold up a hand to block his bare chest, broad shoulders, and chiseled abdomen from view. "Don't take off your clothes." I must be beet red.

"You can spend your whole life in a box and be

happy, but you won't have the chance to be happier unless you step out of the box." He offers his hand as an invitation. "Be spontaneous."

I've been more spontaneous today than I have in my entire lifetime.

"Trust me, Julie."

"Okay. I'm not in a box, though." I slide off my shoes and grab his invitation. Together, we wade into the fountain. My calves go numb. Bubbles tickle my toes. "What are we doing?"

"Trust me." Jack places his right hand on my waist. His fingers saturate the fabric of my dress with heat, stir my hurricane of stomach butterflies into motion. "You're stiff as a board."

This moment should be frozen and described in detail, written at length so I won't forget it even when I'm old and gray—how the boy holding me smells like an evergreen, earthy and wild. His palms are callused, worn from work, and fit perfectly around mine. I'm happy in his arms—that is the element I wish to remember most—and without fear.

Jack waltzes me around the fountain, attempting to dance to the strummed music. We're anything but graceful. He stumbles. I do a belly flop into the pool and drench myself with water. Then, he pulls me close, and I wrap my arms around his neck. We sway back and forth, soaked and shivering, as the fountain's gold spotlights glitter on our skin.

"It's getting late," I whisper when he's close enough to kiss. "My parents are waiting. When they see me like this, I'm going to have a lot of explaining to do."

He smiles. "Let's get you home, then."

Sopping wet, we slide on our shoes and continue the trek.

Every day for the remainder of the week, I sit

with Jack at his usual table and drink coffee. We exempt personal information from our conversations and talk about everything else: books, music, stereotypes, why the world is so messed-up. We're friends—more than a customer flirting with his barista, less than romantically involved. In a few weeks, our friendship will be over. It's better this way. Jack will return to his secretive, complex life, and I'll be uncompromised.

Chapter Four

"If you look for truth, you may find comfort in the end; if you look for comfort you will not get either comfort or truth, only soft soap and wishful thinking to begin, and in the end, despair."

C. S. Lewis, *Mere Christianity*

Savory aromas greet me when I step into the foyer of my house. Food. Chicken. Apple pie. Who kidnapped my parents? Mom doesn't cook. Was she replaced by Mrs. Jones from the commercial? I'll scream if I find that big-haired, clown-grinning woman in the kitchen with a meatloaf in her mitted hands.

"Anyone home?" I toss my purse onto the piano. "Hello?"

"I'm in here, sweetie." Mom hovers over the dining room's mahogany table, arranging silverware next to her favorite set of china. "I thought we'd eat like normal people tonight."

"Why?"

"Because I finished my masterpiece and had extra time on my hands. It'll be fun." She places a vase of gardenias on the table. What's happening right now? Normal people don't eat dinner off china, surrounded by freshly cut flowers. Normal people eat casserole or takeout off paper plates and sit at the kitchen table, maybe in front of the TV when *The Bachelorette* is airing.

"Are you sure nothing else is going on? This isn't like you at all."

"I can be spontaneous if I want, Julie," she says with a huff.

"Yeah, of course." It is better to let people's insanity go unstated—crazy doesn't like to be called crazy. "I'm going to go take a shower. I smell like coffee grounds." And evergreen trees.

"Oh, and uh … put on something pretty." She flashes a smile so casual it reaches the other end of the spectrum. "I like your red dress with the sweetheart neckline."

"Won't that be extravagant for a *normal* dinner?"

She winks. "Never has it been inappropriate for a girl to wear a red dress."

I take a shower, curl my hair. The mirror likes me today—I am eighteen, blonde, and slender, without braces. Not beautiful or pretty. Liked. Desired. With a guy who'd stand in line for me, that is, if there was a line and I removed our friend-zone caution-tape.

The doorbell rings, followed by an outburst of voices. Oh my goodness, it's him. I'd recognize his laugh, his heart-warming drawl anywhere. I clutch my mouth to muffle wheezes. Then, my legs are in motion. They yank me to the top of the staircase. He's in the foyer. His hazel eyes meet mine, accompanied by an altruistic grin. He looks the same: tall and built with ginger hair, fair skin, and a dulcet face. Jon. My brother. He's here. In this house.

"Hey, there's my gorgeous sister."

Whoever said humans can't fly hasn't met me. Jon gives wings, and I soar down the stairs like a cardinal. Everything inside of my chest explodes, jumps, sinks, and twirls. I wrap myself around his neck. He swings me like a pendulum. I don't want him to let go.

"I've missed you, Jules," he whispers. "Have you been okay?"

"No, but I'm better now." I hug him tighter. His skin is warm, smells of sunscreen and laundry detergent—the best scent. "How long will you be in town?"

"I'm on leave for a few days. We have plenty of time to catch up."

If I could, I'd sew us together so we wouldn't have to be apart, so no matter where life takes him, I'll be able to watch his back like he's always watched mine. Is it normal for a sister to love her brother that much? He is my favorite—should I try to find someone from a different gene pool to adore, crave, rely on when the world knocks me down? No, because as long as I have Jon, I have all I need.

"Jules, there's someone I want you to meet." He gestures to the guest waiting with Mom and Dad. "This is my pal, Jack Buchanan."

Cobalt irises invade my peripheral vision, blasting me with butterflies, sweat, and a sinking sensation. Everything freezes for a brief second, and then sucks into a vacuum of time, space, and tunnel vision. The figment sky falls. The earth swallows me whole. I drown beneath the tumultuous waves of my own shock. Jack—customer from The Grindery, Sexpot—is my brother's best friend.

This must be another blood-sugar hallucination. Jack can't be here. He lives in a coffeehouse and wanders the streets, wild and free, mysterious—the way I like him. Can I rewind to when I was painting my lips red, before the tsunami hit? I'll take Jon, sneak off to the kitchen, and escape out the backdoor. We will borrow Mom's Land Rover and drive to Missy's apartment where the world is safe, same, and without beautiful boys wanting to merge lives. Where are the car keys?

"Hello, Julie." Jack tries to shake my hand but resorts to a stiff wave. His cheeks turn white, then red. His voice cracks and then deepens. Cute. Maybe he'll be so uncomfortable, he'll leave. "If I had known I'd see you twice today, I would've brought coffee or something. So you are Jon's little sister?" He says the word *sister* as if it's the mark of death, a curse worth getting his mouth washed out with soap.

"Wait." Jon chokes on a laugh. "You two know each other?"

"Yeah, we met at The Grindery." Jack's recently shaved and is wearing a black jacket with the tag still attached. A casserole is tucked beneath his left arm, meticulously bound in plastic wrap. "We're actually … sort of friends."

"Sort of." More like casual flirts or close-knit strangers.

"That's hilarious."

Hilarious? No, this is downright cruel. Jack was supposed to be temporary, a vault to hold my secrets before whisking them into an oblivion of proximity and whatever else separates two people. But he's here, in my house. The secrets I tried to stow away from Charleston have returned to their place of origin, an ignited fuse to a bomb. Should I run for cover? Would it be rude to grab Jack by his shirt collar and shove him out the front door? He is oncoming traffic, and I'm a deer frozen in headlights, seconds from being flattened into a gutsy pelt. Survival is a question for the aftermath.

"I had no idea you were his sister," Jack whispers as we walk to the dining room. He leans close to my ear. His breath smells like spearmint—I can almost taste it. His smooth cheek brushes mine and chokes me on my own heart. "Believe me, Julie. If I had known … I wouldn't have flirted with you."

What a charmer. "Oh, so since my last name is Stryker, you would've treated me differently?"

"Yes. Haven't you heard of the Guy Code?" He grabs my arm. Geez, is he an electric eel? How does he steal the air from my lungs? "Jon is my best friend. You're his sister. There are rules and boundaries. So yeah, I would've treated you differently if I had known … to respect my friend."

"Okay." I pry his callused hand from my biceps, but somehow, by an otherworldly chance, his fingers intertwine with mine so subtly, so innocently, so absolutely perfect, I step into him. His skin shouldn't feel this good. I shouldn't want to touch him this bad. "Let's try to make it through dinner."

Jack nods and sits at the table, next to me. He has this peculiar smolder, the kind that is neither intentional nor unintentional.

"You're staring." I gulp a mouthful of sweet tea.

"No, I'm not … I'm definitely not." He offers the bread basket. "Roll? They're whole grain, I think. Your mother's into organic food, isn't she?"

I spear a carrot and shove it into my mouth.

"You're my friend. Jon is my friend. I don't see all this as a disaster," he says. "I'm not *interested* in you. You're not *interested* in me. We can be *just* friends." He prods my shin with the tip of his foot and grins when I commence a full-fledged leg war.

"Quit." I stomp his toes. Cold water. Warm bodies. Weird feelings. We danced in the fountain, touching. I wrapped my arms around his neck, fell into his bare chest and absorbed his heat. If being *just* friends is less complicated, why do I have this ache in my chest, a latent longing to be the one he wants?

My heart is too young to rationalize feelings.

"Would you like some pasta and lamb casserole?" Jack heaps ziti and parmesan onto my plate, snickering when the noodle pile reaches an abnormal height. "You're not allowed to say no. I worked hard to make it. Here, eat this." He shoves a forkful of food into my mouth. "Verdict?"

Rude—that's my verdict—and amazing. "This is actually good."

"You're surprised?" He scoffs. His crooked half-smile should be on display. He is the Michelangelo of crooked half-smiles. "Someone like me couldn't possibly make…"

"Okay, okay. I'm sorry for wounding your culinary ego."

"Thank you." He places a napkin in his lap and winks. "You're pretty when you eat my noodles."

"Gross." I laugh and bite my lips to prevent from spewing food across the table.

"Oops, that came out way more inappropriate and assaultive than I intended." Jack clenches his teeth, coughing on a snigger, and shrugs. "My philosophy is this: Say what you're thinking aloud and if what you say is rude, you probably shouldn't be thinking it."

"Hey, Jules," Jon shouts. He waves his arms to grab my attention. "Tomorrow, you're spending the day with me. I have planned awesome stuff for us to do. What's better than quality time with your big bro?" He tilts his head, eyebrows raised. Dang it. He's figured out about Jack.

"Nothing is better than you. What are we doing?"

"It's a surprise."

"A surprise? Last time you planned a surprise, you took me catfish fishing."

"And we had a ton of fun. You learned how to gut a fish. We played in the mud. Our boat capsized." He stuffs a roll into his mouth and mumbles, "You'll like tomorrow. I promise."

Jon's eyes warn me that I'm getting too close, too involved with his best friend. Jack will leave, return to his life before me, and I'll be here, following a routine that once included him. No more coffee dates and book-talks. No more fountain dancing and inside jokes. Goodbye will be a noose around my neck, and Jon will have to cut me free. I should silence my dumb feelings now before I get more attached because it's easy to like people who can't make life miserable, but loving is a different matter— everyone tends to love those wrong for them.

Whatever. I like him. I really, really like him. Jack is a grenade and I'm the good girl who has never been allowed to play with explosives. He has the potential to hurt me. But as much as I'm afraid of being blown to pieces, I'm more afraid of being without him. It's going to hurt.

It's going to hurt because it matters.

"So, Jon, where'd you and Jack meet?" Dad asks.

"At the Marine base on Parris Island. We were assigned to the same squad and fireteam," he says between bites of food. "Jack, at the time, was known as Sergeant Buchanan…"

"At the time?"

"Yes, Colonel Stryker. I'm no longer an enlisted Marine." Jack's expression turns stoic like Dad's and his voice is commanding. What happened to the outspoken customer from The Grindery? "A year ago, during an assignment, I disobeyed protocol for reasons I cannot state. The insubordination led to my dismissal. However, I was honorably discharged."

"How long were you in the military?" Mom pours herself a glass of cherry wine.

"Five years. I enlisted after high school."

"What are you doing now?"

"I'm a freelance researcher. Different people and organizations hire me to analyze business reports and find information concealed from the public. Occasionally, I am even contracted by the military to research and study logistics."

"Jack is the smartest guy I know. After basic training, he was certified in emergency and wilderness medicine, which proved useful when I was accidentally shot during a survival exercise." Jon helps himself to another scoop of potatoes and props his elbows on the table. "We were in the middle of a swamp, struggling to find our rendezvous point. He put a stick in my mouth, pulled a scalpel from his pack, and carved the bullet out of my shoulder. It hurt like hell but ... I didn't bleed out."

"You're a doctor, Jack?" Mom casts her maybe-I-like-you smile.

"More of a combat medic," he says, "and a battlefield surgeon. My profession isn't solely medicine, though. Logistics, analytics, and research—that's what I do best."

Who is this guy? Ex-Sergeant Jack Buchanan? His name sounds like something from a video game or a low-budget action flick. How didn't I recognize this side of him? Sure, we tried not to share too much about our personal lives, at least, he tried—I spilled my guts on day two. But when you give a fragment of your heart to someone, you expect to glimpse their true self when they open up to let that piece of you inside them.

Dad clears his throat. "Where've you been stationed the past few months, Jon?"

"North Carolina. I've been working on an assignment with my platoon."

As my brother talks about his squad and asks about the latest happenings in Charleston, Jack pulls a pen from his pocket and scribbles on a napkin: *Do you like my book? Check yes or yes.*

The question forces me to smile. I check *yes.*

Jack: *What do you think of the main character?*

Me: *He is unbelievably profound for a zombie.*

THE VESTIGE

Jack: *The girl in the story reminds me of you.*

Me: *Really? She's hardcore and blunt. I'm not like her at all.*

Jack: *You underestimate yourself. People have told you you're fragile, weak, and dependent. You believe them. Don't. I see beneath your layers. I see that who you are is a force to be reckoned with. If only you could see what I see.*

Me: *You're a weirdo and a flirt and a total ham.*

Jack: *Maybe. I have many layers.*

He draws the tip of his pen across my hand, writing two words in black ink: *The Living.* "In a dead world, we are alive," he whispers. "You, me, and Jon—we're the *Living.*"

"Are you real?" Stupid. Of course he's real.

"Yes, Julie. I'm not the mystical man from your dreams." He snickers and removes a faded photograph from his wallet. "This is my old squad. We were gathered at the airstrip for deployment when the picture was taken. That's Ezra, Abram, Sutton, and Tally standing on the right. Jon's in the middle with the AR-15. You can't really see it but ... he painted the words *Semper Fi* on his forehead, which mean *always loyal.* They were my family, still are."

"You all look happy."

"We were excited to be out of basic training." Jack leans so close his Old Spice deodorant masks the scent of Mom's gardenias. He places his hand on the small of my back and whispers words I'll probably embroider on a pillow or chisel into my desk. "I don't want to lose you, Julie Stryker. You're the reason I think the world has a chance. Things seem *better* when I'm with you, and I can't risk screwing up something that could potentially make me *better.* Jon won't mind if we're friends..."

"Would you like to have coffee later this week?" I must be the queen of blurting out stuff or the president of red cheeks and awkwardness. "That is, if you're not busy." A tingling sensation spreads across my lips when he smiles. Would it be wrong to kiss him, feel what it's like to squish faces with someone I like but can't love? Yes, kissing would be horribly wrong because it'd be one step closer to falling for him. And people should never *fall in love*. I know from experience.

Everything that falls, gets broken.

****

"Are you moving the rudder, Jon? We're shifting several degrees to the south." I kick off my leather sandals and roll up the ends of my striped capris. The boat tilts starboard. Mist lurches up the bow, spraying salt and foam, and evaporates once it meets my hot skin.

"There are restricted waters ahead," Jon says when he emerges from the cabin with his Marine Corps baseball cap twisted backward. He plops down next to me and offers a can of orange soda.

"Restricted waters?"

"Yeah, Feds are stationed out there twenty-four-seven. Don't know why." He gulps his drink and gestures to the endless stretch of ocean. "What do you think of your surprise?"

"It's perfect. You're like … the best brother ever."

"Yep. In all of history." He squirts me with sunscreen and laughs when I punch his arm. "Sorry I didn't call you last week. My superiors confiscated my squad's communication privileges."

"You're here now. That's what matters." I lie on my stomach and open the can of soda. It fizzes—sweet, citrus, and ice cold. "Did you rent this boat?"

"I bought it."

"You what? Are you kidding?"

"Nope. I named her *Jule of the Sea*, after you."

"That's incredible … a tad cheesy, but incredible. Thanks."

"You know how to sail. If I'm gone and you want to get on the water, you can." He grabs my hand and squeezes it tight. "Okay. Time for a big bro lesson. Listen close. We are where we are. What matters is where we go next. Take my advice. Move forward. It'll save you a lot of trouble."

"Jon, what in the…?"

"Shush. I'm not done." He drapes an arm over my shoulders. His voice heaves with laughter, but his eyes are dead serious. "Life is a constant battle, an unceasing war that sometimes keeps us alive and sometimes threatens to destroy us. Don't give up, no matter what happens."

"You're scaring me."

"There's no need to worry. You're safe." He chugs what remains of his soda. "Enjoy the time you have here. Your life doesn't suck."

"Has the sun fried your brain? What do you mean?"

"We are like boats against the current, struggling to sail forward. If we never recognize the downstream, will we recognize the current? Or will we continue to struggle without knowledge of the struggle? Ignorance is only bliss for a short amount of time. Sooner or later, our stupidity will kill us." He's messing with me. Why else would he be so random?

"Shut up, Jon." I laugh and climb to my feet. "I'll get more drinks."

A huge wave crashes against portside when I enter the boat's cabin. Spinning. Falling. Head hits the linoleum floor. Vision blurs. I slide into the set of bunk

63

beds. Ropes tumble from the rafters above and slam onto my stomach. Pain, lots of it, pulses through my body. Ouch.

"Jules, are you all right?" Jon's voice emerges from the ringing.

"Yeah." Not really. "I might be paralyzed."

"Okay. I'll push you around in a wheelchair and wipe the drool from your mouth."

"Thanks a lot." I drag myself to where his backpack lies, in the room's center. Its contents are spilled and scattered. Sunscreen, granola bar, an extra pair of shorts—I stuff the items into the bag. Then, something cold brushes against my hand. Concealed within a striped towel is a military-issued, G30S Glock. Why is Jon toting a gun while he's on leave?

Wrinkled maps of the United States are also in the towel. They're different from those I studied in school. The country has been colored black with markers, streaked with unexplainable lines and severed by various mathematical equations and coordinates. A large, red circle encompasses Georgia, South Carolina, parts of North Carolina and Tennessee. The word *Severance* is written at the top of each page, scribbled neatly in Jon's handwriting. Maybe this is the vestige of a past assignment, a secret operation.

Maybe nothing is wrong.

I place his backpack on the table and hurry out of the cabin. Endless ocean, blazing sunlight, a cloudless sky—the world isn't complicated.

Everything is okay.

Jon lowers the sails and tosses an anchor over the rail. "We've reached a sandbar, Jules. The water is so clear." He tilts his head and grins. "You're looking at me weird. What's wrong?"

"Nothing. I'm good."

"There are a ton of seashells. Come look."

Sand dollars litter the ocean floor. Silver fish swim past them, oblivious to the treasure. In many ways, the scene is a metaphor. We dart through life without noticing the beauty that surrounds us.

"Who's ready for a swim?" Jon tosses me over his shoulder, ignoring my squeals, and throws me off the sailboat, into the sea. Waves drag me down, sting my eyes. I kick and claw toward the water's surface. Sharks. Lots of teeth. Lovers of flailing limbs. Jon threw me to my death, didn't he?

I cough and suck in air. "You're horrible."

Jon laughs. "Lighten up. You're not going to be eaten." He pulls off his t-shirt and cannonballs, splashing me. Together, we tread slow and steady. Gulls soar past. Waves rock us back and forth, handling our bodies as if they're moored boats.

"Promise me you'll always come back." Water ripples against my skin, warm, silk-soft and alive.

"I can't do that, Jules." He slips underwater and comes up with his ginger hair plastered to his forehead. "You're not made of porcelain. If life treats you bad, you won't break."

"But I might crack a little." He has to come back. I don't know who I am without him. "Why do you think Dad felt the need to drink so much after Sybil died?"

"All the stuff people do to themselves: drinking, cutting, drugs … it's all the same thing, you know? Just a way to kill your memories without having to kill yourself. Dad murdered his pain with alcohol. Mom, with seclusion. It's how they coped. Don't follow in their footsteps. When you're in pain, feel it. Accepting your lot is the only way you can heal."

"Okay, Mr. Wise Guy." I splash him. "We're stopping all morbid conversations, got it?"

For the next hour, we swim laps around the sailboat and search the sandbar for seashells. The sun sets, transforming the sky into a neon display of pink and purple hues. Federal vessels dot the horizon along with something else. Like a mirage, there is a faint glimmer rising from the restricted waters. It resembles a wall of glass and flickers when it catches the sun's final rays. Meteor shower. Gun in Jon's backpack. Stack of maps—coordinates, ink blots, *Severance*. Life may be good, but it isn't perfect.

This world will never be perfect.

Chapter Five

"Men occasionally stumble over the truth, but most of them pick themselves up and hurry off as if nothing ever happened."
Winston S. Churchill

It's Saturday, the box I've had marked red in my planner for weeks, circled, crossed out, and labeled *D-Day* because I couldn't decide on a single way to alert myself of the catastrophic, momentous battle I'd have to face at this moment. I sit on the curb outside of my house. Missy tugs at the wooden beads around her neck, silent. If I could, I'd reach through the veil of reality, grab her by the arm and drag her into the world I want for myself where she and Jack are small infinities I can sit back and admire. But goodbye can't be stopped. It is a knife to my throat.

Even the atmosphere seems to be holding its breath in wait of a tearful conclusion. The air is dense and sticks to us like mud. Mosquitoes hiss before sinking their needles into our supple flesh.

"I'll call you tomorrow," she says. "My stuff is already in Columbia. It shouldn't take me long to unpack. Once I'm settled, we can video-chat or something."

"Sure." Snot drips from my nose like a leak in an old pipe. I clog it with a tissue, but then my eyes start watering, and I give up. No one is pretty when they cry.

"We'll see each other soon." Missy embraces me. Alzheimer's is killing her mom but it's taking all of us. Why has God given us both a painful lot? Can't we have one good thing for more than a few years? Loss—we'll get used to it eventually, that familiar empty feeling, the starving yawn of something that can't be salvaged. "It's time for me to leave."

"Yeah. See you soon."

She moves toward her awaiting car but stops midstride. "Don't forget. I am your go-to person, not that Sexpot guy. Understand?" When I nod, she slides into the driver's seat and cranks the ignition. *See you soon* is worse than goodbye because my gut tells me she won't be the same when I see her again. I'm going to lose a friend in someone else's grave.

Pain stirs within my chest, an agonizing ache, like being hit by a baseball bat. A few pills of ibuprofen or morphine won't get rid of the discomfort. What can I do? Cry? Bury myself in bed and watch reruns of nineties sitcoms? Jon. He'll fix me. He knows how to numb my hurt.

"Jon, are you home?" I shout from the foyer. "Is anyone home?"

Mom kicks open the door of her studio and smiles. Her curly, unkempt hair explodes from her tie-dyed bandana like a bushel of Spanish moss. "He went to the grocery store with your dad, sweetie. They'll be back soon. Anything wrong?"

"No." *Yes.* "I think I'll go for a run. Jon will probably be home when I get back."

"That's a great idea." Mom can't handle more conflict. Once she knows about my problems, they become hers, too. It's easier to pretend everything is okay because recognizing the flaws will only contaminate the false sense of security she's built around herself.

I change clothes and jog to the riverfront.

Charleston Harbor reflects the sky's monochrome hues. Squelching, humid heat consumes the coastal city like an invisible tsunami wave. I run along the Battery. Legs move. Ponytail swishes. Muscles burn. The more I sweat, the less I cry—maybe Missy's departure will turn me into an athlete.

"I almost didn't recognize you." Jack runs at my side, shirtless and soaked. His skin is tan from the sun and glistens with perspiration. "Nice day, huh?" Position him against a palmetto with his arms flexed, pants lowered to show the rim of his underwear, and he could be a model for Calvin Klein. Not fair. He's flawlessly fit, and I'm red-faced and panting. Why are we friends? Pretty people like him were once on my *avoid at all costs* list.

"You're everywhere," I huff.

"I'm staying at an apartment a few blocks from here, remember?" Jack grins. "I run every day at this time." He moves at my speed, refusing to let me gain distance.

"Are you against wearing t-shirts?"

"It's freaking hot out here, Julie." He laughs. His eyes ignite with a perusing spark. "I think you're prettier without makeup. It's the honest truth. I'm not flirting, I swear."

"Go away, Jack."

"What's the matter?" He grabs my shoulder and forces me to stop. "Spill it, Stryker."

"Missy left this morning." I articulate each syllable because a rift will betray my true feelings, but the words create a suffocating weight. I lean against my thighs and gasp for air. Tears spill. Sobs seize. I need to move. I need to sweat before I cry myself to death.

Wet skin wraps around me like a blanket, followed by the musty, potent scent of body odor. Heat absorbs into my pores. His heat. His body, half bare, pressed against mine, hugging my waist. His hand strokes the back of my neck, timid as if I'm a museum statue with a *do not touch* sign. He holds my face in the crease of his chest, lips separated from his heart by flesh and bone. At any other moment, being this close to him would terrify me, but now it returns the ability to breathe. I squeeze him tight and cough on a sob when his cheek stubble scratches my left ear. Dangerous—I like touching his back, gliding my fingers across his shoulder blades, down his spine. Wrongful—I kiss his chest so lightly he probably doesn't notice. Crossed line—is Jack as capable of fixing me as Jon?

"I'm acting stupid, I know. Missy isn't dead. We'll see each other again. It's just … you and Jon are leaving in a few days and without her here, I'm going to be alone. You have to understand. Middle school was awkward for me. I had a hobby that was different from everyone else's. I spent my weekends writing instead of going to sleepovers. Braces, overweight, a fashion statement that consisted of zebra-print sneakers and Jon's holey t-shirts—I was the epitome of awkward. Then, when I was in high school, I cried in the bathroom every day after lunch because of what people said about me. Missy was the first person who actually wanted to be my friend…"

"Stop. You're not an unwanted charity case. There are people who love you, Julie. Understand? You're not alone. You will never be alone. Stop seeing yourself as the past and look at who you are now." He releases his grip and creates space between us. "I've had my share of rejection, believe me, but we don't have to be like everyone else. In fact, I don't think we should. Rebel against society's programmed, cookie-cutter crap. They all look the same and think the same. They're freaking dead, but we're not. We're the *Living*, remember? In a world of zombies, we are alive and surviving."

"Crazy as it sounds, your speech makes sense."

"Yes, I'm a brilliant communicator." He snickers and wipes the sweat from his eyes. Those vibrant, understanding, cobalt eyes. Even the inclination of losing them sends a chill through my chest. Jack reflects the person I wish to be, maybe who I am, and that person fits perfectly with him, the coffeehouse ex-sergeant from who-knows-where. How can I let go of the man who's found a way to reach deep into my heart and change it for the better? Jon said I wouldn't know what love is until I find it—I think this is love but found it at a horribly wrong time.

"I should get home before Mom starts worrying."

"Yeah. Sometimes I forget you're still a kid." He gives me a high-five and jogs ahead.

Huh? A kid? Was he serious?

Air-conditioned temperature washes the heat from my skin when I step into the entryway. Jon's voice echoes from the kitchen. He sits at the antique table with our parents. Dad talks in a hushed tone. Mom covers her mouth with a napkin and sobs. What's happening? Why wasn't I involved?

The floorboards creak as I tiptoe to the staircase. Conversation ceases. Jon turns in his chair and looks at me with bloodshot eyes.

"Hey, Jules."

"Is everything okay?"

"Yeah, we're talking about my deployment. I'll tell you everything later." He musters a smile and gives me an affirming nod. "Go upstairs and take a shower. You don't want to be late for your shift."

Subtle way of getting rid of me, Jon.

I bathe and change into a clean sundress, and then roll my bicycle out of the ivy-curtained alleyway and peddle in the direction of The Grindery.

"Julie, we need to talk to you." Dax and Philip

confront me as I clean the grounds out of the portafilters. "We'd like to promote you to manager."

"Manager? Really?"

"You're the nicest barista we've ever hired. Don't be timid when managing the other employees. They'll walk over you if given the chance," Philip says.

"*Other* employees?"

"Yes, we hired a few teenagers to replace Missy."

A spare tire stored in the back of Dax and Philip's car, used whenever the better one rolls away—that's what I am now, the spare manager. Missy was gone for a moment, replaced in an instant. Change is here. It's as if the coffeehouse walls peel into oblivion, and my nostalgic snow globe shatters on the floor of time. Stop. Bring it all back. Rewind and let me repeat, relive.

"Hi, I'd like a triple-shot of espresso to go. It's been a long day, if you know what I mean." Jack slumps against the counter, t-shirt pulled halfway down his chest, and grins.

"Congratulations. You've officially earned stalker status."

"I can't get enough of you, Julie. If you don't have coffee with me soon, I might resort to waiting outside your house at night with a bouquet of flowers and singing ballads."

"Very funny." That he'd sing to a kid.

"This is for you." Jack hands me a daffodil. "It's a … *make your day better* gift."

"Did you steal this from my neighbor's yard?"

"Yeah, well, I couldn't find anything I liked at the florist and … your neighbor has nice flowerbeds … and your dress had daffodils printed on the fabric the night you let me walk you home." When the customers behind him complain, he steps out of line and peers over the espresso machine's rim to watch me work. "You should tuck the flower behind your ear."

I slide the daffodil into my hair. "Happy?"

"Very." He laughs. It's goofy and honest, the iconic type that turns people's hearts to mush. I've heard it before, but it seems different now—he leans closer, tilts his head back further—as if this certain laugh is meant only for me. "You might find this funny. So I grabbed a to-go coffee before my run this morning and the kid barista asked for my name. Of course, I told him it's Jack."

"Of course."

"Yeah. And he wrote the name Steve on my cup. No joke. He really thought my name was Steve. Now everyone here calls me Steve. That's not even close to Jack, like, what the heck?"

"I'll talk to the newbies about clarifying customers' names." I hand him an espresso. His fingers brush mine. When will he stop shocking me? "You're coming over for dinner, right, Steve?"

"Wouldn't miss it." He winks before strolling to his table by the window.

In all friendships, there comes a time when each person debates whether or not they're attracted to the other because secretly, everyone wants to fall in love with their best friend. I'm in the debate stage. Jack isn't a love. He is a crush. Okay, good. Once the emotions fade, we'll be besties launching origami trash airplanes and arguing about espresso roasts, attraction-free.

"Hey, Julie Stryker, I like you more than coffee and Steve!"

At least, I sure hope that's the case with us.

****

White towers peer over the treetops. Structures emerge—massive, meticulous fortresses constructed among pristine lawns. Another home. Another sameness.

I peddle across the Citadel's campus to the School of Humanities & Social Sciences and move through the maze of hallways to Dad's office. Voices echo from within the room. Is he in a meeting? There's one way to find out.

Dad appears seconds after I knock. He gazes at me, face flushed, and slides into the corridor, sealing the door shut behind him. "Darling, what are you doing here?"

"You left your lunch at home." I give him the brown paper bag. His hands shake like they did at Sybil's funeral. "Are you okay, Dad?"

"Yeah … you should leave now, Julie." He touches my arm—something is horribly wrong. His grip is persistent, protective as if someone is threatening to steal me away from him. He's scared. Why? Who is in his office?

"What's happening?" I stand on my tiptoes to get a better view of the very opaque panel, as if it'll somehow become translucent and reveal its secrets. "Are you in trouble?"

"Everything is fine. Thanks for the sandwich." He kisses my forehead and reenters his study, leaving the door cracked an accidental inch. Standing around his desk is a group of middle-aged men, all high-ranking military. They talk in hushed tones and pore over maps. The most commanding is a man in his early sixties with an array of ornaments pinned to his uniform.

He's a general.

****

Working is difficult without Missy, but Jack eases the discomfort. To see him sitting at his table every afternoon, reading tattered books, waiting for me, somehow makes my grimness disappear. Wednesday night, we stay in The Grindery past closing time, listening to an old-fashioned mixtape, discussing books and the allegorical concept of zombies. He forces me to participate in an espresso-drinking contest that ends with me coughing, chugging a bottle of water, and him laughing hysterically.

"What are small infinities?" he asks as I swish the crema from my tongue.

"They're, like, the things that make life amazing such as fireworks, photo booths at the mall ... and sunshine, you know, when it filters through the treetops and it's so bright and electric, you can almost feel it saturating your soul."

Jack stares at me, soaking up my words with his eyes and smile, as if my response painted a picture worth admiring. He shakes his head and lifts his arms in surrender.

"What?"

"You're incredible for noticing those sorts of things. People like you are my small infinities, Julie." He lowers his voice to a dramatized whisper. "Thank you for making my life amazing."

"Cheeseball." I laugh.

Jack meets me after school. We lie in the green space between Randolph Hall and Porter's Lodge, staring up at the sky's grand Etch-A-Sketch. His hand finds mine, and immediately, my heartbeat is everywhere. It beats in the tips of my fingers, the back of my neck, everywhere. I look at him. He looks at me. We gaze at each other for what seems like hours, neither of us speaking. Conversation is a waste of words. I know him without knowing him, and he knows me fully.

Jon resumes his role of being my big brother. It's almost as if we were never apart. He comes to the Market, fusses when I leave my makeup strewn across the bathroom counter, and drives me to the drugstore when I run out of girly products.

It isn't long until Jack joins our clique. We become the inseparable three—sailing, attending sport events at the Citadel, fishing off the pier. In the evenings, we gather in the living room of my house to play board games. Jon wins every round of *Twister*, Jack is unbeatable at *Chess* and *Battleship*, and I somehow manage to be the champion of *Pretty Pretty Princess*. To see Jack and Jon draped in beads and tiaras causes me to laugh so violently, I fall down.

Mom makes us popcorn and lemonade, and we huddle in front of the television, sharing a knitted blanket, to watch an episode of a Sci-Fi drama. I'm sandwiched between the men—protected, accepted, safe. Sybil watches us from her place on the wall. She's remembered and included. After years of feeling like a broken doll wrapped in duct tape…

I'm whole again.

Chapter Six

"Until they become conscious they will never rebel, and until after they have rebelled they cannot become conscious."
George Orwell, *1984*

Today is the aftertaste of perfection. I lick my lips, savoring the heart flutters and burst of infinite things. Yesterday. The best day. At the beach. Joy cut me loose like a wildfire, and I ran ablaze with my boys. Jack and I buried Jon and sculpted the sand to make him look like a mermaid with ginormous, seashell boobs. We swam to a sandbar, and the patrolling lifeguard blew his whistle at us. From noon to dusk, we worked to enhance our sunburns, soreness, and laughter-induced stomach cramps. And once we were exhausted to the core, we piled into the Land Rover. Jack fell asleep during the drive home. He resembled a corpse, jaw gaping, cheeks sunken into his skull. I managed to drop four peanuts into his mouth before he lurched awake and turned my cheeks hot with his eyes. Then, he wrapped his arm around me, and I drifted off to the thud of his heart. Perfection.

I have known and seen them for real, cherished each millisecond so that when they leave me, I'll have enough of them in my soul to last a lifetime. Close to quota. Not quite there yet.

Clean portafilter. Grind nineteen-ounces of coffee. Weigh. Tamp. Flush. Pull. Steam.

The coffeehouse is quieter than usual. Customers lounge in the main room. Jack's at his usual table, drinking espresso and flipping through a copy of *The War of the Worlds*. He waves at me.

I scribble onto a napkin and hold it up for him to see: *Can't chat today. Need to work.*

Jack smiles. He writes on a piece of notebook paper and lifts it into view: *That's okay. I can admire the view from here.* Flirt. Goofball. My second-place best friend. How will I be able to return to life before him? Impossible. If a leg is chopped off, it doesn't grow back. If someone has sex, they can't get a virginity refund. Before Jack … I would never go back.

Me: *I don't want you to leave.*

Jack: *Me neither. I'm starting to like this place and the people in it.*

Me: *You should stay.*

Jack: *I can't, which sucks because I don't want to have to miss you.*

Me: *Saying goodbye sucks.*

Jack: *You can never love someone as much as you can miss them.* He gestures for me to wait while he scribbles the rest of his message on two sheets of paper. *And I'm going to miss you an awful lot. Let's skip the goodbyes because I am determined to see you again.*

Me: *Okay. See you soon then, Jack Buchanan.*

He holds up his last sheet of paper: *Do you like me? Check yes or yes.*

I draw my answer onto a napkin: *Yes.*

Like? Love? Something mad, honest, and real that gives the ability to throw seaweed and chase crabs with him, and nothing can embarrass or surprise me. What we have is better than any L-word.

Do I have homework due tonight? Biology paper. I still need another resource—will the library be open after dinner? Ugh, these new baristas are so messy—Marguerite didn't clean the steam wand. I really should call Missy after my shift. She was supposed to go shopping with her mom today—oh, I need to go buy a new dress for Dad's military banquet.

My cell phone vibrates with a text from Jon. He's outside, standing on the other side of the road, dressed for our dinner date. The Grindery's arching windows frame him like a pretty picture.

"See you tomorrow, Jack," I yell across the coffeehouse. Not professional, but Dax and Philip won't care. "TV night. Don't forget. Bring the sushi and orange soda."

"Burgers and coffee coming your way."

"I won't let you inside."

"Of course you will," he says and laughs, "because I'm fun to cuddle with."

"Nope. You're banned." I untie my apron and sling it onto the rack.

"Love you," he shouts as I walk out the door. Surely, he meant it as a joke.

A crisp breeze lifts my skirt as I wait on the sidewalk across from Jon. I gather the floral fabric in my fists to avoid flashing the world a glimpse of my granny panties—that wouldn't be a view I'd want Jack admiring. Pink puppies aren't exactly trending in underwear patterns.

"Am I going on a date with Marilyn Monroe tonight?" Jon grins. He looks both ways and crosses the street, walking toward me with blithe strides. "No, that gorgeous girl is my…"

It happens in a single, shattering moment—two seconds for my entire world to fall apart. I'm watching Jon cross the street. I hear a loud bump, splintering, crack. Now, I'm watching his body roll up the windshield of a car. I see him on the ground, in the middle of the road, eyes open and blood pouring from his mouth and nostrils. I hear screaming. It's my screaming. I feel my legs lurch forward. I'm next to him, touching his face, feeling for a pulse, screaming. People gather around me. A voice shouts for help. It's my voice. Someone pounds on my brother's chest. They tell me he is dead. What? Who is dead? Not Jon. It can't be Jon. No, they must be talking about someone else.

Beep. Beep. Flatline. A static hum that resounds through my vacuum of distance where I'm a person in a movie theater witnessing an on-screen death, sad but without pain. Tears blur my vision—why am I crying? Agony slices through my chest as I hold my brother's head—he must be playing a joke on me. The puddle of water beneath him soaks my skirt—why is the water red?

Jon was hit by a car. He died in a flash, without awareness of the end. He wasn't scared. His last thoughts were of me and one day, I might find comfort in that— No, no he can't be gone. These people are overreacting. He'll come back. He always comes back.

"Get up … please … don't you dare die." I sob and cling to the fabric of his shirt. His skin is white. His eyes are empty. I shake him hard and hug him tight, screaming. My hands drip with blood, his blood. I press my palms against his chest and pulse. "One … two … three." My voice slurs as I push my weight and every ounce of my soul into his sternum.

The corpse has mangled limbs, a cracked skull, ribs broken and protruding from its torso like jagged spears. It doesn't look like my brother. This must be a trick.

Sirens blare in the distance. They're going to take Jon away, like they took Sybil. Not again. It was too quick this time. I'm not ready.

"Move." Jack yanks me backward. He takes my place, pulsing until his knuckles are white, and then feels for a heartbeat. "Don't do this, Jon…" He trails off and gazes at the sky with watery eyes. His face drains of color as the sirens grow louder. People crowd around us, and chaos swarms the crimson street and yet he sits in utter silence as if analyzing the situation, processing the hit-and-run, planning his next move.

"Why'd you stop?" I yell. "Keep going."

"He's dead, Julie."

"You just … have to keep trying. He'll come back." I beat on Jon's chest, crying, and bury my face in his crease of his neck. His shirt smells of sunscreen and orange soda. Dust from a crushed sand dollar spills from his pocket. "Don't leave me here alone, Jon. I need you." He's my world.

Arms wrap around my waist and rip me from the body. I kick and claw until I ache with exhaustion. I fight as Jack drags me from the maelstrom and into the alley. Why is he doing this? The police needs to know what happened. We have to help catch Jon's killer.

"Stop, Julie." He clamps a shaking hand over my mouth to muffle my wailing. His stare is stern, flooded with tears. "Get yourself together. Jon is dead. I can't fix him. You can't fix him. He's gone."

Jon is dead.

Intense sobs rattle me. I gasp, but the air is empty. Jack sinks with me to the ground and props my back against a trashcan. When he speaks again, he's on the verge of breaking.

"You're not safe here."

Blood is on my hands, thick as oil. It sinks into my pores and stains me. Jon stains me. The world spins, and acid burns my throat. I vomit behind a pile of garbage, heaving until I expel my organs' contents—there's the orange juice I had this morning. "Get it off me. I can't … get it off." I tremble and show Jack my hands. Asphalt brands my knees with pebble marks when I scoot close to him.

He removes his jacket and cleans the blood from my skin. "Jon was murdered and I'm sure whoever killed him is coming for you, too. I need to get you someplace safe."

Safe? I don't care if a hundred trucks crush me. Someone has to explain Jon's death to our parents, advocate for him now that he's gone. Dead. The word tastes like poison in my mouth. Murder. Who would want to kill Lieutenant Jon Stryker?

Jack squeezes my shoulders and stares into me with brute force. Tears slide down his cheeks, but his expression remains harsh. "You're not safe anymore. Jon would want you to be safe. I don't care if you kick and scream. I'm taking you away from here."

"Why does someone want to kill us? What's going on, Jack?" Panic sends my heart racing to the moon and back. I have more to lose. If the Stryker family is a target, Mom and Dad are in danger, too. "My parents … they're at home. We need to get to them before something bad happens. Please."

"There isn't enough time. Keeping us alive is my number-one priority."

"They're my parents. I don't have anyone else," I shout. "Leave if you want. I don't freaking care what you do. I'm going home and you better not try to stop me." My tear ducts run dry. I stand and stagger toward the street, dripping blood. Mommy and Daddy need me like I need Jon. And if there's one thing I've learned from loss, it's that you lose what you don't fight to keep.

"Don't tell me what I can and cannot do. Jon was my best friend and he'd want you to be safe. Hate me all you want. At least you'll be alive to do it." Jack grabs and tosses my body over his shoulder. "I'm bigger and stronger than you, remember?"

"Put me down!" I beat his back, cursing and

screaming as he walks in the opposite direction. If I don't find Mom and Dad soon, they'll be dead and I will be alone. Worse fate than death.

I bite Jack's shoulder, clenching my teeth until he cries out in pain and loosens his grip on my legs. Then, I'm free, sprinting across Broad Street, through traffic and toward home.

"Life is a constant battle, an unceasing war that sometimes keeps us alive and sometimes threatens to destroy us." Jon's voice echoes through my head as I race through downtown Charleston. *"Don't give up, no matter what happens."*
****

East Bay Street is a stagnant wasteland, void of movement—not even the palmettos sway. It's as if a bomb detonated and all that remains is the shrapnel of a life half-lived. Memories—Jon teaching me to ride a bike on the cobblestone road, Mom showing us the nest of baby robins in her gardenia bush—everywhere like ghosts. I sprint through them, past their smiling faces. Maybe I should stop and stare at them for a while, until they disappear into forgetfulness.

I smother my sobs with a scream when our house comes into view. The windows are covered with plywood. Caution tape circles the perimeter, along with no trespassing signs. A large red 'X' has been spray-painted on the front door. Who did this? Where are my parents? Why is this happening?

Knees buckle. Legs stumble forward. Fists bang against the door. I pry the wooden slats off the nearest window with iron from a flower box and use a discarded brick to shatter the glass. No one is here. They're gone. Why am I climbing into the foyer? They've been taken. I'm too late.

Tears pour from me as I search the building.

Adrenaline and fatigue morph into a cocktail of drugs that gives a hazy high. Emptiness. Destruction. Shambles. The furniture is broken. Mom's paint smears the floor. Dad's office has been cleaned out. Papers, books, photographs—it's all gone. We've been erased. No. Our lives were fine a few hours ago. Dad stayed home from work to grade papers. Mom made oatmeal for breakfast. I fussed at Jon for slurping his milk, and he joked about my relationship with Jack. We all sat at that table, by that window. There are dishes in the sink—proof. Whoever killed Jon and took Mom and Dad didn't blot us completely. Here. We lived here.

Jon is dead.

Pain floods my chest cavity, an emptiness that seeps into my spirit and destroys it. I open my mouth to wail but all that emits is a silent puff. I collapse in the center of the living room among tattered canvases and ripped pillows, and wrap myself in the blanket Jack, Jon, and I once shared during our TV binge sessions. Their arms are around me. Warm. Safe. But I'm alone. They aren't real.

The bad guys took Sybil from the wall. Why? She wasn't a threat to anyone. Couldn't they at least let me keep her? Alone—I've been given a worse fate than death.

A prickling sensation spreads through my limbs. Why can't I move? Maybe this is a bad dream. Maybe I'll wake up. Sleep—that's what'll bring them back.

When my eyes close, the pain fades into a manageable ache.

Jon and I are on the sailboat, drifting toward a magenta sunset. He says everything will be okay, and I believe him because he never lies to me. His laugh rings fresh. His smile inspires hope in a brighter tomorrow. Home-sweet-home. Safe in the same. Happiest place in the USA…

I'm woken by the slam of a door, followed by hands shaking me.

"Dammit, Julie. You could've gotten us killed." Jack yanks me up, quivering with rage. His shoulder is bleeding—my teeth must be sharp. "Are you crazy? The people who killed Jon are coming for you next. They could've been here…"

"You did this," I squeal. Body rolling up the windshield, blood on my hands—it all comes rushing back. Not a dream. "If we'd gotten here sooner, Mom and Dad…"

"There's nothing we could've done." He cups my face in his hands, steadying me. "Listen. I will explain everything later, but right now, we must leave. Do you want to die?"

No is the right answer, but I can't say it. If everyone I love is dead, why should I live?

"We have to go. There's a van waiting outside that will take us someplace safe. If not for yourself, do it for Jon. Come with me." Jack offers his hand as an invitation, and I take it because he's the only person I have left in this crumbled paradise.

Walking through the house is like touching someone for the last time. I shuffle across the floorboards, touch the walls as if they're Jon's skin, Mom's acrylic-blotched hands and Dad's smooth cheek. This is goodbye, isn't it? Goodbye to sameness and safety. Goodbye to a city I thought I'd never leave. Goodbye to the people who matter most to me.

I choke on a sob when Jack opens the front door. He looks back, tears glistening in his bloodshot eyes, and nods. Time to be brave. I'll numb the sorrow and miss them like hell in the morning.

"Now!" Jack sprints to the awaiting van—one of

those white pedophile vehicles moms tell their kids to avoid—and motions for me to follow. However, when I cross the threshold, his expression changes. He stares at my chest, eyes wide with panic. "Julie…"

The way he says my name, as if I'm about to be lost, creates an out-of-body experience, a theatrical scene put to a musical score of heavy breathing and pounding hearts. A red dot hovers between my breasts—a laser, like that on the scope of a rifle. Jack shouts, terrified. I shift my focus from him to the sniper on the rooftop of a neighboring townhome. Oh. This is how I die.

A single shot.

I stumble backward and dive to the right. Too late. A bullet pierces my lower abdomen, sharp like a bee sting. The wound must be worse than it feels because blood, now my own, soaks my dress and forms a puddle on the concrete. There. It's done. I'm dead.

"Dammit." Jack scoops me from the curb as more shots are fired and jumps into the van. "Go, Tally, now!" He presses his jacket against my wound to slow the bleeding. Ouch. There's the pain. Holy crap, that hurts. I was hoping being shot would be like getting my ears pierced—once it happens, the worst part is over, leaving only a sting, and I'd die peacefully, numbed by physical trauma.

Tires squeal as the van lurches forward. Blood surrounds me. It drenches Jack's pants, transforms the metal floor into a pool. When will it stop flowing? How much do I have left in my veins?

I didn't think dying would hurt this bad.

"What the heck happened?" The driver turns to look at me, nose upturned, scowling. Her dark hair is cropped above her shoulders and streaked with red highlights. "Jon sure has an idiot sister."

"Stay with me, Julie." Jack retrieves his

pocketknife and cuts off my dress, peeling away the layers of fabric to expose my gory torso. Puppy panties and a training bra, covered in blood like a horror movie victim—this definitely isn't how I'd want him to see me naked. If I had more plasma in my body, I'd probably blush. Weird to think I may never be embarrassed again.

"Is Jon dead?" Tally asks. "I was listening to the police scanner and…"

"Yeah, he's dead."

She curses. "We're going to make them pay for this. How does that sound, you eavesdropping bastards? What if we … what if we run your friends over with freaking trucks? You can't just kill us. You said if we stayed freaking quiet, you'd leave us freaking alone. You freaking screwed us over…"

"Tally, shut up!" Jack gathers supplies from a plastic bin and squeezes my hand as if saying *I'm sorry I ruined your life*. All those things he said about his job were lies—he was a part of whatever got Jon killed, wasn't he? *Liar.* He and Jon destroyed everything. I trusted them. I loved them. What kind of person tells someone their world isn't unraveling when they're the ones cutting the strands?

"You and Jon did this," I wheeze, "didn't you?" Tears join the puddle. I press my hands to the bullet wound and sob between jagged gasps. "The lies you told me … it might as well have been you who pulled the trigger. You already stabbed me in the back."

Jack's brow furrows and his bottom lip quivers. "What's your blood type?" He yells over the intense rattles and rippling slosh of the red sea. Blood type. Mom didn't tell me. She kept that sort of information stored in Dad's filing cabinet.

"I … don't know." Air leaves my lungs and doesn't return. A metallic liquid pollutes my throat—I choke. I roll over and vomit blood. The floor's star-shaped grooves dig into my forearm, branding me with this hell. Flesh peels off my fingers as I claw at the metal ground. How is it possible to be in so much pain? Am I breathing? Am I screaming? Maybe. Not sure. The tires crunch and squeal. Police sirens wail in the distance. They're alive. I won't be for much longer.

"So if you don't bleed out or die from sepsis, my blood will kill you. Great." Jack kneels with an armful of first-aid kits, flashlights, and alcohol. He braces himself against a stainless steel toolbox and inserts a needle into his forearm, attaches a tube, and then connects the opposite end to my central vein.

My dress gets wetter and the world spins, mixing blood with vomit, faces into the cosmic roar. Angry voices and sharp pain. Dust and crimson plasma. I never got to try the new brand of hazelnut flavoring that just arrived. Where did I put those shells we collected? Jon promised he would keep me safe. Liar. I'll never believe him again.

Jack feels beneath my ribcage. His fingers are vultures picking at my necrotic corpse. "The bullet must be lodged beneath your false ribs, within your external oblique muscle." He uncaps a bottle of vodka. "This is going to hurt." Before I have a chance to respond, he pours the clear liquid onto the wound. A searing pain spreads through me. Yes—I *am* screaming.

Tremors of resilient determination replace the hot agony, and an icy sensation numbs my limbs. Death—this is what dying feels like, isn't it? *Help. Mom. Dad. Jon. Sybil. Save me. Please. Someone. Anyone. Don't let me die. I'm not ready to die. I forgot to take my clothes out of the washing machine. They'll mildew. And what will happen to Missy? When her mom gets worse, she'll need me. Oh, I have a shift at The Grindery tomorrow.*

I'm catering a book club, and the new baristas can't take my place.

Cancer didn't kill Sybil. The car swerved and missed Jon by inches. They're with Mom and Dad in Waterfront Park, watching sailboats drift into the harbor. I should join them.

"You better move fast. She's going into shock." Tally glances back from the driver's seat. "Wow, that's a lot of blood. How is she not dead yet?"

"Be quiet." Jack lifts the vial of alcohol to my mouth and forces me to drink. There must be something wrong with his voice. It's muffled. Wait. Why is his face blurry? Why can't I taste the vodka or feel pain? I really am dying. This is happening. Right now. No, I can't die yet. God, don't let me die. I'm too young. There's so much I've yet to do.

Jack unwraps a package of scalpels. "Stay with me, Julie."

I'm in the ocean, rocking back and forth with a surging current. These waves are safe, warm. They embrace me in a sort of unnatural quiet. I'll stay and swim for a while. Maybe Jon will show up to dive for sand dollars. He likes how they fit in his hands.

Jack removes his t-shirt and tucks the fabric between my teeth. "I don't have any anesthetics, so once I begin surgery, you'll feel everything. The pain's intensity should make you pass out. Stay still. If I make a mistake, you could die." He sticks the blade of his scalpel into my flesh and cuts.

The wad of sweaty, blood-drenched clothing straddles my teeth like floss—putrid, boy-tasting floss. Death sears through my nervous system as Jack digs into me. It's more severe and harrowing than anything I've ever felt. This is torture, torment. Dying might be better. No more suffering. No more heartbreak. *I want to die now. Please let me die.*

Jack curses when a gust of blood explodes from the incision. His bare chest and arms are splattered with red. He clasps a hand over his mouth, clutches his head. He seems to be scared. Because he's covered in me. Because I am about to leave the world. "There's a tear in the abdominal wall. Julie, I need you to be still while I make sutures."

"Make her shut up," Tally's voice echoes with ferocious authority.

"She hasn't passed out yet."

"Duh, that's why she is still squealing like a freaking baby. Do something."

Angry voices. Pain and numbness, sharp and dull—they twist inside me. Something stifles my screams and then eyes. Those eyes, blue. No cobalt. Indigo? Azure? Sapphires? No just cold blue. Hateful eyes. Cold, hard blue eyes. Eyes that were so pretty an hour ago. Eyes that sparkled and laughed.

He removes his hands from my torso and lifts me into his lap. "You're not going to die. I'm a good surgeon. I will keep you alive." His bloody fingers rest directly above my collarbone. "Don't give up. Keep fighting. This isn't over." His grip tightens. The universe spirals. I'm saturated in safe, warm waves—slowly, and then all at once.

SECOND LAYER
Chapter Seven

"There was truth and there was untruth, and if you clung to the truth even against the whole world, you were not mad."
George Orwell, *1984*

I open my eyes and clutch at the sheets. Darkness envelops me. A thick crust cakes my eyelids. Drool glues my face to a pillow. Rot. Dust. The putrid scent of old urine. I blink. A long room with low ceilings and walls covered in puke-colored paper comes into view. Stained medical screens block me from the adjoining space. Not home. Where am I? What is this place? Jon—where's Jon?

Sheets stick to my skin like tape. I claw at the avalanche of blankets in a desperate attempt to escape the fabric prison. The plywood floor creaks with invisible footsteps—who's here? Nightmare. Horror house. This can't be real.

"Help," I croak, squirming under the weight, and remove the mask from my face. Oxygen. Why do I need more oxygen? Tubes trail from my wrist to a bag of saline that hangs over the nightstand. I scratch the IV's insertion site, enhancing the needle's dull ache beneath my skin. Did something happen to me? How long have I been here?

Pain drills into my chest and sucks me clean. My spine arches, and I choke on agony, the blood rush, as if my heart has been hibernating for weeks. The sheets fall away in relent, revealing bruised legs and a battered torso. Bloody underwear—red puppies instead of pink.

Stitches crawl up my stomach, grinning with the tissue of living flesh. A throbbing sensation saturates my brain and my saliva tastes so foul, I gag. A single shot. Blood on my hands. An empty house.

Jon.

Empty eyes. Ribs protruding from his torso and pieces of gray matter spewing from his cracked skull. The images brand each thought that enters my mind, burning me, marking me.

I sob and cover my mouth with a pillow, and then scream and beat my fists against the bed's steel backboard. We were going on a date. He had that dumb smile on his face, the one I loved so much, and wore his favorite collared shirt. Smile is shattered now, in a morgue. Shirt is cut to pieces and trashed. *No, God, you can't do this to me. You can't keep him. He is mine. And if you won't bring him back like Lazarus, take me, too. Kill me. Do it. Please.*

Sunlight spills through the cracks in the window blinds and stings my skin. I cry into the light. Home. A bedroom with plush pillows and ocean breezes. A dream world where Jon dances with me in the kitchen and the coffee tastes like heaven—that's where I live, not here.

He's dead. Dead. My parents are gone. Gone. I am alone. Completely alone. And in pain.

Horrible pain.

The ugly wallpaper draws me into an oblivion without ceilings or floors, only an endless expanse where I tumble deep into grief. My pain is left at the chasm's surface. I am empty. A corpse. Dead and alive. Barely breathing. My heart is the only thing keeping me alive, and I'm pretty sure it wants to give up and join the rest of my body in a slow creep to rest.

Nothing matters anymore.

The screens slide apart hours later—at least, what

seems like hours in my bottomless pit. Jack walks into the makeshift room, a peripheral silhouette. "You're awake," he says. "It's been three days."

Make that four days. Five. A lifetime.

He shuffles forward and stops at the edge of my cot. The outdoors—soil, grass, fresh air—are on his clothes, and I have to hold my breath to keep from puking. "You lost most of your blood. I gave you as much as I possibly could without keeling over but … it didn't seem like enough to keep you alive. You're definitely stronger than you look." He replaces the bag of saline and examines my IV. His callused fingers are sandpaper against my skin and remind me of all I've lost, the lies he told, how I hate him and love him and can't stand the sight of him. "I was able to repair the tear in your abdominal wall and the nick in your large intestine without having to perform a resection. You're going to be all right."

Funny—that's what Mom told Sybil when she was diagnosed with cancer, what Jon said the day Isaac Moore announced to my class that I should be anorexic. *All right* are Band-Aid words people slap on those who look like they're close to breaking.

"Are you hungry?" Jack peels back the blankets to inspect my stitches. He slides his hands across my abdomen, the same hands that held and sliced my organs. Sexy, huh? All girls dream of having their crush surgically remove a bullet from their gut. No. Because that's gross. And weird. "I can bring food, if you want." The more he shocks me with his touch, the more I want to bite off his arms.

I roll over and yank the blankets onto my shoulders. If I'm silent, maybe he'll leave.

"Julie … all this is hard, I know. You're not ready to confront the truth behind what happened. That's okay for now—but soon, you'll need to get out of this bed and face reality head-on. Do you have any questions for me, like, about where we are? Why Jon was killed?"

Nothing matters anymore.

"Talk to me, Julie. Wake up." Jack grabs my chin and forces me to look at him. His vibrant, cobalt eyes glisten with new tears. His bottom lip quivers. "I understand your pain because I feel it, too," he whispers with severe conviction. "I feel it."

Cute—he thinks our pain is equal, that losing a friend is the same as losing a brother. Everyone I love is gone, except him. But the person I thought he was died in Charleston. Now I'm stuck with a liar who kept me miles from the truth by toying with my heart.

Jack leaves and returns a few minutes later with a plate of food. "You need to eat, Julie."

Nope. Food will take me further from Jon and Sybil.

"My mom died when I was a kid," he says, as if confessing his hurt will somehow dull mine. "I watched her die … and I couldn't do anything to save her. We were in a car wreck. Mom was impaled in the trachea by a shard of glass. I couldn't move so as the paramedics raced to our aid, she suffocated. Believe when I say I've known sorrow more than any other emotion. It scares the mess out of me to be this sad, because it seems catastrophic. Grief and fear aren't much different. They both drag us to the brink of extinction where we have the choice to either overcome what destroys us, or be destroyed."

Destroyed sounds pretty good.

Time blurs. I lose count of the sunrises and sunsets. Grief keeps me awake and puts me to sleep, fills my stomach so nothing, not even the broth Jack brings, looks edible. I don't get up, except to drop into the corner and squat over a metal pot like an animal. Jack cleans up my mess—which somehow makes me hate him more. He leaves a lamp at night, as if the light will keep me from slipping further into darkness, prevent ghosts from entering my nightmares. Liar. Backstabber. Jerk…

Who does for me what I once did for Mom. Who shows love, not the gushy love people like to talk about, but the real love that motivates soldiers to charge into battle and wakes up parents in the middle of night to feed their babies. Real love that endures even when it's fought, cursed, and hated.

"Oh, shut up," someone shouts during one of my sob sessions. "I want to sleep. Shut up before I slice your throat." The outburst is followed by a shoe slamming against the nearest divider.

I'm not alone in here.

Jack visits three times a day to bring food and examine my stitches. He talks to me—I didn't realize boys could talk so freaking much—but I block his voice with daydreams of waves lapping at my ankles, silver fish, and Jon's stomach-cramping laugh. Our perfect paradise is a sepia film reel in the back of my head, playing our lives in sync, all the smiles and tears, the blazing sunlight and hurricanes. He was the infinity that made my world spin, the sun and stars. He was everything, and now I have nothing. Nothing but the memories and a deep, deep wound.

"Up, Levi."

I flinch when a German Shepherd climbs from the floor and settles into the space next to me. His body is an oven, burning the deathly cold from my bones. He sniffs me, licks my cheek. Why is he a nice dog? I'd rather he bite because a kiss from him makes me want to cry again.

"He'll protect you," Jack says, "from the memories and anything else that frightens you."

I comb my hands through the animal's thick fur and hug his body. With him I'm warm, safe. Dogs are like that, I guess—they know how to fix you without ever saying a word.

Another sunrise. Another sunset.

Jack lies next to me, denting the thin mattress. "Why won't you talk, Julie?" His breath caresses the back of my neck. "What's going on inside that head of yours?"

Sand swallows my toes as the ocean wars with itself, devouring and dispersing in a schizophrenic display of bulimia. Tourists pass in crowds of sameness, unified in unimportance, but each entity individual and monumental in its own mind. Jon chases Sybil into the surf. They tell me to come join them, and I want more than anything to wade toward their arms.

"You're killing yourself. Why? Do you feel guilty for what happened? You're not to blame for any of this." He shakes me hard. "Julie, you can't quit."

The sea calms to let me inside its wild embrace. I paddle through foam, dive beneath the turquoise surface, and reach out my hand to Jon. *Come on. Take hold.*

"Okay, shut me out. That's fine. You can die if you want, but I choose to stay alive. Whoever killed Jon deserves justice. I'm going to give it to them."

Justice won't bring him back.

"After I lost my sister … I couldn't do that ever again. I *wouldn't* do that again … now, here I am." I sob and roll into his chest, away from death and my siblings' arms.

"You can survive this." Jack embraces me in a protective blanket of flesh and muscle. "Yes, it's going to be scary. Yes, living will force you to endure terrible and amazing things you can't even imagine yet. It will be hard, but I swear, you'll survive."

What were the last words I said to Jon and my parents? I can't remember. It's funny how trivial things never matter until they're the *only things* that matter.

"Listen to me." He tilts forward and strokes my face with a strong touch, as if testing to see if I'm as fragile as I appear. "We'll get through this together. Whatever you can't do, I will."

His eyes are bluer than my imaginary sea and offer an invitation to a different fate. He's here. He can help. When I'm weak, he'll be strong. When I break, he'll fix me. Jon did all of those things, but Jack can do more. He wants to do more. And I want to let him because if life is terrible and amazing, I'd like to experience the ups and downs with someone who might one day love me. I'm not sure if I'll live long enough to see that day or if I even want to, but I do know I want him. Now.

I pull his face against mine. Our lips fit together like puzzle pieces and before I can stop myself, I kiss him hard. It's not romantic or magical, more awkward and sloppy—a casual exchange of saliva. Mouth against mouth. Entangled limbs. Why isn't he kissing back?

Jack detaches and looks at me with his eyes wide, muscles stiff. My breath must smell bad. Oh, gosh, I haven't brushed my teeth in a week.

I twist onto my stomach and hide beneath the sheets. A single tear drips from my chin.

What a stupid waste of a first kiss.

****

Cold sweat breaks across my forehead when gunshots sound. Sniper. Blood bubbling from my stomach. Sirens and screams. Pain gnawing at every fiber of my being like a ravenous dog.

They've found me. They're here to kill me. Run. I need to run.

Smack—I dive into plywood where the only

blood drips from my busted nose and the landscape is composed of a shriveled cockroach and the metal legs of my cot. Great. I've turned into a spaz.

Tremors pulse through my dissolved muscles. I claw at the bedframe, almost topping over when I loosen my grip. Not long ago I was racing along the Battery. What happened to those legs that could take me anywhere, hold my weight without complaint?

Death and gravity don't mesh well.

A single light stream escapes from a crease in the blinds and blazes into my brain. I squint, stagger toward the window, and then lift the plastic panel. Where am I? What is this place? Charleston has been exchanged for rocky slopes and lush treetops. Mountains. I've never seen mountains before. They bite the pale sky and cascade their green fur into the valley where the earth is hard, uneven and without hope for salt and sand. Miles from home. Memories floating deeper into the recesses of the past.

I slump against the wall and hyperventilate, heaving, gasping for substance. I've seen the unfamiliarity, sunk my eyes into the view from someone else's window, a new world as different from mine as the moon is to the sun. And I hate it more than bad coffee and dull books.

Beyond the windowpane is an overgrown yard dotted with weed-infested flowerbeds, rusting lawn chairs, and trailers, all dilapidated and decaying from obvious neglect. People stand waist-deep in the grass. Some sprawl on the ground, shooting at a single dummy mounted on a distant tree trunk. Jack is among them. He lies in the dirt with his head tilted, finger on a trigger.

Not once does he miss his target.

Too much. I can't handle this. Jon tells me to survive with Jack—No, I'm done, finished with the heartbreaking pain and depression, the secrets and intense change. Accept me into the waves. Grasp my hand when I reach out. Let me float into the pool of light where I can be whole again.

Food waits on a repurposed filing cabinet—an egg sandwich smothered in mayonnaise. Disgusting. But my stomach screams with hunger. If I eat, I'll feed my life. One bite won't stop starvation, only slow it. Okay, just one bite.

I cram the sandwich into my mouth and once it's swallowed, I wipe my greasy fingers on my bare thighs. Stupid. Now I'm covered with egg and oil.

Levi sniffs my skin when I climb into bed. He gives a hungry look.

"Sorry," I whisper. "You're a nice dog and if I wasn't dying, I would've shared. I'll make it up to you, though. Next time Jack brings food, you'll get half."

Nausea plows me over like a truck. I hang off the mattress and puke into the toilet bucket. Cramps twist my insides into knots. Acid shoots up my esophagus, lava from a volcano, and burns. I must've eaten too fast. It's been a while since I had a meal—maybe my body has adjusted to the concept of dying early and is doing me a favor by rejecting the egg, bread, and mayonnaise. Ugh, Jack will trash the chunky vomit—another reason for me to hate him and him to hate me.

The screens slide apart. Jack enters wearing a bulletproof vest. His dead lips form a straight line when we make eye contact.

"Get out of bed," he says.

"No." Would it be mean to laugh at him?

"I've been considerate and allowed you to mourn for long enough. You need to know what's going on." He folds his arms. "Get out of bed. I won't be nice anymore." Finally. Maybe he'll shut up and leave me alone for more than a few hours. Better yet—maybe he'll stop trying to cuddle.

"You're not my dad or Jon. You're nobody … so don't tell me what to do." I sink deeper into my avalanche of blankets and grip the bedposts. "Give up and let me die."

"Not a chance."

I raise my knees to kick him when he rips away the sheets. He moves like a charging bull and grabs my ankles. I scream as he yanks me toward the edge of the mattress. Why was I attracted to him? What made me love a controlling backstabber with an insane savior complex?

"Let go," he shouts. With a swift motion, he unravels my hands and drags me off the bed. I land hard on the floor. A throbbing ache pulses down my spine. I dig my fingernails into the wood and crawl toward the space beneath my bed, but his arms swoop me up.

"Stop," I squeal as he moves out of the enclosure and into the main room, which is filled with cots and ragged furniture. This is a new place. I don't want to be in a new place. I like the familiarity of my stinky sheets and hazy window. "Take me back!" I squirm, but his hands bind my legs to his chest. I kick and punch. His vest absorbs my beating fists.

Is the armor meant to protect him from bullets or from me?

"Abram, open the door."

A man rises from the bunker's far corner. He's built like a TV wrestler and has a shaved head, espresso-colored skin. With a grunt and eye roll, he opens the door.

"Don't scream unless you want to embarrass the crap out of yourself." Jack carries me into an outdoor corridor composed of camouflage tarps and stacked branches. People with rifles pass us in a hurry when a siren sounds from somewhere in the sea of mobile homes.

What is this place?

"If you don't stop, I'll bite you again." I try to sink my teeth into Jack's neck, but he twists me forward so my head dangles. If his grip slips, I might be able to nip his wrist, maybe an artery.

"Don't be an idiot. It's embarrassing enough to make me haul you through camp like an angry toddler. Biting the sergeant would only blacklist you as the crazy, vampire chick." He snickers. "Hot panties, by the way."

Heat spreads through me like a wildfire, igniting my toes, singeing the tips of my ears. I want bite him and yank down his jeans so everyone can laugh at his underwear. Knowing my luck, he'd probably be wearing designer boxer-briefs, and people would congratulate him on his good looks instead of blacklist him as emotionally unstable. Life should've come with an escape hatch so I could disappear during moments like this when I'm completely mortified and angry enough to kill.

"You're a jerk."

"I'm pretty sure we're not in elementary school anymore."

"Bastard."

"Better." He smiles.

The passageway widens into a tent-like plaza filled with wooden tables, electric heaters and laundry lines. Soldiers recline against the damp furniture, eating stew from metal bowls and talking in loud, obnoxious voices. They stand up straight when Jack walks past. Their eyes are on my ninety-percent naked body—I must be the queen of memorable first impressions.

Jack takes me into an adjoining trailer—a communal bathroom. Someone gutted a mobile home and installed every cheap urinal and toilet they could find, along with several mildew-infested showers. Yuck. How can these people bear to live in such filth?

He turns on a shower and dumps me beneath the searing, pluvial downpour. I whimper as the torrent burns my skin, my soul, every square inch of me. The sting is boiling water against cool skin, but the pain comes from within, not the showerhead.

"Stop acting like a kid. You're an adult, so grow up," Jack yells. "This isn't an easy world, and it's about to get a whole lot harder for you. There are people who want you killed and if you're not willing to fight for your life, you will lose it. Understand? Jon is dead. You can't change that. The only thing you can do is move forward and deal with your lot."

"Screw you. I'm strong and grown-up, but I lost my brother. My brother. Whom I love. So don't you dare criticize how I cope. Don't you freaking dare." Coughing, I crawl into the corner to avoid the steady stream. It's hot like blood. Jon's blood. "You have no idea how strong I am…"

"You've been trying to die, not cope." Jack adjusts the water's temperature and crouches at the shower's edge. He touches my knee. "Strong people don't lie in bed for a week, hiding from their problems. Strong people get up and keep moving no matter how much it hurts."

"The pain won't stop," I wheeze. "Why won't it stop?"

Jack climbs into the shower and pulls me against his chest. Water beats on his shoulders, rolls down his face. "The pain … it won't leave you alone," he whispers. "You'll miss him forever and nothing, not time or good days or closure, will heal the wound losing him caused. However, you will find that by living your life, remembering him on those good days, the pain becomes a monument … and you'll learn to treasure it like you once treasured him." He squeezes my convulsing body. "You have to wake up and face the world again."

Please wake me up from this nightmare.

I close my eyes to sketch the feeling of him on my memory—his scratchy cheek against my forehead, the breeze of his breath, how the water divides and unifies us in a steady stream. Do I really have a world to face? Yes—Jack's confused, complex world as different from mine as the moon is to the sun. "Why can't you leave me alone?"

"Because," he says, "I care about you."

It's as if we're children at recess and he accidentally dropped the f-bomb. Care, love, feelings—in the adult realm, they're curses in their own right.

"Losing you would break me, so you have to live." He rubs his lips—maybe he's remembering our awkward, wet, one-sided kiss. "Promise you won't try to kill yourself."

Jon and Sybil float across the ocean until they disappear. The waves curl back from the shore. I race after the foaming surf, calling out to those lost in the endless pool, but Jack pulls me back and builds a new home around us. He makes me want to give life a try.

"Okay." I drag my thumb along his jawline, onto one of his dimples. Butterflies fill the hole in my chest. I'm his family as much as he is mine.

"Be outside in thirty minutes. Charlie will escort you to the Command Center." He stands and snatches a towel from the floor. "There are extra toothbrushes in the closet. I'll leave some clothes by the door and another sandwich since you puked up the first one."

A puddle of discolored water forms beneath me. I peel off what remains of my clothes, pump shampoo and lather my hair into a bubbly wad.

CAROLINE GEORGE

Here, beneath the showerhead, my old self is washed away.

Chapter Eight

"The truth will set you free. But not until it is finished with you."
David Foster Wallace, *Infinite Jest*

Eyes dissect and examine me when I emerge from the bathhouse. Does everyone want to look at the crazy little sister of deceased Lieutenant Stryker? What are they saying? Jack left me a nicer pair of underwear. I trashed the red puppy panties. Eyes. So many eyes. That say I'm a freak.

I've stepped back into high school.

Air is plaster inside my lungs, hardening as I half-walk, half-trip through the outdoor mess hall. I tug at the hem of Jack's baggy t-shirt and unstick my boots from the mud. Knees buckle. Legs tremble. An older soldier snickers when I slam against a stack of crates—I try to shield my face with wet hair, but there's nothing where something used to be. A precious body part decided to take a vacation.

Since conditioner couldn't unravel the knots caused by a week of lying in bed, tossing and turning, and poor hygiene, I cut off the matted mess. Now my hair is damp, wild, and wavy, cut short. Instead of falling over my chest in loose curls, it hangs at my shoulders.

Short hair. No makeup. No sundress. Another change.

"Hey, Julie." A wiry boy with tattered clothes jogs from an adjoining breezeway. He grabs my hand and gives it a firm shake. "I'm Charlie Coker. Welcome to the Underground." He's British, but the TV said people don't travel between countries, that everyone is content in their hometowns. If he was content in England, why did he leave?

"The Underground?" I lean against a worktable to catch my breath. Hunger pains swirl within my heart, starving for a bite of home. One mouthful. A whiff of gardenias. A coffeemaker's gurgle. A red dress against my skin. "What is this place?

"The Vestige's headquarters." His teenage face is smeared with mud. "Jack wants to answer your questions. We're supposed to meet him at the Command Center." Charlie leads me to the entrance of a tunnel and lifts its wooden door. He climbs into the chasm, vanishing.

"What's down there?"

His dilated pupils glint in the darkness. "We've built an underground road system. The Scavs fly over frequently and we can't risk being seen. Come on."

If I had a dollar for every question I could ask right now, I'd be filthy rich.

Electric lights brighten the shaft. Scrap metal, concrete blocks, wooden planks and plastic slats—the makeshift thoroughfare stretches in all directions, a lethal maze of pipes and crawlspaces.

It'd be easy to get lost down here.

"Pardon the smell. Some of the tunnels gather leaked sewage." Charlie kicks a discarded soda can and snatches headlamps from a rusting coatrack.

Graffiti covers the walls, floor, and ceiling— *We choose to see the unseen. Truth is a dangerous thing. Remain aware of their lies.*

A shiver wiggles up my spine, giving me a serious case of goosebumps. Did Jon live with these people? Was he a part of the Vestige? What truth did he discover that proved to be so dangerous?

Lights flicker, trapping us in second-long intervals of blackness. Electricity whispers a strained buzz. The generator rumbles as Charlie and I head into the largest tunnel, an old drainage tube trailing off into the complex labyrinth.

Mom and Dad—they're my ticket back to paradise. I'll find them, get rid of whoever wants me dead, and go home to bury my brother, return to the place I should've never left.

"Here." Charlie fishes a laminated notecard from his pocket and gives it to me, along with a headlamp. "It's a map of the tunnel system. Pretty straightforward."

Grime turns my fingernails black. Metal grooves bruise my knees. "Are you a soldier?" I tuck the notecard beneath the flap of my right boot and crawl inches from his mud-caked soles.

"Nah, I'm an apprentice engineer. I work for Nash. He's the tech genius here."

"Did you know my brother?"

"Jon? Yeah, I knew him." Charlie slides into a smaller, mold-infested tunnel. His slender frame navigates the narrow space like a worm or mole, squeezing and ducking with ingrained agility. "We better move fast before someone decides to head this way. Traffic jams are not fun."

"Were you friends with him?" I straddle suspicious puddles and rust patches—it's a good thing I got a Tetanus booster vaccine last month. Darkness becomes too thick for my headlamp to penetrate. Cockroaches chirp from somewhere in the hole, and immediately, my skin starts to itch.

"Yes. He was a good guy." Charlie moves deeper into the maze, winding right and then turning left at a fork. The duct tapers until I can't crawl without dragging my hips along the walls. At least now I know I'm claustrophobic—that's valuable information I wouldn't have known unless someone forced me to stuff myself into a Boy-Scout-made shaft.

"I'm sorry," Charlie says after several minutes of silence, "about what happened to your family." Filthy bandages bind his palms, soaked with what appears to be oil.

"How'd you hurt your hands?" I bite my lip to cage a swell of sobs and power forward into the shrinking abyss. Of course he knows what happened. Everyone must know.

"Eh, I got some nasty blisters while doing maintenance work yesterday. Nash is always creating new contraptions for me to fix, and they seem to get progressively more dangerous to maintain. Here, all work is dirty work. We don't have many luxuries. Our food is bloody awful, we live by the bare minimum, and *make-do* should be our moto."

Terrific.

The tunnel spits us into a cavern-like room with gas lanterns and scaffolding stacked with canned food. Survival gear hangs from the stone ceiling. Not a normal military camp. A rebel base maybe. Or some sort of apocalyptic resort where vacationers come to role-play.

"Hey, it's Coca-Cola."

Two boys who look to be around Charlie's age sit on crates in the corner, rewiring a pair of radios. They stand and amble toward us, feeling my body with their black, shark-like eyes.

"Who's your friend, Cocaine?" The tallest boy's lips curl into a grin so ugly, it should be smacked off his face. He hovers over me and glides a smelly finger down my cheek. If he's not careful, I'll sock him like Jon taught me. Sure, it wouldn't be very ladylike to punch a guy in the balls, but it isn't very manlike to harass a woman because she has different parts and a sweet face. "You're a pretty Lister. If you ever get bored with him, come find me."

"Belt up, Bollocks." Charlie shoves the kid backward. "Keep your scummy mitts off her."

"Come on, Coker the Joker. Lighten up."

"This is Lieutenant Stryker's little sister. Sergeant Buchanan will shoot your head off if I tell…"

"Okay, sorry. I didn't know." He throws his hands up and in a split second, puts distance between us. "She should be wearing a nametag or something."

Guys can be like little boys who throw rocks at girls with the nicest pigtails or middle schoolers who date for a day. Some abuse and betray. But there are those who watch from a distance, give of themselves without asking for a reward. They wait until the girl is the strongest, most empowered version of herself because the challenge of winning her heart is greater and so is its value.

"Who was that?" I ask as Charlie pulls me to a ladder.

"Bellamy Bolstick. He and his mate Brady enlisted last January."

"Why'd he call me a Lister?" Sweat bursts from my pores when I lift myself onto the first ring and then the next. My muscles burn and quiver. How did that cot steal so much of my strength?

"A Lister is someone who enlists in the Vestige after the breach. You're new here, which makes you a Lister," he says. "Push open the door. I'll meet you up there once I fetch supplies for Nash."

I shove my weight against the ceiling panel and clamber from the shaft, out of hell. Soldiers in street clothes move past me with stacks of files, rank patches sewn onto armbands.

Jon lied.

The Command Center is composed of three

double-wide trailers welded together, gutted and remodeled, transformed into a state-of-the-art military base. Computer screens cover the walls, monitoring statistics, news reports, social media, and displaying security feed from various cities. A large map hangs in the center of the main room, pinned to an old American flag. Like the one I found in Jon's backpack, it too is streaked with black lines, handwritten coordinates, and a red circle. Severance.

Let me off this merry-go-round. I gave it a try. Believe me, I tried. But I'm about to get sick. Spinning. Faster. Dirt and strangers. Too much information. Stop the ride before I jump!

Jack hunches over a worktable, inspecting documents. Familiar. Safe. I run through the bustle and collide with his chest. He emits a gasp—I hit him pretty hard—and hugs me without inquisition. His fingers comb through my shortened hair, slowing the whirlwind to a steady pulse.

"I like the change." When I don't release my grip, he squeezes tighter. "You're okay."

The way we hold one another isn't seductive. It's almost as if we both need to be reassured that we're not facing this chaos alone, link our lives together instead of running parallel. And as he tucks a strand of hair behind my ear, our surroundings fade—irrelevant, incapable of damaging us. We're together in some tenuous third-space that can only be visited by touching each other.

"You and Jon lied."

"Yes," he whispers, "to keep you safe."

What hurts more, that he deceived me, or the perfect world we created together was nothing but an imaginary house of cards destined to crumble?

"I trusted you and now … what am I supposed to do?"

His eyes widen when I break our physical connection as if he might be afraid of losing me, as if I'm more to him than his dead best friend's little sister. "I'll tell you everything. No more lies."

"You must be our new guest." A man in his early sixties appears in the crowd clothed in an ornamented uniform. He's the general from Dad's office. "Sergeant, now is when you introduce us."

"Uh ... my apologies, Sir." Jack salutes the man. "General Ford, this is Julie Stryker."

"You have my condolences, Julie. Your brother was a friend of mine. He'll be missed." General Ford extends his arm to shake my hand. It's an empty gesture that stabs me in the chest. "If you need anything, let me know. The Vestige is at your service." His wrinkled face beams with sympathy, but in its dapper creases, hidden beneath his slate-gray irises, are streaks of remorse.

Jon and our parents sat at the kitchen table, whispering, arguing. His backpack held maps and a gun. Dad was terrified when I brought him lunch. It all makes sense now.

General Ford destroyed my family.

"We missed you at the range this morning," Jack says.

"I didn't want to show you up in front of your squad, Sarge."

"Oh, I'm a better shot than you, Old Man."

"Is that a fact?" General Ford grins. "Bet you a hundred bucks..."

"A stick of gum will do just fine." Jack laughs.

"You killed them." Anger tenses my muscles, sends heat stampeding across my skin. "It was you at Dad's office. Whatever secret Jon told our parents ... it was connected to you somehow, wasn't it?" I fly forward, clutch the decorated collar of his blazer, and shake him until his head bobbles. Dead eyes. Empty house. A single shot. "They're gone because of you!"

"What the hell, Julie? Stop." Jack pries me off the general. His scolding stare burrows through my rage. "No one here is your enemy. Jon was part of our family, which makes you family."

"Anyone who lies to me is my enemy." I glare at him and then at the general. The problem with being surrounded by brilliant liars is that I have to assume they're always lying—a lie is only innocent fiction until someone believes it.

General Ford clears his throat. "Sergeant, take her to the Overlook."

Jack nods and drags me to a metal door concealed behind a panel of computer monitors. "No random freak attacks, okay? There's something I need to show you."

The girl who's more explosive than a firecracker—I'm already a stigma.

We go where the world is vast and clear. Birds twitter. Paramount pinnacles crowd the landscape like a mass of rioters refusing to budge. There's so much earth beyond Charleston, but I was happy in captivity, and happiness isn't something to leave.

Jack moves through the sea of dilapidated trailers. From out here, they appear to be uninhabited—abandoned and expired like animal corpses left to rot on the roadside. Tarps and tunnels camouflage all signs of life. Where is everyone? Why are they hiding?

Levi scampers from a muddy crawlspace and joins us for a trek into the woods. He pants and wags his tail, patrolling at Jack's side. Together, we wade through the overgrown lawn, past faded flamingos and a rusting bicycle.

"Where are we?"

"North Carolina," Jack says. "We call this place the Underground. It's where my platoon and I have being living for the past year, our military base."

"You told me you weren't in the military anymore."

"I'm not." He moves toward the trees separating us from miles of woodland. Perspiration beads on his forehead and forms a 'V' beneath the neckline of his t-shirt. "It's time to tell a story."

"Ooh, a story. Sounds thrilling. What's it about?"

He gives a look that says 'you're annoying the crap out of me so shut up.'

Security cameras track our movement as we enter the forest. We push through brush and scramble over rocks. Jack hikes as if he's made this trek a thousand times before. I stumble behind him, out-of-breath, and scrape myself on a vine of thorns. Another wound to add to my extensive collection.

"Dad was a bigwig colonel," Jack says. "He saw me as a disappointment so after high school, I enlisted as a Marine to attract his attention. Within a few years, I passed basic training with letters of recommendation from my commanding officers. I was then recruited into the Air-Ground Task Force." He shoves me up a damp embankment. I clutch roots, claw at dirt. The high altitude burns my lungs—I cough and breathe through the fabric of my sleeve.

Where are we going?

"I aced my Ground Combat training, was certified in emergency and wilderness medicine. Not to sound self-absorbed but … I really was the best … and Dad still didn't notice. I was promoted, ranked a Sergeant, and transferred to Parris Island where I met Jon. We became friends almost immediately…" He trails off, continuing to move at an insanely fast pace.

"Can we slow down a bit? I'm about to die."

"Nope. You need to get stronger." He smiles. "My platoon was transferred to a base in south Tennessee and ordered to patrol a sector of deserted land. I'd been training for years, hoping to be deployed overseas, so it came as a shock when my superiors assigned me to guard an unpopulated town."

"Jack, my legs are cramping." He's such a chatterbox.

"They told us there'd been a nuclear leak from a nearby factory and everyone had been evacuated as a precaution. I knew it was a lie. There weren't any factories within a hundred miles that used nuclear power. Besides, why would the government send their best troops into a radioactive area? We should've been overseas fighting a war. You probably don't remember the news broadcasts eleven years ago, but every country on Earth was facing turmoil—natural disasters, political instability, economic collapses, and then the outbreak of some unknown virus followed by nuclear bombings. The world had fallen apart. And things that are broken cannot be mended with time but effort and sweat."

A wasp darts around me—I sprint past Jack and scramble up a slope before collapsing against a tree. "War? No, I don't remember a war." Bugs. I hate bugs. Especially the ones with stingers.

He laughs. "Wow, you're already getting stronger."

"So … what was the government hiding?"

"The truth." He stops moving long enough for me to catch my breath. "It was Jon's birthday and some of the soldiers had organized a surprise party, just sheet cake and a game of darts. I volunteered to take his night shift and arrived at my post, prepared for the long night ahead."

Mildly intrigued. "What happened?" If I ask enough questions, maybe he'll get so caught up in the story, he won't walk as fast. Is it bad that my legs are numb? Should my head be throbbing? Hmm, I've never had red blotches on my forearms before.

"I found something." He shrugs. "It's ironic, really. All along I'd been protecting the Feds' dirty secret. Once I realized a bit of what was happening, it was too late," he says. "General Ford said to stay quiet about the whole thing so he could protect me, but my discovery was too huge to remain confidential. I told Jon. He told Tally. The information leaked throughout my squad like a virus and infected the entire platoon. Everyone asked questions. Everyone wanted the truth."

"I'm guessing that was a problem." Praise the Lord—Jack is slowing down.

He nods. "General Ford called me into his office days later. He was in a panic, rushing around the room, stuffing things into bags. The Feds were coming to wipe us out."

"You had to run because you knew their secret?"

"Yeah, in a matter of hours, my platoon packed and left base. We traveled on foot for a week, divided into fireteams to remain unnoticed. It was a stroke of luck we found this place—prime location, off-grid. We spent several months digging tunnels and restructuring the camp to camouflage it from aerial view. We titled ourselves the Vestige, which means *surviving evidence*, because we're determined to find what remains of the truth."

"What were the Feds hiding?"

Jack reaches the mountain's peak and pulls me up beside him. "See for yourself."

Wind whips my hair as I tiptoe toward the cliff's edge. Mountains clutter the horizon like waves on a heart monitor. "What am I supposed to be looking at?"

"You see the world for what it is and what it could be," Jack says. "What you don't see is the gaping chasm in between ... and that's what I found." He snatches a rock off the ground and throws it a few feet to his left. Bounce. Hiss. "The gaping chasm in between." He finds a stick and strikes, causing light flickers to appear in midair. Waves of energy ripple across what appears to be a translucent dome, a force field. It slices through mountains and fades into the distance.

Psychologists classify fear as an emotion, but I'm certain it's a physical state. Muscles shrivel inward to protect themselves. Adrenaline releases to prepare the body for action. Heart pumps a surplus of oxygen into the blood. A physical state. That I'm experiencing.

I clutch my mouth as the electrical pulse outlines the dome. Meteor shower. Mirage at sea. Severance. What's going on? Who created the wall? And why has it been kept a secret?

Jack squats and fingers the smoking stick. "I've been searching for answers, all of us have. We've studied the molecular density of the barrier, mathematically calculated its diameter, but other than observations, we know nothing about its purpose. I can only guess."

"What's your guess?" I swipe the tears from my eyes.

"People have always expected *the end of the world* to be a dramatic, thematic event: war, disease, a sudden explosion. But what if *the end of the world* has already occurred? What if our final demise happened slowly, secretly ... and we've been oblivious to it all?" He smiles. "There might be some truth in those end-of-the-world scenarios I read."

"So you're saying this wall ... is protecting us from the apocalypse? You think the world has ended and for some reason, we haven't noticed?"

"It's a theory." He nods. "We live in a multilayered world. The first layer is what you can see. The second, what you know is real. And the third layer is made of things you can neither see nor know are real. That's the world I believe we are living in, the third layer. We've been kept oblivious to it for years and deceived into thinking all is as it seems."

No. This is crazy. "Why hasn't anyone else found the dome?"

"I'm not sure, yet."

"You do realize you sound insane."

"Yeah, but I'm not insane if I'm right."

Any other weird news heading my way, like, that I'm a mermaid or secretly married? I thought finding out Jon had a crush on Queen Bee Rebekah was the most outlandish information I'd ever receive, not that I'm living in an actual snow glob, possibly ignorant to civilization's end.

"You're handling all this like a pro." Jack motions for me to sit next to him. Why is he happy? The world might have ended. We should be getting drunk and talking about the things we won't be able to do. Wait, why am I frustrated with him? Why aren't I screaming and crying like usual?

"Please let me go back to Charleston. I'd rather spend what time I have left at home."

"After *the end of the world*, there is a world. Life doesn't stop. It changes," he says. "Think of it as like living with cancer. As long as you don't go to the doctor and confront the possibility, you can convince yourself it's not there, but you can only live with cancer for so long before it kills you. Wouldn't you rather know what's growing inside of you and fight it?" He yanks me down and wraps his arms around my shoulders. "We can make time and rebuild your home. Don't be an ostrich."

"An ostrich?"

"They stick their heads in the sand. Don't be like them."

"You talk a lot, Jack Buchanan." I laugh and lean against his chest. "Be patient with me."

"I'm used to being patient with you, Julie." He throws another rock at the force field. Bounce. Hiss. His smile shrinks and his grip tightens. "You should know everything about Jon's death."

A breath catches inside my throat—Jon is dead—and the pain comes rushing back.

"Once a month, two of us drive into town to purchase food and supplies. Usually we go to Asheville, but … Jon decided to return home for a few days. He wanted to take you and your parents away from Charleston, bring you here to live with us, keep you safe from the Feds." Jack's cheek brushes mine. His words sink into me. "The first few days, we shopped for our month's provisions. It was a coincidence you and I met when we did."

"So you weren't planning to say goodbye? You and Jon wanted me to come here?"

"Yeah. Tally was bringing a van to drive you, your parents, and your belongings to a house half-a-mile from the Underground. You would've been secluded but safe, had a chance to start a new life away from the Feds' control. Everything had been organized."

In an almost perfect world, we made it. Mom and I hung curtains in our new home, built an art studio made of camouflage tarps for her in the garden Dad and I planted. Jon took me to the Underground every afternoon. We crawled through tunnels, practiced our shooting at the range. Jack came to the house for dinner on Mondays, Thursdays, and Saturdays. He'd bring tapes for us to watch on the outdated television, left me books in the lopsided mailbox. What a happy snow globe that would've been.

In an almost perfect world, we made it.

"Jon told your parents too much. They freaked. Colonel Stryker leaked information at work that traveled to the wrong ears fast. General Ford tried to smooth things over with your dad, keep people quiet, but the Feds became aware of Jon's knowledge and decided the only way to keep their secret safe was to wipe out your entire family."

We were normal people with a mortgage, not names on a hit list. Life has tricked me into believing all is as it seems and now the strings of truth are slowly unraveling.

"This is a lot to digest, I know, and I can't lie and say everything's going to be all right because I'm pretty sure it won't be. The only promise I can make is that I'll do whatever it takes to get your parents back," Jack says. "Once we know what's happened to the world, we can use our knowledge to blackmail the Feds into releasing them."

"Does staying here make me a Lister?"

He laughs. "How'd you hear about that?"

"Charlie told me."

"Yes, you'll be a Lister." He toys with my fingers as if they're alien objects, bending and stretching them. Our right hands press together. Mine is small and slender compared to his callused palm.

Levi lies next to us and places his head in my lap. The three of us huddle together at the cliff's edge, inches from *the end of the world*.

Chapter Nine

"I was a battleground of fear and curiosity."
H.G. Wells, *The War of the Worlds*

"Lunar phases," Nash says between bites of food. "We already know the dome is an electrically charged plasma membrane and uses gravity and some sort of magnetic grid. If its power comes from Earth's gravitation, there should be lapses when the dome isn't as impenetrable. I've already done the research. During a neap tide, we can construct an object to act as a door, insert it into the dome…"

"Yeah, and be fried." Charlie smirks.

"Magnetic fields cannot be terminated but they can be rerouted around objects that conduct magnetic flux. We can create a door."

"Why would we want to leave?" Jack dumps a spoonful of Spam and tomato sauce onto his tongue. Red specks soar across the table as he talks. "We don't know what's happened to the world. Radiation, disease, war—the dome could be protecting us."

"I'm almost done building the drone. It'll be ready to fly in a few days." Nash reaches across me to grab the mustard bottle—does anyone here have manners?

"Not long from now, we'll know if we can leave Severance."

Welcome to the apocalypse. Where *make-do* is a motto and life seems wrong, out-of-place. Where the weak become strong because they have no other choice.

The mess hall is louder than a high school cafeteria and reeks of body odor. Soldiers and Listers sit shoulder-to-shoulder at mismatched tables, eating their mass-produced meals.

Deodorant and air-conditioning must be the unavailable luxuries Charlie mentioned.

I smear perspiration from my upper lip and stab a fork into the mound of undercooked spaghetti. Stupid hands—they can't get the wad of noodles into my mouth.

Jack grabs my arm to steady it. "The flyovers won't begin for another hour. We can go outside, get away from the noise. If you're not feeling well…"

"I'm fine. I know how to take care of myself." Not really. But it's what girls say to make themselves feel stronger, more capable, even when their souls and bodies have gone numb.

"I know that," he whispers. "I just don't want you to have to."

"You care too much. Let me be strong." I uncap my bottle and drink—the fermented liquid is warm like carbonated urine. Strong girls drink beer, right?

After Sybil died and Dad became a temporary alcoholic, I promised myself I'd never drink, not after the pain of losing him, watching his life slowly fade. I made a promise I couldn't keep because now, I need a way to drown out my own voice, to kill my memories without having to kill myself.

"Who are the Scavs?" I swallow another mouthful of beer and gag.

"They're a special ops division of the military. Supposed to be covert," Jack says. "Scav is a nickname we use to warn each other of flyovers. It's only a matter of time before we're found. If they spot a trail of smoke or the tarps of the Overhang, we'll be dead within the hour."

No place is safe. We are the hunted. Time bombs are strapped to our chests, counting down to an imminent zero. Tick. Tick. A day will come when we are discovered, and our strength will be tested. Tick. Tick. Change will rattle the universe once more.

"Hey, everyone. This is Julie, Lieutenant Stryker's sister," Jack shouts before stuffing his mouth with green beans. "Say hello. That's an order."

An explosion of voices greets me like a slap to the face, and I flip my hood as if the invisibility cloak I had throughout middle and high school somehow ended up in my jacket. Has Jack made it his life mission to embarrass me? He's like one of those parents who go from awesome to catastrophically embarrassing in three seconds.

"*She* is Jon's sister?" A girl rises from a nearby table. She resembles a celebrity, not someone who spends each day toting a gun. "Such a disappointment."

"Keep your mouth shut, Lieutenant McConaughey," Jack snaps.

"You're not my superior anymore. Ranks, respect—those formalities ended when we got canned. You call me Sutton like everyone else. Got it?" She bites her bottom lip and slides her hand up his back. He spins to face her, but she clutches a handful of his hair and yanks him to her sculpted waist. "Keep a leash on the new girl, Jack. You know what I do to high-maintenance Listers."

"Don't threaten me. You're here because I allow you to be here."

"Oh, did I insult your god-complex, Sarge?"

Jack slings his elbow into Sutton's belly and knocks her to the plywood floor. "Get out," he says. "I don't want your bad attitude infecting the other soldiers."

She laughs—wow, I hate her. "Aren't you a gentleman?"

"Yeah. You insulted a woman, so I kicked your ass." He dabs his mouth with a napkin and combs his hair into place. "Doesn't get more gentlemanly than that, Lieutenant."

They probably had a fling years ago. Maybe. She looks like his type, the model-turned-soldier who saves the world with a bazooka and lacy pair of lingerie. But he wouldn't hit a girl unless she'd betrayed his respect, forced him to treat her as a soldier gone wild.

In the South, people mask malice with sugary smiles and fake compliments. It's what I've been taught. If you hate someone, hide your feelings in public and gossip behind closed doors. No confrontation, no harm done. At least, in theory.

"Sutton's all bark, no bite," Charlie tells me. "Unlike you."

Jack drapes his arm over my shoulders and pulls down the collar of his t-shirt to showcase the healing teeth marks. "She bites *hard*."

"It's my only defense." I smile when they laugh. "Jack, were you and Sutton together?" Normal question. Not an obvious I-want-you-to-myself giveaway.

"Heck, no. The planet would've exploded."

A sigh breezes past my lips. I suck it back in before anyone notices. If mean, sexy girls aren't his type, maybe I stand a chance. One day. Not now, of course.

"Tally, get over here."

The girl from the van is sprawled on a chaise chair in the corner. She glances at me, eyebrows raised, and fingers the ID tags pinned to the neckline of her tank top. "No. I don't want to meet your stupid new girlfriend," she yells. "Jon wouldn't be happy that you're trying to hook up with his baby sister. Besides, she looked better when she was covered in blood. Was that a sexy experience for you, Jack, sticking your hands into her intestines?"

"You're being rude and creepy. Come introduce

yourself like a normal person."

"Fine." Tally rises from her chair, stomps to our table, and shakes my hand. "Tallulah *Badass* Mason. My friends call me Tally." She digs her fingernails into my palm.

"Ouch." I wince.

"Priss."

Jack glares at her. "Tally, what's wrong with you? Can't you be—I don't know—civil?"

"Nope. I make an effort to be glamorously uncivil to all people. Welcome to the Underground, Priss. We already hate you." She flashes a satisfied smile and walks away.

"Your friends are so nice." I rub the fingernail indentions from my skin and fake the worst, teary smile. "I'm sure I'll like it here … once people don't hate or cut me." The humid air is acid inside my lungs. I cough on a sob, guillotine tears with blinks.

"Some of them are nice," Jack says, "like Nash and Charlie. They're cool."

"We're super cool."

He yanks my arm into his lap and uses a cracked pen to write *The Living* on my wrist. A luminescent smile swallows his face. "There is a difference between accepting a dirty world and allowing it to transform you. You're better than us, Julie, so stay better."

Butterflies twist my stomach into knots. "You want me to be a lonely purist?"

"Duh, of course. I really should be a motivational speaker."

"No, you'd suck."

"Like you at sports and bodily coordination?" He laughs—really laughs.

"Oh, you want to go there? Who said he didn't need to read the directions before putting together my nightstand? Yeah, I'm pretty sure it wasn't meant to look like a wheelbarrow."

"Wheelbarrows are more functional." His dimples and glistening eyes project a foreign language—could someone translate for me? He sighs. "You're going to fit in around here just fine."

He's the lifeguard dragging me from the bottom of a pool, the latte reviving my sleepy brain. In an instant, I emerge from the water and fog. What happened to sadness? Where did Jack hide my fear?

"I believe you." Because I fit with him. And he's here.

A high-ranking soldier built like a mountain enters the mess hall and waves at us.

"That's my cue. I have a meeting with General Ford. See you later tonight." Jack stands, stashes his unopened beer into the pocket of his jacket. "Stay with these guys. They'll show you back to the barrack." He follows the large man into the connecting tunnel and vanishes.

Missing someone is the worst form of torture because it never goes away no matter where you are or what you do with your life. When a person is gone and all you have of them is a fuzzy recollection of what it was like to hear your phone buzz with texts from them, the joy you experienced while in their company, that instance when the bond you shared shattered, you long for all that was lost and could've been gained. You have memories and nothing more. And no matter how much times passes, you still feel the ache of their absence whenever they rise into your thoughts. Torture.

"Who's that?" I ask.

"Ezra Cross, Gunnery Sergeant of the second battalion, sixth Marines, now the Lieutenant General of the Vestige," Charlie says with his nose upturned.

"General Ford offered Jack the rank of Lieutenant General when we first got here. He denied the offer, said he'd rather work and live with his squad. Ezra got the position instead."

"There is one major perk of having Jack as our squad leader. We have the best barrack—no bunk beds." Nash ties his blonde hair into a ponytail. "You're lucky you get to stay with us."

"Jack showed you the dome?"

I nod.

"Good. Knowing the truth is the first step toward healing." Nash's response sounds like a slogan from Alcoholic Anonymous but instead of alcohol, I've been drunk on ignorance for the past eighteen years. Now I'm sobering up.

"Sometimes life really sucks," Charlie says, "but you just have to keep holding out for the moments that don't suck. They'll come around eventually."

We finish eating, navigate the tunnels to the Overhang, and follow the camouflaged thoroughfare to our barrack. Abram sits on his cot, sharpening a pocketknife. Tally throws darts at a magazine cutout of some tummy-tucked actress. Sutton cleans her boots. They stare when I enter the trailer, passing along an unspoken warning—if I'm not careful, they will slit my throat.

Levi tilts his head when I collapse next to him. How am I supposed to change clothes? The medical screens around my cot have been removed.

"Lights out." Sutton flips off the overhead bulbs. Her bedsprings squeak as she slithers into her evil lair of smelly quilts. "Keep your mouth shut, Lister. You never know what might crawl inside it."

Bless her heart.

Darkness cloaks the room, a convenient screen. I

peel off my grungy clothes and slide beneath familiar sheets, into a safe dream world where home is a realistic noun and civilization isn't hanging on by a thread, where things are as they seem.

A gust of crisp, mountain air drifts from an open window. I bind myself in blankets. Why is there fur on my legs, in my armpits? Great. Now I'll obsessively think about my gorilla limbs until I scrounge a razor from the supply closet.

End-of-the-world rules apply.

Mom would have a fit if she knew I was sharing a room with men, sleeping in my underwear because I can't afford to soil my only set of clothes. Jon would tell me to get out of his bed, and then flop onto my belly when I refused to budge. They'd take me back to our pretty house on Rainbow Row, and I'd taste coffee and lipstick while lavishing in a false sense of security.

I have to move forward now and pry my face from the pavement. I have to get up. Memories tell me who I was, not who I'll become. They don't fix the present any more than they fix the past.

The door creaks open. Jack enters and skulks through the barracks. His scintillating lantern floats in front of him, glowing gold. He removes clothes from a plastic trunk, pulls off his boots and wriggles out of his muddy jeans. I was right. He wears boxer-briefs. Black.

His muscles flex as he steps into a pair of cargo pants. Scars streak his spine, arms, and legs. Real courage—living and suffering for what you believe in most.

Fire swells inside me when he leans over to peel off his socks. The ridges of his shoulder blades rise beneath his skin like waves. His biceps bulge. I should look away to respect his privacy. He'd respect mine. Yes, I'll look away. Eventually.

Jack slides a navy t-shirt over his head and wipes the sweat from his stubble-covered cheeks. His eyes latch hold of mine, holding them captive. He smiles as if he's caught me watching a racy movie, playing with matches, or wearing a strappy bodycon dress. "Goodnight, Julie."

"Goodnight." I hide my face with Levi's tail and scoot deeper into the fabric avalanche. He was stripping in the middle of the trailer. What was I supposed to do? Offer to build him a dressing room?

****

Schedules and protocol keep us safe, protected, invisible. No one is allowed to be outside during the Scavs' flyover hours. All lights must be off by ten o'clock. Vehicles are to be parked in the woods and covered with brush. The use of computers is restricted to all personnel unless given clearance by superiors. Patrolling scouts are required to radio the Command Center on the hour.

I can't even go to the supply room to gather rations without asking General Ford for permission.

Listers divide into work crews when the siren sounds each morning and disperse throughout camp. I wash laundry until my hands are so blistered and shriveled, they turn the suds red. Blood. Staining clothes. Abram assigns me to the kitchen where I wash dishes from dawn to dusk, that is, until Sutton notices my crimson sink and threatens to drag me by the hair into the woods. If my body isn't drenched in soap and sweat, I'm plastered with sludge from the tunnels. The more I wash, the less I'm clean. And when I don't think I can last another second, I somehow bear another minute, then an hour. I survive exhaustion, severe muscle spasms, an infection of a thumb sore and dehydration. I live through panic attacks and flashbacks. Jon. Dead. Mom and Dad. Gone. End of the world. Everywhere.

Work harder. Faster. Sweat. Bleed. Survive the pain.

Jack and I hike to the Overlook before dawn. We huddle at the cliff's edge, sip cider from a metal thermos, and watch the hot-pink sunrise cascade over the dome. He whispers a funeral for Jon, tells me beautiful things I wish were real. Life almost seems normal with him, like I'm lying in the green space between Porter's Lodge and Randolph Hall with a sky full of small infinities and a hand to hold.

"Everything is messed up," I mumble when the dome shimmers.

He smiles. "Not everything."

There comes a moment when we must choose how we're going to love someone. Some forms of love leave a sweet memory once they're gone, others leave scars. But there are forms that when stolen, destroy part of who we are—love that transforms us. What if the feelings I have for Jack kill another piece of me once they're gone?

A piercing scream wakes me up one night.

Tally and Abram stand guard in front of the blue tarp separating Jack's living space from the barrack. He screeches—why won't they move? What's going on?

"Wake him up. Move." I lurch from my cot and lift the canvas. Jack's body writhes beneath the sheets of his bed. He wails in a tone that makes me shiver.

"Step one foot in there, Priss, and I'll give you a black eye." Tally grips my shoulder to prevent me from entering the room. Darkness masks her face. "He doesn't want us to wake him."

"Why?"

"The sergeant has a reoccurring nightmare," Abram says. "By experiencing the dream over and over, he thinks he'll be able to conquer whatever is tormenting him. Don't ask me what he's freaked about. I don't know. If the noise bothers you, you can have a pair of my earplugs."

Jack arches his back, tossing and turning like a piece of debris caught in the ocean's surf. He can't be scared. He's someone who fixes broken people, not someone in need of fixing.

Nightmares reveal his weakness as grief revealed mine.

Chapter Ten

"Until the day when God shall deign to reveal the future to man, all human wisdom is summed up in these two words, wait and hope."

Alexandre Dumas, *The Count of Monte Cristo*

Rain drips from my nose, treats me as a stone caught in a rushing river. I crouch in the mud with limbs like chiseled rock and bandaged, blistered hands. The wind saturates my clothes—if I don't stop shivering, I might crack teeth, have a seizure, or lose all feeling in my feet. Do I still have toes?

"Your lips are blue." Jack drapes his jacket over my shoulders to protect me from the cold. Water spews from his mouth and nostrils, streams down his skin. "Ready for takeoff?"

"Yeah, it's ready." Nash and Charlie rise from the ground, plastered from head to toe with grass shards and dirt. "We have a functioning drone."

"Shouldn't we wait for the storm to die down?" I shield my eyes from the torrential downpour. Fog creeps through the trailer park, thicker than smoke. Its ashy tendrils claw at the remote-controlled aircraft. Chunk of plastic and wires. Determiner of our fate.

"Rainstorms are terrific cloaking devices, and since the drone won't be going to a high altitude, the clouds will not hinder our imaging system. We'll have a clear view," Nash shouts over the patter. He pumps a weather balloon with hydrogen and activates the drone's navigation system. "The weather balloon along with a thick coat of paint will prevent a heat signature. We should be off-grid."

Jack stares at the overcast sky with his jaw clenched. He must sense it, too—danger lurking around us like a predator, the stench of change. "Let's head inside."

We squeeze through masses of people to reach the Command Center's main room. Why has everyone come to witness the big reveal? We're screwed whether we live or die.

"Move." I fight through the sea of dirty bodies and emerge at the front of the crowd where General Ford, Ezra, and their crew of logistic officers stand at attention. Someone activates the drone's flight sequence. Static shifts across the monitors before clarifying to reveal aerial footage.

Jack grabs my hand. He's trembling. "Are you afraid?"

For all the strong, compassionate parts of him, there are also scared, broken parts, and until this moment, I've been so focused on the layers I love, I've overlooked the layers that make him human.

"Please. Make me afraid because feeling fear would mean I wasn't numb."

The footage shifts focus, replacing dilapidated trailers with acres of forest, tumultuous whitewater rivers and mountains blanketed in mist. Learning the truth won't destroy Earth in a blink, so why should I worry? I've experienced the worst-case scenario, lost all that mattered to me. The apocalypse can't take or return what's been stolen. It won't leave me any more scarred and changed than I am now.

"Approaching the dome," Nash says. "Increasing altitude."

Silence plagues the crowd like a virus, spreading fast. Some of the Listers appear to be holding their breath. If the drone doesn't pick up speed, I might have a bunch of unconscious people to resuscitate. Jack—he squeezes so tight, my knuckles pop. Why are they freaked? How could life in a world beyond the dome be any better than life inside the bubble?

Reality flickers onto the computer monitors.

Charred buildings rise from the horizon, black as soot, void of vegetation. Stillness. Darkness. Dead. The clouds unspool to reveal cracked highways and mounds of abandoned cars.

There lie the remains of America: skeletal ruins, necrotic residue. The surviving evidence of humankind is all that's left. And it's not enough.

Vomit shoots into my mouth and burns my lips. I must be more afraid than I realized. The end of civilization doesn't confiscate more from me. I am still as homeless and futureless as I was before the drone launched. But I'm indescribably alone. Nobody is outside my snow globe looking in, waiting for the day when I'll be allowed to emerge. Stuck. Trapped.

Footage plays, swirling into an abyss of pixelated imagery. It's as if we're a salvage crew surveying the wreckage of the Titanic, soldiers flying over a battlefield of corpses and knowing we arrived too late. There's no one left to save.

"We know the truth," General Ford says. "It's not an easy truth to swallow. We've been clinging to the idea there might be a life for us beyond the dome. That dream is unattainable. Where we are … this is our home … and it's up to us to make it better."

"It's *the end of the world*," Bellamy yells from amidst the mob. "We're going to die."

Jack releases my hand and shoves his way through the crowd, storming off into the maze of shabby corridors and offices. His warmth dissipates from my palm. Gone. Disconnected.

A pulled trigger.

The walls fold in around me, the ceiling lowers, and the room begins to spin faster and faster until I'm a child clinging to the bars of a playground merry-go-round, screaming out of fear of being ripped into the unknown. I stumble toward the open door, into a crashing torrent of rain.

No, this can't be real. The apocalypse was supposed to be cliché drama, Godzilla roaming the streets and zombies crawling from graves to devour the living. I guess all of humankind wanted to believe they'd end with a *bang* instead of unnoticed silence. We all, deep down, want to believe in a future where our historical monuments and literature hold significance. We want our deaths to be important.

We want to matter.

****

"Aww, why are you crying, Julie? Was all that too scary for you?" Sutton possesses the Overhang like an evil spirit. She breathes down my neck. "General Ford should've only let the big kids see the footage. Listers are too young and fragile to handle the truth."

"Leave me alone." I rest my head on the damp, wooden table. Maybe the introvert position will make me disappear. "Don't you have to go screw someone?"

She emits a growl and yanks me to her waist. "I don't like the way you're talking." Her talons dig into my scalp, and I squeal. "Apologize."

"Let go." I grip her wrists to lessen the tension. Pain pulses across my skull, a sharp, wet sting. Was she born crazy, or did she lose her mind with age? "I mean it. Let go, Sutton."

"You don't deserve to be here," she hisses. "Jon was a nice guy, great kisser, but you're nothing like him. You are weak and ugly … and it baffles me that Jack likes you. I guess it's only a matter of time, though. Dead brother. Dead parents. You'll die, too. And when you're dead, I think Jack might be my next special friend. He has a great body."

"He'd rather die than be with you."

"Let him die, then." Sutton wrenches my tresses and shoves me to the wood. "Jon was a slut."

"Go to hell." Tears puddle on the tabletop. My muscles quiver. No one is allowed to hurt me, debase my brother. I won't let them.

Everything is a battle. You either win or you die.

"We're already there," she smirks. "Welcome to hell."

I rise from the table and with a single punch, send her crashing into a pile of crates. If my hands weren't bandaged, I'd probably shatter a few fingers on her jaw. Worth the pain if I can put a dent in her perfect nose, bust those plump lips that once crawled across Jon's mouth.

Sutton splinters wood and lies in a disfigured wad on the ground. Her expression contorts into a frightening display of rage. "Bad idea." She slams her fist into my stomach, tearing open my scar. Blood soaks my t-shirt in a matter of seconds. Intense pain trickles through my body, draws a gasp from my lips.

I scream and knock her to the floor.

We wrestle in the dirt. I bite her arm. She hits over and over and grabs me in chokehold. I cough, wheeze, entangle my fingers in her long, glossy hair and jerk her forward. She cries out, loosens her hold on my neck. I roll on top on her and strike until her eyes roll back into her skull. I'm hurting someone because they hurt me first. I'm doing this for self-preservation. But even though fighting back may earn respect, in the process, I become like my enemy.

"You're idiots," Tally screams. She yanks me up

by the back of my shirt and slaps so hard, I lose sight for a moment. "Do you want to get kicked out of the Underground?"

"I'm done with bullies. No one is allowed to mess with me, not even you."

She laughs. "You did this to make a point, Priss?"

"Stop calling me Priss." I massage her smack from my cheek. "I'm not a small, defenseless animal you can prey upon. Next time you hit me, I will hit back harder."

Abram and Ezra haul Sutton from the ground. She slumps against the two men, barely conscious, and allows them to drag her out of the Overhang. I caused her wounds. I hurt her like she hurt me. And the more I try to justify my actions, the more I realize how unjustified they were.

Revenge is a lie we fabricate to ease our consciences. But like two negatives can never equal a positive, two wrong deeds cannot make a right. They only screw up the equation.

****

Darkness transforms the tunnel shaft into a place of cockroach chirps, rhythmic drips, and spectral echoes. I scale the ladder into pitch black. Anything could grab me. No one would hear me scream. Since the apocalypse is real, maybe the Boogieman didn't get the *I Shouldn't Exist* memo.

Goosebumps wash across my skin. I reach the bottom floor and immediately snatch a headlamp from the coatrack. A golden glow warms the underground roadway into a less treacherous environment. Tubes. Equipment. Sludge. Nothing too deadly.

It's been four weeks since I had java and detox isn't an option. I'd rather be sipping a latte with a broken leg than be healthy and have no coffee at all.

My priorities are a little skewed.

Moonlight filters into the mess hall from a bare window, illuminating the ancient appliances and linoleum counters. I open cabinets, rummage through the pantry. There isn't a coffeemaker to be found, not even a pack of instant coffee. How does the Vestige function?

"It's kind of early for breakfast, don't you think?"

The florescent bulbs flicker to life. I squint. Jack stands in the kitchen's threshold. His hair is disheveled and his intense, blue eyes are puffy from sleep.

"Why don't you have a freaking coffeemaker?"

"It's two in the morning. Why do you want coffee?"

"I can't sleep."

"And caffeine is supposed to fix that?" Jack snickers and pulls a set of keys from his pocket. "Let's go for a drive. I'll find you some coffee."

"Are you serious?" He can't be.

"I'm starving and the only things available to eat here are canned beans and spaghetti sauce. You'll get your coffee. I'll have a pack of something drenched in sodium. It's a win-win situation."

"Won't we get in trouble for leaving the Underground?" Stupid question. Of course we won't get in trouble. He nearly runs the camp. Why am I sweating? He's Jack, my best friend, my family. I shouldn't blush when he's around. I shouldn't want to crawl out of my skin each time he shows up with messy hair. For once, can I not act like a silly girl?

"Nah, you'll be with me." He offers his hand and smiles when I entwine my fingers with his. "We better get moving if we want to be back before dawn."

Every moment of contact between us seems important—every glance, every touch, every word. I don't understand him, but I know him, and he knows me.

It's this strange connection we share. No matter how often we fight, lie, make mistakes, I choose him and deep down, I think he chooses me, too.

We exit the mess hall and trek toward an industrial building constructed along the forest's edge. Levi appears out of nowhere. He moves through the underbrush like a wolf, quick and silent.

"There are a few perks of living in the end times." Jack enters the metal shed. Vehicles clutter the space: three sports cars, a truck, a van, and a Jeep. His smile widens when he hops into the driver's seat of a red Lamborghini. "Am I totally irresistible now?"

"Oh, yes. Sutton will be all over you when she sees your sweet new ride." I laugh and slide into the vehicle. Jack is here. With me. Looking for coffee. And if a boy can manage to have coffee with me during the apocalypse, I know he cares. There's not a speck of doubt in my mind.

He must care.

Levi settles into the backseat. The garage door lifts. Jack cranks the ignition and drives out of the trailer park, into a wilderness that swallows us whole. Mountains cut through the shadows. The trees reflect the moon's rays, scintillating a dull silver light.

Beyond the Underground, the apocalypse is real and at my fingertips, so close I can touch it. Out here, I am a remnant, not a miniscule cog in some elaborate machine. Coffee isn't worth seeing nothing where something should be. Where are the late-night truckers and sketchy junk cars? What happened to the homes that once lit the rocky ridges like fireflies?

"Scavs rarely fly over after nightfall. We're safe." Jack drives in the middle of the road, slams his foot against the accelerator, and handles the zigzagging highway with daring precision. The Lamborghini's engine roars. Tires squeal as they crest the edge of a cliff.

"There are speed limits for a reason." I grip my seat when the vehicle swerves. After all I've survived, it'd be wrong for me to die in a car crash.

"You do what you couldn't do before," he says, "so the world will seem larger, fuller, and life with have something worth living."

"Speeding makes your life fuller?"

"Everyone loves to speed. They love trying not to get caught." He shrugs. "There's no one around to catch us, though. Not as fun. Stakes aren't high enough. No, I like to drive on the other side of the road because I can." His face loses its humor. Maybe he feels our loss more than he let on.

"Why do you think our end was kept a secret?" I ask once the road straightens and Jack decreases his speed. "If civilization was crumbling, and people were dying, why did the government decide to build a dome here? What made us more special than the rest of humanity?"

"My guess is the Feds wanted to protect and maintain a normal state of life. Maybe our area hadn't been contaminated. Maybe we were the short straw." Darkness shifts across his face. He switches gears, stares at the road with pain in his eyes. "Maybe they decided to keep the rescued public ignorant until things had been reestablished to avoid panic and upheavals. I don't know. Maybe they just like playing God. Maybe we're a part of a massive-scale experiment, fish in a fishbowl."

Jack steers down a dirt road, weaving along the bank of a lake. Houses appear amongst the sea of trees, mostly cottages and boathouses. He parks in the yard of a two-story log cabin, removes a pair of flashlights from the glove compartment, and climbs outside.

Levi scampers into the foliage, unmoved by the

night's eeriness and vacancy.

"I thought you were taking me to a supermarket." Gravel crunches beneath my feet as I follow him to the house. A real home. That belongs to someone.

"Scavs looted the stores but left residential areas untouched. We'll find what we need here." Jack breaks open the cabin's front door and walks inside. "You don't have many personal belongings, so take what you want. Check the bedrooms for clothing. I'll go find a coffeemaker." He tosses me a flashlight.

"We're going to steal?" I cough on dust when we enter the living room, a cozy space cluttered with rotting furniture and faded photographs. "The people who lived here were relocated, not executed. They'll come back. It isn't right to take their stuff."

"Necessity trumps morality." Jack snatches a lighter from the mantel and disappears down a corridor, leaving me to wander at a polite pace.

The nearest bedroom belongs to a teenage girl. It's painted a pale-blue color, plastered with posters of pop singers and actors who are probably dead now. I find a pink backpack beneath the bed and fill it with random, useless things—empty journals, a Polaroid camera, postcards, books, makeup, and a stained quilt. The closet is full of clothes. I sort through the hoard like a zealous shopper at a Black Friday sale, grabbing everything that looks even the tiniest bit appealing.

People took what belonged to me. They ransacked my house because they believed necessity trumped morality. How is what I'm doing different? Am I better than them?

Survival is a passive way of saying "my needs are greater than yours."

Jack waits for me in the kitchen. He's propped against the linoleum counter, drinking from a plastic cup.

"I found a coffeemaker and several bags of medium roast." He gestures to the items piled beside him. "I also found beef jerky and vodka." He swallows the alcohol like a cancer patient drugged on morphine, easing his hurt with a despair-filled gulp.

"Booze has never helped anyone." I pry the cup from his hands and toss it into the sink. If he drowns his pain, he won't heal. He'll become like Dad, and I will lose him. "Let's go sit by the lake."

"You're trying to fix me?" He snickers. "I've spent a large chunk of my life trying to fix people. Not everyone can be fixed. I didn't know how to fix Mom. Jon was too far gone."

"To fix someone, they have to be broken. And I don't believe you're broken."

"What are you trying to do, then?" He slides a hand across my cheek, anchors a thumb behind my left ear. His voice breezes across my skin—I shiver from the shock. "Why stop me from getting wasted?"

"Because there are better medicines." I hug him tight and say everything is going to be okay because it's what I want to say, what he wants me to say. It's what we both need to hear.

The lake shimmers with a million stars and laps at the rocky shoreline like breaths of a sleeping someone. I slide from behind the cabin's screen door and drag Jack toward the dock, through decaying leaves and overgrown shrubs. We have to reach the water and pretend for a moment our world hasn't ended, that we're two people who decided to steal coffee and stargaze. Real medicine.

"Hold on a sec." Jack plucks a daffodil from a weed-infested flowerbed and gives it to me. His lips twist into a crooked half-smile.

Cheeseball.

On a scale from one-to-ten, how wrong would it

be for me to love him, not the sisterly kind of love but real, crazy, all-in love? Maybe a five. There isn't a cosmic rule that prohibits people from falling in love during the apocalypse. But he is Jon's best friend. So maybe a seven. Not too awful. That's like scoring a C on an exam. Passing grade.

"Come on." He jogs to the dock's edge and yanks off his clothes. "We're going for a swim."

"What the heck, Jack?" I shield my eyes and then crack my fingers. His skin glistens from the moon's rays. Goodbye jeans. Goodbye t-shirt and jacket. "You better leave on your underpants."

"If you insist." He snickers. "Be spontaneous."

The hands that say no are peeling off my sweater. I shed clothes until I'm left in an oversized bra and granny panties. Blood burns my cheeks—he's seen me like this before, so why am I embarrassed? He's sliced open my stomach, wrestled with me in undergarments skimpier than these. "Happy?"

"Yes." His gaze sinks into mine and remains there, linking us. "Now I am."

"I should make a *Flirty AF* sign to use whenever you say creepy come-ons."

"Oh, gosh, please do."

People, I have discovered, are layers and layers of secrets. You believe you understand them, but their motives are always hidden. You'll never truly know them, but sometimes you decide to trust them. I trust Jack, but he is composed of layers I can't comprehend. Maybe I'm layered, too.

Maybe we can reveal the truth in each other.

"We've just got to commit, yeah?" Jack bends his knees and rubs his hands together. "On the count of three, we both jump. One … two … three!" He springs from the dock and plummets into the dark water with a repercussive splash.

If I could press a universal pause button and inspect the moment as an onlooker, I'd call myself an idiot for jumping into a lake half-naked because of a boy. Liquid ice sucks me into a freezing cradle, petrifies my muscles, and floods my airways. Bubbles swirl around me as I break the surface. Dummy. Now I'll probably get hypothermia and die. My skin is already numb.

"We'll have to stay in the water for an hour to get hypothermia." Jack floats like a sailboat, rocking back and forth. "And no, I'm not a mind reader. You just look as if you're trying to survive the sinking of the Titanic." He saves my hand from the cold and reels me to his side.

We cling to the ladder, shivering shoulder-to-shoulder with a sea of stars uniting us. Jack looks at me, stares as if I'm something beautiful. His hands glide around my waist—callused fingers against soft skin, hot bodies fighting the cold. Butterflies swarm within me the closer he drifts.

I think I love you. I send this message through my fingers, up his arm, and into his heart. *You're brilliant, weird, and incredibly strong. It annoys me that you always leave your underwear inside your jeans. I hate washing your clothes, and your love for ramen noodles is disgusting. But I'm sure I love you anyway. We make sense. We fit. And I'm subconsciously asking if you could try to love me, too.*

Not kissing him is like fighting the desire to gasp for air underwater.

Gasp. I coil my arms around his neck. Gasp. His lips brush against mine, lingering in our tenuous rift. Gasp. Our foreheads press together, and his oxygen becomes mine.

Time to take the exam. We'll make a passing grade. All we have to do is kiss.

"We can't do this. Not now." Jack releases his hold and climbs from the water, leaving me suspended in a pool of rejection. "I can't kiss my best friend's teenage sister. Don't you realize how wrong that'd be? Not only would I be disrespecting him, I'd be making out with someone who is barely a legal adult. Look at me, Julie. I'm, like, five years older than you. I have a career, a past. Heck, I can get into bars and rent cars. You can't."

Can't was not in his vocabulary when we danced in the pineapple fountain, met for coffee, or held hands in the greenspace between Porter's Lodge and Randolph Hall. He was in line for me. And I tried to get past my crush on him. Even though I was sure we'd end up together. Even though he still had a mighty grip on my heart. *Can't*? He made me love him. He wanted me to love him.

If age and relation drew a line between us, he crossed it weeks ago.

"Stop treating me like a kid. You know better than anyone I'm not a kid." I crawl onto the dock and redress. If I get any hotter, I'll probably erupt into flames. "Say you aren't attracted to me, not that I'm a baby my dead brother has marked off-limits. Now, Jack. Say it."

"There are rules." He slides on his t-shirt, buttons his jeans.

"You didn't say it." A twitchy smile tugs at my mouth and the fear of being alone in a love affair meant for two is replaced by a weird kind of hope, maybe in time and age, maybe in human instinct.

Levi's barks reverberate over the water, sharp and distinct. Silence falls onto the landscape, and a breath gets tangled in my throat. He's howling to warn us. Of what? Scavs? The flyovers won't begin for seven more hours. We should be safe.

"Something isn't right. He rarely makes noise."

Jack walks across the gangplank to where the dog waits. "What's wrong?" He kneels and runs his fingers through the animal's mud-caked fur. As if on cue, Levi whimpers and sprints into the foliage.

"Are we supposed to follow him?" I half-walk, half-hop as I lace my boots. The loose knit of my sweater does little to contain heat—why didn't I choose a hoodie or wetsuit? At least I wouldn't be shivering to death if I was dressed as a deep-sea diver.

Jack reaches into the pocket of his jacket and removes a handgun. Same model as the one I found in Jon's backpack. Which means there was someone worth shooting then as there is now. Someone who wants to kill us—who might be nearby.

"Please put that away." Pain tears through my stomach. Gunshot. Blood sloshing in a pool around me. Stitches. A scar that brands Jon's death to my body. "I can't look at it."

"Guns are inanimate objects," Jack says. "The people using them determine their sins."

"If they didn't exist, people wouldn't shoot other people."

"In a world without guns, people would still find a way to kill one another. History is proof. Native Americans fought with spears and arrows. Europeans used swords, axes, and trebuchets. There are a million examples of murder without guns." He clicks a magazine into his weapon and aims it at the shoreline. "We can blame an object ... but we should blame someone's evil and fight to put a stop to it."

Twigs crackle under our weight as we trudge through the woods. Branches tear at our damp clothes like greedy fingers. I huddle behind Jack because if a monster jumps from the shadows, I'm helpless. Remind me—why are we going toward the scary, dangerous thing?

Levi digs at the edge of a ravine two miles from the cabin. He pants when we emerge from the brush and drops a tiny, pink ballet flat.

"Wow, he found a shoe. Smart dog." I crouch to pet the German Shepherd and smile when he plants a sloppy kiss on my cheek. "Your dog doesn't have a problem kissing me."

Jack gazes into the gulch, frozen. Even in the dim light, his face is stark white. "He found more than a shoe." The tone of his voice is grim, stripped of emotion. Horrified.

I rise from the ground and follow his stare into the narrow chasm.

A layer of putrefying skeletons blankets the earth, bones of all sizes. They're clothed in decomposing rags. Men, women, children—hundreds of corpses are piled in the ravine. Rodents have built nests in their hair. Worms have chewed away their skin.

Vomit burns my throat. I stumble backward, hyperventilating. They weren't evacuated. They were slaughtered. Why? Was the government afraid suspicions would be raised if so many people were transferred to different locations? Did they decide murder was the best way to smite loose-ends? How could this have happened?

Hollow eye sockets lust for my flesh and the life still surging through my veins. They can't have me. I won't be the next addition to their necrotic collection.

"Sometimes you find a lie, and sometimes it finds you." Jack turns from the mass grave and looks at the star-streaked sky, the dome. His bottom lip quivers. "Liars need the thrill of knowing they could get caught, so they leave clues unintentionally. I've spent the past few months searching for a breakthrough, a thread that'd braid information into a single strand. This is the clue."

"People are dead," I scream. "How can you be happy about that?"

"Emotions must relent to cold, hard facts." He returns the gun to his pocket and meets my line of sight with a scowl. "Their deaths will help me stop our world from coming to a total end."

Chapter Eleven

"From now on the enemy is more clever than you. From now on the enemy is stronger than you. From now on you are always about to lose."
Orson Scott Card, *Ender's Game*

"Hand me that roll of duct tape, would you?" Charlie crouches in the threshold of the main tunnel, sweating dirt. His headlamp blinds anyone who dares to look at him. "Hurrying would be good, Julie, since I'm currently being doused with someone's piss."

"Stop whining." I scramble over mounds of excavated dirt and hand him the tape. Dust creates concrete in my lungs—I wheeze, cough, and douse my throat with water from a canteen, but the paste remains hard as rock. "Bellamy needs us in the west corridor. He and the other Listers are digging a tunnel from the mess hall to the Command Center."

"Ugh, I don't like so many people working down here. It's too crowded." Charlie patches a leak in the plastic interior and then slides from the tube like an animal emerging from its burrow. "If you and Jack hadn't found those bodies, we'd still be crawling through our own fecal matter, perfectly chuffed."

Dead maggots with full bellies and rat nests made of hair, hollow eye sockets begging me for a sliver of life essence—I can't dwell on the massacre, think about each child piled in that ravine because now, every tragedy, coincidence, and unexplainable event could be hints, threads raveling to answer the big questions: Who chose us to survive? Why did our world end? What deeper secret was worth murdering hundreds of families to protect?

This is war. To outlast it and save Mom and Dad, I need to relent my emotions to cold, hard facts.

"We're working to secure the tunnels in case the Scavs attack, not because of what Jack and I found. Why are you in such a rotten mood today? Did Tally cut holes in your *knickers* again?" I slide down a pile of rocks to where the ground levels. Blood darkens the fabric around my knees, caused by some unknown injury. Nowadays, I bleed as much as I sweat.

"Knickers are girl underwear. I wear pants." His brow furrows as he marks a red 'V' above the tunnel's threshold, tagging it as repaired. "Something bad is going to happen, Julie. I taste it in the air." He wipes mud from his face and hands me a tool belt.

"No, that's just crap." I laugh. "Let's go."

The clangs of shovels echo through the underground maze. People flow through the pipework like rats scampering through a sewer. Their headlamps fade in and out of sight, brightening and dimming with each passing soldier.

Charlie and I travel to where Bellamy and his crew gouge earth from a new shaft. Their assembly line hauls buckets of soil from the deepening hole. They reek with the stench of body odor and metal, completely covered in dirt so the whites of their eyes are all that are visible.

"Coker, Stryker, pick up a shovel and start digging," Bellamy shouts from the mouth of the tunnel. He peers out and looks at us, grinning. "It's all hands on deck."

I grab a spade from the floor and crawl between makeshift support beams to where Bellamy, Brady, and a few other Listers work. "Make space. Geez, I can't help with armpits and butts in my face." Dirt rains from the ceiling and sends me into a sneeze and cough frenzy.

This is normal life.

Home is a place of claustrophobia and extreme discomfort.

Family are the people still alive.

"Hey, it's our girl, Stryker." Brady gives a knuckle-bump before filling a bucket with rocks. "Is it true that the Feds killed all those people to keep the dome a secret?"

"Yeah." There's no reason for me to elaborate.

"Why would they murder the people they're protecting?"

"They wouldn't." Bellamy stops digging. His eyes search mine for confirmation—they find it. "Which means they're not protecting us."

Jon caught me hiding peaches behind Mom's flower vases when we were kids. I told him I was protecting them from Dad. He said there are very few people who protect something out of goodwill—*protecting* is *saving for later* with the intention to devour once they've ripened to their full potential.

We are the peaches hidden behind glass, safe until we've ripened to the brink of rot.

"Nash and I worked in the research lab and eavesdropped on the council's meeting. They said the Feds need us to be oblivious, continue normal life so our labor will sustain them," Charlie says as he settles into the open space next to me with a pickaxe and lantern. "If we knew about the apocalypse, there'd be chaos and civilization would crumble. We're their workforce. Without us, they'd die."

"We have an advantage, then." I slam my shovel into the wall and yank earth into the narrow shaft. Sweat stings my eyes and creates muck on my skin. Thick muck that weighs down my shaky arms and reeks of sewage.

Abram will have to give me painkillers later. And if Sutton hogs the shower, I'll drag her out by her hair like she once did to me.

"A Lister needs to be on the council. Too many bigwig soldiers in charge," Bellamy says. "It's not constitutional. We don't have equal representation."

"You'd make a great councilman, Bellamy. Want to start a campaign? I'll make posters." Brady snickers and pours fuel into his lantern.

Pain slices through my abdomen when I shove a boulder out of our workspace. I slump against a plastic slat and clutch the scar. Jon's mark. His memory. Engraved on my skin. The ache will subside like always. A few seconds more of hurt. Count to ten and it'll be over.

"Need water, Listers?" Tally tosses a jug into the shaft. She slouches at the entrance with bottles fastened to her belt. "Ugh, you all stink. Maybe I should start toting around soap, too."

"You're a water-girl?" Charlie scoffs. "I thought you'd be assigned a more hardcore..."

"Shut up." Tally glares at him and sits on a stool outside the tunnel. "General Ford assigned me the night shift in the security room and didn't want to give a day job that'd wear me out."

"Don't you have water to deliver?" I uncap the jug and drink until my stomach is full.

"I'm on my break," she says as she cleans the grime from underneath her fingernails. "All this *end of the world* crap is annoying. Everyone is so wound up about the dome and those corpses. The world deserved to end. It was screwed-up."

"Millions, maybe billions, of people are dead. Don't you care?"

"Not really." She shrugs. "I certainly won't lose

any sleep at night thinking about every soul I didn't have the pleasure of meeting."

"Gosh, you're a horrible person." Charlie sneers.

Tally flips him off. "Whatever. I'll live longer than you, Coker."

Filtered, oxygen-rich air is beyond the tube where natural light strikes the incandescent flicker of lanterns. If I can't crawl the fifteen yards, I'll keel over and drown in dirt. Lung pollution has killed three Listers. I can't join the count. I have to survive.

"Must get out. Need better air." I wheeze, but all that enters and exits my mouth is dust. Red specks dot my vision as I dig my fingers into the tilled soil and crawl past Charlie. Heart beats fast. Too fast. "Let me through!"

Bellamy yells for help. The assembly line grips my arms and passes me off like a bucket of rocks. Seven more yards. I'll make it. Jon taught me to hold my breath for two minutes. How many seconds have I been completely without oxygen? Not enough to kill me.

With a final yank, I tumble into the shaft intersection. A girl props me against a crate of shovels, and then leaves. Why isn't the air fixing my body? I should be able to breathe now.

"No wonder Listers have died down here. Those freaks are idiots." Tally squats next to me and smirks. "Open up, Stryker." She plunges her hand into my mouth, down my esophagus.

What the heck.

Mud bubbles up my throat. I lean over and cough the inhaled grime from my respiratory tract, heaving and spewing until the dust is gone. Lungs stretch and contract. The red specks disappear.

"You're welcome." Tally pats the top of my head and then disappears into a connecting tube.

How many times will I have to swish mouthwash

to get the taste of her fingers from my tongue?

Jack climbs from a shaft, drenched in sweat and sludge. He turns off his headlamp and pours the remnants of a canteen onto his oil-smeared face. "There's a tunnel in the east corridor that needs repairing. Want to help, Julie?"

Why is he smiling as if nothing's changed?

I cast him a snarky glare. "Are you sure I'm not too young?"

"Only one way to find out." He leans into the tunnel under construction. "Bellamy, I need you to come help with a repair job. Charlie can take your current assignment."

"Sure thing, Sarge." Bellamy squeezes through the assembly line and removes a tattered backpack from a nail on the wall. "Nobody better do anything stupid while I'm gone. You hear?"

The crew of Listers nods in response.

"We better start moving. The tunnel is on the other side of camp." Jack pulls me to my feet. His hand tightens around mine, lingering before release. "You're not too young," he whispers.

Missy used to say a guy who doesn't fight for a girl's heart isn't worth her time. If I shared what Jack said last night, she'd tell me to move on, get over my love for him, and be secure as a strong, independent woman. I don't need the extra hurt in my life. But I do need him, even if he betrays me, stabs me in the back, and lies to my face. He's my family, and family doesn't give up on family.

What happened to Missy? Is she in Columbia with her mom? Wow, I truly am the worst best friend. Why haven't I thought of her until now? She's as important to me as Jon.

The three of us enter the main passageway,

winding left and right. People slide past. Their bodies crush us against the rigid walls. At least the air is less polluted. At least I'm not suffocating.

"Is General Ford planning to move us underground?" Bellamy asks.

"No, repairing the tunnels is just a precaution. He wants us to relocate inward, away from the dome." Jack's muscles flex. He glances back at me every fifty yards. "The Scavs are searching this area more aggressively. They know where to look and will find us if we don't leave."

The pipes above us rattle. Bellamy stills them with a firm grip and duct tape.

Dirt dribbles from the ceiling in an unsteady stream. Tremors pulse through the tunneled labyrinth and cause the murky puddles beneath me to ripple.

This isn't normal.

"We should turn back." I slide close to Bellamy's ankles when a kid screeches somewhere in the maze. Have the tunnels always been this narrow? "Jack…"

An industrial scream blares through the Underground, grinding, penetrating the layer of dirt surrounding us. Agony shoots through me like an arrow. I clutch my ears and curl into a ball as the wailing continues. Bellamy curses. Jack writhes. Then, the noise subsides, dulling to a distant rumble.

"Please tell me that was supposed to happen." Bellamy's headlight flickers with the quivering of his body. He sandwiches me between him and Jack. "Let's get the heck out of here."

The plastic tube tears apart, releasing a surge of earth. I suck air through my t-shirt sleeve and scream when the intense vibrations rip the tunnel to pieces and toss us into a massive earthquake blender.

Luck must belong to smarter, prettier people.

"Crawl!" Jack lurches into motion when the shaft caves in behind us. Pipes burst, spewing sewage and boiling water. Veins of cracks spread across the ceiling.

We're screwed.

I sob, moan, push, and shove toward the light at the end of the tunnel. It's as if I'm swimming and want to put my feet down on something solid, but the water is too deep and there's nothing to hold me up except my own will to survive.

"Keep moving. Don't stop." Jack presses his back against the ceiling to support the weight. His face contorts from pain and exertion. "Go, Julie. I'll be right behind you."

If he acts like a sacrificial hero, I won't forgive him. There is only one thing in this world worse than dying and that's watching someone you love die instead—you feel their pain with no final solace.

"Don't you dare die for me," I shout. "That's not something you can do."

"Wasn't planning on it." Jack shakes under the crushing weight. His neck veins pop. "Please follow the order, Julie, before you break my back." He jumps into the adjoining tunnel with Bellamy and me milliseconds before the tube shatters into a blockade of dirt.

Burns blister my scalp as I play limbo with dangling electrical wires and straddle puddles of toxic waste. What was meant to keep us safe from the Scavs has transformed into a deathtrap, proving the Underground isn't a place where bad things happen around us but never to us. No haven on Earth. No relief. I'm as vulnerable here as I was back home except now, I'll die knowing the truth.

And it will die with me.

"We're getting close to the—" Bellamy disappears beneath a mound of rock, flattened, swallowed, buried in a screeching instant. Half of his head protrudes from the soil—mouth open, blood gushing from a break in his skull. He's so dead, I don't make a sound or try to dig him out.

Jack rips me backward as the roof collapses. He stares into my eyes for a brief moment, nods, and then commences our mad dash to the main tunnel. Crumbling walls chase us and blow a dusty sigh of disappointment when we tumble into an access shaft with high-ceilings and clean air.

There's a ladder anchored to the cliff face.

A way out.

Heartbeats pound in my ears with heavy breaths singing backup. I claw at the ground and blink the mud from my lids. Blood glides down my forearms—where did it come from? Why are my emotions numb, frozen like meat in need of thawing?

"Your elbows have been rubbed raw. The lacerations are deep, but I can fix them." Jack holds my hand, and together, we climb the metal rungs. "Almost there. We're going to make it, Julie."

I groan from the physical strain and force myself onto the next rung. "Bellamy is dead."

"Yes. He's dead."

"I'm not sad."

"You will be." Jack shoves open the door—I squint as sunlight saturates my pupils. "Fear protects you from sadness and the things that cause weakness. Your fear is what makes you brave." He lifts me from the crevice, onto solid ground where grass laps at our knees.

We dodge soldiers and Listers as they swarm out of trailers, dragging unconscious people into the yard. Shouts and screams lift from the shaking valley, followed by gunfire and a relentless rumble. What's happening? Did Scavs find us? Why won't the earthquake stop?

Jack walks to the center of the lawn with his focus transfixed on the distant summits. Mist swirls over the mountain pinnacles, shimmering with pixels. Movement. A tsunami wave of dirt and trees rises from the earth, cresting the sky, charging toward us at full speed.

The dome is moving.

I choke as the force field slices through cliffs and forests, leaving a chasm in its wake. Trees are uprooted and swept along with the surge. Their trunks snap. Rock crackles. How long until we'll be swept and broken? When will my new home be stolen from me?

Birds form clouds overhead, squawking with alarm—some collide with the dome and are fried like insects in a bug zapper. Deer race from the woods, through the trailer park—they trample several soldiers and rip apart the tarps of the Overhang.

"Get down!" Jack tackles me as a doe leaps over us. Her back hooves scrape my skull. Hard hit. Flash of darkness. Another wound. Can't feel it.

Fear has turned me into a zombie.

"You've been my rescuer enough today. Go." I spit grass and roll over to look at him, the face of someone who may be my last hope. "Do what you do best. Fix this."

There are hundreds of good days in my lifespan. There are also soul-crushing, miserable days when everything seems to go wrong. This day is a bad day, but tomorrow might be good. Tomorrow, we could be happy, rebuild our rebel world, and remind ourselves why we get up each morning to fight for the sliver of truth the powerful want to bury.

"Stay close." Jack squeezes my hand and then joins the pandemonium. He yells commands littered with military jargon and issues assignments to those rushing past.

God, please save us.

"Hey." Jack snatches Nash from the flow of soldiers. "How do we stop this thing?"

Nash shakes his head. He looks at me, and then Jack. Tears drip from his beard. "We can't." He's kidding. Of course there's a way to end the dome's contractions. "We can't stop it."

Can't—I really hate that word.

"Gather everyone. We're moving inward. Tell people to form travel crews, grab what they can carry, and keep their radios close. They need to leave immediately. We'll regroup later."

"General Ford hasn't given the order. He and Ezra are meeting with the council now."

"I'm giving the order." Jack turns to me and places a radio in my hand. His brow furrows. "Go from barrack to barrack. Tell everyone you find, and when you have the chance, leave."

Leave without him? He's the only person I have left. If I let go, watch him drift out to sea with Jon and Sybil, I might never get him back. But he needs me to let go. And I have to be strong enough to rescue myself when the days get hard and life knocks me to the ground. Okay. I'm letting go.

"Move fast," he whispers. "I need you to protect my family. Can you do that, Julie?"

"Yes." I swallow the brick-sized lump in my throat. "I'll protect them."

A severe hurt slices through me as I race away from someone who might be taken in a matter of minutes or days. But I also feel everything, every vein and every bone and every nerve, all awake and buzzing in my body as if charged with electricity. Both of my siblings died, but by remembering our love for each other, I managed to survive the losses because love never dies—it never goes away as long as I hang on to it. I've immortalized them within my heart, and if Jack dies, I'll do the same for him.

"What's going on? Why is the dome moving? Where are we supposed to go?" Brady and the other Listers swarm when I enter the Overhang as if I'm a celebrity caught shopping in a supermarket. "Are the Scavs attacking? Do we need to prepare for a fight?"

"Grab what you can carry and leave. Keep your radios close. We'll regroup later." I climb onto a mossy table to escape the mob. "This is a state of emergency. For us to evacuate the premises without any more casualties, we need effective communication and order. Go to each barrack. Help those who've been injured. Tell everyone you find to form travel crews and head inward, away from the dome."

"Where's Bellamy?"

"Dead." I don't want to see their sad faces so I look around at the tattered tarps and broken furniture—has there always been a rocking chair by the wood stack?

Brady emits a weird, choking sound. "Dead?"

To help myself seem less like a sociopath, I say, "A tunnel collapsed on top of him," as if more information will somehow make the situation better.

"Help. I need help." Charlie crawls from the tunnel, coughing up mud and bile. "It's Tally. The ceiling crumbled and pinned her beneath a mound of dirt. I tried to fix the cave-in with plastic slats, but I don't know how long they'll hold."

Protect Jack's family.

"Be ready to pull us out." I rip the headlamp off his forehead and climb into the hole. Going down alone is a bad idea, and after what happened to Bellamy, I shouldn't ever want to step foot underground again. But this is my chance to save a life. To save, not lose.

After witnessing so much death, I need proof that life is savable.

"Tally, where are you?" I shout once my feet hit the bottom floor. Dust clouds the air, thick like smoke. Rocks cascade off the walls.

"Ugh, took you long enough." Her headlamp flashes in the far corner, illuminating the swirls of debris. "Hurry. I'm not ready to freaking die."

Me neither.

I rush to where she's affixed and dig until my fingers burn. She mutters curses, claws at the dirt. The support beams creak—we have time. The shaking releases another torrential dust downpour—we'll make it out alive. No other option.

Using all my strength, I drag her from the mound and stumble to the ladder. "Charlie, pull us up!"

A hand clamps onto my wrist, lifts me to what seems a lot like safety, past the crumbling walls and into the Overhang. Arms become a cradle when I reach solid ground—strong, alive arms that catch my body when my legs give up. Why is the sky made of faces? Why are the faces looking at me? Charlie. Tally. Brady. Listers from my work crew. Nobody else died.

Tomorrow will be beautiful. The sunrise will ignite the east peak with crimson hues that'll fade to fiery amber. We will wander through forests, across mountains until we find a new place to call home. And when we find the place, we'll build it better.

"Stryker, you look like—"

Dust explodes from the tunnel's entrance in a single, detonated billow. Cave-in. The underground roads are gone. I could've been down there. Tally and I were seconds from being buried.

I writhe in the mud and clutch my stomach as the dirt settles. Tears sprint down my temples, hot and exhausting—Bellamy is dead. Pain ripples through me with each breath—I need a morphine drip.

Wait.

"The ground isn't shaking." I grab Charlie's ankle and slap his calf until he crouches next to me. "The dome's stopped contracting," I sob. "It's stopped."

He smiles and shouts at the top of his lungs, "The dome isn't shrinking anymore."

Cheers erupt from the crowd. People high-five each other in what my dulled brain interprets as slow motion. Home is safe. Most of the family is alive. I can rest now, close my eyes, and fade into a perfect dream world where the Jones Family cooks TV meatloaf and talks about paradise.

"You're a ballsy one. If you'd spent three more seconds down there, you'd be squished." Charlie lifts me into a hug. He snickers as I peel sludge from my skin. "Were you scared?"

What a small word to describe such a catastrophic emotion. Scared. Was I scared? "Yes," I whisper so the others won't hear, "but being afraid is good because it means I still have more to lose."

"Hey, Tally, don't you want to tell Julie thank you?"

"We're even." She steals a canteen from Brady and swishes the dirt from her teeth.

Hunger, exhaustion, and the need to pee turn my body into a busload of whiny toddlers begging for a rest stop. No more near-death experiences. I'm going to take a shower, curl up with a bowl of noodles, and watch TV reruns until my brain hurts.

"It's over." Nash enters the Overhang with a huge grin on his face. "The council is meeting now to discuss relocation. They want a Lister represented at the meeting. Pick your person."

"We pick Julie," Brady says.

People nod in agreement. Why are they nodding?

"What?" I stagger to an upright position and slump against a bench. Their wanting eyes burrow into my soul. No, I must've heard them wrong. They wouldn't choose me as a representative. I'm the new kid with close to no street credit. Jon was a leader. Not me.

"Bellamy liked you. We like you." Brady wipes his eyes and musters a pathetic smile. He plants a hand on my shoulder as if knighting me *Official Lister*. "You'll represent us good."

There's a noodle bowl, television, and toilet calling my name. Hot shower. Clean socks. A whole pack of Band-Aids. I could refuse the position and go crash on the medical ward cot I've befriended over the past few weeks. But they picked me. They want my voice to speak for them.

"Do you accept their nomination?" Nash offers the question like a call to arms.

If only life functioned with a 'do you accept' button, and I could choose what happened to me, which hurt to experience, who died. Existence would be easier, but would it be as significant? Without a button, I'd rather not know what lies ahead because I like the dark. I like thinking there is something good in the places I can't see. And that's not ignorance. That's just hope.

"Yes," I say, because the people I expected to kick me when I'm down have pulled me up time after time. For them. For Jon. "I accept."

Chapter Twelve

"The truth doesn't always set you free; people prefer to believe prettier, neatly wrapped lies."
Jodi Picoult, *Keeping Faith*

New Julie, the version who rescues people and leads minority groups, holds her head high as if she belongs with the ten soldiers who stand around the Command Center's circular, technological table. She studies the pixel diagrams and digital maps flickering on the counter because unlike me, she knows how to decipher them. New Julie enjoys night swims, undercooked macaroni, and advocating for laborers.

Best role I've ever played.

"Three people were lost during the contraction." Abram stands to my right with his muscular arms folded across his chest. "That's three of our people, dead. If we stay here any longer, more will die. There's no denying it. The dome will contract again. We mustn't be here when it happens."

"But there isn't a definite timeframe," Ezra says. "The dome might not contract for months. If we stay out of the tunnels and build above-ground connectors, we'll survive another earthquake and can leave when we see the force field move."

Agreed. Leaving the Underground is a stupid idea.

I tilt my head and take a discreet bite of the protein bar Charlie gave me. Chocolate. I've missed food that tastes good and doesn't look like it could kill me.

"Nash and I need a few more weeks to conduct our research. I'm on the brink of a breakthrough." Jack

163

carries the heaviest presence, one that binds the room in a peculiar sort of engagement. He paces back and forth, slides his fingers along his chiseled jawline. His eyes swirl blue and silver, then gray. Sharp gray that threatens to slice our throats if we don't give our attention.

"We might not have a few weeks, Sergeant." General Ford taps the tabletop screen, enlarging a record of recent enemy activity. "The Scavs haven't had a flyover today, which worries me."

"They knew the dome would be contracting."

"Or they found us and are preparing for an attack. Either way, our camp has been compromised. We must consider relocation options." General Ford fingers the miniature American flag pinned to his uniform—does the country still exist? Can we call ourselves Americans with certainty, or are we playing dress up when we recite the pledge and say *In God We Trust*?

Did we lose that part of ourselves a long time ago?

"This is our home." I twist and pin my hair at the nape of my neck, and then stand with legs wide. It's what Nash told me to do before speaking because men, no matter how many times they profess women are equal, prefer to take direction from bodies like theirs. "I'm here representing the people who dig your tunnels, wash your clothes, the people who sacrificed their happiness to join your fight."

Everyone stares at me with blatant disregard as if I'm a toddler interrupting an academic lecture. Abram rolls his eyes. Ezra snickers. They can try to degrade and intimidate me, but I'm here because New Julie is brave. New Julie won't go down without a fight. New Julie makes men listen to her.

"You're not deciding if we should stay or run. You're deciding what is worth the risk. Make your choice wisely because if you don't fight to keep something, you will lose it. I understand this place is temporary and when threats arise, we'll have to leave. But until those threats are certain, I ask the council to consider staying. Our home is worth the risk."

"Bellamy's dead. He was a Lister, one of you…"

"He was one of *us*," Jack snaps. "We aren't divided into factions but a single unit. We are the Vestige. This is a war we're fighting. Death is to be expected. None of us signed up for easy."

"Yeah, but we didn't sign up to die," an officer shouts. He's fat for a Vestige man. Ketchup dots his belly pouch. "If we want to survive, leaving now is our best option."

"Sir, how can you expect our chances of survival to be better in the wilderness, divided into travel crews with limited rations and communication? Here, we have an effective system. Here, we are united."

Geez, when did I become such a loudmouth?

"Thanks for your input, darling, but leave the world-changing decision-making to the big boys. We're protecting more than our crappy house." Abram laughs and turns his back to exile me.

What a jerk. I am strong and human with a mouth that works like a man's and a more intelligible brain, and I demand to be heard.

My hands are shaking. I ball them into tight fists. There's a crazy pressure in my chest, building, strengthening until the explosion is inevitable. "Do you call your other fighters *darling*, or just the ones with boobs?" There it is—another tension to add to the room's charged, magnetic air.

Men tend to treat women as fragile creatures, but our bodies were built to withstand pain and hard work, think with profound insight. We were created to do what men can't. And if that isn't reason enough for us to be treated equal, I'm not sure what is.

He glances at me, still laughing. "What?"

"You said to leave decision-making to the big boys, but I'm not okay with that because some of the big boys in this room spend more time screwing Lieutenant McConaughey and bossing around tunnel-diggers, laundry-washers, and cooks than actually doing their jobs." Oops, I said it. There's no going back now, not after the screwing and bossing remark.

To cherish my purity and set boundaries are, in my opinion, the highest forms of feminism—a woman who saves her body proves she is strong and secure enough to resist the men who seek to claim her, that she's more than what lies between her legs.

Abram leans forward until our faces are inches apart—I stare him dead in the eyes because there's no way I'm letting him catch a whiff of my fear. "You're treading on thin ice, Stryker."

"I am here as a gladiator for the Listers, and I'll fight for their voice by making sure you don't muffle mine with sexist comments."

"Amazing, isn't she?" Jack clutches a hand over his mouth to hide a smile, but his crinkled eyes and raised cheeks give it away. He plops onto a stool and sneaks me a thumbs-up when no one is looking.

"Enough," General Ford shouts. "Sergeant, explain your reason for wanting to remain at the Underground. All information needs to be offered before the council makes a final decision."

He called me amazing in front of the other soldiers. Amazing. For being bold and empowered.

"Nash and I have been conducting experiments. We found a way to break the dome's magnetic membrane so we could retrieve samples from the outer world." Jack stands and circles the table like a professor pacing his classroom. "Our goal was to find out what caused the collapse of civilization."

I straighten my back when he moves behind me. For that split second, when he's inches from my back, I hold him close in my mind, his subtle dimples and flashy smile, the warmth of his summer-tanned skin. I reach out in our third-space and love him from a tenuous distance.

General Ford rubs the notch in his chin. He watches Jack drift with mild amusement in his baggy, bulgy eyes. "What'd you find, Sergeant?"

"Not only are the radiation levels disastrously high, we detected a toxin in the air—an unidentifiable pathogen. Viruses can't last years without a living host, which means this virus isn't natural. Someone must have mutated and weaponized a strain of a common virus, maybe *Ebola* or influenza, and released it as a universal, airborne attack."

"Strains mutate," Abram says. "Remember the 2009 swine flu outbreak?"

Yes. Jon made me get vaccinated. He was super paranoid about disease after Sybil died and took me to that doctor downtown with the big hands and fake teeth.

"You have to understand—whatever sickness spread across the globe couldn't be identified because until the first outbreak, humankind had never experienced it before." Jack stops at the head of the table, opposite of General Ford. His brow furrows to a dramatic line. "All this didn't happen by accident."

People writhed on the floors of their homes, coughing up blood, fevering until their hearts stopped—not an accident. Cities rolled into waves of dust and rubble while nuclear plumes adorned the horizon—intentional events on a global scale. Why? What's to gain?

"Someone evoked the apocalypse." I sink into a chair and hug my churning stomach. Charlie's chocolate protein bar hates me now. "You think the Feds caused *the end of the world.*"

Jack nods. "Relocating will move us too far from the dome. We must stay here so Nash and I can continue our research. Two weeks is all we need. Once we've gained answers, I will personally pack up the trucks and move us out of camp."

Their pathogen blotted civilization, but we have become its counterpart within a place of safety and sameness where our ideas grow to destroy the secret-keepers and define those willing to listen. We are resilient and highly contagious. Our virus gets people cozying up to the truth before sneezing into their faces. We infect. And we will save.

"Answers to what questions? We know how the world ended. We know who we're fighting against," Ezra says. "We have enough information to bring down Severance."

Bring them down hard. Make them pay for what they've done. We deserve to have our lives back, to sleep without fear of being killed at night, to speak and be heard. We deserve freedom.

I'd kill to see Mom and Dad again.

"No, there's so much we don't understand." Jack patrols the room, arms stretched behind his neck. "This is a mind game. They're telling us what to believe."

Shouts disrupt the order like starbursts of light on a dark canvas. I hold my ears while the soldiers scream in protest. Why won't they shut up long enough to ponder Jack's hypothesis? Why are people so narrow-minded? Even when they consider themselves freethinkers, they're still closed up to certain ideas, chaining themselves in an illusionary box of liberty. That must've been what caused the world's end—people stopped thinking beyond their boxes.

"You're a bunch of crazies!" I throw the half-eaten protein bar at Abram's bald head. Probably shouldn't have done that to a commanding officer. Might wake up in the lake tomorrow. Oops.

"Jack…" General Ford's break of formality silences the debate. He stands, and we sit. "You might be right, but there are too many lives at stake. We must relocate."

"You want questions? Fine, I'll give them to you." Jack keys something into the computer system. Images from the drone's footage flood the tabletop: crumbled skyscrapers, vacant neighborhoods and cracked highways littered with rotting corpses. "Someone caused the world to end. Why? The dome is shrinking. Why? Will more people be killed because they're too close to the truth? What is the government's reason for doing this? What more are they hiding?"

A breath catches inside my throat as the footage pans over a forgotten swing set, now rusted and lopsided. I cough, but the ability to inhale remains wedged within my esophagus like a beaded whim in a dreamcatcher. This is what becomes of us. Our greatest achievements decay and disappear over time, leaving only a footprint of the civilization we built.

Against preservation efforts, we all shall vanish and be forgotten.

"Survival must come first," Ezra yells to muzzle Jack's rant. "There's a town south of here that's off-grid and accommodating. With your permission, General, I'll send a fireteam to scout the area for potential base locations."

"They leave at dawn." General Ford shuts his manila folder as if saying 'case closed.' "Initiate relocation procedures within the camp. Everyone else departs in three days."

"Three days? That's not enough time." I need to wash my hands—they won't stop itching. Maybe the dome's penetration spit the virus into our bubble. "We have to bury our dead, pack, salvage what we can from the tunnels. To prepare, we need a week, at least."

"Four days." He deactivates the table's screen—it dies to black. "You're dismissed."

I clench my jaw to contain the swell of something more complex than fear or anger, something that reaches deep into my chest and makes me shake with adrenaline. I dig my heels into the floor's thin, mildewed layer of carpet to stake claim. This is our home. This is where we bleed and sweat and die.

"Forgive me, General, if I sound disrespectful, but … you know Jack is right," I say once everyone has filtered out of the rickety conference room. "You believe him."

"Yes, I believe him." He tucks a stack of folders beneath his left arm.

"Then, why are we leaving?"

"I must do what's best for my soldiers." General Ford musters a stiff smile that belongs on the face of a politician or Ken doll. "Jack is radical. Not everyone is like him."

"But he's right. You know he's right."

"We're confronted with many different paths in our lifetime. It's not always a fork in the road, more of a major intersection with multiple routes to travel. We can pick a road that follows the rules, gets us where we need to be … or we can pick a road that follows the rules but gets the people we care about where they need to be. The choice isn't always black and white, and it's not always easy. Right now, Jack's path is the route I want to take, but it's not the path that will get my soldiers where they need to be. I choose the majority. Do you understand?"

"Risks are sometimes necessary, sir. Safety doesn't accomplish much."

"Except keeps people alive." He plants a hand on my shoulder and lowers his voice to a gruff whisper. "Would you do something for me, Julie?"

"Yes." If he asks me to make him a sandwich, I'll be pissed. "What can I do for you?"

"Jon's assignment." He opens a filing cabinet, removes a handgun, and sets it in my palm. The weapon is small and heavy, built to use high-capacity magazines. "Protect Jack. His importance to this mission is greater than you'll ever know."

Wow, that's a funny request. Jack has saved me a dozen times, been my bodyguard even when I told him to get lost. General Ford must be kidding. But he looks serious. Why does he look serious?

"I'm pretty sure Jack can take care of himself, sir."

"Yes, but I want to know someone else is looking out for him. He has a gift. He understands things. If we want to win this war, we need him. He's our weapon."

"Why do you want *me* to be his protector? I almost broke my wrist in the shower this morning. Yesterday, I dropped a stack of wood on my feet. He'd be safer with a toddler."

The general casts a fatherly, supportive look—I'm almost convinced he believes in me. "Jack trusts you. It won't be difficult to keep an eye on him. Please. Make sure he stays alive."

"Okay." I trace the firearm's barrel with my thumb. Until recently, the gravity of holding such a dangerous device hadn't occurred to me. But I now know how it feels to be shot, the excruciating pain.

I now know what it means to kill.

"What if he dies?" I tuck the gun into my belt, beneath my sweaty t-shirt. "If I fail, will the Vestige die, too? Our survival can't be reliant on me. I'm not Jon…"

"Be his gladiator. Fight for him like you fought for the Listers today." General Ford saunters to the doorway and glances at me a final time. His crow's feet deepen into cursive signatures, signing Jack's life over to me, the eighteen-year-old barista who shoots targets at the range and still has nightmares about her brother's death. He wants New Julie to protect Jack. But she's fiction. I'm the real version.

And I have no idea who I am.

****

Tarps flap in the night breeze like leftover flags from a battle. I skulk past their writhing hides, into what remains of the Overhang. Crates and tools from the tunnels litter the ground—I have to use one foot to feel for possible stumbling blocks and both hands to grapple gravity. Lights out at ten o'clock. No exception. Not even for Sergeant Buchanan's newly appointed bodyguard.

I cringe when my calf brushes the slimy lichens growing on a table leg. Brady was supposed to scrape them off. They should be in a compost bin behind the Command Center, not oozing down my leg.

A lantern and mud-caked shovel rise from the gaping chasm that used to be a shaft, followed by a chiseled arm and shoulder. I reach for my gun and duck behind a wooden slat. No one is supposed to be out of their barracks. Why can't one thing go right today? All I want to do is eat a meal, wash this filth off my skin, and sleep so I'll feel human again, not get in a fracas with a disobedient recruit.

Jack emerges from the hole with a bag of salvaged equipment slung across his back. He groans and dumps the load. Shadows dart across his body, outlining his shape, giving way to golden beams that crisscross his face and illuminate slivers of skin. Jack. He's working. Past curfew. And he sees me. He's looking at me. Why can't I breathe? What's wrong with my legs?

"Thought I'd get a head start on the relocation procedures," he says after several of the most awkward seconds of my life. His electric eyes peruse me—they have fingers of their own. "You were incredible during the council meeting. The Listers couldn't have picked a better representative."

I force a smile and take one step toward the barracks. One step that seems like a mile because it's one step away from him. But he didn't want me. He chose duty over emotions. He left me in the water, freezing, vulnerable, with a heart that ached for him.

"Speaking against the majority because you believe they're wrong is an intense display of courage." Jack moves toward me faster than I can distance myself from his arms and chest, those soft, thin lips that form the most perfect smile. He grabs my hand, touching me. "When you find a truth that surpasses your desire to fit trends and meet approval, you can be certain it's worth fighting to spread."

He's my weakness. I'd pour out my heart for him.

General Ford must know I'd do anything to keep Jack alive.

"Jon would be proud of you." He lingers inches from me. Sweat rolls down his temples, creating clean streaks in the film of dirt. "I'm proud of you, Julie."

"He wouldn't be proud of me. I'm all grown up now because I've lost almost everything. Fear gives me a sharp tongue, not courage. And I don't know who I am anymore. Why would he be proud of that?" I shove Jack backward and chew my quivering lip when I'd rather be biting his. Pain floods a deep part of me I didn't know existed, a place so buried and intimate, I choke when it's stabbed.

The air between us is charged and unstable like it was in the conference room, as if the universe is holding its breath. I lean my weight against a moss-covered table. Need food. Soap. And lots of sleep. Not a man who makes me wish and dream and hope for the love he won't give.

"I know who you are," Jack whispers. "I've always known you." His hands glide up my arms, from the angles of my wrists to the creases of my elbows. He presses his mouth to my left ear—I shiver from his breath. "You're a force to be reckoned with."

Crema glistened on his upper lip.

Lightning shot up from my toes as he danced with me in that fountain.

His pen drew *The Living* on my forearm, branding me a part of something bigger than my tiny snow globe of sameness and ignorance.

"You don't stay down when someone throws a punch." He squeezes my waist, holds me like a girlfriend, not a sister. "You fight to stand because you've spent enough time on the ground to know the importance of a strong spine."

I dig my fingernails into the tabletop when his hands reach my neck and comb through my matted hair. This is stupid. If he didn't love me yesterday, he doesn't love me today.

"When I look at you, it's as if I'm reading a novel. No matter how much time I spend studying your pages, there will always be more for me to learn, deeper layers of complexity to baffle me, and plot twists that'll leave me speechless." He snickers and draws closer until our chests are fused. His heart beats through his t-shirt, against mine. Together, they make sense.

Together, we make sense.

"You're the person I want to see every moment of every day." Jack cups my face in his hands and whispers a confession that sets me ablaze. "My feelings for you are what keep me going. I know you. And I love you. Even if loving you is wrong. Even if Jon's soul is cursing me."

He makes eating food and maintaining hygiene seem like bad ideas.

"Okay." I dive into him and kiss away my tornado of butterflies. Gasp. His lips move against mine slowly, lingering, strange and perfect and warm like drinking coffee for the first time. Gasp. I wrap my arms around his shoulders. Gasp. He sweeps me up and presses my back against a support beam.

To describe a kiss is to describe a diary entry or a pair of underwear—each is personal and private, slightly awkward. Very awkward. But necessary.

There are fireworks in our tenuous third-space, vibrant bursts of light that turn to skin and thoughts, embers smoldering where light never reaches. I find him there, drifting in the darkness, and when he collides with me, the world becomes simple and clear.

Loving him is an instinctual action, like reaching out my arms to catch myself when I fall, like screaming on a roller coaster ride. First kiss. That seems too natural to be a first.

"You're a great friend, Jack. I needed a kiss goodnight."

"If you want to be just friends after this, I must be doing something very wrong." He laughs and kisses my forehead, then my cheek. "Want to be my girlfriend? Check yes or yes."

"Yes," I say through a smile.

Making out is one thing that won't change even if

civilization fizzles and humanity is reduced to two people. So each time Jack and I kiss, it's as if we're flipping off the jerks who destroyed our planet, as if we're screaming at the top of our lungs…

We know your secret.

And we won't be made invisible.

Chapter Thirteen

"The more I see of the world, the more am I dissatisfied with it; and every day confirms my belief of the inconsistency of all human characters, and of the little dependence that can be placed on the appearance of merit or sense."
Jane Austen, *Pride and Prejudice*

Dr. Rackley, my college psychology professor, mentioned in a lecture that the human mind can protect itself from the effects of a physically and emotionally disturbing event. He said trauma creates chaos in the brain. We can subconsciously flip the switch and turn off the engagement that plants us fully in a situation. The pain hurts less. The memories are dull and obscure like a nightmare.

I am proof of his teaching because when my blankets are ripped off by a man in full-body armor and his arms yank me out of bed, I'm sucked into that safe state of mind, placed within my own mental dome while the end occurs around me. Hazy. Filled with screams that might be mine. What's happening? Why is he hauling me outside? Have the Scavs found us?

A syringe protrudes from my left leg. Didn't feel the needle. I try to lift my arm, but it won't budge. Instead, it dangles over the soldier's back, above a blurred ground. Scream—I have to scream louder and fight before my eyelids grow heavier.

Gunfire is a pounding drum. I roll my head as a group of soldiers are massacred in front of the Command

Center. Two eyes stare up at me from the ground, embedded in a familiar face—Ezra. His chest gapes open, exposing his ribcage and organs. Blood everywhere.

Scavs are here to kill us.

I'm going to die.

Grass embraces me when I land in a mangled wad on the ground. I claw at the dew-dampened soil and muster enough strength to kick once—one kick to my attacker's chest plate. He grips my t-shirt and wrenches me forward. His helmet is ugly like a Halloween mask, jagged and black, an expressionless piece of steel. He presses the barrel of his firearm to my forehead, clicks a bullet into place. Cold metal against warm, living skin. Not for long. I'll grow cold, too.

Whatever was in that syringe burns like acid in my veins. I writhe in the dirt and send my focus racing down the gun's barrel, over the Scav and into the sky where stars are blended into dim specks. *Dead* and *corpse* are familiar words. I've seen death. I'm friends with corpses. This should be easy.

Arms entwine the Scav's neck, forming a noose of muscle and bone. His body makes a violent snapping noise when his neck jerks to one side.

Jack replaces the soldier in my tunnel vision. He's bloody, caked with ash and dirt, but alive. "Fight the drugs. You must stay awake." He pulls me to a standing position and loops my arm around his neck. "Julie, we need to get to the woods."

That's my name. It sounds nice coming from his mouth.

Woods? Where are the woods?

"Your mind will begin to fail," Jack says as he drags me in a sprint toward the silhouette of trees. "Don't let the chemicals take you, at least, not until you're someplace safe."

Ammunition ricochets off the earth beneath our feet, whizzes past our heads. Bodies rise in lumps across the yard. Crimson grass. Pretty. Like a painting.

"Listen, Julie. You have to survive." His face is tight like a knot—jaw clenched, brow furrowed, eyes squinted and filled with tears. "Even if we're separated, you must get the truth away from here."

Why can't I feel my legs, my skin? Where is Mom? She was supposed to bring takeout for dinner. Jon said he'd be home in time to watch that vampire show we like.

General Ford kneels outside the closest barracks with his arms stretched behind his head. A Scav stands behind him with a rifle. The shot rings fresh. Another person vanishes into a puff of red. I should stay to clean up the mess, bury everyone in the old tunnels so they'll rest in peace.

"Hold on to me." Jack scoops up my body and charges toward a smear of green. "Hear me. I love you. We fought hard. Keep fighting, okay? Stay awake. We're almost there." His pounding strides bounce me up and down—I'm going to be sick.

We made out a few hours ago.

There are splinters in my back.

His lips tasted of fireworks and neo-soul music.

A loud *crack* turns Jack's arms to air. I slam into the grass, and the world flashes pitch black. Ringing drowns the gunshot frenzy but can't mask the repetitive thuds, snaps, and whams. I roll over and scream—that's definitely my scream—when a Scav beats Jack with the butt of a firearm. His body breaks and bleeds. No. Stop. He's dying. Please don't take him, too.

"Wake up, Jack," I wheeze. "You have to fight." Pain shimmies up my thighs as I shove myself toward his disfigured form. Tears warm my cheeks. When'd I start crying?

Blood splatters across my face when an axe implants itself in the Scav's helmet. His body collapses. Sutton stands behind him, panting, pale as a ghost.

"Help Jack. Please."

She crouches next to him and feels for a pulse. Her gory nightdress gathers above her waist, exposing her lace thong. "He's gone. We can't help him." Her voice is on the verge of breaking. She runs a hand over his eyes as if switching him off.

The loss of him is everywhere, all at once.

"No," I squeal when Sutton binds her arms around my waist and yanks me away from him. I grab at his clothes and accidentally jerk the ID tags from his neck— two silver plates and a wad of chain. "He's not dead. He can't be dead. I have to protect him."

"Yes." Sutton squeezes the numbness from my body. She grips my chin and makes startling eye contact. "We have to leave, and Jack isn't coming with us. He's been dismissed from the mission."

Dismissed. Not killed. Transferred to a prettier place where he works a nine-to-five desk job and flirts with cute baristas at local coffeehouses. He'll wait for me there, in his Elysium.

"The drugs are knocking you out, Julie. Focus." Sutton yanks me forward. "Run."

Away from death and the life I have left.

Into a wilderness where I'm invisible.

But if the Vestige is wiped out, the truth will die, too.

So I run with tears streaming my cheeks, filled with a terrifying sense of hardness that pulses from my core. Brady and the Listers are killed in a mass execution to my right. Fire devours the mess hall. Sutton's face is blown off in a cloud of crimson mist.

Dismissed.

I snatch the backpack off her shoulder and crash into the dense forest. Branches whip me. Thorns and sharp rocks fillet my bare feet as I crawl up a muddy slope. Then, I'm lying flat on my back, surrounded by foliage that's out of focus. Am I someplace safe? How far did I climb?

Blackness burns my vision like a flame to paper—Mom and Dad lounge on the patio with glasses of wine. I will myself to roll beneath a shrub, but my limbs are dead—Jack dives off the dock, into glistening water. The universe spirals out of control—Jon opens his arms to let me in.

A blazing, orange cloud lifts into the sky like a nuclear plume. It billows over the canopy of leaves, roaring and spooling. I close my eyes—which somehow fills me with relief—and cough on a single, powerful sob. The Underground was bombed. People died.

Jack is gone.

I failed my mission.

He meets me in sleep's sepia haze, appears at his table by the window with a copy of his favorite book and a half-eaten scone. His dark hair is hidden beneath a stocking cap. *The Living* is written on his forearm in my handwriting. He's okay here, in this winter version of Charleston, and maybe a part of me is with him. Maybe he's waiting for me to waltz through those old French doors to begin my shift.

Pain strengthens into a nagging voice that draws me from the darkness. Light blazes red through my eyelids, roasting my brain. I wince and curl into a ball. A twig snaps. Leaves crunch. I'm not in bed. Sutton must've snuck me outside. She was furious when Ezra told her what I said to the council.

Trees appear beyond my barred lashes, swaying

with the morning breeze. I clutch my aching head and prop myself against a trunk. Hunger pierces through me with so much aggression, I cry out. Something horrible happened last night. Sutton didn't drag me here. She saved my life.

Niveous ash rains from the clear sky, a cruel copy of snow. I dust the particles off my pajamas and slither beneath a rhododendron bush. Jack's ID tags are still clutched in the palm of my right hand, imprinting my flesh with his information.

Tears burst from me unannounced. Everything hits at once—like how my body is filthy and reeks of sweat, how my bare feet are blistered, how the people I love are dead. Scavs found us. They used a bomb to cremate the Underground and those in it. Jack is among the warm snow, drifting, settling on the mountain like mist before a storm. He's gone. They're all gone.

I slide to where I woke up and take Sutton's backpack from a patch of ivy. The camouflage vinyl is stained with her blood, fragments of what used to be her face. I swallow a mouthful of bile—there's not enough in my stomach to vomit—and search the bag's contents for warmer clothes and shoes. Inside are nutrition bars, water, filter, a handgun, ammunition, heat packs, a first-aid kit, matches, cable, and a radio, but no clothes. I curse and press the radio to my ear. Static. The signal is weak.

Gnats hiss. A whip-poor-will cries from somewhere in the woodsy prison. I hide my head beneath Sutton's backpack to block the sounds, the inhuman voices that remind me of my seclusion. Nightmare. There's no one left to keep me alive. All I have is myself.

"Jack." His name tastes like ash. I claw at the skin hiding my heart as if to scrape the emptiness from my chest. Jack. Gone. Boyfriend. Dead.

Stop crying.

THE VESTIGE

Remember what he taught you. Remember his instructions.

He is here. Imagine him between those two spindly trees with eyes glistening like blue agate. *He wants you to survive. Do it for him. Live and fight to complete the mission.*

Thunder claps in the distance. I must find shelter before the downpour, before my inward storm becomes a hazardous reality. Caves—I've seen them on my trek to the Overlook. They aren't deep, more of an open space with a rock roof, but they'll keep me dry.

I fasten Jack's tags around my neck and stumble up the mountainside. Ash continues to drift through the green canopy, a predecessor of the torrent to come. I gasp for oxygen as the slope steepens to a severe angle. If there are survivors, they'll try to make contact. I need a working radio. The higher I get, the more of a chance I have at finding a strong signal.

Skin peels off my feet as I shove myself over a boulder. Each step sends anguish climbing up my body. I whimper and moan. Sweat gathers above my lips, cascades down my naked legs and stings the exposed wounds. Infection will set in unless I'm able to sterilize and bandage the injuries. How much time do I have? A few hours? Both feet are swollen and discharging pus. Bad sign.

Foliage acts as a shield. I remove the loaded gun from my pack and limp toward a crevice. Cliffs line the gorge, overgrown with brush. I follow the path to a connecting ridge where the earth is level and the air is thin. It won't be long until rain swallows the mountain—I smell it in the air, sense the building pressure. No matter how far I am from the Scavs and their flyovers, if I'm stuck in a downpour, I will get hypothermia and die.

The sky darkens, and a light drizzle follows. I run

to what was once the Overlook, now a pile of shifted rock, and crawl into the largest cavern. The ceiling is high, but the floor space is narrow, only a few feet in diameter. Plants sprout from the rock interior. Spiders nest in the shadowy corners.

One of my blisters pops when I pry the sticks and rocks from my feet. I wince and pour antiseptic from the first-aid kit onto the wounds. Bloody goo puddles around my left ankle, trickles out of the cave and into a torrent of rain. I gag at the sight of my soles and nail-less toes and would bandage them immediately if I didn't have to let the gashes drain and dry first.

Think of something else.

Think of your pain.

Think of how cold and starving you are, how you'll probably die soon.

I pull out the radio and adjust its frequency. "Calling all survivors of the Vestige. This is Julie Stryker, Niner-Zulu. I escaped the massacre and am awaiting contact. Do you copy? Over."

Static. Silence.

Nash said rainstorms work as cloaking devices. There could be people searching for me, gathering survivors, trying to regroup. I might be able to make contact with them once the storm passes.

Breath curls white from my airways. I remove a handful of heat packs from the bag, shake them to activate the warming agent, and stuff them into my t-shirt.

Jack is here. Imagine his arms looped around your shoulders. He wants you to survive. Do it for him. Live and fight to complete the mission.

I unwrap a nutrition bar and take small, non-nauseating bites. The flavor is supposed to be apples and cinnamon but tastes more like sawdust. I lean against the cavern's only wall and hug my knees. Hunger fades. Goosebumps disappear. I'll live to see tomorrow even though tomorrow holds nothing for me. I'll live for the people who died because maybe, by some supernatural chance, I will find them along the way, in tough choices and happiness, in every defining victory—I will make them alive.

A cloud of mist settles over the mountain, swirling through the trees. Jack and I got caught in a storm during one of our morning hikes. He made me wait in the rain until fog lifted into the forest canopy, said the harder the torrent, the more beautiful the aftermath.

I sure hope he's right.

The brush surrounding the cave's mouth rustles. I reach for my gun the moment Levi emerges and runs into my arms. His fur is matted, plastered with burrs.

"How'd you find me, huh?" I hug his thick neck and sob when he lies next to me. He's a piece of Jack. Alive. Ready to be my protector. "I'll get us someplace safe. I promise."

****

Four days since the attack.

Four days of static and silence.

Four days filled with pain, desperation, and an emptying bag of provisions.

"If we can find a clear signal, we might be able to get the radio working." I tie back my tangled hair with thread and latch hold of the branch above me. "I'm almost there, Levi." My healing feet scrape against the trunk. I tighten the cords crisscrossing my chest and lift myself onto a sturdy limb.

Levi circles the tree like a shark or watchman. He stares up with eyes stretched wide when a stick drops and lands inches from his furry backside.

"Oh, you're fine. Don't give me that look." I

climb toward the bird-dotted sky, into a crisp breeze. "Not like you could do any better, Mr. No Fingers."

The trunk thins into a spindle. I anchor myself to the last supportive limb and unravel a makeshift antenna from my back. It's constructed using a long stick, metal pieces from Levi's collar, the underwire of my bra, Band-Aids, salvaged bolts, a rusty coat hanger I found in the woods and cut into measured fragments, and the cable from Sutton's pack.

Wind molds the treetop into an arch. My stomach twists, jumps to my throat. I squeal and wrap myself around the trunk. As long as I don't look down... Dang it, I looked down. Okay. Focus. Use the backpack strap to bind the antenna to the treetop.

A week ago, Nash and Charlie taught me how to build a receiver. I thought it was useless information, that is, until now. Things I thought mattered so much don't matter anymore. Words I believed would never bear any relevance in my life now enslave me.

Levi barks when I reach the ground. He sticks his mouth into my bag and removes a nutrition bar.

"Stop. Give that back." I snatch the food from his jaws. "There are only two left. We don't know how long we'll be out here. We might starve."

He whines. I sigh and remove the packaging. We split the rations, which I know is stupid since he's a dog and I'm a human, but when I look at him, I see Jack.

Sharing just makes sense.

I drink from my canteen and check the handgun's magazine for the hundredth time. It's full. The sky is clear. No one's watching us, yet. They will search the area. We were Jews in Auschwitz, marched to the gas chambers. We were diaries riddled with secrets, tossed into the fire to burn. We were destroyed because we knew too much, so they will look to make sure we are no more.

Each day I stay in one location is a day closer to being found.

"Say a prayer." I attach cable wires to the radio and turn the knob. "If this doesn't work, we probably won't live much longer so ... let's hope it works."

Static blares from the small speakers and echoes through the woods like a desperate voice calling for help. Then, the frequency clears, dulling static to a distant hum.

Tears blur the landscape, and the atmosphere suddenly seems lighter. I lean against my dirt-smeared thighs—relief is silly because unless someone survived the attack and is monitoring the frequency, I'm still going to die.

Levi nudges my hand as if telling me to speak.

"Calling all survivors of the Vestige. This is Julie Stryker, Niner-Zulu. I escaped the massacre and am awaiting contact. Do you copy? Over."

Silence.

I hold a breath captive and press my lips to the microphone. I'm throwing my last bit of hope into the air—God, please let someone catch it. "Repeat. Calling all survivors of the Vestige. This is Julie Stryker, Niner-Zulu. I escaped the massacre and am awaiting contact. Do you copy? Over."

"Roger that. We read you loud and clear, Niner-Zulu."

"You hear me..." I clasp a hand over my mouth. Every ounce of fear, anxiety, doubt, and heartbreak inverts, becomes a renaissance voice screeching *help will lead you out of the wilderness and then, you will fight like hell.*

"Julie? Do you copy?"

"Affirmative." I dry my face and smile. "Charlie, is that you?"

"Yep," he says with a laugh. "Blast, Stryker. You had me worried. I should've known you'd be alive. A barmy mate like yourself survives everything."

"Who's with you? Where are you located?"

He hesitates—why did he hesitate? "Standby."

"Charlie, come back. Please." I brace my weight against the tree and sink to where a rock protrudes from the roots. He won't leave me stranded. To survive, he needs numbers, people to help keep him and whoever else is still breathing off-grid. "You'll come back."

Levi chases his tail, curling into a ball. He rests his head in my lap, and I hold him like Jack once held me. Once. Not anymore. Because his arms are ash. And our love is frozen in our tenuous third-space.

Why haven't I cried for him since day one?

"Niner-Zulu, this is Headquarters ... or what's left of it. Hello?" Nash's confused accent floods the frequency like music. "Dang it. These headphones are falling apart. Tally, fetch me another pair."

"This is Niner-Zulu. I'm here. Don't sign off." I jump up and grasp the radio with shaky fingers. Even my tongue moves with an unsteadiness symptomatic of fear. "Tally's with you, too?"

"Yes, sadly. She won't shut up." There's a clatter on his side of the connection—maybe he plugged in another headset or dropped a bowl of soup. Food. Hot and savory. Not a nutrition bar.

"Where are you? Who survived?" I shouldn't have asked that last question because the person I want to be alive is without a pulse and body. He's dead like Jon and Sybil, and all I endure now from the loss is a void where my heart should be. The final bit of my humanity must have died with him.

"We've set up camp in a barn eleven miles south of the Underground. During the attack, people got scattered. Tally and Charlie fled with me. We haven't found anyone else."

Because they're all dead.

He clears his throat. "There's a river that cuts through the pasture where we're located. I think it's the same one that starts in the valley. Follow it here and you won't get lost."

"Roger that. See you tonight." I disconnect the radio and stuff it into my backpack. Then, I'm in motion, trekking down the mountain in a maelstrom of mangled feet and drowsy conscience.

Jack's imagined silhouette—the bit of him I've refused to let go—shimmers like the dome at sunrise and vanishes from my peripheral. I've mourned his death my own quiet, shortened, agonizing way. Maybe nowadays I don't grasp hold of someone unless I am sure I'm strong enough to let them go.

Ash wisps across the ground in white puffs, and for the first time since I awoke in this hellhole, the sight doesn't send shivers up my spine. It is evidence of the Feds' catastrophic mistake. Killing turned the Vestige into martyrs, and history is proof...

The dead scream louder than the living.

Chapter Fourteen

"Here's some advice. Stay alive."
Suzanne Collins, *The Hunger Games*

The river's gurgle dulls as I climb the bank. Plush grass swallows my feet like bandages and sends waves of comfort through my aching limbs. I drag myself beneath a fence, into an overgrown pasture. Flecks of stars revolve from horizon-to-horizon in a cosmic, welcoming parade. If they can survive the darkness, I can, too—my light will be magnified by what desires to destroy me the most.

Levi treads at my side, trembling from exhaustion. He casts a pouty glance when I amble across the field, as if begging me to slow down or rest until daybreak.

"Almost there," I say and pat his head. "We're almost there."

A barn emerges from the shadows—large and wooden with a metal roof. Firelight shines through cracks in the doors and windows, illuminating the building like a suburban house during Christmas. Mom used to put candles in the windows of our home that'd shine all December. She'd hang a wreath on the front door—it filled the street with an evergreen scent.

"We're here, Levi." I smile and drop Sutton's backpack. A weeping sound glides past my lips and creates a warm, human halo around me. Good. I'm not numb. My emotions are intact.

"Julie!"

Charlie and Nash rush from the barn's glowing threshold and embrace me so tight, my joints crack. I sink into their arms, against their living bodies. The weeping sound strengthens into full-fledged sobs, but my tear ducts are dry as a desert, maybe because I'm beyond fatigued and underfed, maybe because I've spent the past four days grappling at the concept of being alone.

"I thought I'd lost you all. When the bomb went off…" I force away the memories with the soapy smell of their skin, the softness of their clothes. "You're okay."

"You are, too," Charlie whispers. He wraps his skinny, chiseled arm around my waist and musters a misty-eyed grin. "But you look awful, like, terrifyingly awful."

"Wow, thanks." I play-punch him and mess up his already disheveled hair.

"Come on, darlin'." Nash lifts my pack onto his shoulder and leads me into the building. "We need to find you some shoes. Those feet of yours have seen better days."

A fire crackles in the center of the barn, radiating heat. I slide between empty troughs and old farming equipment, past stalls and into an open space arranged to resemble a living room. There are couches and tables, real pillows that won't give me a neck cramp. Have I died and gone to heaven?

Tally charges out of a stall with a towel draped around her neck. "Coker, you idiot! You used my freaking toothbrush. What the heck is wrong with you?" She throws a red toothbrush at his head and snarls. Her flesh is riddled with lacerations, probably caused by shrapnel from the attack.

"Oops." Charlie raises his arms in surrender. "Sorry."

"No big deal. Just rinse it off." Nash scoops stew from an iron cauldron onto a plate. He hands it to me, a steaming mixture of canned meat and vegetables. Real food.

"Using someone else's toothbrush is basically Frenching them," she yells, "Frenching them so hard, all the tartar from their nasty teeth is now in your mouth." Her pupil daggers shift to me and immediately, they're replaced with something nicer and less characteristic. She folds her arms and pops a hip. "Good. You're here. We needed some fresh blood."

"Swish salt water. It'll get rid of the Charlie gunk." I smile and shovel food into my mouth—savory stew that tastes like Thanksgiving dinner. It's so good, I could cry.

"Go get clean." Nash offers a basin of water, a towel, soap, and a pair of worn sneakers. "We salvaged what we could from the houses down the street. There's enough to last us for weeks."

"You're the best." I sit on a hay bale and tie the sneakers onto my bloody, callused feet. They're a size too big but incredibly comfortable. I soak the towel in warm water and wipe my skin, scrub the dried blood from my legs, brush my hair with an old horse comb.

Ash flakes from my shorts, and I clutch Jack's ID tags to stop myself from slipping into a dark, hopeless state of mind. I might not smell like roses and gardenias, but I'm somewhat clean. I'm no longer alone. There are reasons to be grateful.

Levi plops next to me and laps my leftover stew. He closes his eyes, sighs as if saying 'good job.' I kiss the top of his snout and squirm when pressure expands my abdomen, a sharp and insisting ache. Geez, I haven't stopped to relieve my bladder since I left the caves.

"Where are you going?" Nash asks when I open the main door.

"To find someplace to pee."

Gravel crunches beneath my feet as I move

around the barn to a patch of shrubbery. There's a deserted pickup truck parked among the slithering foliage, half-swallowed by greenery, ancient and decrepit like a museum relic. A person sits in the driver's seat, staring at me with eagle eyes. Zombie. Ghost. Waiting to eat my brains. Why did I leave my gun in the backpack?

I scream and pee my pants a little, and then laugh when I glance at the reflection a second time. Zombie? Ghost? No, that's me after four days in the wilderness—bruised, weak, a savage face on top of a hard body. I'm always me and that doesn't change, yet I'm always changing and there's nothing I can do about it. Fitting—I'm scared of the person I've become.

Goosebumps race up my back with the frigid night air. I crouch behind a bush and unzip my pants, trembling from the soreness in my thighs. Jon made fun of me for weeks after our failed camping trip to Mt. Pleasant. I almost froze to death because of flash freezing and threw a fit when I had to dig my own toilet. He said I wasn't cut out for the woods, but he'd change his mind if he saw me now, that is, after he wet his pants and ran away out of fear.

A twig snaps. I spin around and fall backward when a ginormous shadow emerges from the darkness. His bald head glistens. He's caked with mud, weighed down by packs of supplies and artillery.

"Gosh, Abram, you scared me." I gasp and zip my jeans. Heart returns to a healthy rhythm. Breathing steadies. "I'm glad to see you. It's just … if you're not careful, you might get shot."

He slings the sweat from his brow and grabs me by the shoulder. His plump lips stretch into a weird, genuinely kind smile. "I'm glad to see you, too."

"How'd you find this place?" I cross my legs to stifle the bodily urge. "Where'd you go after the attack? I monitored the frequency for days and didn't hear from you."

Abram scratches his stubble-covered chin and glances behind him at the cluster of brush. "Some blockhead broke my radio." He grunts. "Dropped it in the rain while trying to respond to your broadcast. Now it receives transmissions but can't make them."

"Who are you talking…?" Another person leaves the darkness and freezes when our pupils connect. "Julie." A single sob escapes his mouth as he buries his face in the crease of my shoulder.

Whatever kept my tear ducts dry disintegrates the moment he begins to weep. I crumble into him and cry into the muddy fabric of his t-shirt. He holds me against his chest, squeezing my ribcage until I'm sure it'll break. His face is masked by a newly-grown beard, and he's covered from head-to-toe with bloody dirt. But he has a pulse. And his body is not ash in the wind.

"Jack." I kiss his ear and then his cheek. "How are you alive?" His tears mix with mine as our lips collide, merging into a single stream on a single face. I lost him. Now I have him, and I can't seem to embrace him tight enough. Sutton didn't feel a pulse. He was dead, waiting in an afterlife coffeehouse.

"Abram hauled me into the woods before the bomb hit. We went to an abandoned hospital nearby and used the equipment to keep me alive." Jack wipes the tears from his bloodshot eyes. He touches my face as if ensuring I'm real and not a hallucination. "I was so afraid…"

"Me, too." Beyond afraid. Horrified to the brink of total numbness, the ravenous edge of some essence abyss that nipped at my heels, begging me to tumble into its clutches. I mourned him. I felt the loss of him swell and dissipate from my body. He was in me, then he wasn't, and I fought hypothermia and hunger to keep his mission in motion.

"The thought of you alive put me to sleep each night, but wondering if you died always woke me up." He kisses my mouth over and over. I hold his lips to mine and embrace his neck because if there's even the slightest rift, he might fall away into what could possibly be the cruelest dream.

"Yeah, I'm going inside before I puke." Abram clasps his hands together and steps toward the barn's entrance. "Thought I stopped hanging with teenagers a decade ago."

Jack hugs me tight. Our surroundings fade and we exist in unison, two people who once shared cups of coffee, unprecedentedly ourselves in a changing world. He smiles against my left temple. I squirm—his bristles tickle, caress me like a coarse feather duster.

"Well, you found a beard. Just look at that thing." I grab his facial hair and tilt his head back and forth. "Four days in the wilderness turned you into a bear."

"You're not quite a beauty queen either." He scoffs. "Look at your legs. They have, like, moss growing on them or something. If I'm a bear, you're a centaur."

"I've missed you." I laugh until my belly aches and then slump against him, an action that seems too familiar and perfect to be reality. "Oh, before I forget, your ID tags are around my neck."

"Keep them." He stops me from unclasping the chain. "They're yours now."

"We should probably go inside," I say. "There's a lot we need to talk about."

"Yeah, we should." He drapes an arm over my shoulders and puts weight on me as we trek to the barn's entrance. Light cascades onto him as we near the illuminated doorway. Most of his body is wrapped in bandages. He has braces on his lower back, his right ankle. Stitches crawl along his hairline. Have I been causing him pain? Why didn't he tell me to be gentle?

Levi races from the building and plops in front of us. He wags his tail.

"Hey, how'd you get here?" Jack grins. He winces when we move closer to the shelter. His face appears more sallow in the light. "Did you keep Julie safe?"

"He found me after the attack," I say. "If it weren't for him, I would've frozen."

"Good dog."

"Jack!" Everyone rushes from their places by the fire to greet him. Nash pats his shoulder. Tally and Charlie give him careful hugs. They take him from me, lower his battered form onto a couch.

"How'd you find us?" Nash asks.

"I heard you tell Julie your location on the frequency." Jack sinks into the mound of pillows and sighs. Tension fades from the creased corners of his eyes. "We won't be able to stay here for long. The Scavs might've been able to pick up your transmissions." He pats the space next to him and motions for me to inhabit the dusty sofa. Billie Holiday sings in the depths of my mind as I glide into his arms. He's in love with me. Jack Buchanan. The master of charm and crooked smiles. Loves me.

What a bizarre and wonderful thing it is to be loved by a man.

"You must be starving." Tally hands both arrivers a plate of stew. Her focus remains glued to Jack, scans him with an intent affection that makes me uncomfortable. "Do you need anything?" That gleam in her pupils—I know it too well. She has a crush on my boyfriend.

"Water and soap," Abram says. "Bring a new shirt

for Sarge."

Tally glares at him and goes to retrieve the items. She glances at Jack before leaving the main space. Yep. She likes him. No doubt about it.

Charlie plops down on a barrel and leans against his thighs. "What now?" He rolls up the sleeves of his shirt, cracks his knuckles. "What do we do?"

"Wait for someone to kill us." Tally returns from the darkness. She tosses a t-shirt at Jack, sets a basin of water in Abram's lap, and collapses onto a pile of hay. "We don't have a choice between life and death," she says. "We can only choose how we die."

"Ugh, I can't deal with your negativity any longer. I'm sorry you're angry at the world for screwing you, but quit being so bloody pessimistic, Tallulah."

"What did you just call me, Coker?" She rises like a viper preparing to strike.

"Tal-lu-lah."

"Oh…" Her lips purse and her chest expands with air. She pulls a revolver from her pocket, clicks a bullet into place, and looks at us for permission. "May I shoot him?"

"Grow up. I'm tired of your bickering. If I didn't know better, Charlie, I'd think you have a crush on Tally here. Stop antagonizing her, boy." Nash pokes the fire with a metal rod, sending a swarm of sparks upward in an amber cloud.

"It's my fault this happened. I should have recognized the signs, made everyone leave the Underground while we still had a chance." Jack digs his heels into the dirt. He draws his fingers across my forearm, writing in an invisible language. "I can't wait any longer. We need answers, and I know someone who has them."

"Jack, you don't want to go there," Nash says.

"We don't have another option. If we did, I wouldn't ask this of you … or myself."

"How are we going to get to him?"

"We'll find a way."

"You have a contact? Who?" I grasp my boyfriend's large, callused hand and swivel to look at him. He doesn't break eye contact with Nash. Did I turn invisible?

"Stop! We can't just … move forward," Tally shouts. "Our friends are dead. The world has ended. Nothing we do will change what's happened."

"You're right. We can't fix the past, but we can insure the future is a place worth reaching," Jack says. "Moving forward is our only choice."

She dries her face. Her sadness is mine too, because you never get over the pain of losing people. You just get used to them being gone.

"We need to leave in a few hours." Abram spoons another helping of stew onto his plate. "We'll avoid main roads and places that have security cameras. If the Feds are searching for us, they will have a hard time finding evidence of our existence."

"Who is it we're going to find?" I sit up on my knees, making myself a head taller than Jack.

"My dad," he says. "We're going to find my dad." His expression begs me not to ask questions, so I lower to a sitting position and keep my mouth shut. He has daddy issues—don't we all in some form or fashion? Isn't 'family' a word for 'a collection of vastly screwed-up people who cohabitate and share genes'?

"This is insane," Tally shouts. "I'm not ready to freaking die, and if we keep pursuing the truth, the Feds will kill us. Let's stop while we have a chance."

"If we quit now, everyone dies."

"So what, we have to be martyrs?"

"Yes," Jack says. "We're the martyrs. Deal with it."

A loud, industrial scream vibrates the barn, strengthens into a roaring climax. I hug my knees and roll into Jack's lap, quivering. Bellamy disappeared beneath a mound of rock. Dirt rained from the ceiling. I screamed and crawled toward a flickering light while fear liquefied my insides.

"The dome..." Nash stares past the barn's rafters, into a figment sky. "It's contracting."

Chapter Fifteen

"But there was nothing left to do but continue."
Lois Lowry, *The Giver*

Coffee first. Save the world later.

Espresso machines gurgle. Grinders hum. I slurp the poignant aroma and stand in line, humming, swaying to the acoustic music. I've never been a Starbucks groupie—the type of girl with long hair, skinny legs, a selfie-fetish, and an addiction to pumpkin spice lattes. I'm the girl who envied the Starbucks groupies and their vast collection of friends, and sat alone in my hole-in-the-wall coffeehouse with a big book and sixteen-ounce cup of coco-nutty coffee.

The café itself was once a house, white and beautiful with a large front porch and old hardwood floors. People crowd the space, all bundled in heavy coats and scarves that unify their bodies into a single, rounded, shapeless type. The women behind me chat about their book-club in deeply southern voices. A heavyset man inspects the display of fudge with his lips pinched into a conflicted grimace.

I've missed normal people.

The end of the world has changed a lot, but coffee remains the same. Women are still chatty and fat men still like their sweets. Maybe we stay the same because routine and ignorance keep us safe from what we know will hurt us. Maybe we're all afraid of the new beginning that follows an end.

Justin, the cute barista with curly hair, calls my name and hands me a paper cup. "Have a nice day," he says. His words bait a smile to my face.

First sip spreads heat through my core like an internal blanket. I lean against the wall and savor each gulp, the foam, the texture, the bitter aftertaste. Goodbye, damp chill. Hello, comfort.

"Are you crazy?" Jack hisses. He appears in the under-caffeinated sequence, as clandestine as Tom Cruise in any spy movie. His bandaged hand clamps onto my shoulder and drags me out the door.

Dillsboro is blanketed in murk, frozen by the cold front that moved into the valley last night. Clouds clot the sky, bullying the mist. Cars sling rainwater as they swerve past. I fight to keep my coffee from spilling as Jack pulls me across the icy sidewalk, past storefront windows opaque with fog.

"Let go," I yell and rip my arm from his grasp. "You can't do this, treat me like I'm your kid." Coffee steam merges with my ash-white breath as I take another sip. No regrets, here.

"One rule. We have one rule, Julie. Don't go into stores and businesses unless given permission by Abram or me. You broke the rule!" He slips on an ice patch, and his face turns blood-red, maybe from embarrassment or anger, maybe from a lethal combination of both. "There are cameras everywhere. You could've just compromised our location. Do you realize how serious this is?"

I unbutton my jacket to show him the belt of weapons fastened around my waist—handmade grenades, a gun, two knives, mace. "Nash hacked into the store's security system and turned off the cameras. I made my own bombs. This was a well-thought-out coffee run."

He bites his bottom lip, choking on stifled laughs. "You made your own bombs?"

"Yes."

"To go on a coffee mission?"

"I like coffee. And my bombs are awesome." I

flaunt a sip of the latte and twirl past him. "You must feel awful for underestimating your brilliant girlfriend."

He jogs in front of me and pulls my face into a brief, sweet kiss. "You're awesome."

"Flirt." I swipe the stocking cap off his head and slide it onto mine, and then laugh when he slips again on the slick pavement. "How'd you find me?"

"I saw you through the coffeehouse's window on my way back from the downtown bar. Went there to watch the news. As of yet, the Feds haven't released our faces to the public." He loops an arm around my waist and smirks. "Our lives are so normal."

To the people driving past in their ice-slinging cars, we're a couple who probably met as kids at the Baptist church down the street and fell in love, two lovers who'll stay where they were born and live a blissfully simple life in their home-sweet-home. Wouldn't that be nice—to close my eyes and exist without thinking about the apocalypse and whether or not my boyfriend will stay alive?

Jack gulps a mouthful of my coffee as we follow train tracks away from town. "Ugh." He coughs. His face contorts with something close to offense. "What'd you put in the espresso?"

"It's a latte. I put milk in it."

"Why the hell would you do an awful thing like that?" He laughs and holds my hand while I balance on a frozen rail. "So this is how it feels…"

"To do what?"

"Be on a date with you. Kissing and coffee are pretty much the definition of a date," he says with a wink. "Of course, I'd rather take you somewhere super rad, like Budapest or Krakow." His eyes shimmer with the visage and for a fleeting moment, I can see what he sees, the aged clock tower and cobblestone roads. "You and I sit at an outdoor café in the city square after dark, sipping strong European coffee as street performers twirl fire and stretch accordions. That's how I would start our relationship, Julie, if the world was bigger than we can touch. I'd give you a memory you'd never forget so even if you decided I wasn't good enough for your future, you'd still remember me—I would exist in your mind as the man who aced the first date."

Heat stings my chilly cheeks and makes me sweat. "That's a nice thought." But depressing because the world isn't bigger than I can touch, and Europe is no longer viable. We're stuck with kisses and coffee on deserted railroad tracks, and twisted, not-normal lives.

"Aren't dreams supposed to be nice?"

"The nicer a dream, the more hurt it inflicts when it's proven to be an illusion." I force away the thought of us at a Hungarian or Polish café, and then jump onto a patch of gravel. Better not to dream too big, hope for too much. Better to be grateful for what's left and pray it won't be stolen.

"You're going to hurt me a lot, then."

"No, I swear—I'm one of the few people who won't give you pain. We've both been hurt too much to hurt each other." I stand on my tiptoes and kiss his cheekbone. "Tell me more about your dad. Why are you afraid to see him? What did he do to you?"

Jack shrugs and releases an angst-filled sigh. "Senior year of high school, I came home late after a swim team meet. Dad had locked me out of the house— not unusual of him—so I found the spare key, went inside and found him having sex on the living room couch with a woman I'd never met before."

"Gosh, I'm sorry."

"That's not what sucked." He pockets his hands, gazes down at the passing wooden slats. "Instead of apologizing for his actions, Dad grabbed a fire iron from the mantel and beat me until I crawled out of the room. Fractured my scapula and thoracic vertebrae, severely bruised my face and back. I didn't go to school for weeks so ... I was kicked off the swim team, failed several exams, and didn't get to take a girl I liked to the prom." His focus shifts to the mountains, and his heartthrob voice fades to a haunting whisper. "I'm not afraid of him, Julie. I'm afraid of what I'll do to him when we get to Albany."

I swallow the sharp lump in my throat and drift into Jack's bandaged side. "Is he in your nightmares?" What else can I say—*sorry you have a demonic dad* or *let's slap him silly*? Maybe I should've just kissed him and held his hand, not unearth more painful memories.

"Sometimes." Jack clenches his jaw. "Sometimes he shows up to beat the crap out of me."

"Not anymore. I'll blow him to pieces with my bottle bombs. No Mentos in these things."

He laughs.

****

Cars dot the interstate in steady streams. Road signs rise from civilization, ready to command people who have pretty lives, eat at restaurants, and go to school and work, and then their trendy homes. There's a shopping mall at the next exit—I'd give a kidney in exchange for a set of impractical clothes and high-end makeup. Have I always been this superficial? Organs are more useful than designer shoes. I should know by now that luxuries won't save my life any more than they'll help it.

Metallica music beats, pops, and grinds with such magnitude it rubs my skin like grains of desert sand tossed up by an aggressive whirlwind. I sink into the vinyl lounge chair and stroke Levi between the ears. He too must hate the music because he emits a grumbling sigh and collapses on the RV's linoleum floor, paws crossed.

"It's ruined." Nash curses and leans back in his seat. He stares at the microscope we salvaged from an abandoned hospital. "My last sample of the virus ... it's ruined."

"How? What happened?" Tally twists her head to look back at us. She slouches in the driver's seat, forming an arch that would make Mom give a lecture on posture, self-respect, etiquette and whatever else she could weasel into the talk. "What'd you do?"

"I was performing a viral DNA detection test to better understand the mutated virus's genetic properties. The solution I was using to break down the viral envelope's glycoproteins backfired and completely destroyed my sample. Goodbye, weaponized mystery strain." He ties his long hair into a ponytail and groans. "I wanted to create a vaccination so one day, we might be able to live beyond the dome. Wouldn't that be nice, to have the whole Earth available to us again?"

"How cute." Tally snorts. "You actually think we'll have a life after all this is over."

"You don't?"

"The world has ended for us," she says. "Sure, it will begin again one day in the future, but not for us. We're like Israelites wandering in the desert—our descendants will reach the Promised Land once we die to pay for our mistakes. Accept your lot, Mr. Optimistic. You won't be getting anything better."

"We didn't cause the apocalypse..."

"But we were too dumb to see it," she snaps. "That was our mistake."

Sirens blare in the distance, wailing a tune that turns my stomach to rock. Blue light flickers in the rearview mirror. No escape. Can't outrun them. They've found us.

"It's the police," Nash states in an equally unnerving tone. "They want us to pull over."

"No. If I stop, they'll recognize us." Tally looks at me with glassy, red-streaked eyes. A vein bulges on her forehead, pulsing, throbbing. "What should I do?"

There was a sniper on the roof and blood on the sidewalk. A bullet sunk into me, breaking flesh with a sound not unlike the parting of kissed lips. Ice, dark and deadly, crept through my veins until I could see and feel nothing, until the world morphed into shadows.

"Stryker?" Tally slams her fists against the dashboard. She pants, heaves, begs me to take charge, and give her an order. "Should I try to outrun the cop?"

"Give me a second." My fingertips tingle, and a hollow pressure saturates my brain and chest. Lungs grow still. Heart screeches. I turn in my chair to have a better view of the pursuing car's boxy outline and the shaded face of whoever sits behind the windshield. This can't be the end of us.

This isn't how I choose to die.

"Keep driving." I snatch our radio from the floorboard and press its microphone to my mouth. "Come in, Headquarters-Actual. This is Niner-Zulu requesting backup. Do you copy? Over."

"Roger that, Niner-Zulu. What is your situation? Over."

"Sergeant…" I smear the sweat from my upper lip. "We are currently being pursued by a government-issued vehicle. Awaiting orders. Over."

"Do you have possible escape routes in sight? Over."

"Standby." I scramble into the passenger seat and scan the surrounding stretch of tree-lined asphalt for side roads and exit ramps. Nothing. So unless we somehow manage to swing the RV over the median and outrun the squadron of cops sure to follow, we're screwed. "Negative."

"Pull over," Jack says after a minute of uncertain silence.

"Say again," I wheeze. Pain ripples down my throat and pools in the pit of my stomach. I brace myself against an armrest and claw at the vinyl to steady my hands.

"Pull over," Jack repeats. "Do you copy, Niner-Zulu?"

"Wilco. Out." Acidic tears rush down my cheeks as the death sentence resonates. I clutch our radio to my neck and hyperventilate through gritted teeth. "Do what he said. Pull over."

"If we stop, we die." Tally stares at me as if I'm about to hang her from a noose. "The Feds won't give us a spanking. They'll exterminate us, tear our bodies to pieces with their machine guns, throw us into gas chambers and fill our lungs with poison…"

"Pull over." I buckle my seatbelt as if it'll somehow protect me from the dangers she listed. "Stop whimpering like a baby and follow orders, take the risk. We don't have another choice."

Tally grips the neckline of my shirt and yanks me close to her. "I swear … if we die … I'll blame you." Her hiss is as poisonous as the daggers in her pupils. She presses the brake, and then slows to a halt on the roadside. "There's always more than one choice. Always."

Nash mutters a Catholic prayer when Tally rolls down her window. His words saturate the air with a relentless fear, a surrender to death that plagues me with goosebumps. I unsheathe the gun from my holster and conceal it between my thighs. We won't be taken—I'll make sure of it.

A policeman appears outside the RV. He's middle-aged, handsome, dressed in a standard uniform with the Scavs' crest ironed onto his right sleeve. "Miss, your license plate is expired." His dialect is formal and pronounced, similar to my old cell phone's robotic voice. "May I see your ID and registration papers?" He smiles, but his expression remains glacial and stiff.

Tally removes a wad of documents from the glove compartment. "Here you are, Sir. I'm sorry. I didn't know my license plate was expired."

"Where are you headed?"

"Albany," Nash says. "To visit parents." Sweat flattens his beard. He taps his foot, writhes in his seat. Mistake. If any of us appear nervous, the cop will become suspicious and make a call to the station, and then he will know who we are and our bluff will be just that, a groundless, hopeful deception.

I cling to Jack's ID tags and stroke the indented letters until my panic subsides. "We'll find you a bathroom in a few minutes, Nash," I say loud enough for the officer to hear. "You could use the RV's toilet and flush it once we're hooked up at the campsite."

"Uh, yeah. My bladder thanks you." He winks as if saying *very clever* and teeters into the vehicle's bathroom. Why doesn't the cop stop him? Isn't there a protocol we have to follow?

"You will get a new license plate." The policeman steps forward until his beak of a nose crosses the windowsill. "You will drive safely. You will not put other citizens in harm's way." His lurid eyes are probes, small and enticing, vivid in color. "Understand?"

"I understand," Tally whispers. "I will get a new license plate and drive safely. I will not put other citizens in harm's way." She straightens her back and shifts her focus to the interstate's yellow strips.

"Good day to you all." He tips his hat and returns to his car.

"It's over." I gasp once the engine rumbles to life. A crushing weight leaves my body. "Tally, we're okay." I shake her shoulders, but she doesn't respond or move. "Tally?"

"I'm fine." She slaps my hands and leans away from me. Her face is white as a sheet.

****

A severe silence shears the living room when a key clicks into the main lock. I crush myself behind the leather couch, next to Charlie's bundled frame, and hold my breath as a silhouette moves through the entryway. Floorboards creak. Keys clatter into a metal plate. Light flickers throughout the house, transforming the shadow of a figure into a middle-aged man. He's an older version of Jack, shorter, but has the same build, mouth, nose, and hair.

His eyes are dull hazel.

Jack emerges from behind the closed door and presses a gun to the man's temple. "Hey, Dad." He clicks back the hammer with obvious spite.

Colonel Buchanan snickers. His face crinkles with an offensive sort of humor. "If you'd called to give me a heads up, I would've made dinner or something."

"We both know you wouldn't have done crap." Jack signals for us to leave our hiding places, and then shoves his dad forward. He was right to be afraid of this resentful version of himself—I might be a bit scared of him, too. "I have questions for you."

Abram and Tally seal the windows with dark fabric and duct tape. Nash and Charlie reinforce the locks. I'm supposed to do something. What was my assignment? Search Colonel Buchanan's effects for bugs and GPS chips? Monitor the military base's security feed on Nash's laptop?

"We could act like civil adults, sit at the kitchen table with a few bottles of beer…"

"If you want to survive the night, you're going to answer my questions. I'm not bluffing." Jack binds the colonel's wrists with a zip tie. He glances at me, and the hate in his eyes dissipates because we both know a righteous monster is a monster just the same.

"This isn't a good idea, son."

"Yeah, well, I haven't had many of those, right, Dad?" Jack gestures to me. "This is my girlfriend, Julie. She'll be assisting with your interrogation."

A few months ago, I would've been nervous meeting the father of my boyfriend. Heck, I'd probably spend all afternoon fixing my hair and picking the perfect dress. Now the opinions of others hold little importance because when I lost the illusion, I discovered the face behind my mask was one I liked, felt proud to own. Colonel Buchanan doesn't have to fall in love with me. I have his son's love, and soon, I'll have the answers I need to help fix this screwed-up world. Good enough.

Kirk Buchanan snickers. "She's a little young for you, boy. How old is she, sixteen?"

"Eighteen."

He crinkles his nose. "You've had prettier girlfriends, Jack."

I slam a knee against his thighs, and then shove him to eyelevel. The sensation of making someone grunt with pain is strange and uncomfortable, like getting legs waxed. But it is necessary to prove I have a voice, I'm a reckon-worthy force—men will not belittle me by attacking my appearance. "Careful. You really don't want to piss us off, especially me. I might not look like much but if I have to choose between killing you and saving my unit, I'll kill you without hesitation. Underestimating me was your first mistake. Don't make another."

"That's why..." A smirk creeps across his Jack-mouth. He tilts back on his calves and stares at me with a gleam of something close to interest in his dreary pupils. "You don't need to be pretty."

"Go set up the interrogation room," Jack says loud enough to shut up his dad. He lifts my chin and plants a strong kiss on my lips. Show off. PDA isn't the best way to tell me I'm attractive.

Nash and Charlie monitor the military base's security footage from their makeshift command center in the bedroom. Tally goes outside to patrol the perimeter. Abram and I clean the counters, arrange tools on a platter, and soundproof the walls with slats of Styrofoam.

"You will tell me what I want to know." Jack binds his father to a wooden chair in the center of the kitchen. His jaw clenches, and his brow furrows into a single, overstated dash. "I'm not under federal jurisdiction anymore. I can do whatever I want to you."

"And what is it you want to know?"

"Tell me about the dome."

"The dome? What's that?" He blinks on repeat, musters an innocent smile.

"Don't patronize me, Dad. I found what the Feds are hiding. Why do you think my battalion and I disappeared? Did you ever wonder what happened to us? To me?"

"I didn't think too much about it, figured you'd done something stupid."

Hurt flashes across Jack's face and then morphs into an expression hard as rock. He tips the chair onto its hind legs. "Why is the dome contracting?"

"You're going to prison, kid. After all this is over,

you will go to prison."

"Answer the question."

"I'm not saying a word."

"Fine." Jack snatches a bundle of tubes from the platter and shakes it in front of his father's nose. "Remember these? They were your punishment of choice. When I'd disappoint you…" He doesn't finish his statement. Instead, he grabs the pitcher from Abram's hands. "You're disappointing me, Dad."

There was once a boy roped to a chair whose father choked him with water, drilled plastic down his throat until he screeched and his eyes bulged with fear. There was once a boy with a secret abuser and scars that never completely healed. He grew into a man, but the fear and scars remained the same. Instead of existing solely as streaks on his spine and screams in the night, they manifested as something deeper, bloodier, an unforgiving lust for revenge that now turns the air cold.

"Waterboarding?" Colonel Buchanan laughs. "During my first tour in Afghanistan, I was captured and tortured by rebels for months. Do you honestly think your amateur tactics will break me?"

"You'll break."

I turn toward the tapered window when Abram pries open the man's mouth. Gagging. Coughing. Wailing. We're better than this, right? Is torture a harsh reality of our situation? Maybe. But I don't want to become callused to it. I don't want inflicting pain to be normal.

"Look," Abram shouts at me. "This is what the Feds will do to us if we're caught."

Jack pours the pitcher's contents into his dad's lungs, making the man convulse and spew water like a fountain. "What are the Feds hiding?" He rips the tube from Colonel Buchanan's throat. "My people were massacred. I watched them die … and you know why they were killed. Tell me." He throws punches against skin and bone, striking over and over until blood streams down the prisoner's face. "Who caused the apocalypse, released the virus? Why is this happening? Talk."

"Stop!" I swallow a mouthful of bile and clutch my aching stomach. "There are other ways to make someone talk. Don't be like him, Jack."

"You're all fools." The colonel's laugh resonates like a chuckle in a haunted house. His smile is red with blood. "Look in the mirror, son. The truth has been with you the whole time. It is you."

"What do you mean?"

"You are one of them," he says. "You're not human."

Chapter Sixteen

"No one would have believed in the last years of the nineteenth century that this world was being watched keenly and closely by intelligences greater than man's and yet as mortal as his own; that as men busied themselves about their various concerns they scrutinized and studied, perhaps almost as narrowly as a man with a microscope might scrutinize the transient creatures that swarm and multiply in a drop of water."
H.G. Wells, *The War of the Worlds*

"Not human?" Jack laughs. He leans against the kitchen counter and crosses his arms. "Enlighten me, Pops. What am I?" He frowns when Abram and I don't laugh with him.

"You're half-human, half-alien."

"This is low … even for you." He reaches toward me, grabs my hand, and squeezes tight. His eyes are wide and desperate. "I don't look like an alien."

"And what are aliens supposed to look like?" Colonel Buchanan squirms in his chair. Crimson spit oozes from his mangled mouth. "Your girlfriend knows I'm right."

No. Maybe. I'm not sure. I might've considered the possibility of aliens one sleepless night, same as I wondered if zombies would rise from graves—if nothing is as it seems, then anything and everything is possible. So I'm not certain, but I'm also not surprised.

Jack unravels our fingers when I don't respond. He punches the colonel so hard, the chair cracks. "You're insane," he screams. Pain ripples down his back in sweaty tremors. "You're screwing with me."

"Why would I lie? Test your blood. You'll find

that your genetic makeup is much different from any of ours. Look in the mirror. Haven't you ever wondered why your eyes are brighter than most, why it's easier for you to get what you want? You have extraterrestrial blood in your veins."

"Aliens aren't real."

"Your mom was one of them."

"Shut up." Jack clutches his head and sinks to the tile. I try to comb a hand through his hair, down his neck, but he slides away from me as if I've betrayed him.

"Tell us everything," Abram says. "Start from the beginning."

"That might take a while."

"We have all night."

I sit a few inches from Jack and place the tip of my pinkie on his thumb. He doesn't bat it off, so I go into our tenuous third-space and think of small infinities like fireworks and cold watermelon, fountain dances, and photo booths. He'll see them, too. He will hear me say in a figment, supernatural voice *I love you* and *nothing said will hurt us*.

"Intermarriage was the first step in their invasion process," Colonel Buchanan says. "Their goal was to blend races, slowly weed out the humans until all that remained were people with the alien genetic marker. My battalion and I were recruited into their marriage program. Our job was simple—we must have offspring with members of the Pureblood class. I met Lavinia at an art gala in the City. She was the most beautiful person I'd ever seen. We talked. She agreed to be my wife and two months later, we were married. It was shortly after our union that we had a son—you, Jack."

"Disgusting prick."

"I didn't have much of a choice. You see, they have the power of persuasion. As long as I was ignorant, they could make me do anything. Awareness is dangerous—it makes people immune to their power. They can't control those who know the truth," he says. "When I finally realized the extent of their abilities, and came to my senses, Jack was already seven years old."

Grandpa choked on a grape after church one Sunday while relieving himself on the toilet. His decision to eat and poop at the same time has never made much sense to me, but he did eat and poop, and a grape did get lodged in his esophagus. Mom gave Jon and me the news during dinner that night. We both laughed because we thought she was joking—Grandpa couldn't have died from something as petty as a quarter-sized fruit. Hilarious. Impossible. As unimaginable as aliens taking over the planet and toying with our minds. As novel-worthy as my boyfriend turning out to be from space.

"How long have these aliens been on Earth?" Abram asks.

"Decades. They invaded slowly, secretly—it's been a game of strategy for them. They raised their children to be influential citizens and placed them in the government and military. They caused events that led to the outbreak, World War III, the end of the world."

Jack slumps against his knees and without breaking from his fugue-state, he slides his hand onto my wrist. *Nothing said will hurt us*—it will even if we fight like hell, reject the colonel's verbatim account and create our own softer version of the truth. We will be hurt because we're different now in so many inconsequential and catastrophic ways. We have been changed.

"What about the dome? What's its purpose?" I straighten my back to an unnatural angle and press Jack's hand deep into my skin as if to keep the old version of us from slipping away.

"Containment," Colonel Buchanan says. "Before

the virus was released, they constructed the dome to contain a portion of the human race. Like I said before, ignorance gives them power. They created the illusion of normal life so we'd keep civilization and production alive, remain calm and obedient. They need us to be their laborers because they don't have a large enough population to sustain themselves yet."

I bite my bottom lip. If I ask more questions, maybe I won't be scared, maybe I won't want to crawl into a hole and suffocate. "Why didn't people become suspicious when they couldn't travel?"

"Commercials that use the aliens' power of persuasion are aired in every city. The propaganda brainwashes people into staying near their homes."

The Jones Family remained in their American Dream paradise, a home-sweet-home concocted from meatloaves and manicured lawns, pretty things and pretty words. Has anything in my life been real?

Abram grunts. "Why is the dome shrinking?"

"I'm guessing they don't need all of us anymore," the colonel says with a shrug. "Think of the dome as a balloon, all blown up to its full size. You release the air, it shrinks, and when you blow it up again, it grows larger than before. The aliens use the dome as a measuring tool. As their population and stability increase, the dome shrinks and we decrease. Our people disappear and no one notices or makes a fuss. And one day soon, the human race will be completely replaced with a species that looks, sounds, and acts like us. They're parasites. They absorb into the culture they're invading. Imagine a few years into the future. People are sitting at coffeehouses, going to work, waiting in traffic, having dinner with their families, except the people aren't human. They're aliens who stole the lives we created."

"These beings ... what are they called? Where are

they from?"

"They don't title themselves or talk about their origin. In their minds, they are just a new breed of human. Those who have unmixed ancestries refer to themselves as Purebloods, but they're usually the ones with high-ranking positions and live within the City, their hub." Colonel Buchanan spits a wad of mucus from his mouth. When he resumes speaking, his voice is less hostile. "This isn't some tacky Sci-Fi film, Jack. Aliens aren't little green Martians with big heads. They're intelligent beings who make humans seem like runts in the universe's litter. We're inferior, and in a few years, we'll all be gone … except you. You'll survive because of the DNA your mom gave you."

"No, you're lying!" Jack lurches from the floor. He wrenches his dad upward. "I've spent the last year of my life fighting against the Feds and now, you're telling me I am one of them, that I'm some sort of half-blood alien freak." His eyes flicker with an electric light, and his mouth twists into an ugly grimace. "You've beaten, ignored, and treated me like I'm worthless. Now, I know why. I was your dammit doll. You'd get mad at the Feds and instead of practicing self-control, you'd come home and abuse your alien son, let him take the punishment for his race." A single tear drips from his chin and when it hits the tile, his pain becomes a bone-cracking ache in my chest.

"You are not one of them." I place my hands on his shoulders to reassure him that we're not facing this chaos alone, linking our lives together instead of running parallel. "You've never been worthless."

"General Ford knew about you, Jack. I told him myself. How else would you have risen ranks so quickly? You were his secret weapon." Colonel Buchanan puffs out his chest and grins in a degrading, self-impressed sort of way. "Remember. Everyone is a liar. We all do what's in our best interest."

"What's wrong with you? Are you incapable of showing decency?" I shout. "Jack is your son. He has your DNA, too. Be a man for once in your pathetic life and treat your kid with respect." My eyelid twitches. Sweat springs from my pores and drenches my clothes in minutes.

The truth was supposed to rescue us, act as leverage and save my parents. I thought life would be better after today, not worse. Not hanging by a fraying thread. Not begging to pluck the last love from my side. Until this moment, I've never wished to lose the thing I wanted most.

Jack slides from my hands and then kicks the chair sideways. He leaves the kitchen, and a quiet voice within my thoughts says I'll never get him back, at least, not all of him, not the coffeehouse stranger and my brother's best friend, not the man who'd steal daffodils and write on my skin. He must know I still choose him. He must know I love him—I've shown it more than said it because love is deeper than three words.

"From now on, the only person you'll speak to is me." I lean toward the colonel until our noses are inches apart. "You've hurt Jack enough and if he's allowed to question you again, he will kill you. Everyone in the Vestige would love to put a bullet in your chest, including me ... but I have decent self-control. You won't die under my watch. That said, I offer you protection in return for information. Help me formulate a plan of attack, and I'll keep you alive."

"You're not a soldier. How can you insure I won't be murdered in my sleep?"

"I'll keep you alive. You have my word."

"She's a fighter," Abram says. "She'll keep you

safe."

"Do we have a deal?"

"You have no idea what you're getting yourself into." Colonel Buchanan glowers like an angry toddler. "The Feds, as you call them, won't react kindly to your uprising. Their invasion has taken a lifetime to complete. You'll have to sacrifice everything…"

"I already have," I say. "Almost everything."

****

Passing headlights illuminate the RV's interior like strikes of lightning in a storm-fogged sky. Flash. Charlie tosses his broken radio onto the stained couch. Flash. Abram's bald head glistens. Flash. Tally and Nash become spectral silhouettes in the front seats. They whisper, but their words carry less discretion and more gossip, more worry, more prejudice.

I tilt my head over the lounge chair's armrest—Colonel Buchanan lies on the floorboard, bound and gagged. He squirms and groans, squints his eyes into a poisonous stare. Levi lies next to him, which seems unfair because the dog doesn't deserve to share the plot of linoleum with such a horrid man.

"Do you think Jack's all right?" Charlie stumbles across the walkway and squeezes his bony frame into the space next to me. "We shouldn't have let him travel alone. It's not safe."

"He needs time to think." I lean my head against Charlie's razor-sharp shoulder—the kid really needs to eat more food. "Right now, he's confused and hurt … but he'll be okay … eventually."

"Do you think it's weird?"

"What?"

"That he's an alien?" Charlie lifts my jacket from the floor and balls it into a pillow. He tucks it beneath my head to cushion the space between my skull and his shoulder.

"Jack hasn't changed." Lie. Of course he's changed. Of course the fact he's half-alien is weird, but why would I choose not to love someone because their blood is different from mine?

"Yeah, but he's an *alien*. There are *aliens* on Earth."

"Crazy." I blink as if wiping my vision will somehow get rid of the spaceships and ray guns that keep popping up in my imagination. "Why should it matter, though? He's not a Fed. He's one of us."

"You know that. I know that. But does Jack know that?"

"We have to make him know," I say, "every day."

Charlie sighs and sinks into the chair. "I don't understand how we missed seeing an alien invasion. We've been fantasizing about one for long enough. You'd think we would've been prepared."

"We don't look for things we believe could never exist. We're stupid like that, I guess. The world is always as we see it and nothing more." I swallow the brick-size lump in my throat and swivel to face him. A familiar numbness pricks my mind, but I fight it for the first time. I fight to keep the hurt because it's one of the few normal things I have left. "Sometimes life really sucks … but you just have to keep holding out for the moments that don't suck."

"They'll come around eventually."

Dawn is a faint glimmer on the horizon when we arrive at the old relocation destination—a foreclosed farmhouse on multiple acres of property with a working generator and well. The bank that owns the estate is trapped beyond the dome, probably reduced to a pile of looted rubble. No one has touched the three-bedroom, gently dilapidated home in a decade. It's something forgotten in a place it should be remembered, something dead in a world created to look alive. Isn't that who we are now, though—the forgotten ghosts in a gasping civilization?

By noon, we've unpacked the RV and set up the Command Center. Everyone disperses throughout the property. I lock Colonel Buchanan in the cellar. Charlie builds an antenna and manages to get the television working. People huddle in the living room to watch a rerun of *I Love Lucy*, and I take a shower and change clothes.

Jack pulls into the gravel driveway hours later. He retreats to the mobile home and no matter how many times I bang on the metal door, he doesn't speak or let me inside. Why is he dividing us? We're meant to go through this together, be the voice in each other's ears yelling *get up* and *stand on your own two feet*.

"Damn your pride, Jack Buchanan." I slam my fists one last time on the RV's door and then drift toward the house. My face springs a leak, soaks skin and fabric with steamy heat. It's almost as if his fingers are somehow hollowing my chest one handful at a time, and I moan from the pain.

We weren't supposed to hurt each other.

But he's hurting me.

Rumbles reverberate across the pasture and vibrate up my calves, expanding into an animalistic growl. The horizon shifts from a linear plain to a jagged ridge flickering with light pixels. Another contraction. Another step closer to the end.

"Julie, would you trek to the gas station? We need more supplies," Nash yells from the front porch. He tosses me a backpack. "Get toilet paper."

"Sure." I massage my black-blue knuckles and tighten the backpack's straps. Leaving is good. Maybe when I come back, Jack won't be in pieces. Maybe he'll be able to glue himself back together without me. Maybe we don't really need each other to survive.

Sunlight breaks through the ceiling of clouds—Earth is fighting to keep us all. Mud cakes my boots like concrete—we're trudging forward because we've seen the unseen, we've become the unseen, and until the figment veil has been torn, we'll always live in darkness.

Jon used to hide things in the visors of Mom's Land Rover—sprigs of dried lavender, autumn-painted leaves, notes and pictures, bizarre trash he found on the roadside. He wanted to give Mom fragments of him so that when his leave was over, she'd be left with more than a memory. I'd like to fill my pockets with those memories. I'd like to leave some of my own.

A bell chimes when I enter the ramshackle gas station. There isn't a security camera in sight, but I slide a *God Bless the Second Amendment* cap onto my head as a precaution, and then grab cans of soup, a bottle of shampoo, toilet paper, matches, and a sleeve of Oreos. The two dirty construction workers and pregnant cashier don't even look in my direction as I saunter up and down the aisles.

This place probably failed its health inspection. The dropdown ceiling is stained a putrid brown color. Cockroaches writhe in the corners, and I'm pretty sure each item of food I touch has been expired for weeks.

"How you boys doing this fine afternoon?" the cashier says when three men enter the building. They're wearing military uniforms with the Scavs' crest ironed onto their right sleeves.

"We are quite well. Thank you for inquiring." A soldier with shimmering gray eyes takes a beer from a cooler and pivots toward me, shifting his pale gaze from the rack of jerky to the refrigerators.

I drop behind a shelf packed with candy and press myself against the tile. Heart drums. A metallic taste contaminates my tongue. Dust rolls back and forth from my mouth. Okay. I'm stuck. They'll leave eventually, right? Dang it—Nash forgot to give me a gun. What did he expect me to do in an emergency, turn into a psycho ninja? I can barely change the song on my relic of an iPod while running.

"Do you have a wireless jump starter? Our vehicle's battery no longer functions."

Window of opportunity—the bathroom door is cracked wide enough for me to slither through unnoticed. If I can crawl to the next aisle without drawing attention, I'll have a decent chance of survival.

"Yes, there's one behind those tire pumps. You need a mechanic?"

"No. The jump starter will suffice."

A throbbing sensation pulses through my body as I half-scramble, half-slide into the neighboring canyon of trail mix and potato chips. Sweat makes my skin cold, my hands slippery. I shift from elbow to knee to avoid the sticker sound of damp flesh peeling off dry tile.

One wrong move will finish me. The Vestige made a pact—put the mission's needs above our own lives, do whatever is needed to ensure the unit isn't compromised. Being captured and interrogated isn't an option. I can't let the Scavs silence us, bury the truth in an even deeper grave. No, if I'm found, I'll have to make sure they can't get a word out of me.

I'll have to silence myself.

"Add three beers and a handful of razors to our bill," the youngest Scav says. His gelled head crests the donut case, and his shoulder dips into the aisle's threshold.

"What're y'all doing out in these parts?"

"We are performing surveys for the government."

Surveys of the human population. Surveys that'll result is mass murders and dome contractions. I don't understand—how can they interact with the people they're devising to kill without remorse? In their shimmering eyes, how is our species beneath theirs?

I remove a hook from the chip rack and crouch in a sniper stance when the entourage appears in the framed space beyond the crevice of shelves. One alien hands the pregnant cashier a stack of money. He flashes her a luminescent smile, calls her a 'swell doll.' The other Scavs confront the two construction workers with similar grins twisting their faces.

Good. They're distracted. Now is the time to move.

"Do me a favor." Pale-Gaze Scav rips open a package of razorblade refills. "Test the sharpness of the blades. I must know they are efficient." He gives each human a metal piece and snickers.

A supernatural stillness crashes into the room when he says, "Slice your throats." The victims caress their gullets with the blades, eyes vacant and hands confident. I open my mouth to scream for them to stop, but all that emits are hyperventilated gasps. I try to move, but my body is heavy like a rock. They can't be saved. The command has been given.

Blood trickles from their windpipes and stains their shirts. The cuts are deep and accurate, as if they knew how to make themselves unfixable. Their expressions remain unchanged even when they hit the floor, and the vacancy in their eyes becomes a permanent exhibit.

Ringing resounds in my head as the last breath trickles from their nostrils. I clutch my mouth and scoot down the aisle, away from the corpses and their laughing murderers. Run. Get out. Where's an escape? Help. They'll come for me next. And I won't be able to let myself survive.

The doorbell chimes.

I roll from my hiding place after half an hour of silence and sprint from the gas station. Tears stain my skin like blood, and each step creates a slit of pain in my chest, a violent throbbing. My hands shake as I walk up the winding driveway to the farmhouse. Why won't they stop? I need them to stop before someone notices.

"Julie!" Jack emerges from the RV and jogs toward me. The moment we're in reaching distance, he sweeps me against his chest. "My parents lied. Everyone lied."

"You're not defined by their mistakes." I can't seem to coil my arms his neck—they claw at the air instead, flailing away from his DNA and striking, spooling irises.

"But I am," he whispers. "Everything that I am … is what I've fought against, what I hate." His stubble scratches my cheek, and I shiver. "The only thing I like about me is you."

Waterfalls of blood cascaded down their necks, drained the innocent life from their bodies. They sacrificed themselves like animals because of a single command. What if I've been manipulated, too? Colonel Buchanan said his ex-wife made him love her. What if my feelings for Jack are a lie?

"You're flushed. Did something happen?" His touch makes my skin crawl.

Jon rolled up the car's windshield and catapulted across the street in a broken, bloody wad. Sutton's face disappeared in a cloud of red mist. Bellamy was flattened beneath rock in a single crunch. Jack was there when they all died—he questioned the system, so everyone he charms is murdered. I can't trust what we have is real. I'm not willing to risk everything for a potential illusion.

I'm not willing to risk my heart.

"Get your hands off me." My throat constricts once the words are spoken. I avoid eye contact because a moment of connection between us will surely shatter my strength and composure.

It'll hurt to keep him. It'll hurt to let him go. I must protect myself. This environment isn't safe. Our lives are a battlefield and existence is survival of the fittest, every man for himself. No one's looking out for me. I am my own guardian. Releasing him releases the risk of pain.

"What do you mean?" He takes a step backward and surrenders his hands.

Tears blur the pasture into a green smear. My chest aches. I speak fast to rid myself of the discomfort, like ripping off a Band-Aid, but the pain grows. "I didn't think any of this would bother me, but it does. You haven't changed, I know, but our situation has. We're not the same. And I don't think I can have a relationship with you, not for a while. It's too hard."

"Uh … you said we were in this together." He tilts his head, furrows his brow as if I've asked him to solve an impossible equation. "You said you wouldn't hurt me. You said you loved me."

"I do love you, but it might not be real. You could've…"

"Made you love me?" He scoffs. "You can't explain what we have, and I can't prove my genetics didn't influence our relationship. But I love you. Doesn't that mean anything?"

The pain in my chest morphs into a piercing, all-consuming sting. He is the only man who has ever loved me. I thought we'd grow old together, spend the next sixty years of our lives kissing and drinking coffee. I wanted him like he wants me. Not anymore. I have to sacrifice the future we might've had for better odds, a chance to survive as a whole entity, not fragments.

"We're done," I say. "We have to be done."

"Fine. I get it. No one can love the half-blood alien freak, so why ask, right?"

"Don't be dramatic."

"Dramatic?" He smirks. "You're the one who's making a big deal about this. I would give you everything, Julie, if you asked. Why can't you overlook the questions, get past your delusional suspicions, and accept that what we have is worth keeping?"

"Because every time I look at you, I see *the end of the world*," I yell. "You're a constant reminder of who ruined my family, what happened to my home. I don't want to love you. I don't want to kiss and spend time with the worst thing that's happened to me." Too far. Not true.

Jack emits a faint gasp, the sound someone makes when they're punched in the stomach, and grits his teeth. "You're a liar." Water turns his eyes to glass. He leans forward until our faces are inches apart. "I'd rather not love the thing I'm waging war against."

"Same here." I turn and tromp up the hillside. Heartbreak burns through me, and sobs rattle my body before they reach my mouth. We're done. Over.

I've made a huge mistake.

****

"Eat." I lower a platter to the damp, concrete floor. "It's time for us to have that talk."

Colonel Buchanan yanks his chains and props himself against the rusty bunk bed. He glares at the rifle propped against my shoulder. "Do I look like an idiot to you? I know how these sorts of things work. Once I tell you what you want to know, you'll kill me."

"No, I won't. It's not good business."

"Why else would you have brought that gun?"

"To protect myself."

A single bulb illuminates the scarcely furnished storm cellar and shelves of canned produce, swings pendulum shadows across his weathered face. He rattles the chains. "I'm not going anywhere."

"Pardon the precaution." I fish a notebook and pen from my pocket and toss them to him. "Give me the location of the City and its layout. List all possible entrance routes."

"There's no way to prevent what's going to happen." He fingers the pen and paper as if they decide his fate, which in all honesty, they do.

"Let's say there is a way. If you had a chance to attack the City and smite the aliens in their own backyard, how would you do it?" When he hesitates, I drag a chair toward him, just out of reach, and sit. "You're a bad man, Colonel Buchanan, but you could be better. Help me. Do it for Jack. I know you love him in your own strange way. Please."

"You don't ask easy questions."

"I don't want easy answers."

Colonel Buchanan scoots to the mattress's edge and snickers through a toothy grin, one that cuts through me like a poison-coated knife. "Atlanta is now their City. It's protected by a smaller dome. Getting through the force field will be impossible." He sketches a map of Severance.

"We already know how to get through."

"Really? How?"

"There are some cards I'd rather not show before I play my hand." I tap his paper with the rifle's barrel. "Continue."

He tilts the notepad and points to the crudely drawn city in the dome's center. "The City is unlike anything you've seen or experienced. You and the Vestige will have to alter your appearances, mannerisms, and speech to blend in with the Pureblood population."

"You can help us with that."

"Maybe," he says, "but I can't fix your genetics. Before entering a building, taking transportation, or making a purchase within the City, one must place their hand on a tile-like scan that searches their DNA for the alien genetic marker. Those who have the marker are allowed clearance. Without it, they're dead." He scratches his chin and stares at the paper. "Only two of you will be able to enter the City. Jack will have to give you transfusions each night to insure the genetic marker stays within your system."

"It is possible to trick the scans, then."

"Yes, it's possible." He writes notations in the margins. "Your attack must be silent, an infiltration. There aren't enough of you to win a war, but you're smart. You can ruin them from within. Strike where they're strongest, and they'll crumble." He sets the notebook beside him and connects with my line of sight as if to verify that what he said is true. "Give me the night to strategize. Tomorrow morning, I'll have a plan of attack."

"You're cooperating. Why?"

"We have a common enemy. Besides, I owe it to Jack." His words are pretty, but believing them would be like gulping a drink leftover from a frat party.

"Thank you." I stand and grab a few of the diagrams from his lap before leaving.

When did I become the girl who hurts others to save herself? Did Jon's murder change me, or have I been using his death, the kidnapping of my parents, and the bullet in my stomach as excuses for the transformation that's come from seeing the dark and twisty truth and not caring about how it darkens me? Interrogations, bloody necks, aliens, and the apocalypse—I have to be better, I can't become a lie.

An ink-black sky greets me when I exit the cellar. Flashlights coruscate near the tool shed, where Nash and Abram help Jack secure a satellite to the roof. I move parallel to them, zip up my jacket, and toy with his ID tags like a bad habit.

They're cold against my skin.

He became the person I'd catch fireflies with on hot nights when the cicadas hissed and the bullfrogs croaked, the person who told me to stick my head out the car window so I could feel the estuary's breeze on my face. He became my everything in an instant and now haunts the recesses of my memory as a profile, a silhouette, glimmering eyes and a deep dimple, warm hands that reach out for me to take hold before their offer expires. I'm no longer ignorant. The hold is broken, yet I still love him. I love him so much I don't know how to tell him without it seeming inconsequential. What's wrong with me? He is the one. He has always been the one. Why can't I get past my fear and just be in love?

"Come help us, Julie," Nash shouts. "Don't you want to be a part of the action?"

Jack sits at the roof's edge with a wrench in his hands. He looks at me, and I pray he can still read my face like a book. I need him to know the truth. I need him to see past my layers.

If I seem to not want to be with him now, it's only because love scares me too, more than manipulation, because love is a choice I make and not something forced upon me. I trust him, but I don't trust myself. I must have time to trust myself so I can completely love him.

He's the grenade. I'm the grenade. We'll blow each other to pieces…

Together.

Chapter Seventeen

"We did not ask if he had seen any monsters, for monsters have ceased to be news. There is never any shortage of horrible creatures who prey on human beings, snatch away their food, or devour whole populations; but examples of wise social planning are not so easy to find."
Thomas More, *Utopia*

Nash hovers over the worktable to my right, measuring and cutting strips of metal from the support beams we salvaged from a nearby warehouse. "You're a quick learner, Stryker," he yells over the roar of fire and grinding metal. "I ain't never seen someone pick up the skill so fast."

"If we're able to fix the world, I guess I could work as a welder." I use the torch to fuse together the doorframe's lower left-hand corner. Sparks dance across the steel surface, fleeing from molten iron and flame. Sweat bullets drop from my mask and fizz, turning to gas.

"Nah, you can't leave me, darlin'. You and Charlie are my crew. I'll never find better sets of hands," he says, "or better listeners."

"That's me: good hands and ears." I unstrap my helmet and lift the windowpane—a gust of air chills my saturated flesh, crisp and fresh like jumping into a pool of mountain water. I haul another iron strip to the workspace. It kidnaps the yellow glow of electric lighting and ignites with rust hues.

"We'll be finished with the frame in a few days." Nash removes his mask and writes notations on a crudely drawn blueprint. "Good thing, too. We're approaching a neap tide. The dome will be at its weakest gravitational lapse." His fingernails are black with accumulated dirt.

"Better than waiting a month." I replace my gas cylinder and check its gauges. "Does our frame conduct enough magnetic flux to reroute the force field?"

"According to my calculations, yes, but we won't know for sure until we insert it into the dome."

"So there's a strong chance we could be fried?"

"There's always a chance we could be fried," he says with a laugh. "That's the beauty of it."

Hinges squeak when Charlie enters the building. He combs his hair into place and pockets his hands, and then sways back and forth as if on the verge of slipping back into sleep.

"Finally decided to show up for work, did you? That bed of yours must be mighty comfortable if you'd rather sleep than help me build stuff. Julie was here at dawn. I might promote her…"

Charlie yanks a gun from his pants and pulls the trigger.

Nash crumbles to the floor.

Blood splatters my shoes, converging in a puddle beside me. A red pool. Like the one that submerged and almost drowned me. But I'm supposed to be safe here. Friends don't kill friends.

Jon wades to the shore with his hand stretched toward mine. Take it—I should. Follow him into the waves where I'll be protected from assassins and lies—the choice seems decided. I'll follow him and Sybil into the depths, through a magenta horizon and halcyon sea, and blood won't stain me anymore, neither will love or hate or fear. I'll be safe from it all.

A bullet soars so close, it nicks the top of my scalp. I blink Charlie into focus and clutch my ringing ears. Sunlight outlines his bony frame in a silhouette reminiscent of an electrical pole.

"Get down on your knees."

"What've you done?" I scream and press my fists against Nash's chest to slow the bleeding. His breaths are jagged and labored like Sybil's before she died. "Charlie, how ... why?"

"I couldn't let the Vestige enter the hub," he says with his brow furrowed, face scrunched. "You left me no other choice. If he dies, the way through the dome dies with him."

Pain tears through me when his eyes ignite with a familiar gleam. Why haven't I noticed it before, that vibrant shimmer of a second-layer something?

"You're one of them." I lean more weight against Nash's chest. Blood oozes through my fingers, and his heart beats against my palms. "You're a spy."

"Took you long enough." He aims his gun at my face. "Scoot toward the wall."

"How could you do this, Charlie?" I cast him the most pitiful look and crawl in the designated direction. Nash will bleed out in a few minutes—his skin is already whiter than his teeth. I won't last much longer, either. Maybe someone heard the gunshot. Maybe they'll come before it's too late.

"This isn't what I wanted, really. Assassinations weren't a part of my assignment. I was meant to infiltrate the Vestige and relay your findings to those in the City. I'm a mole, nothing more ... that is, until today. You see, the Special Ones like their humans to believe in freedom—more information is leaked that way. It's an illusion, like all things in your world. We are excellent at creating your ideas and society, your rebellion. We control it all."

I shiver from the ache of betrayal and slide a hand up the back of my t-shirt to the weapon belt. "The drone's malfunction, the attack—you caused them, didn't you?"

"Among other things. I damaged the tunnels before the dome's first contraction so they'd collapse. I jammed the radio frequency after the Underground was bombed. I told the Special Ones about Jon's plan to move his family to the Underground. They killed him for me, of course. I would've hated to do it myself. Jon was such a nice human."

"Charlie…"

Tears burn my face, hotter than blood. He was my partner in the tunnels. I trusted him when I should've been beating the guts from his body. Because of him, almost everyone I love is dead.

"Don't look at me like that. I do like you, Julie." He crouches and presses the gun to my forehead—another bullet inches from my brain. "We were friends, truly, and I wouldn't be doing this now unless it was absolutely necessary. You won't feel a thing. I'll do it quick. Really, I'm sparing you from a lot of unneeded suffering. You won't have to witness the final stages of the invasion."

I claw at the gun tucked into my belt—it won't budge from its pouch. "Please. Don't do this. I'll say the shooting was an accident. We can save Nash and … you can stay with the Vestige. We're not trying to destroy your people, Charlie. We just want our race to survive."

Sweat stings my eyes, and I flinch when he clicks a bullet into place. Another minute is all I need to unsheathe the Glock and fire a blast through his alien chest. Almost there. Forty seconds.

"Were those gunshots? Is everyone okay?" Abram and Jack race into the shed and then slide to a stop when Charlie points the gun in their direction.

Idiots. Why didn't they bring a weapon?

Jack lifts his arms. "Whoa, what's with the semiautomatic?" His focus shifts to the dying man, and his jaw clenches. "You're a spy."

"Seems that way, doesn't it?" Charlie smirks and mumbles something in a foreign language. "You've made this a lot harder on me. Only two people were going to die. Now, I have to kill four."

"You don't have to kill anyone," I shout.

"Put the gun down." Jack steps forward. "We're your friends…"

"You're enemies of the Special Ones," Charlie says. "You have to die."

A bullet hole appears between his eyes, followed by a puff of pink mist. He crumbles to the ground without a thump or clatter. Dead. No chance of resurrection.

Sobs and laughs tickle my lips. I lean against a worktable's leg, roll onto one side, and hug my stomach. "Thank you, God. It's over." Over. The traitor is gone. And we're alive for now.

Jack and Abram stare at me as if I've grown a second head.

They stare at the gun in my hand.

****

In the room's corner, where floral wallpaper peels into ribbons, there is a splatter of pink paint, a dusting fine as blasted brain matter. It watches over Nash and me like a monument, refusing to let either of us forget the ice-cold gun, dead eyes, and heart that won't beat again.

"What happened?" Nash groans and claws at his bandaged chest. "I thought I was a goner." He writhes in the avalanche of blankets. His gaze flickers to mine, and immediately, his eyes fill with tears.

"Jack was able to fix you. He's pretty good at fixing people." I snatch a bottle of aspirin from the nightstand and dump a few pills into my shaky hand. The same hand that fired a bullet into Charlie's skull. Dang it. Why can't I breathe? "Here. I'll go get you a cup of water."

"Don't bother." He swallows the capsules dry. His bottom lip quivers, and tears cascade down his stubble-covered cheeks. "Charlie's dead, isn't he?"

I massage my tinkling face and nod. "Abram's burying him now."

"You did what had to be done."

"But killing for a good reason doesn't make me any less of a killer," I say. "It only makes me a killer with a good reason. And a good reason won't help me sleep better at night."

"Charlie was a spy," he whispers. "We have to accept the truth."

"Betrayal is a truth I'd rather not believe."

"People will always disappoint you, Julie. They'll lie, betray, and hurt you in ways you never thought were possible. And you'll do the same to them." Nash smears his tears and musters a small smile. "I loved that kid as if he were my own. People just … don't realize that love has the power to kill them." He swats the tags dangling from my neck, and his expression dies. "Or turn them into killers."

A hollow sensation punctures my core so deeply I lean against the rotting mattress to put pressure against it, to fill the cavity with something more than guilt. Charlie had my back long enough to stab it, so I shot him. My body reacted out of instinct and necessity, not because murder is a reflex I've developed. Earlier this morning, I would've thrown myself in front of a bus to save him. I would've sacrificed myself for the person I just killed, the person who would've killed me.

Everyone gathers in the cellar two hours later for a mandatory meeting. We form a disfigured circle around a table blanketed with Colonel Buchanan's notes and diagrams.

"Why'd you call us down here, Jack?" Tally folds her arms and rubs her bloodshot eyes. She positions herself away from the pendulum glow, in the mildew-infested shadows. "Shouldn't we talk plan of action after we finish burying Charlie?"

"Julie was the one who called the meeting," he says with obvious skepticism as if I should be incapable of rational thought after performing my first kill, when the truth is, rational thought is the only thing holding me together.

"Our time is running out. The dome's contractions are more frequent, and the neap tide is approaching." I move to where Colonel Buchanan sits in his wad of chains. "Using his knowledge of the City, the colonel has devised a plan of attack. Listen to what he has to say."

"You have the floor, Dad." Jack won't look at me, not even when I offer him a hand-drawn diagram. I disappointed him, lied, betrayed, and hurt him in ways I never thought I could. And he's doing the same to me now because repaying pain with pain is supposed to heal what's broken, at least, that's the lie we all tell ourselves. If he knew how much I love him, maybe he'd change his mind. Maybe he would view me as a scared girl instead of a lying traitor.

"I spent last night writing down every bit of information I've gathered over the past two decades. I have a plan—don't know if it's a good one, but it might work." Colonel Buchanan shuffles through his notes. "Infiltration is our best option. Two agents will enter the City. The rest of us will set up a Command Center outside the inner dome, monitor their progress, and send scouts to neighboring towns to spread the truth. We'll get people to notice the unseen and keep them calm until the operatives complete their tasks within the hub. That said, stopping the aliens' invasion won't happen overnight.

Our timeframe, I'm guessing, is a month or two. It'll take a while for the agents to establish themselves, make connections and carry out their assignments."

"Who will we send into the City?" Abram asks.

"My son…"

"No surprise there," Jack says. "You need my blood."

"And of course, Julie."

"What? No. Why me?" My knees buckle, and the air drains from my lungs. He must be joking. Tally would be the better candidate for a covert agent, but then again, she has a crush on Jack, and nothing brings two people closer than a top-secret mission.

"Out of everyone here, you bear the closest resemblance to the aliens. With a little coaching, you'll blend with the Purebloods better than Jack," Colonel Buchanan says.

Sure, let the teenager masquerade as a posh alien and infiltrate the extraterrestrial beehive with her hybrid ex-boyfriend. Sounds like a brilliant idea. Better yet—I should start riots in the streets with a confetti cannon and walk around with *Leave Earth, Martian Scum* posters.

"How do we know you won't flip sides once Julie and I are in the City?"

"You have to trust me." Colonel Buchanan leans against the tabletop and shifts his attention to Nash who is perched on a wooden stool. "How long until the doorframe will be ready to use?"

"If people help me, I can have it done in a couple days."

"Okay. Good. That concludes our council meeting." Colonel Buchanan clasps his hands together. "I need to speak with Jack and Julie alone. Everyone else, please leave my cell."

Jack steps closer to me, but not close enough. He

avoids the sight of my face as if it's the ugliest thing in existence. "It'd be easier if we didn't have to do this together, I know. We both need space, and to be honest, it's difficult for me to be around you. In the City, we probably won't see each other often, but I'll make sure you're safe. You won't be alone, not for a second. Even when we're apart, I will ensure that your needs are met. One phone call, and I'll be at your door."

"You deserve to be mad." I touch his cheek, fit my thumb in his left dimple and force him to look at me. "I'm a messy person who does messy things. You just have to know that about me. When life gets scary, I run away and make a fool of myself—it's what I do because I'm screwed-up and insecure—but I always come back, and in my heart, I love you all the time. I'm sorry for hurting you. I'm sorry for not standing by your side when you needed me most. I'm sorry ... and I ask you to forgive me."

He relaxes against my palm and lightly kisses my wrist. Something close to relief removes the creases from around his eyes. "Be my friend again. I can forgive a friend."

"But you can't forgive someone you love, someone who loves you." The heartache returns more intense than before, and it takes all my strength to refrain from lapsing into a full-fledged cry session.

"No," he says, "not for a while."

"Okay." I imprison a sob behind my gritted teeth and nod. "Friends."

"I've formulated profiles for you both." Colonel Buchanan jingles his chains to capture our notice. "You'll be brother and sister—Jack and Julie Lefèvre, which was Lavinia's surname. Your parents were killed in a car crash. You lived with your father's brother in the suburbs until Jack got a job at the Department of Homeland

Security."

"But I don't have a job."

"Some of my friends in the City are sympathetic with your cause. They'll give you work," he says. "Your assignment is to find out where the dome's generator is located. Rent a penthouse in the City. I need you to be as close as possible to the Military Command Center. Julie, you'll work as a secretary for the District and live at the boarding house in Druid Hills. It's owned by distant relatives of Lavinia. Tell them you're her daughter. They'll believe you."

"What's the District?"

"The government. When the world ended, it was condensed to fit into a single building. The President, Congress, Supreme Court—everything is at the District, which makes it a perfect target. Apply for a job. You'll get one. Keep your ears and eyes open, relay all information back to us, and when the time comes, you'll bomb the District. Once their political system and military are gone, and the domes are in our control, the invasion will be over."

"What about my parents? If they aren't dead, the Feds have them locked away somewhere."

"We'll find them," Jack says, "once the mission is complete."

Electricity hisses. The lightbulb dims before brightening into a ball of fire that washes the cellar with fiery radiance. Shadows sink into oblivion, revealing mounds of debris and moldy canisters. Jack and I will do the same, won't we? We'll be the grand revealers.

"You can't break character. No one must know your true identities. Don't talk about yourselves. Don't have personal relations with anyone who isn't essential to your mission. And there is to be no physical contact between you of any sort unless vital to your survival."

Jack laughs.

"I mean it. The only time you're allowed to touch her, Jack, is when you give her transfusions and even then, you're exclusively allowed to hold her arm when you stick the needle into her vein. Understand? There are eyes everywhere."

"Then where are we supposed to do the transfusions?"

"I'll think of a place," Colonel Buchanan says. "Play the parts of brother and sister. Keep in contact with one another. Meet for dinner, go to parties. Blend with the environment."

"Who'll take care of my dog while I'm gone?"

"That big guy with the bald head will take care of your dog."

Jack sighs and paces the room. After his third loop around the table, he plops onto a stool. "Okay. I'll be your spy and mobile blood bank even though I'm still not sure why I'm following your orders."

"Good. I'll create some pamphlets that list various addresses and important information. You'll need to be taught about the Pureblood's customs, speech habits, mannerisms, style, the layout of the City and available transportation." Colonel Buchanan props his elbows on a stack of maps. "You haven't said much, Julie. Are you willing to do this?"

Willing to live a dangerous lie for two months? Willing to be alone in a metropolis, surrounded by aliens who want to destroy my race? Willing to see the things I haven't wanted to see?

Mom and Dad would want me to let someone else play espionage, but this is the chance I need to reclaim my life, finish Jon's fight. If I succeed, they'll live, and I will, too. Stakes are high, but my hope is higher. I'll cast the dice and play my hand.

"Yes," I say. "I'm willing."

The next few days are spent in the cellar with Jack and his dad. We're taught proper etiquette, common speech habits, and are forced to memorize our profiles, maps of the City. On the second day of training, Colonel Buchanan cuts my hair with a pair of shears and attempts to apply makeup to my face. He revises my mature, rugged reflection and transforms me into someone pretty and innocent, vibrant with youth—everything I once hated about myself but now find to be a paean to the past.

I helped make a door to a new beginning.

Now it's time for me to walk through and begin.

****

"Don't be calm for my sake." Jack drums his fingers on the steering wheel and tugs at his vintage tie. Sweat beads on his smooth cheeks, enhancing the evergreen scent of his aftershave. "Let's talk. Being quiet … it's freaking me out." He leans over to inspect the blood bag dangling from the BMW's dashboard, the tube attached to my forearm.

"Stop fiddling with the bag. I'm being transfused just fine." I shoo away his hands and squint when golden sunlight blasts through the windshield. It saturates my silk dress and curly hair, acts as a spotlight drawing my reflection to the rearview mirror—red lips and bright eyes, bleached teeth that shimmer stark. "We've memorized our roles. What's there to talk about?"

"Once we enter the City, we'll be limited as to what we can say to one another. Now is the time to get it all out, you know?" He squirms in his seat and glances at each billboard as they fly past.

"I don't want to be your friend, okay?" Heart drums double-quick, stomach churns, eyelid twitches— my body didn't get the *you're a fearless spy* memo. "If I ever fall in love with someone else, it'll be because something in that man reminds me of you. Isn't that weird? Don't you see how messed-up I am? You can't make me love you, mold with you, and then disappear from my life, Jack, because now, I'm irreversibly different and stamped with you."

At any other time, confessing such an intimate part of myself would make me keel over in mortification, but knowing I could be dead in a few hours makes restraint and embarrassment seem like luxuries. We will enter the Third Layer tonight. And there's a high chance we may never exit.

Jack rubs his mouth to hide an obvious smile. "Stamped?"

"Yes, stamped."

"So I, like, tattooed you or something?"

"Yeah, I have an embossment of your face on my butt."

He laughs. "Well, let's hope the aliens don't body-search you."

"What, you don't think it's normal for a sister to have her brother's face permanently sketched on her backside?" Involuntary tears blur him into a watercolor smear when I lean onto the console and drag my index finger up the crease of his sleeve. I miss him when I touch him, even when he looks me in the eyes and talks as if we're coffeehouse strangers-turned-friends. He'll forgive me one day, won't he?

Traffic thins. The loud roar of civilization becomes a steady buzz, a dying pulse and then, silence. Cars fade into Earth's background, and we're left on an empty stretch of asphalt with ruins around us, a snow-globe world behind us and the truth looming in the distance.

"I'll have to pull off the main road in a few miles," he says, "so the Scavs won't track us. Nash and the gang should be waiting at our designated entry point."

"What if I'm not ready? What if … the Purebloods see through me?" I remove the needle from my arm and stop the bleeding with a handkerchief. A lump stretches my throat until I can hardly breathe.

"They won't look, so they won't see." Jack places his hand on my knee and gives an affirming nod. "Let's beat those bastards at their own game."

After speeding through a maze of back roads, we arrive at our meeting place—the empty lot beneath an arching overpass. Garbage is everywhere, shifting with the wind like debris caught in an ocean's surf. I shiver from the cold and unload my half-empty suitcase from the car's trunk.

The RV emerges from the desolate suburban set minutes later and rolls to a stop. Nash, Tally, Abram, and Colonel Buchanan emerge with the iron doorframe in their arms.

"We need to hurry," Nash says. "The dome is at its weakest level of gravitational strength."

Everything seems to happen in flashes of time and movement. I'm swept up to the dome-protruding overpass. With a single shove, Abram and Colonel Buchanan propel the frame into the translucent barrier. There is an eruption of sparks, a hiss of protest, and then nothing except for a single door in the center of a forgotten road.

"No freaking way," Tally squeals. "It works!"

Colonel Buchanan hands us earpieces, voice recorders, and small radios that resemble cell phones. "We'll set up our Command Center in an empty shopping mall a few miles from here. Make contact with us every night. Relay all gathered information…"

"Yeah, Dad, we know."

"If you are unable to make contact using these

devices, find a pay phone and call my personal number—it's written inside those pamphlets I gave you. The Feds will be able to monitor what is said between us, but neither phone can be tracked. Be selective with your words."

"We'll contact you once we're settled."

Jon took me fishing last summer. He loved to fish. I tried to match his enthusiasm, but when our rusty tin-can of a boat capsized, I lost my ability to fake excitement. His cup of bait was in my hair—worms in my hair! Not the small garden worms. The slimy, gigantic, I-am-going-to-terrorize-a-city kind of worms. I screamed and splashed. Jon laughed so hard, he almost drowned.

Memories. I want more. More misadventures with Jon. More dance parties with Jack. More espresso-drinking contests. Before I die. But it might be too late.

"Goodbye" sneaks past my chattering teeth as if it has a mind of its own. I hug Nash and Tally, give a firm handshake to Abram and a glance of trust to the colonel. Then, it pushes me over the frame's threshold, plants my heels in gravel and grass where they'll stay.

"Don't look back," Jack says when Abram pries the door from the dome. He swings our suitcases onto his shoulders and begins the trek up a hill. "We can do this, Julie."

"Your optimism is cute."

Stuck. No going back. There is a mission file with our names on the tab. We are operatives, pawns in a game bigger than any individual. If we fail, humanity disappears.

No pressure.

The slope levels, easing the ache in my sweaty thighs. I stagger forward and almost collide with Jack, who is frozen at the edge of an old bridge. He stares into the abyss of space with a gleam of something close to awe in his eyes.

"There it is…" His lips quiver before molding into a smile. "We're here."

Before us lies the City, a glittering oasis in a sea of blackness. Skyscrapers, sleek and remodeled, flood the horizon. Small aircrafts zigzag through the cluster of high-rises, glowing blue and white. A ginormous structure rises from the center of the metropolis, ablaze with lights.

"We've reached the Third Layer."

THIRD LAYER
Chapter Eighteen

"No matter how big the lie; repeat it often enough and the masses will regard it as the truth."
John F. Kennedy

Jack surrounds me. His eyes. His charm. The uncanny charisma that beams from his face and the faces of those on the sidewalk. I hold my head high to match theirs, emerge myself in the doppelganger sea where the women are pretty and the men sway like sleek tycoons. Their bodies slide across me in brief caresses of drop-waist dresses, pearls, striped suits, and black-and-white shoes. Nothing old or overused. Not a wrinkle or glimmer of emotion to be seen.

Buildings rise on either side of the street, shimmering with lights and mega screens. Cars, designed to resemble vehicles from the 1920s, speed through the metropolitan maze and electric sky. Why did I agree to come here? What made me think I'd match the Purebloods, blend into their nostalgic City? Oh no, they're noticing me now—a woman with finger curls smiles when she bumps against my shoulder, and the teenage boy selling technological newspapers tips his hat as I hurry past.

They look, but they don't see me.

I stumble into Jack when a Model-T replica swerves close to the curb. He shoots a warning glance and then nods his head toward the bus station across the avenue. There it is—our divide, the end of a line and beginning of another. The question is, whose line is about to end?

"You will be in good health. No harm shall come to you here," Jack says once we're inside the station. He reaches out his hand to touch mine, but instead, stuffs it into his blazer's pocket. "We will not be apart for much time. All will be swell." His mouth quivers, and his eyes turn red.

"Will you pay me a visit tomorrow?" I yell over the uproar of beautiful voices. "I would very much like to see you." My nostrils tingle with the thick scent of cologne, and my heart rolls within me like a wheel thrust into motion. I know our mission backward and forward. I've spent hours engraining each move into my head, but theories differ from reality. A theory says, "Here is how you could save the world." Reality says, "Here is what will happen if you try."

"If all goes as expected, I will visit you tomorrow evening." He tenses and motions to the cluster of security cameras above the terminal. "You must be cautious. Their eyes are all around. They will be observing you always."

"I will be most careful." *Because I need to be with him again. Because I really want to live.*

Steam billows through the structure when an aerial bus lowers to the road and opens its doors for entry. Purebloods flock to the vehicle's mouth in a single surge.

"You best go before the bus fills with passengers." Jack returns my suitcase. He fakes a conclusive smile as dazzling as post-baseball fireworks. "Until tomorrow, sis."

My hands ache with the need to touch him, trace the creases of his forehead and the lump on his nose's bridge, to be glued to him so we won't be separated. Theory liked us. Theory made us seem in control. Reality, on the other hand, turns us into lone soldiers on an outnumbered battlefield. It reverts us from spies to scared kids who dream of nothing more than to have a decent home.

"Until tomorrow." I join the swarm before my knees turn to stone, and I waltz into the bus's belly. A green light flashes when I place my hand on the scan. Accepted. As a Pureblood passenger.

I drop into a padded seat by the door and browse the outdoor terminal for Jack. He waves from the platform as if he's sending me someplace nice, maybe college or summer camp or spring break vacation. He waves like Jon did when I left for an overnight camping trip with Missy.

Tears dilute him into a mistakable blot. I press myself against a window as the bus lifts into flight and the last member of my family slips into the distance.
****

Streetlamps illuminate the repaved sidewalk of Druid Hills and turn the dead of night into a reading-capable glow. I unfold the pamphlet Colonel Buchanan gave me and trace the boarding house's address with my thumb. It shouldn't be far up the road, maybe half a mile. A few hundred yards until I reach my assigned location, become a lie. A few minutes of walking alone through a rich neighborhood that looks an awful lot like those outside of Charleston.

Luxurious new mansions crowd the stretch of manicured lawns and flowerbeds, pop up like weeds between old cottages and seventies abodes. Why weren't the aliens more original with their architecture? They were supposed to invade Earth in a fleet of spaceships, fight a bloody war, and build colonies out of plastic pods, not construct their world to look like our past.

I smooth my skirt with shaking hands and reapply red lipstick—it makes my mouth taste and smell like blood. Jon would be brave and complete the mission, wouldn't he? After all that's happened, would his desire to save the world trump his shaking hands and pounding heart? Be like him—that's what I have to do. I must be my brother's substitute, absorb the conviction that made him strong.

Escape is but a pretty thought.

The boarding house beckons me toward its red-brick entryway and ivy-covered walls. I go to the front door situated between spiraling topiaries and pound the lion-shaped knocker. Oops. I did it. Jon and I used to play dingdong-ditch on Halloween. I should take this opportunity to practice ditching.

A woman resembling an actress from a 1950s sitcom opens the door. "Good evening." When she smiles, I almost expect a commercial twinkle to appear on her bleached teeth. "May I help you?"

Help? Yes, that'd be nice. I'd like to be helped back to my comfy life of classes and coffee. I'd like help tearing apart this City, the dome, every newspaper and magazine with Pureblood propaganda. I'd like someone to help me stay alive.

I swallow the cannonball-size lump in my throat and return the smile. "Yes, I am in need of a room to rent. My name is Julie Lefèvre. I am the daughter of Lavinia Lefèvre."

"Why yes, I recall meeting Lavinia years ago. She is my husband's cousin. Please, come inside." The woman wipes her hands on her floral-print apron and steps aside. "You must pardon my appearance. I am making dinner for my family." She takes the fur wrap from my shoulders and hangs it on a coatrack. "My name is Margo Lefèvre. You have arrived at an optimal time, Julie. Several of our rooms are now available to rent. It would be quite a pleasure to have you live here with us. How is your mother?"

"She died several years prior to now." The first of many fibs.

Margo emits a faint gasp and then touches my arm. "You have my sincerest condolences. Please, come and enjoy a cup of tea in the apartment. You must meet my husband and inform him of your mother's passing." She places my suitcase near the stairs and leads me into a private section of the house. "What brings you to the City?"

Here is my chance to recite the lies Colonel Buchanan created. Julie Lefèvre is a crumbled piece of paper riddled with facts and timelines. She's a theory, and I'm her reality. I put a face to her name.

"I came with my brother. He works at the Department of Homeland Security," I say as she takes me through a personal living room. "His quarters are quite small, which is why I decided to come here. Mother often spoke of the loveliness of this house and your amiable company."

"How very kind of her." Margo blushes when we enter the vintage kitchen. "This is my husband, Jed." She gestures to the man seated at the breakfast table. He could easily be a cutout from a Norman Rockwell painting— gelled hair, a clean shaven face, spectacles, and a yellow sweater vest. "Jed, this is Lavinia's daughter, Julie. She will be renting one of our spare rooms."

Jed glances up from his crossword puzzle and grins. "Gee, that is swell. I was unaware that my cousin had a daughter. We have not spoken in many years." He sets his teacup on a lace doily and adjusts his wiry glasses as if to get a better view of me, probe my face with his shimmering eyes.

"Both of my parents were killed in a car crash when I was a young child. I do not remember them well. My brother and I were raised in the suburbs by our father's brother." Sweat drips down my back—better beneath clothes than streaming my temples. I lower into the empty chair across from Jed and meet his vibrant gaze. Let him look. He won't see.

Margo births a plate of desserts from the cupboard and places it between her husband and me. "What a tragic experience. If we had known of your misfortunes, we could have been of some condolence to you and your brother."

"How unfortunate for you both." Jed sinks his teeth into a rose macaroon, sprinkling his vest with pink shards. His humanoid jaws clench the European sweet tight, and then part into a smile matching in indulgence. "Let us now be of some help to you, Cousin Julie."

"You are most kind." I pick at my fingernail cuticles and gulp my tea like a shot of vodka. Did the room get smaller? Why is the air heavy and hot? Bleached teeth, bright eyes, alien housewife and husband—I've been to haunted houses less scary than this place.

"Mother, I am hungry." A little girl, probably eight or nine, wanders into the kitchen from an adjoining room. Unlike human children, she is fully proportional. Her dark hair hangs in curls at her waist. "When will dinner be ready?"

"Adalene Margaret Lefèvre, it is quite rude to interrupt a conversation. We have addressed your offensive habit many a time. Apologize to our guest."

Ada sighs and throws me a haphazard glance. "I apologize for my interruption."

"Very good." Margo unties her apron and motions to the kitchen's exit. "Let me show you to your room, Julie. You shall have the best available."

Floorboards creak as Margo leads me up the main staircase, down a decorated corridor. She sweeps her fingers across shelves and countertops as if checking for dust—maybe that's what she's doing. "There are to be no male suitors in this house. Loud music is prohibited past eight o'clock."

"Do not worry, Cousin Margo. I am a quiet person ... and I usually keep to myself." Because loving a boy and causing commotion would silence me forever and put an infinite end to the mission. I'll keep my head down. I'll follow the rules, at least, for the time being.

"Marvelous." She sighs when we enter a bedroom with poppy-stamped walls and plush furniture. "The laundry room is in the basement. We eat dinner together on Saturdays. If you would like to cook food, please take advantage of the community kitchen on the main floor. Hot plates are unnecessary fire hazards." She sets my suitcase on the queen-size bed and clasps her hands into a neat ball. "Charis LeBlanc lives next door. She is pleasant company. If you feel lonesome, pay her or me a visit."

Great idea. I'll pay an impromptu visit to the aliens who'd string a noose around my neck if they knew the truth. I'll sit in their frilly parlor and let them look at me long enough to detect my human genes. Sarcasm, of course. I really should stop being bitter and impudent. Dead brother, dead friends, dead world—those are decent excuses for snarky thoughts, right?

"I am grateful for your hospitality. Family is of utmost importance."

"Quite." Margo touches my arm as if I'm her sister or child, a real relative, not some stranger she found on her doorstep. "Pleasant dreams, my dear."
****

Life became a checklist the moment I passed through the dome, a collection of segments all bound together by a moving body and focused mind. The small details of time slip into a void—I don't remember what I had for breakfast, whether or not Margo said, "Good morning," if someone sat next to me on the bus. Trivial things like that don't matter when I'm alone, which is a normal state nowadays. Life is a checklist, and soon, it'll be complete.

The District claws through the pavement of metropolitan Atlanta and plumes into the sky, shimmering with glass, joining what remains of an old space station in a slow creep toward the clouds. I become a vein in its monochrome body when I enter the plaza and join the surge of suit-wearing Purebloods. They move in diagonal lines on either side of me. Their briefcases slap my hips. Their horrible, beautiful faces remain stiff and straight, as if noticing someone for a split second would be a violation of conduct. But I'm invisible. And to be a shadow is to have a shield.

I scan my hand and enter an atrium that echoes with the patter of feet. Workers crowd around transparent screens to read the day's news and weather reports. Milkmen exit the cafeteria with empty wire baskets. A receptionist sits at her kiosk in the center of the lobby, hands folded and eyes bright. Her red lips lift into an overenthusiastic smile as I approach the desk.

"Greetings. Are you in need of assistance?"

"Yes. I am here to inquire about a secretary position within the District. Where must I go for an interview?" It's good I didn't eat breakfast this morning. I'd probably send it soaring onto her blouse.

"Mr. Alastair is no longer in need of a secretary in the Congressional Budget Office." She tilts her head and dims her smile to a frown. "I apologize for the inconvenience this information may cause you."

Inconvenience? More like a death sentence. Without the position, my mission is compromised. I'll be an inoperable agent, left in the inner layer penniless and alone. There must be an available job somewhere in this building. What can I tell the receptionist to make her advocate for me?

"Brother said I am required to work. Would you please search the database for job openings? I do not wish to leave the City because I am without a position." I scratch the back of my neck where hair recedes to hot, sweaty skin. Light spots float across the room like fish in an aquarium, darting in figment schools, spiraling up to the arched ceiling. Knees buckle—I should sit down in a chair before my butt hits the floor. Eyelid twitches—no one will hire me if I look freakish.

"All departments have reached quota," the woman says. "If you leave your contact information with me, I will alert you when a job becomes available. Have a pleasant day." She spins around in her chair and resumes work without offering a pen or paper.

What a passive way of telling me to screw off.

I trudge across the lobby, into sunlight that turns my silver dress into an oven and blasts through the maze of steel and concrete, reminiscent of a projector's beams in a dark theater. I collapse onto stone steps overlooking the space station—it lies dormant amidst skyscrapers, flickers with beacons—and press my skin against cold rock to ease the heat ache.

Over. Done. Failed. Jack is the only active agent. What am I now, a weapon stored away for safekeeping, a good card on hold for the right move, frozen like almost-spoiled hamburger meat? Dang it, I won't be able to make rent next month or buy food. Maybe Colonel Buchanan will let me live with Jack, eat from his pantry. Maybe I won't be a useless deadbeat...

"Excuse me. Are you Julie Lefèvre?" A girl taps my shoulder and stumbles backward when I turn to confront her. She's taller than most Purebloods, beanpole skinny, with mousy brown hair teased into a bouffant, and high-arching eyebrows. Not perfect. But pretty in a nice, comforting sort of way.

"Yes, I am Julie. Who are you?"

"Charis LeBlanc." She smiles and sits next to me. Her severe posture relaxes into a casual slump. "I saw you leave the boarding house this morning but did not have an opportunity to introduce myself. May I inquire as to why you are here?"

"I came to interview for a secretary position. Unfortunately, the job is no longer available."

"Are you in need of work?" Charis smooths her floral-print skirt. She glances at me with something close to friendliness in her blunt, brown eyes, something that doesn't make her seem like a killer. "Do you know how to work an espresso machine? I work at the District Coffeehouse. If you wish, I will get you a job there. We are short-staffed and in need of another worker."

Thank you, God.

"Oh, my goodness, that'd be swell." I throw my arms around her bony shoulders and rock her side to side. "I work espresso machines better than computers. You should taste my steamed milk and see my latte art. I'm, like, a well-trained barista. Coffee should be my middle name."

She flinches, probably from the informal outburst and taps my back—the break in character, glimpse of my true identity, mustn't have alarmed her too much. "Does this mean we are friends?"

"Sure." I laugh. "Of course I'll be your friend." Because she's put me back in the spy game. Because in a few weeks, I'll help bring down her pretty little world.
****

Curiosity is like chickenpox. People give you a

list of all the reasons why you shouldn't scratch the pox: infection, scarring and spreading, the wrath of your germaphobe mother. But in the end...

You scratch them anyway.

"Who left the note on my door?" I tiptoe through patches of shadows, into the boarding house's backyard. This probably isn't the best idea, but I brought a gun. If a monster or murderer jumps from the hedges to grab me, he or she will get a bullet in the head instead.

"Cousin Julie, I am over here." Ada crawls from beneath a shrub, smeared with dirt. Her hair is matted into a woodsy knot. "I plead you to be quiet. If we are heard, my operation will be destroyed."

"Your operation?" I choke on a laugh and cross my arms. Cute. She's pretending to be a spy. Maybe that's why she left the note on my door, to pull me into her game of make-believe.

"Yes. I trade secrets. I see people do things and hear their conversations. No one notices me because I am small." She grips my hand and pulls me into the darkness. Her eyes glint in the dim light like animal pupils. "I have a secret to trade with you."

Fine, I'll scratch the pox. "What do you want for the information?"

"Your barrette," she says after a moment of thought.

I unclasp the pearl clip from my hair and place it in her small fist. "What is the secret?"

"There were soldiers at the house earlier today," she whispers. "I saw them when I came home from school. They were talking with Mother and Father ... about you."

Chapter Nineteen

"Seldom, very seldom, does complete truth belong to any human disclosure; seldom can it happen that something is not a little disguised or a little mistaken."

Jane Austen, *Emma*

Jack never came to visit me.

He sends the blood bag and tubes by messenger each evening so I can transfuse on my own. First night, I stuck myself fifteen times before striking a vein. It got easier to perform the procedure after that, because I knew if I failed, I'd become a mouse in a snake tank. On day three, I mailed him an encoded letter—never received a response. Maybe he's afraid our cover will be blown if we're seen together. Maybe he's busy with work. Maybe he thinks… I'm not sure what he thinks anymore.

Loneliness settles within me like a fog on day five. Sun down. Sun up. Coffee brewing. Coffee serving. Needle prick. Blood. DNA supplying me with more time, but what if I don't want more time? What if I'd rather trudge back to the dome and wait at its perimeter until the invasion is complete? Could I quit? Do I have the power within me to say "Fighting for others no longer matters?"

Nash and Tally call me on the radio at night, once the sun sinks deep into the horizon. They talk about the Vestige's progress, how they've recruited messengers to travel from town to town, selecting people from communities and briefing them in secret so that when the time is right, they'll be able to bring the citizens of their towns out of the dark and into the light. Change happens in the world I left behind while I snoop around desks and eavesdrop on conversations.

"They told us to be wary," Margo whispered to Jed when she must have thought I was out of listening distance. "Julie must leave. I did as you requested and had brunch with her, but spending time with your cousin did not prevent her presence from being any less unnerving. We are unaware as to why the Special Ones are interested in her. She could be harmful."

"Do not fret, my love. Julie is not a danger to us," Jed said in an equally quiet tone. "The Special Ones shall prevent my cousin from performing malicious acts. We are secure."

Suspicion is poison. It'll kill me. Soon.

Death takes everyone. It doesn't pick and choose. Good people die. Bad people die. Little girls die. My sister—I visited Sybil in the hospital, laid in her bed while black goo poisoned her tiny body. She'd sleep, vomit. I'd watch cartoons and draw flowers onto her bald head with Crayola markers. My brother—no matter how many times I wash my hands, his blood still warms my skin.

Death is the one thing in this universe that unites us all.

****

Screw it. Jack and Colonel Buchanan won't give orders—they've left me waiting for too long, treated me as a back-up plan, a spare tire in the vehicle that is our mission. I can get the information they need. Yes, I'm in a prime location for espionage, and no one will suspect the young barista delivering coffee. Two departments. Ten minutes per floor to prove myself as a Vestige operative. If I'm caught snooping—I won't get caught.

"Eleventh floor, Congressional Budget Office." I squeeze myself and a full coffee tray into the lift. Feds cast me smiles so fake, annoyance shimmers in their frigid pupils like sparks from an electrical socket. They cross their arms to avoid touching me.

I steady the tray on a gold rail. My knees buckle from the pull of gravity, and my organs writhe within me as the designated floor approaches. Ten minutes. Timer starts when the doors open. Move fast.

Don't stop.

The elevator fades into a room of empty cubicles, and buckled knees become legs with determined strides. I blink to adjust my eyes to the florescent light, the new landscape. Where is everyone? Lunch break?

Jon snuck me into the Citadel dormitory a few years ago, when he was still in college and Dad worked as an adjunct. I was sure I'd be discovered and escorted off campus—it's not like I could hide my age, gender, and status—but Jon told me to walk with purpose, said I could make myself invisible by acting as if I belong. That day, a sundress-wearing girl became a shadow in a place she should've been a target. Lesson still applies—I will belong, and no one will see.

I reach Mr. Alastair's vacant workspace and place a cup of espresso on his desk, next to a stack of pixel newspapers. A manila folder protrudes from the pile with *Financial Report* printed on its tab.

Jackpot.

Murmurs pollute the space near the vending machines and drift toward me in unconscious pursuit. No, lunch is supposed to last until one o'clock. Who the heck are these overachievers?

Coffee washes across the countertop—I must've knocked over the cup. Sparks explode from the newspapers like fireworks, crackling and hissing as they crest the cubicle's rim. The manila folder disappears into a squealing beacon of electrical fire. Gone. Ruined. By me, the clumsy idiot pretending to be Jason Bourne or

James Bond.

What made me think I could do better?

I clutch a handful of coffee cups, sacrifice the tray to an empty trashcan, and then, with my body scrunched to my knees, I scurry down the neighboring aisle and out a set of doors. There isn't a single security camera beyond the lobby. Purebloods will say the fire was a misfortune, an innocent accident.

No one will suspect me.

The Department of Health and Human Services is a reset button on my operation's fictional remote. I deliver coffee to various workers who fill the desks and type on translucent computers. No eye contact. Only shifty smiles, the occasional nod of acknowledgment.

Security footage flashes onto a monitor as I give a woman her cappuccino. The small text in the lower left-hand corner reads: *Human Reproduction Institute.* Reproduction, as in, babies?

Doctors appear on the screen, mixing serums in a lab. Footage from a courtyard shakes into focus moments later. People in white scrubs fill the outdoor space. Some play chess at small tables, others eat packaged sandwiches. Many of the women are pregnant. Some have infants strapped to their backs.

"Mom ... Dad." I choke on the words and grip a divider to support my weight. Bile gurgles up my throat. Heart rattles my chest. If the Feds didn't have a use for Mom and Dad, they would've killed them in Charleston. That's their purpose now, isn't it?

They're being used as reproductive specimens.

"Are you well, Miss?" A middle-aged Pureblood catches me when I stumble into the walkway. His face is Botox smooth. "Do you need medical assistance?"

"No, I am quite well. Your concern is appreciated." I slide from his frigid hands and trudge toward the exit. Smears of monochrome replace the room, but the door remains in full clarity. Escape. Before they see through my ruse and turn me into a surrogate. Before my body is used to breed half-bloods. Before I'm forced to reunite with Mom and Dad.

Pain shimmies up my legs and strengthens until I can hardly move. I drop the last few coffee cups and wheeze, gasp, suck empty air. What's the point? Half-blood children won't determine the Purebloods' survival, so why create them? Why exploit the enemy race? What more do they want from us? They've taken everything, and we've let them.

"Please rest. You appear faint." A teenaged assistant rushes from the blur with a chair. She makes me sit and then dabs the spilled coffee from my skirt. "You are in need of a cold compress."

A digital map of Severance projects on the far wall with a red clock in the upper corner—336:21:05. The time shed seconds and minutes as it counts down to some cathartic event.

"What does that clock mean?" I massage my forehead as if to erase the thought of Mom waddling down a sterile hall with a round belly, unaware that the child inside her is half-alien.

"Once the time runs out, a virus will be released on the remaining human population," she says through a toothy grin. "In two weeks, the invasion will be complete."

For the longest time after Sybil died, I'd say, "I've done harder things," when confronted with a challenge because I figured I'd never receive worse news, feel worse pain, or conquer anything as catastrophic. However, coping with a two-week timeframe and lab-rat parents—yeah, this seems harder.

"Thank you for helping me." I rise from the chair.

A sinking sensation drags down my stomach. Isn't this what I wanted? I searched for information to validate my abilities, and I found it. Colonel Buchanan will give me assignments now that I've discovered our true *end of the world.*

I ride the elevator down to the atrium and amble into the District Coffeehouse. Charis asks me something when I slide behind the counter, but her words get lost in the tangle of my thoughts. I snatch a bag of cookies from the pastry cabinet and then lock myself in the supply closet like a normal person.

Tears slice my cheeks when I curl into a ball on the floor. I sob into a cookie, press my face against the cold tile that replaces warmth with needle pricks. No one can ruin my life more than they already have as long as I stay in the darkness, away from the line of yellow light outlining the room's exit.

Mom and Dad are test subjects. A fatal virus will be released in two weeks, and humankind will fade into extinction. I can't change the *now* but maybe I can shift the *then*, and drive reality back to theory, but to do that, I have to stand up.

Cookie crumbs imprint my forearms as I drag myself to an upright position. I take the cell phone-lookalike radio from my dress pocket and tune into the Vestige's frequency. Static. An indistinct melody. That sounds an awful lot like home.

"Calling Headquarters. This is Acorn. Do you copy? Over."

"Roger that, Acorn. We read you loud and clear," Nash says. "How're you doing in there?" His voice is loud and chipper—it brings another rush of tears to my overworked ducts.

"I've been better ... but I'm still alive ... and that seems to be a rarity nowadays. Uh, is Colonel Buchanan nearby? I need to talk with him."

"Yeah, he's in the corridor. I'll fetch him for you."

Charis taps on the door—I tell her to give me a few more minutes to gather my composure, that something upset me. She doesn't ask questions because Purebloods mind their own business and don't lie to each other, at least, not in common ways.

"This is Colonel Kirk Buchanan. Do you copy, Acorn?"

"Affirmative." I crawl behind a stack of boxes and cup my hand over the microphone to minimize my voice's reach. "I've discovered information vital to the Vestige's efforts."

He clears his throat. "Are you in a secure location?"

"This is the most secure I'll be."

I wait until a surge of customers creates a ruckus outside before telling him about Mom and Dad, the two-week timeframe. As I talk, my words lose their weight within me, and they float into the radio frequency like balloons from a child's birthday party, meaningless until they pop in someone's face.

"Your job was to wait for my orders, not go rogue," the colonel says after I finish the brief.

"But you didn't give me orders. I've been on my own for the past week."

"Oh, well, that changes everything. Of course you should break protocol because you're lonely and bored." He chuckles. "Your mission is to wait and listen, submerge yourself in Pureblood society…"

"I found information we need to bring down Severance. My objective has been to gather intelligence from the District. That's what I've done—I've gathered intel. Use me. Don't give Jack all the work. I might not have military background, but I sure as hell can do my job."

"What does my son think of your perspective?"

"He won't meet with me. I've been doing the transfusions on my own."

"Not anymore. You and Jack were supposed to act as each other's handler. Go to the penthouse on Peachtree Street this afternoon. I'll radio Jack and tell him to expect you."

"He doesn't want to see me."

"I don't care." Colonel Buchanan slams his hand against something hard and emits a pained grunt. "There's a general I want you both to track tonight. His job is to manage the security of the dome's generator. Jack has been following him for the past week, trying to locate the force field's source. Unfortunately, he hasn't had much luck. You will join him. That's an order."

"Fine." I shove another cookie into my mouth but spit it out when the texture becomes like ash leftover from a hard rain. Pear and rosemary, the one Pureblood cookie concoction that can't offend me with nostalgia of after-school snacks and picnics by the harbor, now make me cringe. Sweet—Jack was once sweet. A craving—Jack used to want me as much as I wanted him, endured my hurt instead of letting me bleed alone. "Over and out, Colonel."

What can I do to prepare myself for the confrontation? He'll look at me, but the look will be empty. The girl who drank coffee with him at the battered table by the window, the girl who fell in love with him when every odd was against her—she won't exist in his eyes.

How do I cope with being invisible to the one person I thought would always see me?
****

The space between us in a canyon too wide to jump, too uneven to bridge. I press myself against the passenger window. Jack leans left, wedges his body between the steering wheel and door, but the distance doesn't seem like enough. Or maybe there's too much of it. I won't be the one to mend the gap. Not me. I threw myself onto a tightrope, reached out to him as the strand frayed, but he cut the cord and watched me fall into what could've been something beautiful.

"General Augustus is changing routes." I tuck my hair into a cloche hat and lean a few inches off my cliff to have a better few of the GPS tracker. "He just turned onto Piedmont Avenue."

Jack swerves the Duesenberg Model-J into a connecting lane, presses the accelerator, and watches the speedometer rise. He glances at me quickly, as if to hide the cobalt flash, to make sure I believe I'm more invisible to him than air. But he did look. Because he wanted to see me. And sooner or later, he'll also have to speak more than a few words.

"Why'd you decide not to do the transfusions together?" I tighten my seatbelt as we weave through the constipated flow, past Purebloods in their on-ground vehicles who appear unbothered by the traffic and our aggressive driving. "You didn't even respond to my letters. We're supposed to be friends and … you haven't treated me like a friend."

"Adjust the scope. Set the zero at one hundred yards." Jack shoves his sniper rifle into my lap. "If the general thinks we're following him, things could get messy." He slams his foot on the brake when a food truck pulls out in front of us—I slingshot forward. Pain blasts through my skull. A red flash saturates my vision and then bubbles into a swarm of floaters when I unstick my forehead from the dashboard.

"Target is three hundred yards ahead. We'll have visual once we turn the next corner." He grabs my shoulder and holds me in place as the car makes a sliding turn onto Tenth Street. His fingers linger, hesitate. They lift from my skin, lower, and then return to the wheel. "General Augustus's Bugatti Royale Victoria is three cars in front of us. He usually travels with an armed protection unit."

"Well, I'm a decent shot. Perk of growing up in a military family." I adjust the rifle's scope and snap a refilled magazine into my handgun. "No touching each other, remember?"

"You're the one without a spine. I thought it'd be nice to protect that brain of yours." Jack reaches into the middle console and removes a scarf, a vintage baseball cap, and a pair of sunglasses. "Here. My car's windows are tinted, but if we get close enough, they might see us."

"You still haven't answered my question." I tie the scarf around my face and inhale heat.

He rolls his eyes. "We are agents. This isn't a friendship slumber party where we … play Truth or Dare and paint each other's nails. I'm not your friend here, Julie."

"True. We're not friends. I don't think we can be friends."

Jack flinches. His glance is longer this time, more severe. "Why?"

"I'm sure you know the answer."

He nods because saying the memories of who we were before everything crumbled won't affect a digressed relationship would be like claiming Earth is the center of the universe even though science has proven otherwise. "Crap."

"What's wrong?"

"The driver made eye contact with me. He knows

we're following them. They won't lead us to the generator now." Jack curses. "I'll have to dump this car and find a new one."

"Are the plates registered to you?"

"No." He sighs and decreases speed. "The Purebloods' military intelligence is top-notch. I've been analyzing their department intel for the past week. Their protocol is flawless. If they sense their assignment is in danger, they switch routes, plans, everything. They're like government-issued computer software, constantly regenerating passwords and firewalls to prevent hackers."

Skyscrapers line the street and cage the atmosphere in a narrow, blue block. A tunnel—that's what this place has become—without a light at its end. Maybe there isn't an end to this madness at all, only deeper holes and weeks spent trying to forget about the darkness.

The general's motorcar spirals in the road's center, whipping itself in an illegal U-turn. Cars swerve. Tires squeal—I might've squealed, too. Windows roll into their cuticles, and Scavs appear in the empty spaces with guns aimed in our direction. A puff of smoke lifts from the asphalt as the Bugatti Royale Victoria charges at us with bullets flying from its interior.

"Holy crap. Go back. Go back." I duck my head when bullets shatter the windshield and flood the air with shards. Glass. Bullets. Cars moving fast enough to disintegrate a small animal in a cloud of pink mist. Yeah, there's no way I'll walk away from this alive.

"Stay down." Jack shifts the car into reverse and speeds backward through the maze of forward-moving traffic. I scream as the vehicle spins a complete one-eighty and lurches into motion. Jack drives against the stream of vehicles. A taxi tears off a rearview mirror. A transit bus rams against the hood and causes the automobile to fishtail. He jerks the wheel, catapulting us over the median and into the neighboring lane.

Pain shoots up my neck—dang it, I must have whiplash. "Are those mobsters still following us?" I grip the middle console and peer through the rear window. "Yep."

"Now's the time to use that sniper rifle, Julie." He smears the sweat from his brow and gazes at me with eyes wide, pupils dilated. "Take them out."

I swallow a mouthful of stomach acid and roll down the passenger window. Wind whips through the automobile, tosses my hair into a frenzy. Okay. Kill to survive. Simple concept. Easy to apply.

"Aim for their heads."

"Yeah, yeah I know." I unbuckle my seatbelt and swing the lightweight rifle into my arms and then lean out of the car with the adjusted scope pressed to my right eye. Horns blare—they strengthen in sound and fade as cars shoot past. Bullets whizz around me like mosquitoes or gnats.

"Fire," Jack shouts.

"I want a clean shot."

"You won't get a clean shot. Fire the damn gun, Julie."

I place my finger on the trigger—Charlie slumped into a puddle of his own brain matter. I blast the general's windshield and execute his driver—people survived because of me, because I killed someone who would've killed me first. The vehicle swerves for a moment but stabilizes when another Pureblood climbs into the front seat—self-defense is different from murder, isn't it?

A milk truck skims past, scrapes the car with its rearview mirror. Jack yanks me into the passenger seat seconds before my face becomes a smear on the trailer.

"Where's my gun? Did you drop it?" he yells

once I've uncurled from a fetal ball.

"Maybe. That truck must've knocked it from my hands." I buckle up and scan the congested highway for signs of the rifle. "Don't whine. Just … drive faster."

"This thing can't go much faster." He shoves his foot onto the gas pedal and propels our vehicle down a narrow side road lined with older buildings and factories. "So…"

"What?"

"There's, like, a bump up ahead."

"A bump?"

"Uh, yeah." He shrugs and wipes his mouth. "You might want to grip the door handle." His voice is squeaky—why is his voice squeaky?

The road comes to an abrupt halt only yards ahead of us. It drops ten feet into a concrete ravine.

"No, Jack." I brace my knees against the dashboard, grip the door with one hand, and entwine my other arm around the seat's headrest. "You aren't."

"Yep. Sure am." He pumps the gas one last time and drives us off the cliff.

Pause. Slow it down. Frame by frame. Let me witness my final seconds, that is, if I'm about to die. I'd like to remember that gravity didn't hold Jack and me before we crashed into cement, we lifted off our chairs, and his slate-gray tie flopped in front of him like a bib. I'd like to remember these moments, because after months of hurting myself to save others, I should die with something, anything.

We plummet into the ravine. Airbags explode. Blackness strikes like a viper. I close my eyes to ringing and pain, and open them to a clear sky and trash-piled alley.

"You're okay." Jack unravels the scarf from my face. Blood trickles from his nose. Puke stains his white shirt. "We're safe. The general and his thugs didn't follow us."

"How far did you drag me?" I moan. My entire body aches, stings, and throbs.

"Not far." He plops onto the asphalt. His arms tremble—I want to steady them. "We shouldn't stay here for much longer. The Feds will search the area soon."

"Then tell me before we leave and disappear from each other's lives." I drag myself to where he sits. "Why didn't you come visit? What made you decide to cut me from your mission?"

"You really don't know?" Jack massages his neck and looks at me in a way that says *I see you*. He frowns, but his dimples smile. "Julie, it would've been too hard."

"Hard? Druid Hills isn't far from your apartment. I could've met you…"

"Gosh, no." He leans close to me and sighs, not out of frustration but something else. "Dad gave me an order and … I knew if I touched you … I wouldn't be able to stop."

Chapter Twenty

"If you tell a big enough lie and tell it frequently enough, it will be believed."
Adolf Hitler

Jack tilts back his seat. I brace myself against the headrest and coil my arms around him, melt against his chest. He eases his lips against the side of my neck and then kisses me. Not a cordial peck before saying goodbye, not some middle school first-base action. This is an oh-my-goodness-I-never-thought-it'd-be-this-good kind of kiss.

"Margo serves dinner in a few minutes. I should probably…"

"No. Stay." He combs his hands around my waist, up my back, and through my hair. His mouth stretches into a grin. "I still love you, you know?"

"I love you, too." Heat swells within me until I can no longer breathe. I cup his smooth face in my hands and kiss him again. He's here, beneath me, between my fingers. "But I should go before she gets suspicious. We've been parked out here for a while."

"They don't ask questions." He leans forward, pressing my back against the wheel. His eyes connect with mine and create a tension within me, like someone squeezing my heart. "Dad was right."

"About what?"

"Touching you is dangerous." He laughs and kisses my chin. "Go now before I take you captive."

"Oh, you're planning to kidnap me? I'm pretty sure there's a law against that."

"Eh, I've broken worse laws." Jack unlocks the

doors. He lifts a sweater from the passenger seat and wraps it around my shoulders. "I'll come do the transfusion with you tomorrow."

"Sounds good." I blink away a rush of tears and give him a tight hug to absorb the dimensions of his chest and the warmth escaping through the weave of his shirt. He has no idea—I thought about him every time I took a shower because being naked and stuck under a flow of water didn't offer many distractions, I wondered over and over if I'd exaggerated our relationship into some brilliant love story when all along it was nothing more than a weird bond between two lonely people.

There were some days I begged God to reveal what Jack thought about me, write it on the walls, make the truth so obvious, I'd have to accept it.

"See you tomorrow." I kiss his bottom lip and scramble out of the car. Air on the verge of freezing hits me like a wall as I scurry up the boarding house's cobblestone path—it makes my skin burn with a need for Jack's skin, his heat, closeness.

Charis blocks my path when I enter the foyer. She folds her arms and furrows her pristine brow. "You are late to dinner, Julie. Margo is displeased."

Good. Let her be displeased. Food means nothing compared to the hot make-out session I just had with my boyfriend, at least, I'm pretty sure he's my boyfriend again.

"She has my sincerest apologies." I slide off Jack's sweater and move to the staircase. The soft weave smells of him—Old Spice deodorant, evergreens, espresso. I hold it against my cheek like a rebel or daredevil. No touching. But we touched. Like we did that night in the Overhang. When I got splinters in my back. "I shall join you all for the meal once I place my effects upstairs."

"We left the District at the same time. I have been here for quite a while." Charis follows me up the stairs. Her heels tap the hardwood in a pursuing patter. "Where have you been?"

"With my brother."

"You are lying," she says in a tone loud enough to freeze me in place.

"Perhaps you are mistaken." I clutch my knotted stomach and pinch my quivering lips. How could I have been so stupid? I broke the rules. Disobeyed an order. Surrendered my safety to the enemy. Suspicion is a death sentence. Lies come back to bite.

"No. I saw you in the car." She saunters toward me like an executioner ready to swing an axe. Her face is blank, a scorched oasis. "The way you were kissing him … it was most improper."

Tears and sweat sting my eyes. I slump against a doorframe. Options—what are my options? I could try to escape before she contacts the Feds. I could kill her—no, I won't kill her.

She smiles and grips my shoulders in what might be considered a hug. "Why did you not inform me of your suitor? We are friends, are we not?"

"Uh, yeah." I sigh and laugh as if she's discovered a secret affair, not two spies violating their cover identities in the front seat of a car. "My relationship with the gentleman is volatile at the moment. I planned to inform you once the courtship is secure." Good lie. Believable.

"How wonderful." Charis follows me into my bedroom and plops into an overstuffed chair. She smooths her skirt out of habit. "I have yet to see two Purebloods so … engaged with one another. Conduct between lovers must be quite different in the suburbs than here in the City."

"What do you mean?"

"Emotions are not a part of our lifestyle. To be frank, I have not witnessed two people demonstrate feelings beyond the frame of amiable relations."

"Do Purebloods not fall in love?"

She blushes. "I doubt there is such a thing."

"What do you feel, then?" I shouldn't have asked the question because it divides me from her, sets us apart when we're supposed to be one in the same, but the curious part of me needs an answer, to understand what drives the Purebloods' invasion. If they do not love, they cannot hate. And without hatred, they couldn't have destroyed billions of lives.

She flips open a book of poetry and squirms in the chair. Her eyes spark with something close to sorrow or angst. "I am not certain. I do not have a word in mind."

"But you have emotions?"

"Yes … I think I do … because of the injections. Do you not receive the vaccines?"

"No." I sit on the windowsill and rub Jack's sweater between my hands. A knot twists my stomach, makes me crumble forward in pain. "These injections … do they give you feelings?"

Charis cups her crimson cheeks and flashes a smile. "I feel what they wish me to feel, Julie."

Voices rise from the floorboards. Male voices. Shouts. The stomp of feet on the staircase. No, this can't be happening. I have at least two weeks of life left, not two minutes.

I squeeze my eyelids shut and choke on air. The room becomes a smear of color, cream and poppy red swirled into a hallucinogenic kaleidoscope. "Charis, did you tell anyone about my boyfriend?"

She shakes her head and glances at the closed door. "Did Margo invite guests to dinner?"

"They won't stay for long." I grab my radio and gun from beneath the mattress and then stumble to the frosted pane. It lifts without protest and floods the room with a frigid breeze.

"Julie, what is happening? Why do you have a weapon?"

My heart drums within me so fast, my brain aches. I slide on Jack's sweater before draping my tingling legs into midair. Run—there isn't another option. Time—the Scavs will be here soon. I can't let them take me. I know too much about the Vestige. If I'm captured, the resistance will be silenced.

Ada barges into the room, panting. "There are soldiers downstairs, Julie. They are here for you." She runs across the space to hug me. "They wish to transport you to prison."

I kiss her head and motion to the dark gap beneath the bed. "You and Charis must hide. The soldiers will hurt you if they find out you let me escape."

"What have you done?" Charis yells. "Why do they wish to imprison you?"

"I'm human." The truth is sweet, like cotton candy or lavender lattes. I've missed the taste of it. "If they catch me, they will kill me. Prison … is a lie."

The girls stare at me as if I'm a ghost, the monster in their closet that's been revealed to be a pile of clothes. Maybe the same concept applies to all of us—we are told who and what to fear.

"We shall pray you survive the night," Charis whispers. "Go now. Time is not on your side." She leads Ada to the wardrobe and together, they hide behind it.

A shiver trickles through me when I wedge my feet into the ivy-covered lattice. I claw at the tangles of foliage, press myself against the building's side. Okay. All I have to do is climb to the ground. Easy. Jon used to take me rock climbing on the days Mom and Dad locked themselves in their bedroom. This isn't much different, right?

Wood splinters above—the Scavs must have kicked open my bedroom door. Rifle lasers flash through the window like spotlights in search of someone to fry. Wood splinters beneath me, too—I fall and slam against the earth with a loud, bone-shattering *crack*.

Pain as intense and harrowing as the agony I experienced during the emergency van surgery pierces through my torso, ripples across every fiber of my body. I wheeze, dig my fingernails into the dirt. Then, I can't breathe at all, only release jagged exhales.

Military aircrafts soar across the black sky. Their turbines growl and their spotlights strike the lawn in search of me. I have to breathe. I have to run, even if I die in the process.

Gasps and sobs leave me as I climb from the grass and wobble into the shadows. Cramps rip apart my insides. The ache of broken bones sends tears cascading down my cheeks, but I run. Through backyards, over highways, in and out of sight—I sprint until my legs collapse.

Concrete slaps the final bit of strength from my frame. I curl into a ball and squeal into my bloody skin. The Vestige will help me, won't they? Colonel Buchanan won't leave me in this bubble for the Feds to find, torture, and kill. I'm a loose end that needs to be tied.

Wires stab my fingers when I reach into the sweater's pocket, and a suffocating weight settles within me. I scrape the radio onto the pavement in fragments.
****

At two thirty-five in the afternoon, light would hit the sunroom's glass in such a way, it'd fill my house with oval rainbows. Sybil said they were pieces of a promise, gifts from God. She'd run up and down the hall, trying to fit the small spectacles into her fists. Her laughter rang like a boat's sail clanging against the mast. She's here. Now. Running through the City in search of me. I know it's all a delusion—her laughter, the rainbow fragments that appear on buildings and lift from streets—but part of me would like it to be real.

"Come on. Keep moving." I stagger across a deserted parking lot and screech when my pain magnifies into something close to death. Vomit dribbles from my lips. Sweat soaks me as I convulse with an unstable violence. "Don't stop. Fight. You're almost there."

Rainbows flicker onto a blank billboard.

They're not real.

I trudge into the gut of downtown but remain in the shadows where light cannot reveal me. Purebloods sashay on the illuminated sidewalk. Their sleek figures pass without so much as glancing in my direction.

Emergency protocol is to contact Colonel Buchanan, find a secure location, and wait for orders. To reach him, I'd have to use a pay phone, and I can't risk revealing myself to the Feds. I might be safe at Jack's apartment for a while. The lease was signed under another name. We'll be off-grid for a few hours, maybe a day or two, enough time to mend my body.

"Julie?" His voice melts my level ten pain into a seven. "What happened?"

I blink Jack into focus. He fills the doorway of his penthouse, disheveled from sleep. His hands draw me into a narrow foyer. Soft hands that can fix me.

"Oh, gosh, you're bleeding." He peels off the sweater and gasps. His brow furrows. His mouth twists into a frown. "Your shoulders … they're pitch black. Did you walk here?"

Yes. I'm not sure. How did I get to the apartment

building? Elevator? Bus? Rainbow fragments? Jon might have helped me, but I'm not sure.

"I'll patch you up," Jack whispers when I collapse against his chest. "You're safe here." He gathers my limbs into a neat wad and carries me into a postmodern living room. "Who hurt you? Was your cover blown?"

"Scavs came." I wince as he lowers me onto a vinyl couch. The upholstery crackles like bones—maybe the sounds are from my own torso. "Fell out a window."

"Have you coughed up blood?"

"No." I trace a finger along his stubble-shaded jaw, up to the dark circles encompassing his eyes. "We're not safe anymore. Radio the Vestige. Tell them…"

"Shush. Let me take care of you." Jack crouches and rubs his hands together for a solid minute. He rolls up the sleeves of his t-shirt and then unzips my dress. Curses slip from his mouth as he probes my stomach and spine. "How'd you manage to get here? You're a mess."

"Wow. Thank you." I suck air between my teeth and press my heels into a cushion. No matter how I position myself, pain continues to ripple through me. "Everything hurts."

"Don't move. I'll go get the first-aid kit."

Sweat beads on my skin even though the room's temperature is low and the stained dress is gathered at my hips. Rainbows dart across the ceiling—they echo with Sybil's laugh. Has physical torment fried my brain? Am I dying?

"Help. Come back." I pant for oxygen, sob, and shiver. "Something's wrong."

Jack emerges from the kitchen with a blue box tucked beneath his left arm. He sits next to me and squeezes my hand. "Your parasympathetic nervous system is reversing your fight-or-flight response. Think of it as like … detoxing from a drug." He fills a syringe with a clear liquid, taps the tip, and squirts a short stream into an empty mug. "Hold still."

I flinch when he injects the morphine into my forearm. It's like hot coffee rushing through me. The rainbows grow brighter until they saturate the room, and then, they vanish with my pain and sweat. I lift my legs as if they're toothpicks. Nothing has weight. Not my body. Not the world.

"You have several fractured ribs and severe bruising on your spine and abdomen. It'll take a good amount of time for you to heal so … I recommend toting around a bottle of pain killers." Jack pulls the dress over my torso and zips it into place. His grimace morphs into a full-fledged grin while he stares at me. "You look like roadkill."

"Are doctors taught to laugh at their patients, or did you just miss the lecture on bedside manner?"

"Rule of thumb—be nice if a solider is dying, act like a jerk to the maggots who'll recover."

"Why?"

"Because if you say enough mean things to someone, they'll try their best to get well enough to kick your butt." He laughs and strokes the hair from my face. His touch is like stars and feathers, air streaming from a hole in a balloon. "Has the morphine helped?"

Snow forms a halo around Jack's head and then dissipates into a flurry of sparks. The room's shadows turn to white blurs reminiscent of cigarette smoke. I squeeze my eyes shut to block out the hallucinations and roll into his lap where warmth isn't a side effect.

"The brightness will fade in a few minutes." He eases his lips against my cheek. His espresso breath drifts nearby, somewhere in our secure third-space—it sends mental photographs showering from above, pictures of our coffee-stained table, his tattered novel and luminescent smile. "We'll have to leave in the morning. Dad won't let us stay in the City now that our presence has been identified."

I nod and hug his waist to moor my head and shoulders in place while the rest of my body suspends in an invisible water of sorts, drifts with a current. Shouldn't I be bothered that the spy game has come to an end? Mom and Dad will be left in the Human Reproduction Institute—why can't I be mad or upset, terrified our odds have run out?

A wave slams against my butt, rolls me back and forth. I claw at Jack's t-shirt and laugh when he smiles. Lots of teeth. Whiter than white. And dimples—what's the point of dimples? How do some people have them? Why are they perfect accessories to a face?

"You're pretty."

"I'm pretty?" He raises his eyebrows—they're like fuzzy caterpillars.

"The prettiest." I press my hands against his cheeks. They absorb my fingers like gelatin and jiggle when I touch them. Weird. Gross.

"Well, if you keep slapping me, I won't be pretty anymore." Jack grips my wrists and pins them to the couch. He snickers. "You like the morphine, huh?"

"Why is your face scratchy?"

"I haven't shaved yet. Does it bother you?" He rubs his chin and mouth. Lips. Nice lips.

"Kiss me … and we'll find out."

"Gosh, you're high. I should've given you a smaller dose."

"Want to know a secret?"

"No."

"I'm going to tell you."

"Please don't."

"Jack…" I climb up his torso and lean against his

shoulder. He has to know my secret. He likes the truth. Lies are bad. "I'd marry you if you asked."

"Oh, dear." He chokes on a laugh. "You need to sleep."

"Do you forgive me?"

"We can talk in the morning." He lifts us into the sky, far above the living room where constellations dance in unison. But I don't have a parachute. If he drops me, I'll die.

"Please, Jack."

He sighs. His smile shrinks into a straight, understanding line. "Julie Stryker, I've been in line for you since day one ... so why the hell would I let you go?"

Chapter Twenty-One

"Never attempt to win by force what can be won by deception."
Niccolò Machiavelli, *The Prince*

Mom must be washing clothes downstairs—that dang machine has vibrated my bedroom since Jon squeezed himself into it during a game of hide-and-go-seek. What time is it? Why is she doing laundry in the middle of the night?

I roll over and scratch the sleep from my eyes. Drool puddles on what could be a pillow, wets my cheek. This can't be home—the air is too cold, the rumble matches a plane's turbines better than a jacked-up washing machine. Where am I? What happened after I arrived at Jack's apartment?

Darkness accommodates the light stripes penetrating the shaded windows. Not sunlight. Or the glow of electricity. Something else that burns red. A vicious crimson.

"Jack?" I claw at silk sheets, stretch myself across a bed wider than a dining room. The nightstand's alarm clock blinks 2:30 AM—how long have I been asleep? Why am I not in pain?

The low growl climaxes into a hiss, and the bloody light condenses into two circles like eyes anxious for a peep into the penthouse's bedroom. I prop my back against the metal headboard and press a button on the built-in tech panel, lifting the shades into their cuticle.

A chunk of jagged metal fills the window frame. It hovers outside, close enough to touch.

Faceless silhouettes watch me from the cockpit.

Guns eject from the fighter jet and twist into gear.

"Oh, crap." I throw myself off the mattress as the vibrations reach an all-time high and then fall flat on hardwood when my feet slam against flesh and bone. The tear-jerking ache of injuries spears through me—I choke when it reaches my chest and throat.

Jack cries out and clutches his stomach. He writhes on his floor pallet, knocks over a trashcan filled with old ramen noodle containers and notebook paper. "Julie, what's the matter with you?"

"Move," I screech. "They've found us."

Bullets blast the windows inward and spray the bedroom with glass and lead. I curl into a ball as shots tear the mattress into a wad of stuffing and explode plaster from the walls in ashy puffs. The Underground ended in a scene like this, with machine gunfire and red light. So many people died. Sutton became faceless like the jet's pilots. Puffs of human ash fell through the trees at dawn.

"Hold your ears." Jack crawls to the wardrobe. He removes a grenade from the bottom drawer and yanks out its pin. "Get under the bed." His body shakes like mine, and his lips quiver between pants.

I squeeze into the shielded gap while bullets ravage the space. Sound fades into a single pitch hum without variance. No more explosions. Just a constant ring. I press myself against a sliver of wall and pluck the glass from my knees and elbows. Pain. Good. It means I'm alive.

The floor quakes. Fire ripples across the carpet before disappearing into smoke wisps. Is it over? Did the grenade put a stop to the violence? Where's Jack?

"You better not be dead." I cough soot from my airways and mow a path through the rubble, from beneath the tattered bedframe. "Jack?"

"I'm in one piece." He stands where the window used to be with nothing but a metropolitan chasm behind him. Shrapnel protrudes from his left shoulder, soaks his shirt with blood. "We need to leave. That was only the first wave. They'll come back."

"This is my fault. I should've known they'd track…"

"You saved us. We'd be dead right now if you hadn't trampled me." His mouth twitches into a smile. He removes a duffel bag from the bookcase and uses a dirty towel to slow his bleeding. "Let's go. We can't waste time."

"Where will we go? The Vestige can't help us here." I follow him into the living room even though moving defies my instinct. I'd rather stay beneath the bed because luck runs out—no hot hand can roll successful pairs of dice forever.

"Trust me. I have a plan." Jack slides on striped socks and sneakers. He removes a handgun from beneath a couch cushion and tucks it into the lining of his sweatpants.

A blazing, orange cloud lifted into the sky like a nuclear plume and billowed over the canopy of leaves. The bomb, the energy surge carried a sound unlike anything I'd heard before, a distinct sonic boom. It's come back to haunt me. Now. When the main door flies off its hinges. The sound returns.

Smoke bombs clatter across the threshold and diffuse fog throughout the room. Scavs rush into the penthouse with their rifles and lasers aimed in our direction. Loud voices. Bright lights. Bullets—why can't the shots be silent, less terrorizing? Didn't weapon designers consider the effects those sharp claps would have on people's psyches?

"Go to the balcony," Jack shouts. "Snap out of it,

Julie. Move." He charges into the wave of soldiers, fires his gun at the gap of armor between shoulders and necks. That sound—why won't it stop? Blood—who'll have to clean up this mess? Not me. I won't touch blood. Never again.

I pitch a nearby mug at a Scav's head and then sprint out the backdoor, onto a poolside terrace overlooking an ablaze skyline. My lungs burn, so do my knees and elbows. I gasp for air, stumble past the glistening water as pain chews into my gut. No escape from up here. The only way Jack and I can protect the Vestige's mission is to jump.

"Get on the ledge!" Jack flies from the fog and forces me to climb over the concrete rail, onto a thin platform. "Fight the morphine. Focus."

Wind lifts my skirt, slaps hair into my face. I wheeze and grip the rail until my knuckles turn white. "Okay. I understand. We have to jump…"

"Gosh, no." He pulls on a pair of gloves and grips a metal beam trailing twenty-five stories to the earth. "Hold onto me," he says, "and don't let go."

The City folds around us like wrapping paper, curls toward the sky and ravels into a knot of buildings, cars, and concrete. I glue myself to the wall. My heart pounds and the world spins into a blur—the atmosphere burns my insides with a dizzying toxin. We can't slide twenty-five stories. Impossible.

Oh, I'm going to be sick.

Jack pries me from the rail. I give him a koala hug, entwine my arms around his neck, legs around his waist. Okay. Good. Not dead, yet. But the ravine is deep. Up and down don't exist anymore. There is a single direction—we will either escape or become bloody pancakes.

"Be still. We have to do this slow and steady." He

leans into midair—I pinch my lips to cage a squeal—and drops from the balcony.

Shots fire overhead, somewhere in the wrapped parcel of space and metal. I smush my face against Jack's shoulder. I pant into the cavern between my neck and his back as wind pushes us upward and gravity drags us in rebel decent. Down. Fast. Past window smears. Through howling gusts.

"You're choking me," he shouts.

"I don't want to fall." I squeeze tighter and squirm as my knees slip to his hips. Thank you, God, for jeans and their bulky belt loops. "Hold on. Let me reposition myself."

"When'd you get so heavy?" He groans. His neck veins bulge. "Like, I know I'm not much taller than you but … you shouldn't be this heavy."

"Geez, I realize you're stressed, but you don't have to be a jerk."

"Sorry." He scrapes his feet against the building and slows to a stop in front of a narrow ledge. His body shakes with fatigue. "Get off." When I climb onto the platform, he hands me his gloves. "The drop is too extensive. We won't make it to the ground unless we bear our own weight."

Bear our own weight, as in, slide alone? No, no I'm not coordinated or strong enough to control my decent. Heck, I couldn't even ride the fireman's pole on my elementary school's playground. But I don't have another option. If I slide, I have a better chance of survival than if I jumped or waited here for the Feds to find me.

"Hurry. We don't want the Scavs to meet us at the bottom." Jack latches himself to the beam and drops six feet. "Put on the gloves. Chop-chop."

"You'll hurt your hands."

"Don't worry about me."

I put on the gloves, grasp the joist, and take a deep breath. The wall is friendlier than the ground—yeah, I'll stare at the wall for a while. "All right. Slow and steady."

Jon and I had a fight a few years ago, on the day I decided to finish high school at home. He stormed into my bedroom while I was unloading my backpack, ripped a textbook from my hands and threw it so hard it dented the wall across from my desk. He yelled for an hour straight—I can't remember everything he said, only a few phrases. He told me I have to be strong enough to stand up on my own, that I can't use other people as crutches or depend on their strength to make me strong. If I spend the rest of my days running from pain and risk, I'll lose what I'm trying to protect.

So with tears dripping from my face, I lower from the ledge.

I depend solely on my own strength to keep me alive.

"Faster," Jack yells from several stories below. "You can do this, Julie."

Sweat drenches me within seconds. My muscles burn as I descend into the chasm. I spit bile, blink sweat and tears. The more I slide, the more I have to fight the numbness in my hands, my quivering arms. They'll quit working soon. I have to slide faster.

Blood and chunks of flesh smear the girder, streak the steel in vertical lines. Jack's palms must be ripped to shreds. How is he still holding on? Will his fingers be intact by the time he reaches the ground?

Ten floors to go. I'm close.

Cars fly past in swarms of light and color. Engines roar. Wind beats against my back like a sledgehammer. I press the beam to my chest even though it rips my dress, tears skin. Pain surges from bruises and fractured ribs—the morphine must have worn off. I need more. So much more.

"Eight … seven … six," I scream, "five … four … three … two…"

Gravity sucks me into a cosmic vacuum where the landscape moves at an incalculable speed. The wall becomes a blank sheet of matter. Industrial lights merge into a spooling constellation.

"Let go," Jack shouts. "I'll catch you."

Chaos concedes to darkness—maybe I passed out. Arms replace air in a neck-jerking blow. Then, I'm on my feet, supported by Jack's battered frame and fleshless hands.

"I have you," he whispers. His lips ease against my cheekbone. "I have you."

Purebloods engulf us in a mob of red lipstick and pinstriped suits. They swarm from the fighter jet wreckage, scream questions until they're blue in the face. Don't they see Jack's injuries—blood paints a target on his shoulder, flesh hangs from his wrists like corn husks? Why won't they offer help?

Jack cups his hands over my ears to dull their voices' brunt. I relax against his chest, and the pain gnawing at my every physical fiber fades. No more shaking or watching reruns of memories I'd like to drown in the sea. He gives clarity—if only I could fix him like he so often fixes me.

Guns fire when Scavs emerge from the residential building. They charge into the masses, break apart the protective barricade of bodies with bullets and punches. They won't stop, will they? Not until Jack and I are dead. Maybe it'd be better if we had jumped off the skyscraper instead of postponing the inevitable because…

I don't know how much more of this I can take.

****

Charleston is a bastion, a dig-in-your-heels-and-hang-on kind of city. It has stood, fallen, and been rebuilt after hurricanes. It has modified itself but remained largely unchanged. It is delicate, rugged, and strong. A survivor, that stands even when it's lost everything.

That completes its mission no matter the cost.

"When we arrive at Homeland Security, we'll have to move fast. I should have access to the plane, well, unless my clearance was revoked." Jack increases altitude and merges the stolen car with aerial traffic. "We'll have to park on the lower deck and travel the rest of the way on foot. The landing pad is surrounded by an energy grid that prevents privately owned aircrafts from…"

"Timeout." I slump against the dashboard, hide from city lights and traffic. My eyelids dip—no, I have to keep them open because if I drift asleep, I'll lose the adrenaline keeping me intact.

"You're supposed to say something when you call a timeout. That's how it works. It's not a mute button." Jack drums his fingers on the steering wheel and twitches like a terrier during a thunderstorm.

"We'll get through this, you know?" He fakes a smile and then places a hand on my thigh.

We won't make it out of the City alive.

Our hovercraft circles over Homeland Security and approaches the lower flight deck, a limited stretch of runway lined with aeronautical lights. I grip Jack's wrist as the vehicle lands.

"When the engine cuts off, exit the car and run." He looks at me with dilated pupils. Breath leaves his mouth in short huffs—he knows what I won't say, the facts of our situation. We move forward because we can't move back. We stomp into death without another choice. "The motion detectors will send a signal to security.

We'll have a maximum of six minutes before the Scavs reach the roof."

Six minutes until we join the list of casualties.

Six minutes to fight like hell.

Then, when our hourglass runs out of sand, the sea will calm to let us inside its wild embrace. We'll paddle through foam, dive beneath the turquoise surface, and reach out our hands to Jon and Sybil. All of this will end. The Purebloods will complete their invasion. Nothing'll matter anymore.

"Countdown starts now." Jack cuts off the engine, and together, we lurch out the doors, onto the illuminated tarmac. He leads me in a sprint across the runway and up a metal staircase.

"How much time do we have left?" I wheeze and rub the sting of wind from my face. A burning sensation slices through my calves—it'll go away soon, once a Scav fires a bullet into my skull.

"Doesn't matter." Jack wraps an arm around me when the plane comes into view—a serrated fighter jet. He squeezes tight as if to say goodbye and then opens the cockpit's pilot hatch. "Get inside."

"You want me to fly the plane?" I crawl into the chair and fasten my restraints.

"It functions on autopilot. You won't have to do a thing. Trust me." He plops into the passenger seat, flips several switches, and keys something into the navigation system. "Once we've passed through the dome, type the Command Center's coordinates into the controls. You remember them, right?"

"Of course." Because Colonel Buchanan made me write them five thousand times in a notebook and pinpoint them on a map. "How much time do we have left?"

Jack glances at his wristwatch. "Three minutes."

He smiles when the machine rumbles to life and its turbines spin to takeoff speed. "Don't pull any levers. You might disengage the vertical stabilizer or activate the gun system."

There is an escape, and we've found it. Tomorrow, we will wake up in a makeshift military base, have cups of stale coffee and eat powder eggs with refugees who haven't showered in weeks. Colonel Buchanan will boss Jack and me around while Tally tells him to screw off. Life will be normal.

We'll be home.

"I love you." Jack flips one last switch and then climbs out of the plane. He stands outside as both hatches lower and lock. Wait, why isn't he leaving with me? What's happening?

"No, Jack!" I bang the door until my knuckles bleed. Tears pour from me, and my chest aches with a new pain. This isn't right. We're supposed to stay together.

"The Vestige needs a contact in the City. I have to stay," he shouts as the plane's turbines spin faster and batter him with a torrent of air. "You can do this, Julie."

"Get inside," I scream. "You're not leaving me, Jack. You're not." Pain twists my stomach, makes me groan. I slam my fists against the digital control panel—maybe the hatches will unlock.

"I'll find a radio and make contact." Jack places his hand on the window closest to me. His transmuted voice sinks through the thick glass. "I have to stay. You have to go. No one is going to see the truth unless we make them. No one is going to fight for our world unless we inspire them. You and me … we are the Vestige."

"They'll kill you." I lean my forehead against the hatch and breathe condensation onto the barrier. "You can't die. Jon died. Everyone died. Not you. Please don't let them take you, too."

"We'll get through this, I swear." Jack wipes his tears and moves away from the jet. Idiot. Jerk. I won't watch strangers lower his body into a grave. I won't be the girl crying oven his open casket. If he dies, most of me will die with him—why should I attend my own funeral?

"Damn it." I sob as the plane's engine hisses to a climax and the tires roll forward. There has to be a way to stop this thing. Somehow.

Energy ruptures through the jet. Speed pins me to the chair. Vibrations turn to weightlessness. Then, I'm in the sky. Clouds spool across the windshield and reveal the landscape below in flashes—skyscrapers, hovercrafts, bustle that moves through the streets like molten lava in the depths of a volcano.

A power outage drains the City of its glow. The electric lights turn off in quadrants, piece by piece until only a conjoining strand of illumination is left flickering.

Drawn across the metropolitan hub in resonating, scintillating writing is the letter 'V'.

The Vestige has made their presence known to the Feds.

They've declared war.

Chapter Twenty-Two

"Most people don't believe something can happen until it already has. That's not stupidity or weakness, that's just human nature."

Max Brooks, *World War Z: An Oral History of the Zombie War*

Vibrations morph into a roar, then a piercing squeal. Suction smashes me against the chair. I gasp for air and grip armrests as the jet angles upward, shoots into a dark swirl. The rumbles will liquefy my insides if they don't subside—I have to disengage the autopilot, but I can't move my limbs. What's happening? Aircrafts don't inhabit the atmosphere.

"Dear God," I mumble on repeat, "help me."

Pain stabs through my head like a needle, and pressure slams against my sternum. I open my mouth in a silent scream. I squeeze my eyes shut as fire licks the windshield and curls up the nose. And then, all at once, the stress ends in an abrupt lift of pressure. Silence replaces the industrial howl.

I open my eyes.

A black void filled with billions of stars surrounds the jet. Constellations swirl and move around me, preceded by the faint chime of spectral light filtering through the great beyond, connecting the celestial sketches in an intricate pattern of rays and effervescence.

Tears float to the ceiling. Up, not down. Glassy beads instead of wet splats. I choke on the sheer horror that comes from being thrown into nothingness, and I sob when exhaustion ripples through me as a tingling ache. I cannot move three feet in any direction without having the eyes sucked from my skull, air vacuumed from my lungs. There isn't another soul within a hundred mile radius. Alone—that's what I am now, totally and morbidly alone.

The plane rotates until Earth comes into view. Sunlight ignites the sphere with color. I've seen so little of the world and now, I see it all at once—every ocean, mountain, continent, all vulnerable and small compared to the infinite universe. It's different from how I imagined. Instead of the green and blue globe that plagued my textbooks, the planet is various shades of brown. The ocean is still blue, but the land masses have lost the chloroplast vitality of vegetation.

I savor recirculated air—what if the oxygen runs out? Why did the autopilot bring me into space? Holy crap, I'm in space ... like an astronaut ... but I don't have a spacesuit. Jack is going to get an earful when I get back to Earth. How do I get back?

Domes appear on the planet's coffee-colored surface like fungus bulbs, adorning each continent with a civilizational fragment. Those in sunlight shimmer green while those in darkness flicker with city lights.

Severance isn't the last pocket of humanity.

There are more of us.

We were preserved by those who sought to destroy our race.

I shield my eyes when dawn sizzles over the horizon and saturates North America with the warmth of daybreak. Severance ignites with a florescent blue haze. Home. A cobalt flame.

The jet's autopilot must be programmed to transport me to one of the other colonies.

"What is this, *Star Wars*?" I swing my weightless arms forward and key the Vestige's coordinates into the digital control panel. The screen floods with satellite images, maps, and pixel flight routes. It sorts through the database of information before reprogramming the autopilot.

"Okay. Going home." I tighten my safety restraints when gravity latches hold of the plane. It happens all at once—North America increases in size, flames sweep across the windshield, and vibrations pound me like a sledgehammer. I blink away the stars until cotton-ball clouds fill the atmosphere.

Turbines reactivate and send the jet soaring over radioactive ruins of a crumbled city. Craters dot and char the landscape. Dust fogs the air, parts in sporadic gasps of clarity. Dilapidated rooftops, congested intersections, an old Walmart, and a vacant Starbucks—welcome to post-apocalypse America, where the things that once meant much no longer matter.

Severance looms is the distance like a distant mirage and swallows me when the jet pierces its magnetic barrier. Trees and overgrown fields replace monochrome rubble. Cars trickle up and down interstates, zigzag through mazes of country roads.

I've seen the truth, all of it, every wrinkle and crack.

****

Adults and teenagers rush from their stations in front of a deserted grocery store and pry open the plane's hatch with a crowbar. They aim their rifles at me, the Pureblood lookalike.

"Don't shoot." I slide from the cockpit with my arms raised but stumble when my feet meet the pavement. I'd melt into a puddle if a kid's AR-15 wasn't around to act as a rail.

"At ease, soldiers. She's one of us." Abram emerges from the committee dressed in camouflage pants and a bulletproof vest—normal, Vestige clothes. He pulls me into a tight hug. "You look like you've been to hell and back, Stryker."

"Yeah … hell sucked." I squeeze his cocoa shoulders and rest my cheek against his armored chest. He smells like smoke and whiskey, those bottles of shampoo hotels leave in their bathrooms.

He smells like home.

"Tally will know how to mend those lacerations … and that crazy hairdo." Abram supports me as we waddle to the store's entrance. He tilts his head to make eye contact with the recruits. "You know the drill. Disassemble the plane's navigation system. Be thorough. If the Scavs locate us, we're all dead."

"Julie Stryker." Colonel Buchanan strides from the temporary Command Center, followed by a posse of older men. He dons a smile and gives me a bone-crushing handshake. "Welcome back."

The acidic stench of body odor and spoiled milk makes me cough when I follow Colonel Buchanan into the store. Garbage clutters the linoleum floor—food wrappers, empty bottles, used medical supplies. I shuffle through a pile of bloody newspaper—who the heck bled all over the *New York Times*?

Refugees and recruits dwell within rooms made of empty shelves. Lanterns illuminate their austere, sunken faces. They perch on tepid iceboxes like ravens, curl up in beds made of rags and tattered cushions. Comfort exists in denial, so they chose the truth, to live in a makeshift compound where the air reeks of morning breath and beef stew, and people are no longer enslaved to lies.

I smear the sweat from my face and move through a warren of stopgap aisles. Lottery-ticket dispensers stack the check-out counters to create a work platform of sorts, artillery covers every available shelf—a few years ago, this was a civil place, but *was* is as significant as the dead.

Colonel Buchanan crushes a cockroach with the heel of his boot, leaving a pool of legs and exoskeleton fragments in its place. "I'll have Tally fetch some decent clothes. We need to scrub the City off you before someone mistakes you as a Pureblood and puts a bullet between your eyes."

They'd kill me because my lips still bear a faint trace of red, because I might be an alien? No, the Vestige's goal isn't to smite the Pureblood race. We fight for our freedom, our world. We seek revival, not to hurt those who've hurt us. If we become like them when they became like us, we lose our right to a fresh start. We will abdicate our place on this planet.

Jed and Margo are proof that ignorance is two-sided.

"Something happened on my way here." I grab Colonel Buchanan's arm to still his eager legs. "There are more colonies like Severance. I saw them. We're not all that's left of humanity."

"Are you sure?" When I nod, he mutters a paragraph of mind-blowing profanity and slumps against a shelf. "More humans … and more aliens."

"More world." I flinch when Levi plops next to me and rubs his wet nose against my thigh. "Good to see you, too." I hug his thick neck and bury my face in his fur.

"Ugh, that stupid dog got away from me." Tally jogs from the maze of corridors. "I was trying to chain him up in the storeroom and…" She pauses when I rise to my feet. Her cheeks flush. "Oh, it's you … you're back."

"My cover was blown."

"Thank you, God." She throws her arms around me in a chokehold embrace and laughs. Her collarbone stabs my neck. "You have no idea what these freaking idiots have put me through. Are you okay? Where's Jack? Nash is going to piss himself when he sees you."

"Calm yourself, Lieutenant." Colonel Buchanan pries me from Tally's grasp and clears his throat. "The Vestige has been hard at work. We've recruited and sent out messengers to surrounding cities and towns to meet with influential people in secret and deliver the truth. We've opened Command Centers in four other locations. Mind you, it's been a quiet operation. With only two weeks until the virus releases, we can't jeopardize our efforts by revealing ourselves to the Feds."

Home—the word has gained a new meaning. It doesn't refer to a place of comfort or safety, a building with central heating and clean sheets. It isn't a paradise of sameness—nothing is the same anymore, not my house on Rainbow Row or the people who filled it. Home is this, the snarky soldier who now considers me a friend and the filth that strips away my hold on the past. Home is with Jack and the Vestige. Home is where I can be the most honest version of myself.

"I'll take Stryker to the medical ward now, that is, if you're finished gabbing."

Colonel Buchanan glares at her. "Yeah. You do that."

Tally leads me to the medical ward, which was once an employee break room. The on-call nurse wraps my ribcage and sliced knees. I'm given a set of clothes, a bowl of soup, and a spare bed in the guest bunkroom. I change. I eat. I try to sleep but every time I close my eyes, I have nightmares. After being alone with my thoughts for a good amount of time, I tie on sneakers and shuffle through the store, down empty produce aisles that stink of rot.

His hand pressed against the jet's window, fingers

flattened into strips of skin, veins flexed. He staggered through torrents of wind like a piece of debris caught in a tornado. And when the plane rolled into motion, his face tightened into a display of desperation and resolve as if watching me soar toward the horizon was too painful for him to conceal from expression. He made me leave— why can't I be angry? What happened to the agony that made me scream and beg for relief?

Empty is good. Empty is strong.

"It's mighty nice to see you again, darlin'." Nash lurches from his desk when I enter the Communications Control Center. He grins and gives me one of those brief side-hugs encouraged at church youth groups. "How you holding up?"

"Not too well." Awful. I'm crumbling to pieces.

"This'll help." He lifts a half-filled pot of coffee from its hotplate and pours black liquid into a *World's Best Father* mug. "Have some apocalypse brew."

"Bless you, Nash." I clutch the mug to my chest and shove through the forest of box stacks and outdated technology to a rusted lawn chair. Tension dissipates from me as I lower into the seat. No more weight on my shoulders or pressure in my chest. Only coffee—the same instant powder my rich, dead grandparents used to have in their kitchen. I gulp the bad imitation and scrape my tongue to lessen the grotesque aftertaste.

The remains of my lipstick leave a bloody crescent on the mug's rim.

"I spoke with Jack a few minutes ago and told him you're here." Nash pulls his hair into a ponytail and keys a line of code into the computer. "He located a radio and moved someplace where the Feds won't find him. He's working now to locate the inner dome's generator."

"At least he's alive." Because I can't cry over another grave.

Will the future consist of bad coffee and leftovers? Nothing new. Nothing profligate. Only the necessities. Am I the bloody crescent painted on my cup's rim, tasting only a poor substitute of a known luxury because I, too, am proof of a plush life that no longer exists?

Have I become the pathetic remains of a perfect illusion?

Tally slides into the threshold. She leans against her thighs, panting like a runner after a marathon. "Come quick. The messengers from upstate have arrived."

Loneliness played with my mind more than I care to admit. In the City, while I sat at the Lefèvre Family's dinner table and rode the bus to and from work, I fantasized about the moment I'd waltz into the Command Center. I expected the homecoming to be filled with grainy clarity and warmth, people swarming me with cheers and questions, a sense of pride in a job well done. The play-by-play is still vivid in my thoughts. I prefer it over reality, because here, the air is stale, the world is matte and human interaction is like communicating with puppets. I need sleep. Rest will revive my senses, right?

Nash and I follow Tally through the makeshift military camp, past cluttered check-out counters, and into an entryway protected by vending machines and cheap games. A teddy bear with dull, button eyes leans against the glass of a claw machine and stares at me—creepy bastard. I try not to look at it. Dull eyes are dead eyes, and I've seen too many dead eyes.

White light pours in from the fogged storefront windows and illuminates a crowd of silhouettes. I squint and shield my eyes as they approach.

"Julie!"

I flinch when arms entwine my waist and jerk me into a hug. Braids slap my forehead and an endowed chest smashes against my sorry excuses. That voice—I'd recognize it anywhere. The scent of hair oil and rosemary—I used to joke I'd be able to smell her a mile away.

"Missy?" I open my lids but keep eyelashes feathered over the breach. Her face comes into focus—dark skin, thick lips, gold-tinted cheeks. Impossible. She can't be real ... but she's hugging me. Missy. Best friend from Charleston. Here.

"Hello? Earth to Julie." Missy laughs. She cups my face in her long, slender hands and probes me with her dark pupils. Her mouth pinches into a straight line—she must see it, the pain and scars within me, the unmistakable presence of loss. "I've missed you."

"What are you doing here?" I squeeze her tighter. I'd cry if my tear ducts worked.

"I was recruited to be a messenger a few weeks ago. Colonel Buchanan held a clandestine meeting at my new college. When he mentioned you ... I knew I had to enlist."

"How's your mom?"

"Not good. How are your parents?"

"I don't know. I haven't seen them in months."

She nods as if the information is matter-of-fact. "Lots of people have been separated from their families. At the meeting, once Colonel Buchanan told us about the aliens and the dome, my roommate realized her dad had been missing for years."

"We'll find them." At least, that's what I keep telling myself.

"Yeah." She musters a smile and drapes an arm over my shoulders. "I can only stay here for the night. My squad is on tour. We've been trying to spread news about the invasion. Hey, you should tag along, that is, if you have some spare time."

Jack doesn't want me in the City. I don't have work to complete at the Command Center. Why shouldn't I go on vacation and take advantage of my inactive state?

"Sure. I could use a few days of R&R."

"Great." Missy clasps her hands together and scans the indoor refugee camp. She gives me a you-have-so-much-to-tell glance. "Sexpot isn't here, is he?"

"No. He's still in the City."

"Are you two ... a couple?"

"It's *the end of the world* and you want to talk about boys?" Of course she wants to know my relationship status before we debrief each other. Most girls would rather talk about romance than military protocol and apocalypse scenarios.

Yes, it's true—single, love-scared Julie Stryker is dating the quirky weirdo she met at work. Dating ... are Jack and I dating? We are together, yes, but dating means something different. Normal people date, go to restaurants and movies. Jack and I skipped that step and went straight to a relationship level I can't classify. I love him ... even when he locks me in a jet and sends me to outer space.

She folds her arms and lifts her chin. "I knew you'd end up together. I just knew."

****

Three days—that's how long it takes for me to forget about our diminishing timeframe.

Missy and her squad travel to various locations to spread news of the aliens' invasion. Tally acts as their guard, and I do whatever is needed, which isn't much. Uselessness is a relief. I don't have to be strong and together. I can be exactly as I am without putting anyone at risk. While they meet with mayors and business owners, I distract myself with distracting things: books, magazines, television, Starbucks, and outlet stores that smell like expensive perfume and money.

To be surrounded by a pretty world, distanced from obvious danger and my weighty collection of problems, makes it easy to forget.

Comfort makes it easier to keep my eyes closed.

"Good evening, ladies and gentlemen." Missy stands in the center of the chlorine-polluted room, behind a podium. She shuffles through her notes and recites the introduction of her truth spiel.

Members of the local Homeowner's Association pack the neighborhood pool house, located in some suburb of some big city. They encircle plastic foldout tables and stab forks into slices of store-bought Key lime pie, the same brand Mom used to buy for Thanksgiving and Christmas.

Tally emerges from the bathroom. She rolls her eyes when I hand her a brownie. "No use kissing my butt, Stryker. I called shotgun for the whole trip. Chocolate won't make me give up my seat." She wipes the sweat from her pale face and guzzles water from a plastic cup.

"Are you feeling okay?"

"Of course. Why wouldn't I be?"

"You look awful."

"Priss." She scoffs and rubs the splotches on her neck. "I'm fine. Mind your own business."

"The world has ended," Missy shouts in a crescendo climax. "We've been invaded by aliens."

I plug my ears before the civilians pitch their fit. Wait for it. Ah, yep, here they go. Murmurs and laughs spread through the room like wildfire, at least, from what I can tell by the many gabbing mouths. People spring from their seats and squirm—the sight is funnier mute.

"Are you insane?" The bald man next to me throws a plate at the podium. His megaphone-loud voice slices into my silence. "Is this a joke?"

The truth is crazier than lies because lies are required to stick to possibilities—the truth isn't.

"You're a bunch of freaking idiots." Tally slams her fist against a tabletop. "This isn't a freaking joke." She swipes her sweaty bangs and then staggers sideways. A yellowish goo oozes from her mouth.

"Tally…" I grab her wrist. It's cold and clammy. Shivers quake her arm, ripple across her body and onto to mine. What's wrong with her? Why hasn't she told anyone about her illness?

"Outside. Now. Don't make a scene." She meets my line of sight and clenches her jaw as a saliva dripple cascades onto her t-shirt. "Get up … and walk out the door."

Now is when I should prepare myself. The news festering on her tongue isn't good, neither is her puckered expression or fear-glazed eyes. She will say what I don't want to hear like the nurses who told me Sybil died or Jack when he declared Jon's passing. Her mouth will deliver the next blow.

I rise from the chair, and together, we leave the building and trek across a parking lot crowded with squeaky-clean mom-vans and sports cars. Lampposts draw trails across the tennis courts, create a path to lead us from the pool house to our mud-caked van.

"You're sick, aren't you?"

Tally climbs into the vehicle and collapses next to a toolbox. She clutches a rifle to her chest as if it's a teddy bear. "I don't get sick." Her teeth chatter. "I'm tired, that's all."

"Sure, and I'm President of the United States." I sit on the van's stoop. A warm breeze tousles my hair—it's drenched with the scent of brake fluid and carbon monoxide. "Do you have any more unlikely things you want to say?"

"Gosh, you're obnoxious." She scratches her neck—it's covered in boils, a discolored rash.

"What the heck?" I brush her hair to the side. A wad of dark strands fills my hand in a tangled clump. Soft. Like Sybil's. Before she died. "Oh, Tally…"

"Don't touch me." She bats my fists and scoots into the crevice between seats. "I rubbed against a vine of poison ivy a few days ago. It's no big deal."

"You're lying."

"This isn't something you can fix, okay?" She chokes on what might be a sob and then rubs her eyes until they turn red. "You can't help me, so don't try."

"What's wrong with you?" I grip an armrest so tight, my knuckles lose their color. Pain expands within me until I can no longer sit up straight. "Fine. Be stubborn. Don't tell me. I'll take you to the hospital and … someone there will be able to help."

"I didn't recognize the symptoms in time." She squeezes my knee and wipes a tear from her cheek. "The radiation has already infected my bone marrow. No one can fix me."

"You're joking." I flash a smile to enforce the statement, to ease the sudden squeal of panic in my head. "You can't have Acute Radiation Syndrome."

"The dome is thinning, I think, and my body has absorbed some of the leaked radiation. I checked the patient logs at surrounding hospitals. There are fifteen current cases." Her voice crackles like a fire until all severity burns to a desperate crisp. She stares at me—it's about to come, that horrible news I predicted. "Julie, I'm dying."

It happened in a single, shattering moment—two seconds for my entire world to fall apart. I watched Jon cross the street. I heard a loud bump, splintering, and a crack. Then, I watched his body roll up the windshield of a car. I saw him on the ground, in the middle of the road, eyes open and blood pouring from his mouth and nostrils. I heard screaming. It was my screaming. I felt my legs lurch forward. I touched his face, felt for a pulse, screamed.

Not again. Tally will be fine. Maybe she has the flu or pneumonia. Doctors can fix her like Jack fixed me. They'll stick an IV in her arm, and everything will be fine. She has to live because no matter how much I deny it, I will be the girl crying over a casket.

"No," I wheeze. "You can't die. We buried Charlie and … the Scavs killed our friends … so I can't watch you die, too." Tears burn my face as I wrap her in an embrace. If I hold her close, maybe she won't slip away and disappear. Maybe I can keep her alive. "The aliens might have a method of treatment in the City. I'll go back."

"You'd be better off if I died."

"How can you say that?"

"Because…" She breaks free and curls into a fetal ball. The whites of her eyes fade from bloodshot pink to a necrotic yellow color. "I love Jack."

Rewind. Repeat. Over and over. Tally, the girl who slept in the bed next to Jon for years and groaned as I bled oceans in the back of her van, is in love with my boyfriend?

"He saved my life, you know." She coughs and then speaks in a dry rasp. "Both of my parents overdosed on drugs so … I was put in foster care. When I turned eighteen, I was left to live on the streets. I slept on park benches and worked odd jobs. One night, after I'd swiped a few beers from a drunk guy, I attempted to rob an apartment. The owner was home. He caught me."

"Jack?"

"Yeah. Jack." Tally smiles—I hate everything about it, how her teeth glisten with thoughts of him, how her sunken face glows. "He gave me food and said if I enlisted in the military and did something productive with my life, he wouldn't press charges. So the next day, I enlisted as a Marine."

I slide toward the open door and drape my legs over the step. A new kind of discomfort twists within my gut, a dull pulse that makes me squirm. She's been close to him from the start. I knew she liked him. Why wouldn't she? He's her commanding officer and best friend. A crush comes with the territory, but love? Love is different from like. Love is committed. Love doesn't back down.

"You don't have to worry, though. He doesn't feel the same way. I told him once and … he looked me dead in the eyes and then pretended I hadn't said a word." She drags herself forward, latches hold of an armrest. "He picked you, Julie."

"So why would I be better off if you died?"

"I can't be happy for you. If you marry Jack, I won't come to the wedding. If you both end up in a house with a cute picket fence, I'll throw toilet paper all over your front yard because … I'll wish it was mine. You get that, don't you? I want to be a good person and a not sucky friend but deep down, I'll always be the one he didn't choose, and I won't be happy for you."

"That's okay. Don't be happy for me." I heave a jagged breath when our sight becomes a single, connected line. "Live long enough to be happy for yourself. Love him. I don't mind because … no one can be loved too much. Tally, you can toilet paper my yard over and over. I'll help you."

She laughs. Snot runs down her chin. "Can we stab forks in the grass, too?"

"Of course." I sandwich one of her slender hands between mine. "The domes are thinning for a reason. It might be a warning. Maybe the Feds want to reestablish their supremacy. I don't know, and it doesn't matter, but other people are going to get sick. We need to radio Colonel Buchanan and tell him to issue a warning, supply potassium iodide tablets to as many towns as possible."

"Not good enough," she says. "You have to go back to the City and fulfill your mission. It's the only way to prevent further damage."

"The District."

She nods. "Blow it up."

Chapter Twenty-Three

"Imagining the future is a kind of nostalgia… You spend your whole life stuck in the labyrinth, thinking about how you'll escape it one day, and how awesome it will be, and imagining that future keeps you going, but you never do it. You just use the future to escape the present."

John Green, *Looking for Alaska*

Sacrifice—I used to think the term meant *quitter*. Martyrs, instead of fighting for their lives, willingly gave themselves to gain a status for their cause. I wanted to believe those sacrificial people had other options—they just couldn't see them. Now, I understand there are moments in our lives where we are given only one option, one path, one fate. We don't always have the choice between life and death.

We can only choose how we die.

I clutch an embroidered purse and tap my foot against the floorboard. Passengers flood the transit— pretty people in their pretty city. A little girl sits across from me with her mom. She flips through a vintage picture book and toys with her sundress's pleated skirt. A young couple holds hands a few rows ahead. They're all happy. They have lives and memories, experiences I might never have. Not after today.

"Are you sure you want to do this, Julie?" Nash asked as Colonel Buchanan squirted dye into my hair. "There has to be another way."

"There isn't," the colonel said on my behalf. "Tally doesn't have much time. Heck, none of us do. I checked with hospitals. Hundreds of people are experiencing symptoms of radiation poisoning." He plastered his fingers to my sopping scalp and tilted my head until our eyes locked. "I contacted that girl from the boarding house: Charis LeBlanc. She sent us a bag of her blood. The new genetic marker will allow you to travel through the City unnoticed."

"Have you told Jack?"

"No, for obvious reasons."

Nash stretched a tape measure across my chest to fit me for the bomb-vest. "You will wear the explosives into the District, ride the elevator down to the basement, and activate the bomb. You'll have five minutes to escape before detonation."

Colonel Buchanan steadied my trembling arms with his still hands. He crouched next to me, furrowed his brow into a dash. "I don't know how to tell you this because you're my son's girlfriend. I want you to be safe but ... the mission must come first. If you're given the choice between..."

"The mission comes first. If the need arises, I'll die to fulfill my objective."

"Good girl." He held a mirror in front of my face to reveal dark-blonde hair and tired eyes. "Remember. We are an entity of fragments, traces of something on the verge of extinction. You hold the truth, Julie. You are the Vestige."

Needle pricks race down my spine when the aerial bus lowers in front of the District. I follow protocol, exit the bus, and confront my target. Every nerve and cell within me tingles as if charged with electricity—I better move forward before I talk myself into turning back.

Purebloods with gelled hair and ironed suits pass me as I climb the familiar stone steps to the building's entrance. They'll die because of me, won't they? Their families will cry over caskets and graves because I decided the lives of others were more important than theirs. Murder is wrong—there's no way to justify it—but self-defense is survival. I'll pay the price to keep my people alive, even if guilt rots my bones, even if I vanish into flames.

Tick. Tick. Tick.

Each pulse ripples across my chest, gnaws at my living heart—it presses a figment knife to my throat and whispers over and over, "You will die today."

I understand what scares me. I've explored it within the confines of my mind, but knowing a fear doesn't remove it—it only makes the fear more rational.

The ticking vibrates my core with a bass-like sound. Someone will hear it if I'm not careful. I should hum. Yes—what's a good song? I better be wise with my choice. Whichever composition I choose could be the last to leave my throat. "I'll Be Seeing You" by Billie Holiday—that's a good song to hum before going up in flames, right?

"Salutations." I join a group of white-collar workers by the elevator and sweat. Pain, an intense sting, spreads up my back. I adjust the vest's straps and pretend I'm wearing an uncomfortable bra. Dang, I forgot to put on nice underwear. Why can't I die in lace, not drugstore panties?

The elevator doors part. An armed guard waits inside with a hand-scanner. He skims the palm of each boarding passenger and denies those without high-level security clearance.

Retreat. Abort.

I slide through the crowd and fast-walk to a translucent screen. Broadcasts flash across the panel, video footage and rolling text. Normal people read the news. No one will suspect I'm an enemy operative. Time—I have enough of it to inspect the atrium, the guards at the main entrance talking on their communication devices, the shifting security cameras overhead. They've created a cage. If I try to leave or reach the basement, they'll catch me. If I make a scene, attempt to activate the bomb here and now, they'll shoot me before I've unclipped the vest.

One option. One path. One fate. Better me than Jack. Better me than thousands of innocent people. I can do this. It'll happen so fast, I won't feel a thing. I'll never feel anything again.

Jon and Sybil, I'll be seeing you.

Light reflects from the tile floor and envelops me in warmth. I move to the bathroom in what seems like slow motion, through a sepia haze of seconds, faces, inhales, and exhales. I'll be okay. The people I love will be okay. I can do this for them.

A weird kind of resolution—something I can't pinpoint—settles within my muscles, warm and comforting like hot chocolate on a cold, rainy day. I lock myself in a stall, unzip my dress and remove the bomb. A single press of a button will activate the device. A single press will decide my fate, the fate of humanity. Can I do it? Am I brave enough to sacrifice my own life for the lives of others?

I press the activation button and wheeze as the timer begins its countdown. Five minutes until detonation. Five minutes until the end, the beginning. Five minutes until my life's erased and the world is stripped of its deceptive layers. Five minutes.

Tears mix with sweat and stream my temples. I hug the bomb because the closer it is, the faster and more painless I'll die. Jack—I didn't get to tell him goodbye. What'll he do when he finds out what happened to me? Who will he become, the wounded soldier who sleeps with a light on at night because his dreams kill him slow and steady, someone who tries to come back for me even though there's nothing left for him to find?

"Jack," I shout into our disconnected third-space. His name hurts me in a way I didn't think was possible, a deep cut in a deep heart. "You probably can't hear me, but I need you to … somehow … hear me. I'm going to die soon. We won't see each other again on this Earth, which is why I need you to find me in your thoughts, open your ears and listen to my voice. Last words are cliché and overused so I won't waste my time presenting a profound final lecture, but I do want closure, if not for me, then for you."

A woman clops into the bathroom and occupies the neighboring stall. Her skirt creates a fabric puddle beneath the divider.

"You have to stay. I have to go. No one is going to see the truth unless we make them. No one is going to fight for our world unless we inspire them. You and me … we are the Vestige."

Two minutes until detonation.

"Oh, gosh. Time's almost out. Hear me. I love you. I love you."

Memories flicker through my head like slides in an old projector. I'm a kid playing on the beach with Sybil, burying our dad in the sand—I am scaling the staircase in my taffeta gown to meet Jon in the foyer—I am dancing in the kitchen, singing at the top of my lungs while I bake cookies with Mom.

Jack and I lie in the green space between Randolph Hall and Porter's Lodge, staring up at the sky's grand Etch A Sketch. His hand finds mine and immediately, my heartbeat is everywhere. It beats in the tips of my fingers, the back of my neck, everywhere. I look at him. He looks at me.

"There you are," I whisper aloud. A smile burns

my cheeks. "Goodbye, Jack."

Seconds left. I squeeze the bomb and take one last breath, but as the timer crests a half-minute, the stall door flies open, and a Scav in full-body armor yanks me into the center of the bathroom where soldiers wait with rifles ready. No, I won't let this happen. My mission cannot end in failure.

I lunge at the smallest Scav and manage to slide past him, the barricade of armored muscle, and escape into the lobby. I sprint to the atrium's center and then dig my fingers into the bomb's bundle of wires and tear them apart. The aliens destroyed my world, but they will not destroy me. I fight back. I give everything to save everything.

"Come on. Work." I slam the explosives against the tile floor.

The bomb deactivates.

"What? No!"

Scavs rip me to my feet and take the bomb's shattered remains. They contort my arms behind my back, cuff my wrists. No. Wait. I'm supposed to be dead. Humanity is supposed to be safe. I couldn't have failed. Failure isn't an option.

****

"They'll torture you first," Jon's figment voice echoes through my mind as I watch the City melt into the distance. "You have the information they want." He's right—the secrets in my head will be the aliens' final weapon. "You know what has to be done, Julie."

Skyscrapers glisten with magenta hues and then shrink into once human-owned businesses, now pieces in the Purebloods' dollhouse illusion. Turbulence rattles the hover car—instability causes a rift between *what is* and *what could be*. I press my heels into the floorboard's thin carpet, scoot into the middle seat, and slam my handcuffs against the console.

"Quiet down back there." The Scav taps a Taser against the dashboard and then resumes his conversation with the shiny-haired chauffeur.

Now is my chance to give Jack time to locate the dome's generator, protect the Vestige's voice and raise their odds by lowering my own. The war will end when I leave this vehicle.

I won't be a failure.

A glass bottle of distilled water glistens in the side door's groove. If I act fast, it won't hurt as bad, right? More pain than the bomb, but not as severe as the gunshot wound. Two motions—that's all it will take to tie a loose end and then cut the strands all together.

Glass slices my bare ankles when I dislodge the bottle with my feet and slam it against the middle console, shattering, spilling. Water and blood drip down my legs. Weird—why am I not in pain?

Shiny-haired chauffeur slams the brakes. The Scav twists in his seat and attempts to stop me.

Too late.

I grab the largest chunk of glass and with a quick, stinging motion, I slice open my wrists. Blood pours from me—obscure DNA and overworked hemoglobin. I let out a brief cry and then smile because pain is evidence of my victory. Death will save my world and end theirs.

"You failed." I slump against the backseat with blood pooling around me and stare at the Scav's masked face. "You can't have my home. It's not yours to take." Pain ripples through my nervous system, makes me arch my back and writhe. "The Vestige will ruin you. Once people know the truth, your pretty set-up will unravel and … you'll be killed by the people you sought to destroy. We won."

The Scav removes a pen-like device from his belt

and stabs it into my thigh. I wince as the sharp pinch grows into an acid-like sting, and then settles into a hot numbness. My eyelids grow heavy—dammit, he drugged me. I roll onto my side and scrape my slit wrists until flesh peels away and blood coats my body like a blanket. If I sleep, the Scav will keep me alive. No. I have to die.

Sacrifice—I used to think the term meant *quitter*. I don't anymore. When done for the right reasons, for the right people, sacrifice is an act of war. It requires bravery—a will to fight and never relent. It requires someone to love life so much they're willing to give it to preserve it. I'm not a quitter. I demanded the truth and now, I set it free.

No more layers.

No more deceit.

Gravel crunches somewhere beneath me. I lift the bricks that used to be my eyelids and cringe when streetlamps saturate my pupils with golden rays. Pain—still there, not faded by death. Shadows—they fill the front seats. Trees surround the hover car instead of clouds.

"No, no." I lurch into an upright position and examine my wrists. Gauze binds the cuts in thick strips. Handcuffs merge my hands into a skin and fabric ball. How were they able to fix me? I mangled my wrists beyond repair, well, what I thought was beyond repair.

Death would've saved Jack. Now he's in danger. Everyone is at death's door because I couldn't manage to work a bomb or sharp object. Geez, am I totally and completely incompetent?

An old mansion, ablaze with lights, comes into view. The main façade is formal, made of stone and stucco, surrounded by terraced gardens and topiaries. Cars clog the cobblestone driveway. Purebloods flock to the immaculate entryway, draped in expensive garments, furs, and jewelry.

What is this place? Why am I here? Are the aliens going to torture me with their outdated dialect and fancy attire? Out of all the locations to commit a murder, why'd they choose a soirée?

I curl into a protective ball when the car rolls to a stop in front of the servants' entrance. A Scav opens the nearest door. His gloved hand clamps onto my right shoulder and pulls me from the warm interior, out into air colder than ice. I shiver and bang my wrists against the car's trunk because of the slim chance I might get a clot and drop dead.

"Misbehavior is not permitted within the President's home." He lifts his visor, revealing a handsome face and sharp, green eyes. "Acting impolitely will result in immediate punishment."

"What will you do? Kill me?"

He tightens his grip on my shoulder and drags me into the house.

Servants, carrying platters of gourmet appetizers, create a traffic jam within the stark, narrow corridors. My guard shoves through the chaos, into a culinary kitchen. Steam clouds the space with rich aromas—my mouth waters, and a new ache fills my belly. Cooks hover over wood-burning stoves. A butler discusses dinner wine with a server.

"Move." The Scav knocks a platter of silverware from a waiter's hands. Forks and knives bounce on the tile, clatter, and flash their sharp edges. I could grab one and end this nightmare for good. Even as incompetent as I am, I should be able to silence myself with a steak knife.

"Pondering another suicide attempt is futile. You shall not succeed." He whisks me up a steep flight of service stairs to the mansion's main level. His chest bumps against my back as we move. His stale breath drips down my neck and makes me cringe.

Ornate wallpaper parts in sporadic gaps to showcase Monet and Da Vinci. Michelangelo sculptures adorn the lavish indoor sunroom. Human art. Human history. None of it is the Purebloods' to claim. How can they absorb our identities when they killed us because they hated who we became? Sick—that's what they all are, sick in the heads.

I bite my bottom lip and focus on the tap-tap of my feet against the marble floor, the glittering chandeliers overhead, not Jack and Tally, everyone who will die because of me. But how can I not think about Jack? How do I prevent Tally's boil-covered neck from popping into my thoughts? I love them. I love each and every person fighting this fight. Traitor—I'll become like Charlie when the Purebloods pump me with truth serum, and betraying my family is a fate worse than death.

We cross the loggia and enter a salon. Sheer, white curtains blow inward from the windows. Pink roses clutter the countertops. A lean woman in her early thirties stands amidst the Parisian furniture. Her steel-gray eyes are like knives embedded in her face, pointed in my direction.

"The human is in disrepair," she says to my guard. "You cannot expect her to meet with the President in such an atrocious condition. President Duchene requested the girl be brought uninjured."

"She attempted suicide on our journey here. I have already attended to her wounds."

"How was she able to cause herself harm? Were you not ordered to watch her keenly?" The woman sighs and redirects her attention to me. "Your appearance must be corrected." She whispers into her communication device and then pins the hair from my face with one of her jeweled barrettes.

"What, does my blood offend you?" I conjure the snarkiest expression possible, which means I cross my arms and raise my eyebrows. Snarky has never been my strong suit. "Why clean me up if you're going to kill me? Makeup on a dead girl doesn't make her any less dead ... or any prettier."

"No harm shall come to you here."

"Yeah, right. I believe you." Snarky isn't my strong suit, but I don't suck at sarcasm.

A maid scurries into the room with a pair of satin gloves and a tea-length gown covered in pedal-like frills. She drapes the pieces over my shoulder as if I'm a store window mannequin.

"Would you please change your attire? I apologize for the inconvenience, but it is necessary for you to blend with the guests downstairs." Knife-Eyes motions for the Scav to unlock my handcuffs. She musters a smile, well, more of a dog-like sneer. "Please. The sight of a lovely girl covered in blood would cause an awful disruption, and I would prefer the party to continue without such a problem."

"Her request is a formality. You do not have a choice," the Scav says.

"I figured as much. Most of what you people say is a formality." I peel off my dress and slip into the borrowed frock. If I wasn't hyped on adrenaline, I'd squirm in their violating stare, turn red from the moment of nakedness. But I *am* hyped on adrenaline, determination and a type of anger that makes my hair stand on end. They want me to be afraid and submissive, but by playing dress up, they've revealed they need me for something more than information.

To be needed is to have power.

She dabs the smeared mascara from my face. Her

angled bob swishes back and forth as she strides to an embossed door. "You may now meet the President."

Bile shoots into my mouth when the threshold becomes an empty void, a threatening invitation. I swallow the stomach acid—where else could I put it? Pain melts down my esophagus like molten lava.

How do I confront the person responsible for ruining my life? How do I look him in the eyes and not want to rip his throat apart with my bare hands? I've been stripped of all that once held me together, forced to stand alone in a cast of my own making. What if I can't hold up in front of him? I've already failed my mission. I can't stigmatize the Vestige as crybabies, too.

Jon checked me out of school the day Andrea Murphy wrote *pigs belong in the zoo* on my locker. He was silent as we walked to the Land Rover, didn't say a word until we were a mile down the road. I asked him how I could show my face there again, and he told me to give them something to look at, hold my head high, and be the girl who takes punches and throws them back.

That's who I have to be now, the girl who takes punches and throws them back.

I clasp my hands together to conceal their shaking and amble into a grand, old-fashioned library. Bookshelves climb two floors to the cathedral-like ceiling. Flames crackles in the fireplace, overshadowed by a portrait of Queen Elizabeth I.

"Rhys and Mariah have had their way with you, I see." A woman rises from the presidential desk. She smiles, framing perfect teeth between plump, red lips. "You look ravishing, my dear. The gentlemen downstairs would fall over each other to make your acquaintance." Her slender figure sashays toward me, dressed in a backless gown.

Heat slashes through my body when I look into

her ginormous, baby-doll eyes. They're dark like chocolate, the same shade as her glossy curls. Why isn't she monstrous, cold, and easy to hate? Why couldn't she be a white-haired man in a crisp suit who reeks of cologne and rot?

"I am President Gemma Duchene." She cradles my hand in hers and giggles—yes, she giggles—as if I'm a cute puppy on display at the pet store. "It is a delight to meet you."

"You're young to be president."

"Not as young as you might think. I have been blessed with a youthful face." She caresses my cheek with her warm index finger. "I see now why no one recognized what you are. You either bear a close resemblance to us or … we bear an awfully wonderful resemblance to you."

"Well, I'm an original, not a human copy." There, I threw back one of her many punches. She can pucker her lips and giggle all she wants—I won't be swayed by her manipulation tactic. I know the truth. I've seen and felt, given my all to protect it.

This is a ruse. She must be a monster.

Her breath cascades over my face, sweet like a floral bouquet. She twists my hair around her pinkie finger—I'll rip her scalp apart if she continues to play with mine, I'll grab an iron stoke from the fireplace and thrust it through her chest. "You are quite pretty."

"Why am I here?" I grit my teeth as she floats around the room in a blur of crushed velvet and porcelain flesh. "What do you want from me before I meet the torturer and executioner? I expect you'll send me to them once we've had our chat."

President Duchene toys with her diamond necklace. She frowns as if my blunt behavior has hurt her manufactured, injected feelings. "I desired to meet one of the people responsible for causing the upheaval in the suburbs. You must understand—the Vestige is not a welcome faction in our new society. We like peace. You do not."

"You're trying to exterminate my race," I say. "Peace isn't an option."

She entwines her arm around mine and pulls me to her side. "We have much to discuss. Come. I will take you someplace where we won't be disturbed by the party."

Someplace quiet. Someplace out of listening distance. Someplace she can kill me.

Chapter Twenty-Four

"Yet do not miss the moral, my good men.
For Saint Paul says that all that's written well.
Is written down some useful truth to tell.
Then take the wheat and let the chaff lie still."
Geoffrey Chaucer, *The Canterbury Tales*

"Hurry. If they witness our departure, they will follow us. We must reach our location before our absence is noticed." President Duchene takes me down a flight of steps to the basement. Her guard follows at our heels as we breeze past beautiful, laughing people in fringe dresses and beads.

I dig my fingernails into the hand cuffing my bandaged wrist and cough on what might be a sob when we move through dressing rooms and a large space covered in tiles. A swimming pool replaces the floor. Guests jump off diving boards, squeal, and shout while servants bathe them in champagne.

We are the lies we tell, and they tell grand, luxurious lies.

"Why do you shake, my dear?" President Duchene smiles and holds me against her hip. A strand of her glossy hair gets caught between my teeth—a trace of arsenic. "Do you not sense the peace within this house? Here, no one fears the suburban turmoil. I keep my children safe."

"You keep them ignorant." I press my elbow against her side, out of spite. Maybe she'll cry out, grunt with pain. Maybe I can hurt her before she hurts me again. "Lies aren't a shield. They offer as much protection as a rowboat in a hurricane."

"A liar is someone with malicious intent," she whispers. "Metaphorically speaking, I cut up their food so it will be easier to swallow. I allow their lives to be without worry."

"You're a dictator."

"No, I am a mother. They are, in essence, the same."

Partiers tip their hats at us, kiss our cheeks. They look at me but only see an ornate dress, big eyes and satin gloves, a pretty thing in their pretty world, their paradise of sameness, their home-sweet-home.

"Where are we going?"

"It is a surprise ... a nice surprise." President Duchene leads me out a backdoor and across the south terrace, away from illuminated balconies and a manicured esplanade. She treads on her tiptoes and squeezes my hand as if we're best friends sneaking from the party to share secrets.

Moonlight filters through the treetops and reveals a brick wall severed by an open gate. Millions of flowers and plants arrange the garden beyond in art deco designs.

"Our destination is up ahead." President Duchene walks me beneath vine arbors and then pauses in front of a brick and glass structure—a conservatory. She arches her back and huffs as she pries open the main door. "My soldier will stay outside. We will be alone."

Alone? Is she stupid? I could tear her to pieces, kill her with a single punch to the neck. Yes, she's taller than me, but I am thicker, stronger, and less disgusted with getting my clothes dirty. Doesn't she know—even a glorified beanpole can be snapped in half?

I step across the threshold into an indoor jungle. Greenery pours over the walkway, stacks shelves, and christens the glass ceiling. Fountains trickle into stone basins with a spectral chime. Where are the torture devices and executioner axe? What happened to the nightmare I've been preparing myself to face? Death will be different here. There will be pain, terror, and then, there will be nothing. No sound. Nothing. Moonlight will fall through the windows, onto me, into me. I will breathe in the air, the light, and die with peace, beauty.

"Breathtaking, is it not?" President Duchene drifts through the foliage like a phantom. Her dress's train sweeps the floor. "Your race took this for granted, but we know the value and rarity of such living things. Those who are deprived treasure what they are given, which is why we will be better humans."

"Your kind destroyed most of the planet. You're no better than the people like me."

Tally would bash President Duchene's skull with a pot, and then attempt an escape with the hope a Scav would put a bullet in her back rather than pump her with truth serum. Where's a brick or a shovel? If I act fast, the President won't be able to react.

"We had to create a clean canvas so we could learn to be better. Come. You must see your surprise." She drags me into a connected greenhouse where high tea waits on a cluster of white patio furniture. "Do you enjoy cucumber sandwiches and sweet morsels?"

"Not enough to betray the Vestige. That is why we're here, isn't it? You expect snacks and civil conversation to give me a loose tongue."

"On the contrary. Indulgence gives me, as you say, a loose tongue." She sits and pours tea into a pair of painted porcelain cups. "You must have many questions for me?"

"I'm not scared of you." Creeped out, maybe, terrified of what she could do to the Vestige, skeptical of her charm but not scared—fear comes from a personal will to survive, and I no longer have it.

"Wonderful." She offers a cup and flashes a smile of pearls. "Ask your questions."

There it is, every answer Jack and I have been wanting, all tied up in a red-lipped, velvet-wrapped package with my name on it. I expected this moment to be more climactic. I thought the truth would offer an ultimatum, not wish to have tea with me.

"Explain how all this happened." I lower into the chair across from her and shiver when a palm branch scrapes my back. Death will come for me soon—I've never been surer of a theory—but if I'm to become one of the many martyrs for this mission, for this truth, then I'd rather know everything.

She laughs. "You are a saucy intrigue, are you not? Most young women would rather have a mouthful of chocolate than hear how their petty world ended."

"I don't know any women who've watched their family and friends die for chocolate."

President Duchene plucks a lavender sprig from a flowerbox and crushes it between her hands. She stares at me until the room's temperature drops a few degrees. "My people have been on Earth for almost a century. Our invasion was a slow, strategic process. We did not wish for a war or sudden chaos. It was better to end humanity over time. My grandfather, the first Pureblood President, recognized the instability of the human race. He used their weaknesses as a weapon. Mind you, *the end of the world* took many years to complete. We caused an economic collapse, turmoil in the Middle East that led to a Third World War, and later released an airborne strain of a mutated virus."

Her voice makes the truth factual, not some conspiracy delusion I've allowed myself to believe.

"Various domes were constructed before the war's final nuclear bombing. Pockets of humanity were kept alive to preserve the culture and civilization. Their ignorance was and is easy to maintain." President Duchene scoops a sugar cube from a ceramic basin and pops it into her mouth. She stores it in her right cheek, lets its sweetness dilute the bitterness of her words. "Here, in the City, we produce food, clothing, and other products for the occupants of the outer layer. All it takes is a *Made in China* stamp to create the illusion of a normal, importing nation." She dabs sugar crystals from her lips and furrows her brow into a sympathetic arch. "The time has come, though. We do not need your race's services any longer. I do wish we could live together harmoniously, but the world is not big enough. Your time of existence has passed. It is our turn to take your place, make humanity better than before, revise your accomplishments, and make them our own. Please say you understand."

There was a flash freeze in Charleston a few months ago, the night Jack and I went to a music venue downtown. He turned up the heat in his rented Jeep until I couldn't distinguish air from skin, and then plugged his phone to the speaker system and activated his favorite playlist. We sat in silence, tilted toward each other at an attracted angle and gazed at the flickering dashboard in an industrial darkness. His profile caught the bluish light, became a perfect sketch of stubble, dimples, and a ball cap. He mouthed the song's lyrics as they played on repeat: *Give you up—I'd rather die, for you are my battle cry. Give you up—I'll never give you up.*

"Do you understand?" She pounds a fist against the table and snaps her fingers to regain my attention. Her pupils shrink to dots, and her smile becomes a cartoon-like grimace—I'd laugh at her if she wasn't talking about the extermination of humanity. "Your time of existence has passed."

I smooth my skirt and force a smile. "Listen here, you small-minded witch." Oh, explosive. This is a new characteristic. "Our little tea party is cute, but it doesn't fool me. You are a manipulator, a devious politician who has controlled most of my life from behind an invisible curtain. You destroyed my illusion, and you let me see you through the smoke and rubble. I am not a traitor. I will not negotiate such behavior. Torture, kill me—I won't betray the Vestige because their mission, the truth, is worth every ounce of pain you could inflict. I mean, come on. You think your kind is better than mine? Look around. You've become the part of us you hate while we strive to fight the poison that ruined our system."

"Do you not like what we have done with your world? It is beautiful now. No crime. No unreasonable behavior or complex feelings." She rubs her foot against mine as if physical contact will somehow shrink my rage into a manageable temperament. "Julie, my love, your conviction would make a brilliant addition to our society. Listen. I shall make a deal with you. Tell me what I wish to know about the Vestige, and I will allow you to stay here. The Special Ones will not protest my offer."

"Go to hell."

Her brow furrows, creates creases in her forehead. "I do not have to be a hospitable host, Julie. The Special Ones requested I send you to the labs immediately, but I wanted to offer you a chance to be smart." She corrects her posture and bites into a cucumber sandwich. "Be smart, Julie."

"Smart people are tearing away your layers. Smart people discovered the truth and are fighting to reveal it," I yell. "You don't want me to be smart. You want me to be a coward."

"Humankind was dwindling on the brink of extinction before Purebloods arrived. People lived in their nice little towns, oblivious to the chaos occurring in other continents, terrorists invading their country, and the slow crumble of their governments and society. They believed what was told to them. They not once dared to question what they considered truth. Is that not stupidity? Should stupid people be left alive even after they have earned their deaths? We hurried your demise, nothing more. We are not the villains. We are the new beginning. I can give you the life you want for yourself. The truth is dangerous. It will destroy you. I want you to live. Please. Let me save you."

Saved from death to exist in a universe without Jack, to inhabit a place where I'm a miniscule minority dwelling side by side with the parasites who sucked the identity out of my race? No, thanks. Even the thought of pretending the invasion never happened, going about my days with a distinct knowledge that humankind switched genetic makeup, makes me want to choke on a creampuff.

"I've made my decision."

President Duchene shrugs. She smiles in a sinister, I'm-going-to-gut-you-like-a-fish sort of way. "So … what will you do if you survive the night?"

Find Jack. Kiss Jack. Rescue parents. Save the world. Buy a latte.

In no exact order.

A rusted nail tears my skirt as I squirm in the chair. I tear off my satin gloves and toss them to the ground. "First, I'll get my parents out of your disgusting Reproduction Institute."

"Oh, my dear, you are greatly mistaken. Your parents are not in my Reproduction Institute," President Duchene says with a laugh. "They are dead." She waves her pinkie and gulps her tea.

Breakfast waited in the kitchen. Mom hovered

over the stove. Dad sat at the table, reading the newspaper and drinking his daily cup of Italian Roast. Jon entered the room with clarity glittering in his eyes. He plopped next to me, made my stomach ache with joy. I laughed with him hours before I cried over him. I sat beside Mom and Dad in a house on the verge of becoming a ghost town.

"I had them killed the day your brother was assassinated. They are buried in a mass grave fifty miles north of Charleston. If you do not believe me, I have pictures I can show you."

Sea Foam was the color I'd planned to repaint our dining room—Jack found a swatch in the Underground's supply room, taped it above my cot to act as propaganda for hope. I knew Mom and Dad wouldn't be the same once I rescued them. I'd have to fix them again, rebuild their minds while we rebuilt our home. If Mom was pregnant, I'd take care of the baby.

A single burst of laughter slips from my mouth without warning and then reverses into a convulsive sob. I clutch my chest when a shutter of pain moves into my heart. Empty pain. Evidence of loss. The hollowing torment of acceptance.

"You poor, foolish child." President Duchene pouts her lips and scoots her chair closer to me. She rubs my hand until I jerk it away. "All this time you thought them to be alive."

Dead—it's the truth. They are gone. I must've known, which was why I didn't fight to retrieve them. I clung to the unachievable dream of our future because I had nothing left but memories and scars.

"You might as well have tea. You must be hungry after such a long day of attempted terrorism." President Duchene pours hot water into a cup and forces me to take it. "Cheers."

I shake with occasional sobs like an engine sputtering to life and inhale steam. The tea is drugged, I'm sure, but I want to drink it. Unconsciousness will save me from the pain, numbness and sorrow. I'll wake up and after being interrogated, I'll die. Easy.

"Drink your tea." Her face sloughs into a canvas of wrinkles and smeared makeup. Her baby-doll eyes lose their luster, become cold as glass. "Go ahead. Take a sip."

Jon's blood oozes down my fingers in hot, thick globs. It's not real. I can escape it. I can escape these walls. The Scav is outside. I'm alone with the President. There are many exits. I have a chance to survive. Do I want to keep fighting? What will I have if I live? Jack. I'll have Jack. I won't be alone.

"Drink your tea." President Duchene drums her polished fingernails on the tabletop. Her voice shifts into a gravelly tone, reminiscent of Grandma's before she died.

"Swallow your own tea." I throw the cup at her face and lurch from my chair as the vessel bursts into a firework of painted porcelain. She squeals when I sprint out of the greenhouse and into the conservatory, howls like a banshee in an old horror movie. I shove through the maze of greenery, stumble into moonlight and shadows. Plants wrap their ivy tendrils around my arms—dang it, I peed a little.

"Oh, Julie," President Duchene shouts in a singsong voice. "Where did you go, Julie?"

No time. She's coming. Her footsteps echo all around me. Where can I go? How do I get out?

I duck beneath a counter of rare flowers and press my body to the sludge-covered wall. Air stings my throat, lungs, and then lessens its pressure as my heartbeat quiets. If I breathe or move, she'll find me. If I let fear overcome my senses, I will lose the fight.

A spider drops onto my shoulder and crawls across my skin—I flinch, cage a scream.

"You cannot hide forever. I will find you." President Duchene drifts past like a ghost or demon. Her gown brushes the stone floor, gathers leaves and petals in a processional puddle. She pants—I swear, her breath lowers the conservatory's temperature ten degrees. "Oh, Julie. Come out, Julie."

I roll from beneath the counter and race in the opposite direction.

"There you are," she hisses.

Sweat or tears stream my cheeks as I swat brush, dive through darkness. I turn right—President Duchene waits at the end of the aisle. I sprint down a narrow path—she confronts me, laughing, with a cup of tea in her right hand. I slam my weight against various doors—they're locked. I beat my fists against windows and crawl over workbenches—her sinister smile greets me at each intersection.

Give you up—I'd rather die, for you are my battle cry. Give you up—I'll never give you up.

I reach the main door and yank its knob as the President soars in my direction with her arms outstretched. It swings open, but a Scav blocks the threshold. He clasps his gloved hands around my throat, tosses me to the ground, and pins me in place.

No. This can't happen. I was too close.

President Duchene kneels at my side and lifts her cup to my lips. "Drink. Your. Tea."

The Scav pries apart my gums and forces me to gulp the liquid. It warms my mouth and eases my hunger pains. Then, a pressure washes through my body, and the world spins out-of-control.

"Do not be afraid. You will go to sleep, that is

all." She cradles me in her arms and strokes my hair. Her face hovers beyond my lash-barred eyelids, a puzzle of brown, red, and white. "Shhh, Julie. Do not fight it. Embrace the rest, darling. You will not wake again."
****

Classical music resounds in the space surrounding my body, enhanced by the crescendo of an orchestra, a violin's cry. Peroxide saturates the air with a poignant stench. Footsteps patter to the right, and then tread into silence. Why can't I move? Should I be conscious? Are they going to kill me while I'm trapped in the dark, aware but not awake?

Beep ... Beep ... Beep ... Beep.

Death claws its way into my chest and sits there, waiting. I didn't know it would hurt this much. I didn't realize all the good in my life would be emptied out by it.

Beep ... Beep ... Beep. Flatline.

Wait. What's happening? Oh, I'm dying. Help. Please.

Someone, bring me back to life.

Chapter Twenty-Five

"That's why we have memory. And the opposite of memory—hope. So things that are gone can still matter. So we can built off our pasts and make a future."
Isaac Marion, *Warm Bodies*

I am almost dead.

It's not so bad. The darkness is brighter, and the only physical sensation I have is a tingling in the back of my head. I do hate limbo's wait music, though. Flatline—it's a steady, mechanical scream, a one-melody soundtrack. I'd like to press the universal skip button and listen to an eternal replay of Frank Sinatra and Bob Dylan. Wait. What's wrong with me? I don't want music. I want to live.

Stop. This is okay. I'm okay. My family is waiting for me. I believe in God and heaven. I believe in life after death, which makes this whole ordeal less scary. I'm not ignorant, optimistic, or religious. I just see the truth because in a world of layers, the truth is the only thing worth seeing.

Pressure pulses through me, a sharp and relentless ache. Fingers imprint my chest, air fills an empty void—someone is trying to resuscitate me. Please, whoever you are, don't stop. I know you're there. Come on. Push harder. Fight for me, so I can come back to you.

A beat ripples through the darkness and floods it with warmth, a steady pulse. I gasp when more air is shoved down my throat. Electricity vibes through me in a single wink.

I claw at a metal tabletop when light penetrates my head like an axe, and the one-melody soundtrack fades into repetitive beeps and florescent buzzing. Ceiling tiles appear, their pattern broken by dark hair and cobalt eyes, a face smeared with dirt and tears.

"Praise God." Jack slumps over the surgical table, boxes me in a protective room of flesh, muscle, and bone. He slides his hand over my cheek, one finger anchored behind my left ear, and silences our jagged heaves with a kiss. His lips quiver between mine—they're not a dream. He isn't an illusion.

Whatever has kept me together these past few weeks unravels into mush. I wrap my arms around him, gather wads of his t-shirt in my hands, and cry like a baby. I kiss his neck, his stubble-covered cheek. I hold him tight, but I can't get close enough to satisfy the ache in my heart.

"Geez, your lips are blue." Jack kisses me again and then pulls back far enough to reveal medical equipment and glass cases. He dries his bloodshot eyes. "You were down for five minutes. I didn't think I'd be able to bring you back. I was afraid you'd end up like…"

"I'm here," I whisper in a raspy, oxygen-deprived voice that sounds more like Abram's than mine. "Where are we? What is this place?"

How are you here? How are you real?

Jack squeezes my hand. "The Human Reproduction Institute." His cheeks flush white for a split second, and his Adam's apple bobs. "They didn't do anything to you, at least, not the kind of stuff they usually do to people here. The equipment in this room is meant for hormone extraction, you know, the stuff they use to make emotion injections."

"So they took my hormones and killed me? Those jerks…"

"Your body will recover," he says through a smile I didn't think I'd see again. An electrical glow frames his face—he resembles a dream more than a living, breathing person. I can touch and talk to him, but a part of him is missing. Maybe it's me. Maybe part of me is missing.

"If we don't get your blood circulating, your limbs may die." He unstraps my wrists and ankles, and then helps me roll over. "You have to move no matter how much it hurts."

There is death within me disguised as weakness—I hate its weight.

I moan as pain pulses through my head, ripples up my calves like fire or shots from a nail gun. I writhe as Jack bends and extends my legs. "How'd you find me?"

"Nash hacked into the City's security system. He was monitoring the video footage and saw you here. I was a few blocks south with Tally, Missy, and Abram when he radioed. I was close, which is good because if I'd arrived any later..." He rubs his neck as if trying to massage away the thought of losing me and then steps over a collapsed man in a white lab coat.

"What'd you do to him?"

"I whacked him on the skull with a centrifuge." Tally appears in the open doorway with Missy and Abram at her side. Most of her hair has fallen out, leaving bald patches. Dark circles encompass her eyes. "He didn't go down easily, though. Screamed and kicked a lot." She leans against Abram and clutches her rifle, out-of-breath. "I'm glad you're not a stiff, Stryker. That'd freaking suck."

"Back at you." I smile. Tears blur their figures into silhouettes. "Why are all of you in the City?"

"The Vestige is making an attack," Abram says. "We're waging war."

War? Now?

"Come on. We need to leave." Jack lifts me to a standing position. I cling to his arm, shaky and barefoot.

339

My legs struggle to support my weight as he leads me to the laboratory's exit.

"You don't, by any chance, have a change of clothes with you? Or an extra pair of shoes?"

"Sorry. We left our wardrobes at the Underground." Tally smirks. "Couldn't fit all of our panties and boots in our backpacks."

We move through the Institute, down stark corridors and flights of stairs. The electric lights seem brighter. They reflect off the floor, the walls, everything.

"The Vestige has entered the City. Hundreds of Purebloods have already joined our effort," Jack says as we leave the Institute and rush through the old space station. He checks his wristwatch. "We have t-minus five minutes until the District explodes."

"What? How'd you manage…?"

"One of our spies was able to plant a bomb in the building's basement," Abram says. "In five minutes, Severance will be without a government. And once that threat has been annihilated, the inner dome's generator will be shut down. Our mission is on the verge of completion."

"Don't forget about my treatment," Tally shouts. "I'm going to die if I don't get some sort of cure soon. Do you see these oozing bumps? They aren't freaking zits, people!"

"We'll get you the treatment, Tally. Don't worry," Missy says. "That's where we're headed now, right, Jack? To the hospital across the street?"

"Yeah, but we need to hurry. All hell's breaking loose."

I touch the slide of my handgun and inhale until my lungs are on the verge of exploding. We're almost there. We can't give up. The dream is collapsing. The truth is an uprising. Reverse. Reverse the end of the world. So close. We're so close.

We reach the space station's ground level and stride across the cramped, colorless lobby. The security guard at the front desk commands us to halt, aims his gun at the back of Abram's bald head. An explosion sounds, followed by a puff of red mist. The guard slumps forward, dead.

Tally holsters her firearm and snickers at my expression. "Get used to it, Stryker."

Jack takes us outside where the sky has turned to shifting steel, where the surrounding skyscrapers and asphalt pathways are flooded with panicking Purebloods. Aircrafts, serrated jets, surge overhead. Gunfire, smoke, explosions—the City has transformed into a war zone.

I wait on the crowded curb while tanks weave through the congested traffic, unclogging the thoroughfare like a colossal plunger. The letter 'V' is spray-painted on the machines.

Aerial war machines buzz like a swarm of bees, twist into an aerial plunge and fire bullets in our direction. We lurch into a mad sprint as ammunition ricochets off the asphalt beneath our feet. I duck my head and dodge the flying shrapnel as Jack leads us across a vacant, overgrown lot. The pavement scratches my feet. I cringe from the ache in my pounded chest.

"Get down." Abram does a belly flop behind a rusted dumpster. We follow, concealing ourselves milliseconds before the jets fly past. Missy emits a single, nervous sob. Tally wheezes and slumps against my shoulder.

Jack checks his watch. "Two minutes." Sweat soaks his t-shirt. His muscles flex. "The hospital is up ahead. If we hurry, we should be able to find some sort of treatment for Tally's radiation poisoning."

"I can't run," Tally says between gasps. She gazes

at us from her dark eye sockets and purses her boil-lined lips. "Go without me. I'll only slow you down and … you can't risk not reaching the rendezvous point."

"Don't be melodramatic. I'll carry you," Abram says. "Nobody gets left behind."

I prop my back against the dumpster. Laughter wells within me, but I hold it in. I'm shoeless. Again. People I love are dead. Again.

"The perimeter is secure. Move out."

With Tally draped across Abram's back, the five of us travel through what was once downtown Atlanta. Traffic is thick. Cars swerve as we sprint across the main intersection—some wreck and explode. Abram carries Tally to the opposite curb, and Missy follows. I dodge the vehicles and trip on my own feet, which is stupid and totally like me. I fall forward and slam against the pavement. Tires squeal. A taxi slides to a stop inches from my body.

"Do you have a death wish or something?" Jack drags me onto the median. His heavy breathing drowns the City's metropolitan roar. "Did you trip on those big feet of yours?"

"Shut up." I lean against his chest, his heart.

A tremor washes through the City. I turn to confront the cityscape as a plume of fire lifts into the sky. A cloud of ash spools over the District, black with soot, red with sparks.

The Federal building crumbles into a pool of screams and rubble.

I am a panning camera—I see myself, Jack, the horror on our faces as we observe the grand act of war. I savor the stenches of burning rubber, molten metal, and flesh. Flesh. We killed our enemies, but in the process, we stole innocent lives. Innocence. I think I've lost mine.

I think I've lost my mind.

Purebloods flee from their vehicles. Tanks blast jets from the sky. A transit bus crashes into a nearby building and disappears into a cloud of fire. Death. Destruction. Heat and debris.

Jack slides his hand into mine. *This had to be done,* his expression tells me. *We didn't have another choice.*

The vibrations intensify as the dome flickers with pixels. Like an opening door, a splitting contact lens, the force field dissipates.

We've removed the Third Layer.

"Let's go." Jack leads me to where Tally, Abram and Missy are stationed. "Dad will arrive with the second regiment in a matter of minutes. With the dome and government gone, it won't be long until a full-fledged war breaks out. The hospital is just up the block. We'll have to move fast but ... we can still make it there and find the treatment."

"Things are already crazy," Tally says. The dark circles around her eyes have blackened. More of her hair has fallen out.

"If we don't reach the meeting place, we'll be sitting ducks when the second regiment attacks. Jack ... Sergeant, you know we can't risk not being there. Missy has to join her squad. They're in charge of retrieving the virus from the labs. Without her, they won't be able to complete their objective. And what about you and Abram? You're leading the advance against the Pureblood army." Tally coughs. More of her hair drops to the ground. "We. Cannot. Afford. To. Take. Risks."

"Yes, we can," Abram says, "for you."

"What's our timeframe?" Missy asks.

"We have ten minutes max."

Abram nods and remounts Tally on his back. "Then I guess we'll have to run."

The City has morphed into a lethal, unorganized deathtrap. Bombs detonate. Smoke fogs the air. Purebloods swarm the streets like ants fleeing from a stomped anthill.

I weave to avoid chunks of building, severed limbs, and shattered glass. I block the bloodcurdling screams and sirens from my cognizance. I enjoy the run because running is the one thing I can do without feeling dead inside.

Jets battle each other overhead. They twist and plunge, fire endless rounds of bullets. Shrapnel rains down from their aerial attack. I cover my head and gasp when a plane collides with a skyscraper, knocking down the building as if it's nothing but a flimsy house of cards.

"The Vestige commandeered several of the Scavs' aircrafts," Jack says as we sprint through the masses of frantic civilians. "Our guys know which planes belong to us. They can distinguish friend from enemy. The aliens aren't as fortunate. They're firing at everyone."

A hospital comes into view. Ambulances crowd the curb, flickering with warning lights. Medics roll survivors through the main entrance on stretchers.

"We made it." Tally sighs.

Mechanical squeals echo through the City, and the hiss of dying turbines follows. We stagger to a halt as a jet spirals over downtown, burning, smoking, falling at a steady decline. The plane hits the hospital like a missile, exploding in front of us, blotting our destination into oblivion.

I curse and scream as Tally's last hope burns to the ground. Why? Why must everything I care about be taken from me? Is this some kind of sick joke?

"Move!" Jack leads us into an alley as blocks of rubble are tossed from the eruption. Detritus flattens cars and cracks sidewalks—a young boy is stabbed in the throat by a metal shard, an elderly woman is knocked down and leveled by a concrete chunk.

"It's gone." Tally sobs as Abram lowers her gaunt frame to the pavement. She squirms in my arms when I try to hug her. "I'm dead."

I hold her tight. I can't let her go. If I do, she might never come back.

"No." Jack paces the backstreet with his arms stretched behind his head. "This is just a setback. There must be other places that have the treatment. We'll keep searching."

"The radiation is destroying my system at rapid speed," she yells. "Even if we somehow manage to find the treatment in a few days, it won't work. My body is shutting down. I'm dying and … there's nothing any of us can do to stop it. You know I'm right, Jack. My fight is over!"

"No," he shouts. His bottom lip quivers. He ceases motion and stares at her, quieting his voice to a protesting murmur. "No. You are not going to die. Not you, too."

"There must be another way," I say.

"In the labs, there's probably a treatment for radiation poisoning," Missy says. "When I go with my squad to retrieve the virus, I'll look for it."

"Yes. See. You have a chance." Abram crouches next to Tally and touches her bony arm.

She shakes her head and turns to Jack. "Sergeant, I am asking to abort the mission. I also request to be discharged from active duty, due to my state of health."

He stares at her. There's a lasting pause between them, and I sense their wordless communication is the depths of Jack's and my third-space. She loves him and in a different sort of way, he loves her, too. I accept their emotional bond because Tally deserves to be loved before she dies, if not by her friends and future boyfriends, then by Jack.

"You can't waste time trying to save me. I'm a soldier, your soldier … and soldiers die in battle. This isn't something worth fighting. It can't be fought. I have a week or two until my body shuts down. That's time. I have time." She hesitates as if her tongue has said things she doesn't fully mean. "I want to live … but that's not really an option anymore … so this is how I choose to die. Please. Give me the freedom to make this choice. You gave me a life, Jack. Now let me choose how it ends."

"Affirmative. You are relieved of your current station, Lieutenant Mason. I thank you for your service to this country and humanity." Jack clenches his jaw until his dimples become deep crevices.

"You're going to quit?" Abram yells and kicks over a garbage can. His mouth is angry, but his eyes are sad. "I've lost Sutton, Ezra, and Charlie. You will not join the list, Tally."

"Don't be a freaking idiot. You can't command me to stay alive. That's not how this whole death thing works." Tally sighs and leans against my shoulder. "At my funeral…"

"We're not having that conversation right now," Jack says. "When the war is over, you and I can talk. Okay? We need to start moving again. The rendezvous location is several blocks south." He lifts her from the ground and onto his back. "Hold on tight."

Tally and I want the same things: life, Jack, to open our eyes and breathe in the clarity of a mask-free world. She doesn't hate me for gaining what she has lost but loves me in her own sarcastic, hidden way. I've known many types of love in my life, none of which have ever been as selfless as hers. She proves people are different from how we perceive them, that love can be demonstrated in hidden, undramatic ways every day. She proves sacrifice isn't always a *kill myself to save them* circumstance but a relinquishment of something personal to aid someone else, an unapplauded choice to swap life to give others time. She is a hero. She is brave. And I wish with every fiber of my being that I could pump her dying body with life and sacrifice for her like she is doing for me.

Life is dark and dirty, but at least it's real. At least I'm not wandering around in the dark, ignorant to the possible light. At least I can recognize friend from enemy, truth from lies, myself from a deceiving reflection of my own making. I know who I am. I see the truth and choose to reveal it.

Missy fires bullets at a pair of Scavs, killing one of them.

Abram grabs her arm. "When you're at the labs, I want you to search for the treatment," he whispers. "I won't let Tally die if living is an option."

She looks at him, and then at me. "What? You really thought I wasn't going to search for a cure? Oh, come on. Tally isn't getting away from us this easy."

It's as if the floodgates have been flung open. Human soldiers charge up the street with their weapons and mismatched uniforms. Some drive military vehicles, tanks. Others ride in minivans, on motorcycles. I smile at the sight of them.

Our odds are good. We have a chance, and a chance is all we need.

Jets continue to battle overhead. Missiles blow the streets to pieces. I dodge the blasts, bleeding and aching with pain, and follow Jack and Tally through the surge of armed forces. Scavs emerge from the crowd. They attack the approaching Vestige, fire bullets, and throw grenades and futuristic charges.

Jack waits for me next to a tank that has the American flag dangling from the main gun. Colonel Buchanan emerges from the metal hatch and lifts Tally into the machine.

I shuffle toward them as hunks of building pound the earth like meteors and people race past me in spectral blurs. I squint my eyes when sunlight filters through the gap of high-rises.

Even in the midst of war, the sun still sets and rises—there are infinite things in a finite world.

"Are you all right?" Jack scans me for injury and touches my face. "You're going with my dad. He will take you to one of our outposts. You'll be safe there."

"What? No. I'm staying with you."

"You're hardly wearing any clothes."

"Easy fix. I'll get a pair of pants."

"Julie."

"Jack," I say, "I don't want to leave you."

"You need medical attention."

"No. I'm fine. You patched me up real good. Give me a protein bar and I'll be ready to take on a whole army of Purebloods."

His expression softens. "I need to know you're safe. People have tried to take you from me too many times, Julie. Not anymore. While I'm fighting our enemies, risking my life for what we both believe in, I must know you are waiting for me, that even the aliens cannot destroy what we've created. Do this for me. Please. I'll come for you tomorrow morning, once my mission is complete."

I will obey him because I love him. I love him so much it hurts.

"Hurry up. The Scavs will begin their advance any second. We can't be here when the real fighting starts." Colonel Buchanan speaks commands into his radio and clicks a refilled magazine into his machine gun. "Son, you still need to reach your rendezvous location."

"I know." Jack holds me closer. "Trust your instincts, Julie. Don't follow commands just because they're given to you ... and stay alive."

"That won't be a problem. I'm good at staying alive."

"Yeah, because I'm always around to save you."

"We have a great thing going, Jack Buchanan." I climb up the side of the tank and squeeze myself halfway into the hatch. Jack pulls himself onto the hull and kisses me so deeply I cannot tell who is breathing for who. His lips merge with mine so perfect, so real, so uniquely us.

"That's enough." Colonel Buchanan forces us apart. "Get inside, Julie."

Jack jogs alongside the tank. "Dad, make sure Tally and Julie are both decontaminated and given doses of potassium iodide," he shouts over the grind of the road wheels. "Tally needs to be given a treatment of either Neupogen or Neulasta. The granulocyte protein might buy her more time. She also needs plenty of water and pain medication."

"I'll take care of your girls," he yells. "Now stop your fussing and complete your assignment, Sergeant. Your task force is waiting for you."

I'm shoved into the tank's main compartment and forced to sit with Tally behind the turret seat. The air reeks of gasoline and body odor. Men and women work at various stations within the tank, all controlling an aspect of our movement and artillery.

"The outpost is on the opposite side of the City. I'll take you there once I make my scheduled stops." Colonel Buchanan seals the hatch and crawls to where we sit. He stumbles when a bomb's detonation causes the machine to shake. "It's starting."

I hug my knees and count the repetitive blast of gunfire, the rumble of distant explosions. They're closer than they were a few minutes ago. "How long do you expect the war to last?"

"What we're fighting today is only one of many battles. The other colonies will retaliate once they learn of our rebellion. They'll pound us with missiles or release the virus. It will happen. If not today, then maybe tomorrow." Colonel Buchanan squats next to Tally. "Nash needs someone to help with communications. I'm assigning you the position."

"I've been discharged." Tally props herself against the uneven wall. "Look at me. I'm dying. Nobody in their right mind is going to want me working for them. One glance at my face and they'll toss me into the sick bay."

The colonel grabs an oil rag from an overhead compartment and fastens it around her head, creating a bandana-like cap. "No one has to know." He smears oil across her face to camouflage the red welts. "These last moments of your life will either define you as a victim or as a hero. They will define your place in history. You don't stop fighting. Ever. You don't let them win. This is a war we're facing. As long as you're breathing, you're fit for work. Trust me. Keep fighting."

She stares at him with tears in her eyes and nods.

"None of this will matter in a few years. Yes, because of our actions, humanity will survive, Lord willing, but I'm sure as soon as things get back to normal, once your kids and grandkids grow up in a comfortable world, they'll go right back to being as ignorant and vulnerable to deceit as we were."

"Then, why are we doing this? Why risk our necks to just prolong an inevitable end?"

"Because of the slim chance things could be different."

Chapter Twenty-Six

"The end was contained in the beginning."
George Orwell, *1984*

"I don't feel good about this, Sarge." Nash tightens his grip on the bundle of computer hardware. He gazes through the windshield at the empty streets, the piles of debris and deserted traffic. "We don't have backup. If something goes wrong…"

"It won't," Jack says. "I've studied diagrams of the building. I could navigate the corridors in my sleep. We can do this, I'm sure. We're more mobile as a small unit. Trust me." He touches my knee and nods to confirm our mission, to assure me that whatever happens, our efforts won't be in vain.

After today, I can go home. With Jack. With my nasty scars and battle wounds. I will heal with him and the Vestige in my pretty house on Rainbow Row. Life will be beautiful again. It must be.

Jack leans forward to have a clear view of the Illusion Complex—it houses the people and equipment responsible for the aliens' deception. A fireteam discovered the building yesterday during the initial attack. "We have an entrance. At my signal, we move." He slides open the passenger door and motions for us to exit.

With Nash sandwiched between us, we leave the van, and rush across the sidewalk and through a blown crevice in the building's exterior. Electric lights flicker as we skulk through an office. Old magazines and newspapers litter the tile floor, breezing between cloned desks and chairs.

Here, the aliens created the first layer.

"Where is everyone?" Nash asks as we cross into an adjoining hallway. He fidgets with the bundle of software. "It's quiet. Too quiet. It shouldn't be this quiet."

"Bombs have a tendency to get people moving," Jack says. "Nobody wants to die."

I clutch my automatic rifle and grit my teeth. To see where my world was manufactured, to be close to the liars who wrecked my life—it all becomes undeniably real. I've known about the illusion for months, but now I'm at its source, its origin, and I must destroy it before it destroys me.

A security guard emerges from one of the many rooms—old, confused, and covered in dust as if he slept through the attack and awoke to find a vacant building. He draws a handgun from his holster, but before he has a chance to fire, I shoot him in the head. It's instinctual. A single shot. A single death. He crumbles to the ground, into a puddle of his own blood.

Jack looks at me with his brow furrowed, jaw clenched, as if I'm the evil twin of his innocent girlfriend. "That easy, huh?"

"Yeah. That easy."

"It shouldn't be, Julie. I don't want you to change into someone you hate."

"Would you still love me, though, even if I did change?"

"Of course," he says, "but I worry you won't."

Nash taps our shoulders and points to the devices bolted into the corners. "The security cameras—they're active. See the green lights? Someone could be watching us. We need to hurry."

I'm not ready for the conversation to end. I need another minute with Jack to prove I'm still me, that I haven't changed completely. To think I've disappointed him makes me want to curl up in a ball and cry. I don't want to be a monster. I just want to live.

Jack leads us through a revolving door and down a hallway lined with various print ateliers. Magazines, books, newspapers—everything that falsely extended the confinements of our colony were fabricated here, in these rooms. Skinny women with glossy skin and perfect hair, the models I envied and used as a rubric to grade my own beauty, were created on those screens. They were an illusion, a layer, and because of my insecurities, I fell for the ruse.

"Dang it," Nash says when he lifts a tattered book from the floor. He smears the debris from the cover. "I guess the next installment won't be released any time soon."

"Sometimes it's better not to know the ending," Jack says, "because you can at least hope for the best possible scenario. Knowing the truth hurts. And a book shouldn't make you hurt."

I stride into the enclosed overpass connecting the complexes. The glass walls glisten with sunlight and warmth. I stop for a moment to gaze out at the stretch of urban decay as a fire plume rises in the distance, followed by a sonic blast. Several bombed skyscrapers collapse and create a massive dust cloud.

We're nearing the end of this story, and I'm not sure I want to know the ending. Wouldn't it be easier, less painful to quit now and believe in the best-possible scenario?

Jack walks to the opposite end of the overpass. With a tug, he unseals the entrance to the connected building. Nash and I follow him through the factory, past boxes of clothes, kitchen supplies, and merchandise with fake import tags. Robotic arms paste lids onto cans of food, seal bags of coffee—civilization is manufactured by machines and label-makers.

The sight makes me sick.

"We're not alone," Nash says. "The machines are being controlled by someone. I feel them watching us. You feel them too, don't you, Julie?"

"You're paranoid," Jack says.

"Paranoia is what's kept me alive this long."

We leave the factory floor and climb a flight of stairs to the studio level. Static blares from the speaker system. Electrical surges cause the lights to spasm, illuminating the vast space in flickering gasps. Surrounding us are sets of popular television shows and newsrooms, cameras, film equipment, and wardrobe racks. Bodies litter the floor of the editing lab. Why are these aliens dead? Who killed them?

"Yep, I knew it." Nash curses and stumbles backward. "We're gonna die."

Jack kneels to inspect a corpse. "They've been dead for a few hours."

"What happened? Did they commit suicide?"

He shakes his head. "These people were shot with military-grade weapons."

"But we didn't kill them," Nash says. "So who did?"

"They knew too much. The government didn't want us finding any of their loose ends."

"The Scavs?"

"Yeah. The Scavs. Be on your guard. They might still be in the building." Jack, with his gun aimed at the encroaching darkness, leads us to the building's core.

We reach the main broadcast studio. Nash goes into the control room and hooks up his equipment to the computer system. Jack adjusts the cameras and lighting, reorganizes the set.

"Are you nervous?" I ask.

Jack shrugs. "I haven't had time to be nervous."

"What will you say?" I bite my cheek and wipe my sweaty palms on my thighs. "When the cameras start rolling and you have everyone's attention, what will you tell them?"

"The truth," he says as he drags a desk into the soundstage. "It's enough."

"I'm hacking into the broadcast signal right now," Nash shouts from the control room. "It might take a while, though. There are a ton of firewalls."

"Work fast. We're running out of time." Jack straightens his t-shirt and restyles his hair. He turns to me for approval. "Do I look okay?"

"Yes," I say with a smile, "you look okay."

It happens in a single, shattering moment. Two seconds for my entire world to fall apart. The studio doors are kicked open. Scavs rush into the room with their weapons aimed and open fire, spraying the soundstage with lead. I watch as Jack is pelted with bullets. Blood gushes from his torso, soaks his clothes. He takes one step forward and crumbles to the ground. I hear myself scream. I feel my body lurch into motion and my finger press the trigger of my rifle. This can't happen. Not again.

The next few minutes are nothing but flashes of violence, a montage of blurred movements. I charge at the armored soldiers. I kill the first two with shots to the neck. I tear the helmet off the third alien and break his skull with a blow to the head. My mind doesn't register what I do, and maybe that's a good thing. Maybe it is better that I don't understand what I'm capable of inflicting.

When my cognizance resurrects, I am standing amidst a carpet of bodies, trembling, with tears streaming my face. Nash stares at me from the control room in shock, but I don't care. He is alive because of me. Alive. Surviving. Because of my transformation.

"Jack…" I stumble to his side and kneel in the puddle of his blood. "Don't do this to me, Jack. Don't you dare do this." I curse and cling to his hand. His flesh is white. His breathing is labored. He's dying. "You hold on. You keep holding on and you don't let go."

Jack gazes up at me, writhing. "Four times. I was shot four times." He moans and struggles to lift his shirt. "My leg … my shoulder … twice in my abdomen. Can you find exit wounds?"

I inspect the holes. "You were shot clean through the shoulder and … one of the bullets grazed your ribcage." I roll up his pant legs, struggling to lift the fabric past his knees. "A bullet is lodged in your left femur. And I can't find an exit wound for the bullet in your abdomen. Tell me how to fix you."

"I'll go find a first-aid kit," Nash shouts.

"No, stay there," Jack commands in a weak voice. "Keep working." He looks at me and motions to the open threshold. "First, make sure the doors are locked."

I scramble to my feet, slide a tripod through the door handles, and use every bit of my remaining strength to pile furniture against the panel. "Now what?"

"Unclasp my belt," he says, "and tighten it above my leg wound."

I remove the strip of leather from his hips and lasso it around his thigh. My hands shake as I take the knife from his pocket, cut his t-shirt into bandages, and use the fabric to bind his shoulder and waist. His blood stains my skin. I watch him squirm. He can't die. I won't let him.

"You patched me up real good, Julie. I'll be fine. I promise." He touches my cheek to redirect my attention from the wounds to his eyes. "I won't die today. Not today. But because I look so bloody awful, you have to be the one," he whispers, "to tell the truth. It has to be you."

The thought of being on television, my voice projected throughout Severance, sends a stampede of anxiety through my body. I shake my head. "Jack…"

"It has to be you," he says. "You know what needs to be said. Do it for me, for Jon."

"I'm scared."

He squeezes my hand tight. "Me, too."

"I've hacked into the broadcast signal," Nash shouts. "Let's do this."

****

The world is composed of layers. We are composed of layers. Everything in the universe is an interwoven web of truth and lies, hope, belief, the choice to see past the vast stretch of constellations and into the core of what unites us all. I can do this. I can take a stand. For Jack. For Jon. For myself. Because of our efforts, history will remember us. Humanity will survive because of our open eyes, our sacrifice. The Vestige will be a symbol of awareness. For the rest of time.

I lean my weight against the desk, vulnerable to the many cameras. Jack watches from within the control room. He's propped in a metal chair, slumped forward with bags beneath his eyes. If I had to choose between saving the world and saving him, I'd save him. I'd keep saving him.

"You can start talking once the cameras flash green," he says into the microphone. "Don't be nervous. You got this. You're pretty and persuasive. If you can win the Listers' allegiance, you can rescue humankind. I have faith in you, Julie. A ton of faith. What you say will save the world."

"No pressure." I swallow the lump in my throat and fidget with a discarded pencil. My heart is a bird trapped in a box, fluttering, ramming against the walls of its enclosure, trying to escape. Has my tongue always been this swollen? I can't seem to remember my name. Did it start with the letter J—Julio, Jane, Janice, Jenna?

Static echoes through the soundstage. Nash types on the keyboard. Jack works with the sound-system. I grip the desk's edge as the surrounding screens buzz to life, gain color, and clarify to reveal multiple faces, a conference table crowded with official-looking Purebloods. Their vibrant eyes glow and gaze through my attenuated skin like X-ray machines.

"What's happening?" I shout. "Is this a public broadcast?"

"No, it's a private feed transmitting from somewhere in England," Nash says. "Their system is overriding our signal. They've blocked my hack."

"Greetings. We are the Special Ones," the gray-haired woman at the end of the table says in a crisp, emotionless voice. "It appears you and your people have surmounted our armed forces. Congratulations. You must be most pleased with yourselves. To have accomplished such a feat with so few fighters is admirable. Our invasion has been occurring for decades and yet you managed to cease its progress in your colony within a matter of months. With sincerity, I applaud you and your people's insight. You have proven that your race is not one to be underestimated."

President Duchene waltzes into view, clothed in a lace tea dress. She sits next to the elderly woman and casts me a smile. "Good morning, Julie."

"You fled the area rather quickly," I croak.

"Yes … well, I could not risk being injured by your little rebellion."

Jack bangs his fists against the Plexiglas window and lifts the microphone to his mouth. "You," he shouts with rage dripping from his tongue. "You're the whore I caught sleeping with my dad!" He clutches his stomach wound and glares at her. "That night I came home from swim team practice, he beat me up because I saw you two on the couch. But it wasn't because I saw him *doing* you. He hurt me because I saw you … the President. Oh. My. Gosh. You slept with my dad!"

"Jack, dear, you have always had such an awful temper." President Duchene sighs and inspects her buffed nails. "I put your father and mother together. You were born because of me. And after Lavinia did her duty, it was only fair for her to give back what was mine. Be honest with yourself, darling. You are not angry I slept with him. You are angry he slept with me, knowing the truth."

"Enough, Gemma. Banter is unnecessary." The elderly woman corrects her posture and gazes at me with daggers in her eyes. "You might have won your temporary freedom, but you shall not live for long. My people dislike threats. We will retaliate, and you will all die. You are a weak species. A virus outbreak or radiation leak…"

"Bring it on," I scream. "Unleash the whole damn arsenal! It doesn't matter what you do. We will survive, and you will die. Have you learned nothing from this? You can lie and become better liars, but the truth … the truth will always come to light and when it does, you will crumble. There's no security in an illusion. There's no way you can win this war unless you destroy the Vestige, because we won't stop telling the truth until the world is aware of your layers. So come after me. Come after us." I grit my teeth and ball my fists. "Bring it on."

"You will die. War will kill you."

"If that's true, then how could I die better?"

"By not dying."

"Everyone dies. The goal is to die in the best way possible," I say. "And the best way isn't the most comfortable way, but the way that changes the most."

"Fine." She places her hands on the table and nods. "Let the war for Earth begin."

"It's already begun."

Nash manages to override their signal and end the transmission. He looks at me, wide-eyed. His cheeks flush. "You probably shouldn't have dared them to attack us."

"I'm dumb when I'm pissed."

Jack steals the microphone. "Don't listen to him, Julie. You were brave. You proved our strength." He smiles as if to hide his pain. "Ready to save our piece of the world?"

I take a deep breath and return the smile. "Bring it on."

Throughout Severance, people are watching television, listening to the radio, and in a few moments, they'll be watching and listening to me. Life won't be the same after today, but that's all right. I see our horizon, obscure and bright in the distance. I don't know where our future is or where it will go, but I believe it's somewhere, and I pray it's beautiful. We will make it beautiful.

The cameras flash green.

****

There are certainties, small infinities this world offers like ocean breezes, skies streaked with white lines like mega Etch-A-Sketches, people's voices as they rush like currents through civilization. Life will forever exist, no matter what happens to us or around us. The sky will remain blue, wind will still blow, and somewhere a voice will mutter.

Jon said my obsession with simple things is cute.

I roll over and stare through the dark lenses of my sunglasses at the manicured green space nestled between Porter's Lodge and Randolph Hall. Students still lounge on the lawn and car horns still blare from the streets outside the College of Charleston, but there is a different smell in the air, a different look to the world.

It's been four months since my broadcast aired. The initial panic has calmed. The world has a new pulse, a new perspective, yet people continue to move forward with their lives. Our oasis of civilization is thriving, and so are we. And even though our moment of security will not last for long, we have found peace in the obscurity, in the truth that has set us free. The Vestige has taken control of the government. The Purebloods have joined human society without much protest. We're healing, uniting. The past is composed of facts, but the future is hope. Together, we're clinging to the hope of a brighter tomorrow. We will move forward. We will survive. Together.

Captain Jack Buchanan of the U.S. Marine Corps strides across the green space in his uniform, adorned with medals and ribbons. He sits next to me and places his white hat on my head. "Hi."

"Hi." I adjust the hat's brim and roll onto my side. "Don't you have to be on a plane in an hour? President Buchanan needs you in the City…"

"Dad can wait," he says. "You're more important."

"Wow. I'm more important than the President? I should put that as the bio on my Instagram."

He laughs. "Yeah. Definitely."

Jack scoots closer to me. Our foreheads press together. His hand finds mine and immediately, my heartbeat is everywhere. It beats in the tips of my fingers, the back of my neck, everywhere. I look at him. He looks at me. And I smile because the world is no longer diseased with ignorance. The layers have been revealed. We cured humanity. We were the cure.

During the final attack, Missy retrieved the virus from the labs and found a treatment for Tally's radiation poisoning. They're both alive and live with me in my house on Rainbow Row, along with Nash, Abram, Levi, and occasionally Jack, when he isn't working for his father in the City. They fill my house with voices and keep my family's memory alive. I'm not alone. When I have bad days, nightmares, freak-outs, they surround me and share the weight of my pain.

Normalcy is impossible, but I've found an attainable proximity. I've resumed college classes and my job at The Grindery. On the weekends, I volunteer at the new government outpost and issue housing assignments to Pureblood transfers. Normal. I'm almost normal. My boyfriend is in the military. My family was killed in a war. My friends are loud, messy, and they love me. Besides the fact I can't wear red lipstick without flashing back to my time in the City, I dress the same, look the same. And although I suffered from a severe case of PTSD a few months ago, I'm handling the adjustment to civilian life well.

"Julie?"

"Yeah?"

"Did you hear what I said?"

"No. Sorry," I say, and crinkle my nose. "Tell me again."

Jack props himself on his elbows, staining the sleeves of his uniform with grass. Sunlight filters through the treetops and illuminates his cobalt eyes and bleached smile. He's beautiful. I know men aren't supposed to be, but he is. "I was saying I found a new zombie novel we should read."

"You're still talking about zombies?"

"Hey, we must be prepared for all possible end-of-the-world scenarios."

I lean over and kiss him. His stubble-covered cheeks scratch my skin. His lips fit with mine, connecting us, fusing our bodies together. "I love you. I'm so, so in love with you."

He wraps an arm around my waist and rests his mouth against my cheekbone. "I love you more."

"Not possible." I comb my fingers through his short hair. I'm home. The end was my beginning—I see that now. Because of death, I've learned how to live.

After *the end of the world*, there is a world. Life doesn't stop.

It changes.

And it changes me.

The End

www.authorcarolinegeorge.com

Evernight Teen ®

www.evernightteen.com

CPSIA information can be obtained
at www.ICGtesting.com
Printed in the USA
LVHW091306160919
631210LV00001B/23/P